TWO SHADES OF BLUE

A novel by
Sydney Gibson

Two Shades of Blue is a work of fiction. Names, places, and incidents in this book are either the product of the author's imagination or are used fictitiously. Any resemblance to actual persons, living or dead, events or locales is entirely coincidental.

Copyright @ 2021 Sydney Gibson

All rights reserved.

No part of this book may be reproduced or used in any manner without written permission of the copyright owner except for the use of quotations in a book review.

First Print Edition 2021

Published in the United States by Lights Out Ink, LLC.

ISBN: 978-1-914152-15-3

eBook ISBN: 978-1-914152-16-0

Cover design by Rafi De Sousa

Lights Out Ink is an independent publisher of serialized, digital, and printed fiction.

Visit www.lightsoutink.com to discover our full library of content.

Special Thanks to Virginia for all of your hard work and dedication in turning this mess into something that made sense.
*To Lanae, my writing buddy. Thank you for enduring my crazy moments during the editing process, I'm looking forward
to your book!*

And to all of my readers, thank you for the continuing support!

Table of Contents

Chapter 1 1
Chapter 2 19
Chapter 3 33
Chapter 4 49
Chapter 5 61
Chapter 6 75
Chapter 7 97
Chapter 8 119
Chapter 9 133
Chapter 10 143
Chapter 11 155
Chapter 12 165
Chapter 13 175
Chapter 14 191
Chapter 15 203
Chapter 16 211
Chapter 17 219
Chapter 18 231

Chapter 19..257
Chapter 20..269
Chapter 21..279
Chapter 22..289
Chapter 23..297
Chapter 24..305
Chapter 25..323
Chapter 26..339
Chapter 27..351
Chapter 28..363
Chapter 29..371

Chapter 1

If I stared long enough at the ripples of water, I could almost see my reflection. With each distorted image, I wondered, how did I get here? The ever-popular question to the universe. Along with Who am I? Where am I? And Why is McDonald's breakfast the best?

Before the lake had a chance to answer, someone tapped me on the shoulder, breaking me out of my thoughts. "Excuse me, Detective Tiernan?"

I turned to acknowledge the young, almost baby-faced police officer looking up at me with immense respect. "I'm sorry to bother you, Detective, but they're ready for you now." He stepped back, a nervous smile covering his face.

I took a deep breath and smiled at him, wondering if they'd lowered the minimum hiring age. He gave me an awkward nod, then merged back into the crowd of blue-clad officers over my shoulder. I glanced once more at the lake, taking another breath of clean air before turning towards the clump of blue ahead.

I took my time walking over, pushing through the crowd of officers. Yellow crime scene tape cordoned off a large square. A large square filled with death. In the center of that square lay a white sheet covering the one thing I'd been avoiding since I pulled up to the scene: a dead body.

I frowned as I pushed past the officers to step under the tape. My occasional partner, Aaron Liang, was bent over, holding up a corner of the sheet. The entire thing was riddled with dark red stains. He scowled at the body with disgust and frustration, his typical look at any crime scene, no matter the gore.

"So, Aaron, what do we have here?" I pulled on a pair of nitrile gloves, and crouched next to him.

Aaron was younger than me by five years, handsome with a swimmer's build, and a kind heart. He was of Chinese descent and his jet-black hair was always perfectly styled, no matter the hour or type of crime scene we were called to. His hair was always pristine. I'd make fun of his hair any chance I got, since it was his pride and joy. He'd shake his head and flash his million-dollar grin, taking the edge off any insult I could throw his way.

Aaron was quite possibly the only person in the department who was truly kind to me. We worked well together whenever the Captain forced me to have a partner. I'd avoided being permanently assigned a partner for years. From road officer to Detective, I weaseled my way out of having a partner any chance I could, until I met Aaron. He stood out from the moment I shook his hand. He was the only person in the department who understood how I thought and that I preferred to work alone. He didn't pester me like the others to go out for after-shift drinks, or talk endlessly about a personal life I had little interest in hearing about. He accepted my antisocial nature, and I loved him for it. But I'd never ever tell him that.

"Hey there, Lieutenant." He offered a polite smile before turning back to the body. "It looks like a nasty murder with an attempted body dump into the river." He motioned towards the edge of a nearby industrial complex. We stood in front of a rusted warehouse that ran along the edge of the south side of Chicago. The river wove around it, leaving little dock-like areas in between the bulky metal buildings. Perfect places to dump bodies, drugs, cars, and any other critical piece of evidence that could make my job so much easier.

"Looks like they didn't quite make it." He pointed at the drag marks that led right to the body. Aaron squinted at the end of the lot where it dropped off into the river. "Less than twenty feet to get the body into the water. How lazy can you be?"

I shook my head; Aaron was right. For as much work as it took to murder someone, why not follow through and dump the body with all the evidence it carried? "No murder is ever simple, Aaron." I cocked an eyebrow. "Give me the details."

Aaron turned to the body, his hands moving as he spoke, highlighting the key bits of evidence I always looked for. "It looks like a middle-aged white male. But it's hard to tell. There's a tremendous amount of blunt force trauma to the left side of his face. We'll probably have to rely on dental records or DNA for positive identification. We haven't found any significant defense wounds, so I'm thinking he was caught by surprise and knocked out." He paused, indicating the head. "The severe beating has me worried. Not all thugs waste time on beating an unconscious mark. They take the money and run."

I focused on the areas Aaron pointed to. The victim was unrecognizable. His face was so swollen from blunt force trauma to his eyes and forehead, he barely looked human. Add in the blood from said trauma, and I couldn't readily see any distinct injury to explain why there was so much of it. I'd have to wait until he was on the autopsy table to get a better idea.

Aaron lifted the sheet higher. "Here's where it gets weird."

He pointed with a gloved finger to the area near the victim's head. Bits of torn paper soaked in blood were tucked under the victim's right ear, stuck to the concrete. "The techs removed one large piece already. Said they look like pages ripped out of a book and purposely placed under the head. It looks like the head was positioned in a way to draw your attention straight to the paper. I told him to leave the rest until you got here. I keep staring at them, Lieutenant, but I can't figure out what the hell they are."

I bent down to get a closer look and recognized the words instantly, having been forced to study the language for most of my primary education. I leaned back, glancing at Aaron. "It's Latin. The pages are ancient Latin. Possibly from a religious text, maybe a Bible."

I motioned a crime scene tech to bring me a set of tweezers with an evidence bag. When both were in hand, I gently pulled the pages out from under the victim's head and placed them in the bag before sealing it and handing it back to the tech. "Take this to the lab now. Tell them I want the blood test done ASAP. Then call Cavanaugh and have him get started on analyzing the paper and ink. Rush the lab reports. I'd like to have the results by the end of the week, if not sooner." My tone was far harsher than I intended, but I was tired, and the number of homicides around the city were stacking up every day. Stacking up on my shoulders, practically smothering me with the weight. "Where's the Medical Examiner?" I scanned the crowd. I wanted to move the body and search for more evidence.

Aaron rolled his eyes. "Dr. Willows is over rubbing elbows with the local media. He's keen on running for Mayor next year." He yanked a garish bumper sticker out of his pocket. *Willows in 2024* shouted in my face in garish red, white, and blue.

"Please throw that out." I sighed, already irritated. Cursory looks were never enough. I didn't want to waste more time standing around waiting. "Can you please get his ass over here? I don't want to spend my entire day at this scene while he shakes hands and babies."

"Sure thing." Aaron grinned, running to the media corralled at the far end of the yellow tape.

I stood up, stifled a yawn as I walked towards a patrol officer standing at the tape. "Please find me when Dr. Willows graces us with his presence."

The officer nodded. "Will do, Lieutenant."

Heading back towards the sanctity of my cruiser, I left the scene as my shoulders hunched in exhaustion. The unmarked sedan was far enough from the crowd of looky-loos who obviously had nothing better to do but stand around at a crime scene. Gawking and getting in my damn way.

The abandoned docks were a few blocks away from the old meat packing district where I'd spent most of my patrol career, chasing drug dealers and taking my own turn pulling perimeter duty at gruesome crime scenes.

The docks always had bodies. Criminals picked it as the perfect place to dump a body or kill someone. What made me laugh was how rarely any bodies ever made it into the lake. Leaving me to wonder what stopped the person from taking that extra step and shoving the body into the water? It would've saved me a lot more time and trouble if criminals weren't such lazy bastards.

I shook my head at the morbid thought, born from exhaustion.

Sliding back into the driver's seat, my mind filled with how truly jaded I'd become over the last few years. They always say the life of a police officer is hard, but the life of a homicide detective is ten times worse. Many became ten times more addicted to any vice that could numb away the things you saw. The only addiction I had lately was being exhausted and semi-bitter if crime scenes took too long to process. That and iced green teas with seven sugars.

Other than the handful of negative aspects of this job, I was living the dream to the outside world. I had the job I always wanted. I was the youngest Detective Lieutenant in the department, and my star was on the rise. Or so my bosses told me.

I leaned my head against the window and closed my eyes with a heavy sigh. The sound of the water pushed through the small crack in the driver's side window and calmed my headache as I drifted to how I got here. How it all started and how I ended up hiding in a car, silently avoiding a crime scene, hoping Aaron would just take the lead on this one.

I was tired and desperately wanted to keep my eyes closed for a few more moments. Or days. Either way, my memories took over as I tried to stay awake.

I exhaled, indulging in them for longer than I should've.

* * *

I was fourteen when I mugged the wrong person in the dark alleys of the Motor City. I'd been a street kid for far too long. Scrounging and fighting for the basics needed for survival in a gritty city like Detroit. I couldn't remember what happened to my parents, only that I didn't have any and spent years being bounced in and out of foster homes. I spent my childhood in places shoved full of too many kids, handled by social workers who had too many cases to handle with care.

On the day of my fourteenth birthday, I'd run away with a small group of kids from our filthy foster home. I didn't know any better and followed them blindly. I was a shy girl, always hanging in the back while the others stole, robbed people, and broke into cars and buildings. All petty crimes that afforded us just enough cash to buy cheap gas station snacks that kept our bellies full.

One sticky Detroit summer night, they pressured me into committing my first mugging. The other kids got in my face, shouted that it was time to carry my own weight and contribute. So, I stood outside a local bar next to the largest downtown casino and waited. I waited for hours, scared shitless to select a mark and rob them. I hoped to squeak by another night without doing it, using the excuse that no one came down the alley.

It worked for a few hours, until the oldest kid threatened to beat the living shit out of me if I didn't come back with at least twenty dollars and a wallet full of credit cards.

I was just about to quit and face my beating, when a well-dressed man walked past the alley. His suit was an expensive one, meaning he had money and a fat wallet full of credit cards.

I let him pass, building up the courage before I slowly followed him as he walked towards the casino parking deck. I waited until the shadows were in my favor and rushed him, throwing all my one hundred pounds of skin and bones into his side.

As we smacked into the trunk of the car, I poked him in the back with a cigarette lighter. "Don't move! I gotta gun. Gimme all your money!"

Even to this day I'm not sure what happened. But within an instant of tackling the man, I was on the ground with a shooting pain in my head. The man was huge as he stood over me with the broken BIC lighter in his hand. I tried not to cry, but the pain was too much, and I started to bawl.

I received no pity from my intended victim, even with tears streaming down my cheeks. He hoisted me up by the collar, my feet dangling a few inches off the ground. He glared at me, ready to hit me if I made the wrong move. "How old are you? And why are you trying to rob me with this stupid plastic lighter?"

I couldn't answer. I just sobbed, snot running down my face.

The man bent closer to me, his eyes black with anger. "Did you hear me, boy? What in the hell were you thinking?"

He pulled me into the light. I winced, waiting for the beating of my life. Then he saw my face. "Jesus Christ. You're a girl." His tone immediately softened.

He set me back on the ground and I collapsed next to the car, curled into a ball, still crying uncontrollably. The adrenaline dumped out of my body like I'd pulled the plug on a drain, and I was terrified. The man knelt, reaching for me. I flinched, afraid he was going to hit me again.

He held up his hand, digging in his suit pocket and producing a shiny black wallet. "No! No! It's alright! I'm a cop. I'm not going to hurt you." He opened the wallet, and showed me his badge and ID card.

I could barely see through tear-filled eyes, only making out the star shape. I wiped my eyes, staring up at the man. After having many badges shoved in my face on my recent crime sprees, I knew it wasn't a Detroit police badge.

I mumbled through sobs. "You're a liar. You ain't a Detroit cop."

The man smiled with a nod. "I know. I'm not with the Detroit Police Department. I'm from Chicago. Here, take it and look closer." He grabbed my hand, setting the wallet in my palm. I held it up in the light and read Chicago Police along the inner circle. I shoved it back at him, still not trusting his words. I was headed to juvie. No point in dragging this out.

The man took his badge back, and held out his hand. "Come on. I'm going to take you home. I need to at least tell your parents what you're up to tonight."

I shook my head furiously. "I don't have a home. I don't have parents," I mumbled around gasping sobs. I was embarrassed I couldn't control myself, trying to wipe the tears away, but they came out faster than I could swipe them away with a dirty sleeve.

The man took in my appearance. I was a street kid and definitely looked the part. Dirty face, dirty hair, and dirty clothes that were too small and too torn to do anything more than act as unique decoration on my painfully thin frame.

He took a deep breath. "Well, let me help you up. I didn't mean to hit you so hard. I thought you were a boy. How old are you?"

"Seventeen." I tilted my eyes down as the practiced lie fell out.

"Seventeen, my ass." He chuckled, reaching down to gently grab my elbow. I continued to shake and didn't have the strength to run from him.

"You gonna take me in?"

He stared at me for a second, clearly assessing if I was worth the trouble. "I might. But I think you need to eat more than you need to be booked right now. What do you think?"

My stomach jumped at the mention of food. It'd been a long time since I'd eaten more than a few bags of chips and candy, but I tried to play it tough. "I don't care. They'll feed me in juvie."

He saw right through the tough kid act. "Fine. I'll make you a deal. I'll feed you then take you in and turn you over to the officers there. That way I know you had a decent meal before the night ends. They stopped serving food in juvenile hall a few hours ago. So, come on."

My roaring, empty stomach took charge, and I shrugged and let him take me by the elbow, sit me in the passenger seat of his car.

I pushed myself into the furthest corner away from him. His car was so clean, I felt like I was dirtying up the seat by just sitting on it. I also didn't want to look at the cop who was taking me in and dumping me like trash into the worst dumpster in the city. Juvenile Hall.

I was so caught up in my own defeat, I didn't notice he was taking me out of the city. Leaving the dirty alleys, broken streetlights and distinctive smell — rotting garbage mixed with motor oil — for clean sidewalks, trees and brightly lit storefronts. I sat up in the seat, clutching the armrest. "Wait, this isn't the way to juvie. Where are you taking me? Are you kidnapping me?"

The man chuckled. "I'm not kidnapping you. I told you I'm a cop, but if you don't believe me, call and give them my badge number. Here." He tossed his cell phone and wallet in my lap.

His kindness and gentle way of handling me was confusing. Every other cop I dealt with treated me like an inconvenience and usually told me to shut up. I grabbed his phone and started dialing, "Where are you taking me, so I can tell whoever answers?"

"I'm taking you to the diner by my hotel. I'm going to feed you then I'll take you in. Make sure you tell the desk sergeant my name when he answers. Detective Edward Tiernan."

The Chicago police department confirmed Edward Tiernan, badge number 1786, was indeed a homicide detective and was currently in Detroit for a conference, but I could leave a message for him, or hang up and call 9-1-1 if it was an emergency.

Fear edged with relief ran through my shivering body. He really was going to take me to juvenile hall. I hung up, slowly setting his phone in the middle console.

He glanced at me. "Now that you know who I am, will you tell me your name? I'd like to know what to call the girl who mugged me with a busted cigarette lighter."

"Emma." I was curled up in the far corner of the seat again, shaking with pure panic.

"Emma? Just Emma? You don't have a last name?"

I shook my head. "The city just gives you case numbers if you don't have a last name."

Edward frowned. "Of course. Well, I'll have to find out if your case number leads to a last name or a family."

I looked out the window at the passing freeway. It'd been a long time since I'd seen outside of the city. "I told you, I ain't got family."

Edward didn't ask any more questions until we pulled into the parking lot of an all-night diner.

Inside the quiet, clean diner, I must've eaten fifty dollars' worth of food while he drank a few cups of coffee and picked at a plate of toast. As I ate, I took a good look at the man I'd tried to rob.

Edward was a handsome man with strong features and lines that showed he laughed a lot and worried just as much. He wasn't as big as he seemed on the street. He was athletic, but not as large as he looked when he clocked me. His dirty blonde hair was cut in a modern style but reminded me of men's haircuts I'd seen in encyclopedias from the forties. He had deep green eyes that were soft for a cop; he didn't have the hard edge look that came with always looking over your shoulder. He looked a little like how I thought a father should. I wondered if he had kids, and if he was a good father. I wanted to ask, but instead filled my mouth with another stack of pancakes.

While I devoured half the menu, Edward asked random questions about where I was from. I gave him bullshit answers. I didn't care. I was going to juvie in a few. I'd never see him again.

But Edward didn't take me to juvie that night.

He made a few calls while I shoved a hot fudge sundae into my already stuffed belly, then told me the downtown center was overcrowded and wasn't taking anyone else in.

In later years, I found out he was lying, but at the time, I was a tiny fourteen year old, sleepy from the twenty pounds of food I'd eaten.

Edward took me back to his hotel that night. He got me my own room next to his and explained that if I tried to run, he would arrest me. Again, he was lying, but it terrified me enough to stay out of trouble. Turns out Edward really was in town for a police convention, at the casino he was leaving when I rushed him.

Boy, did I know how to pick them. The kids would make fun of me and the big one would probably punch me for not bringing back at least twenty dollars or half the food I ate.

Over the next few days, I stayed at the hotel with Edward. And each day Edward told me he was trying to find where I belonged and if I had family willing to take me in. I knew he would come up empty but grew a little attached to him. He was kind and made sure I was taken care of, and never said no when I asked for ice cream.

I often thought, maybe this is what it's like to have a parent, but I wouldn't let myself daydream. In time, Edward would take me back to the city, drop me off on the street and drive away, leaving me to the streets like everyone else before him.

After the fourth day of enjoying hot showers and more food than I could ever remember having eaten, Edward told me he'd been assigned my temporary guardian and I was going home to Chicago with him. I was shocked, nervous, knowing it was another temporary solution in my life. Soon, I'd be back on the streets, no matter how much my gut told me to trust this man.

Truth was, he'd found my records. Found no one wanted me, that I had no family other than my dead parents. He also found my short school record telling him I was an above average student with an increased sensitivity to others. Even though my recent actions contradicted it, I had an overwhelming need to help others. Probably why the other kids always took advantage of me.

Edward had taken a heartfelt interest in me and wouldn't let me fall back into the system. He spoke to the courts and they gave him temporary guardianship. Since I was only fourteen and a burden to said state, they handed me over with a bow. Washing their hands, and me out of the system.

I remember staring at him as he explained what was happening, wondering why I was going to a juvenile hall in Chicago. I even asked him outright. He laughed, telling me not to worry about it.

Edward took me home to Chicago, to the western suburbs, where his wife Maggie welcomed me with open arms. She was a tiny woman, with short dark blonde hair and a strong demeanor intensified by her piercing dark blue eyes. Many people politely commented on how much I looked like her, thinking she really was my mother. People also commented on how much I looked like both Edward and Maggie, which always made me laugh. I look nothing like either of them: dark honey blonde hair, and icy blue eyes that grow lighter depending on my mood. Let alone the fact I grew quickly with good meals, ending up at least a foot taller than Maggie and almost four inches taller than Edward. Edward often joked I looked like they adopted a Serbian supermodel, not a kid from the streets of Detroit.

Edward and Maggie made sure I went back to school as soon as they could enroll me in the local high school. I excelled and graduated with honors. I then went on to Northwestern where I graduated magna cum laude with a degree in medicine but transferred to Loyola to finish my Master's in psychology.

To date, I'm still only a few classes and a few clinical rotations away from a slapping 'Doctor' before my first name. But it wasn't meant to be. Even with my education, with opportunities to work in the largest and best hospitals around, I followed in my adopted father's footsteps and became a Chicago police officer.

Edward protested, saying my education was best suited for cleaner work, but I knew it was where I needed to be. I applied for the police academy on graduation day. I excelled there too, graduating at the top of the class, and was assigned to my father's old district.

Five years into my stint in road patrol, I took the Detectives test and was promoted straight to the homicide unit.

There, I found my talent for profiling and cracking the most unusual murders Chicago could offer.

The day I got my gold badge, the pride on my father's face filled my heart with so much love and acceptance. I knew I was doing the right thing, becoming a police officer. To this day, I see it in his soft green eyes, the same green eyes that first stared at me over a plate of eggs when I was fourteen and nothing more than a broken shell.

* * *

A gentle tap on the passenger window startled me. I nodded at the baby-faced officer who had collected me earlier, I grabbed the keys from the ignition, slowly removing myself from the now stale air of the cruiser. Walking around the hood to meet with the young officer, I glanced at him. He was eager, making it clear as day this was his first big crime scene.

"Detective Lieutenant Tiernan, they're ready for you."

I pulled my long, honey blonde hair back into a ponytail, grumbling. "Just call me Lieutenant. No need to get bogged down in titles." I motioned for him to lead the way to the yellow tape. He jogged ahead of me. Aaron stood by the bloody sheet, waving me over. "Tiernan! Get your ass over here! The medical examiner is *finally* letting us look at the body."

I took a deep breath. "About damn time." I was grateful to continue the investigation, and to stop thinking about my past.

The medical examiner, Dr. Willows, always looked like a smarmy car salesman to me. I was not a fan, and hated having to engage him in any way. His teeth were too white, his handshake felt like a wet, dead fish, and he squeezed too hard. Determined to non-verbally state his dominance over you. I took a deep breath, grumbling his name between clenched teeth. "Dr. Willows."

"Did you touch the body?" He didn't look up from the notepad in his hand.

"No. I moved the sheet to look but didn't touch. A few scene techs recovered critical evidence around the body, but they were careful not to disturb anything of importance." I rolled my eyes. This guy was such a dick.

Without looking up, Dr. Willows chastised me. "Touching the sheet is technically touching the body since it's resting *on the body*. You know you're not allowed to touch anything unless I'm present or have released the body."

I was already agitated that it took him a half hour to make the scene, and I snapped. "Well if you could manage to show up and talk to us instead of sucking up to the media, I wouldn't have to move the sheet to look at the body to continue my investigation. Your personal career goals compromise my case and the precious time I have to find the murderer."

I hit a nerve, a good one, judging by the color rising in his cheeks. The good doctor wouldn't look at me, only clearing his throat as he stood. "I have a heavy workload lately."

"We all do." I shook my head and watched him stare at the body, his face still flush with embarrassment. He handed his field notes to Aaron, not wanting to confront me again, and issued quiet permission for us to proceed with our investigation.

Aaron stood next to me, reading Dr. Willows' preliminary notes out loud. "Time of death was between three and four thirty a.m. No signs of sexual assault. Defensive wounds on the hands and legs. Indicating the victim fought hard against the attacker. Cause of death: excessive blood loss due to blunt force trauma. Other than that, we have to wait for the techs to finish collecting fibers, DNA, and all that jazz."

The scene techs went about their job collecting evidence in rigid routines. Sometimes I envied them. They were able to simply collect the evidence, hand off what they found, and move onto the next case. They never got too attached to the victims, never had to tell families their loved one was dead, and never had to dig into the deepest, darkest secrets of people they didn't know. I lost myself for a second in the never haves until I heard Aaron repeat my name.

"Emma? Emma?"

I snapped back to reality. "Sorry, I drifted away for a minute. We still need identification for this one. How long before they're done?" I motioned with my chin towards the techs.

"About three hours. The scene is still fresh and seems confined to the immediate area. What do you say we leave them to it, head back to the station while we wait for Dr. Willows to get us a solid identification?"

I sighed and flagged down a patrol officer. "You. Call me immediately when they've finished, and the evidence has made it back to the labs." I pointed at the body, before pointing at the officer. "You're in charge. You go where they go, nowhere else unless I say so."

The officer swallowed hard. I had just assigned him to babysitting detail. "Yes, Lieutenant."

I nodded. "Thank you, and please don't call me unless there's a lab report in your hand waiting to be set on my desk."

The officer nodded, mumbling under his breath as he turned away and shuffled over to the techs.

Aaron shot me a grin as he stood up, peeling off his gloves. "You're such a ballbuster, Lieutenant."

I rolled my eyes. "I *am not* a ballbuster, Aaron. They know I'm serious about my work and my work alone. I don't need friends or bar buddies."

He pointed a finger at me. "And this is why you're the Ice Queen of Chicago PD."

I grimaced. "Thanks for reminding me." The stupid nickname had started a few months ago, when I began to focus more on my work and less on my coworkers, creating a general disconnect from everyone. I was overwhelmed with the new homicide cases coming in every day, and I hadn't really been myself since Elle died.

I stripped off my gloves, crumpling them into a self-contained ball, and cleared my throat to change the subject. "I'll meet you back at the station. Have the medical examiner's office rush the autopsy and tox screen. I want to get a jump on things before the evidence starts dying. I'll start the paperwork on this one." I blew out a breath. This was the ninth body in the last two weeks. Adding to the growing stack of brown file folders perfectly perched on the corner of my desk. Waiting for me to put the pieces together and solve the puzzle of why people felt the need to kill each other.

"Sure thing, Emma." He tossed his gloves into a red bio bag behind him, smirking at me. I gave him a dirty look for using my first name at the scene in front of other officers. Aaron was the only coworker in the entire police department who dared to use my first name, but then again, he was the only person I trusted and could honestly call a friend. Aaron had proven his loyalty to me during one of the hardest times of my life, and I never forgot it.

Aaron ignored the dirty look. "I heard the Captain wants to meet with you? Something about you getting a new partner?" His smirk grew bigger as I glared at him. He knew how much I hated having partners.

I groaned and leaned my head back. "No. No. No." I wanted to shake my fist at whichever God thought this would be a perfect time to burden me with more stress.

Aaron held up the crime scene tape for me to step under. "Oh yes, yes, yes, Emma. You can't keep escaping this. Captain Jameson has run out of patience with you and your solitary ways, and the entire unit is struggling under our increasing caseloads. If it makes you feel any better, my new partner starts tomorrow." Aaron patted my shoulder. "It was only a matter of time."

I folded my arms over my chest, huffing. "Then why can't they just put us together? You already know how I work, and more importantly, when to leave me alone." My mind raced through several scenarios and logical reasons of why Aaron would be a better fit than a fresh-faced uniform who just passed the detective exam. I started crafting every excuse I could to throw at the Captain to justify either leaving me alone or making Aaron my partner.

Aaron laughed. "Face it, we're both getting rookies. The unit needs new blood. Captain's exact words."

I said nothing, dropping my head down as I walked back to the matte black cruiser I'd left facing the lake. It was a worn-down old patrol car re-purposed to serve the Detective fleet as a take-home car. I'd managed to claim it as my own and spent a week disinfecting the entire interior so I could stand to sit in it without gagging.

I pulled the door open and dropped down into the driver's seat. Resting my forehead against the steering wheel, sighing hard.

A partner. I didn't want a partner, dammit.

I slammed the keys into the ignition and drove back to the station.

Chapter 2

The station was in the middle of the city where anything and everything was less than a five-minute walk from its front door. I pulled my car into the garage and took the elevator up to the homicide unit.

My office was in the far corner of the building, on the fourteenth floor. It looked out onto the lake and I loved it. Normally, newer detectives would be assigned a desk out in the common area, but I'd won the corner view in the yearly retirement raffle.

The retirement raffle was the division's way of making a little cash for the police athletic league. Whenever the previous inhabitant of any office on the floor was about to retire, their office would be raffled off. The tickets, at ten bucks each, were put into a patrol hat and drawn by the retiree to be

Last year, I was the lucky winner, but what most didn't know was that I spent two hundred dollars on raffle tickets. Giving me a significant chance of winning. Aaron gave me crap for spending that much, but it was for a good cause. The view was the only reason I came to work, most days.

My office was also the only space in the unit that was neat and orderly. The bookshelves around me were full of various science textbooks intermingling with the necessary law books.

But the law texts were slowly being replaced with more science books. I'd begun to take an interest in forensic science and research over the last few years. My high and hungry IQ was in constant search of current information to sate its hunger. My poor mind was starved for anything other than gruesome crime scenes, autopsy reports, and endless witness statements. I was burning out as a police detective and I needed to re-energize my mind, until I was eligible for early retirement.

I sighed as I sat down. Maybe I should've gone to medical school instead of the police academy.

Staring blankly at the computer screen, I sorted through bland department emails until my phone rang. I answered with a grumble. "Detective Lieutenant Tiernan."

"Hello, Emma, it's Betty. The Captain would like to see you in his office, about twenty minutes ago." There was a sarcastic tone in her voice, followed by a soft chuckle. Betty was Captain Jameson's secretary, a lovely older woman and the only other person in the station I allowed to use my first name. Only because she would've slapped the dirty look off my face if I ever tried to give her one.

She once asked me why I hated being called Emma. I told her I felt I had to maintain a border between my work life and personal life, the linchpin being my first name. It was far too personal, in my mind.

I ran a hand over my eyes, pressing the heel against them to relieve some of the tension they held. "Please tell him I'll be down in a minute." I hung up the phone and grumbled to myself. I knew the second I stepped into the Captain's office, I'd be meeting the new partner I *did not* want.

I grabbed the coroner's report from the hands of an intern who was on the way to my office and flipped through it in the elevator down to the administrative floor. It was a preliminary field report highlighting the victim's external injuries. The full autopsy wouldn't be done until later in the evening.

I was far more interested in that other report, but wanted some paper to fill the case file, to feel like I was moving somewhere with this new body. I glanced over the minute details Aaron shared with me, locking them into my memory for future reference. The elevator dinged as I finished the one-and-a-half-page report, and the door opened on the quiet hum of the administrative floor.

The admin floor was cleaner than the rest of the station and was always in a state of renovation. The public spent more time on this floor than anywhere else in the massive old building and deserved a clean, shiny place to complain about how little we were doing to solve the crimes against humanity.

My smile was genuine as I stepped closer to the Captain's office and saw Betty at her desk. She returned the smile, and stood up to meet me at his door. The closer I moved towards it, the more clearly I heard his voice. He was proudly boasting random impressive facts about the department in the stupid political tone he sometimes used when babies and city officials were nearby. Waiting to be kissed and shook. I sighed hard and nodded to Betty as she pushed the door open. I followed her in and saw her motion to the Captain, to let him know I'd finally arrived for this fateful meeting.

I might have been a little more fearful of Captain Liam Jameson if he hadn't been an old friend of my father's and practically watched me grow up. Because he was a friend of the family, he always treated me with respect, and often ignored my unique ways of working and my constant requests to be partner-free.

Liam was as old as my father, but his hair had gone pure white a long time ago. His somewhat movie star looks were amplified by his perfectly tailored white, blue, and gold police uniform. And if you squinted, he looked like Clint Eastwood.

As Liam made eye contact with me, he broke out a wide grin full of shiny white teeth. "Ah! Detective Lieutenant Tiernan, so glad you could make it." He motioned for me to take a seat next to someone I barely looked at.

I knew they were my new partner, and I secretly hoped the less I looked at them, the quicker they would get fed up with my icy demeanor and disappear. I sat down, crossed my legs and set the case file on my lap. I smiled, throwing on my best attempt at an even tone. "Apologies for being a little bit late, but Detective Liang and I caught a new case over on the Southside docks."

Jameson leaned against his desk nodding. "Ah, perfect! This will be a great start for you two. Detective Lieutenant Emma Tiernan, I'd like you to meet your new partner, Officer Sasha Garnier." He waved his hand at the person sitting to my right. "Oh, pardon me, I meant Detective Sasha Garnier."

I sighed at the way Liam was laying it on thick, and looked at my new rookie partner.

What I saw caught me by surprise. I was expecting a young hotshot male patrol officer. Instead, I was staring at one of the most beautiful women I'd ever seen in my life. Sasha Garnier wore crisp patrol blues, and her light brown was hair pulled into a tight regulation bun. But her eyes, her eyes were an incredible hazel color. copper in the center, with green edges and dapples of silver when the light caught them. She grinned at me, holding out her hand, pulling me away from staring deeper into her eyes.

I clenched my jaw, knowing in one look that grin would have a profound impact on me if I continued to stare at it, and her. Both elegant and cute, Sasha had a Midwestern girl-next-door appeal. I felt my cheeks grow warm from studying her features. Regardless of my Ice Queen reputation, I was a sucker for a beautiful woman, especially one in uniform, a secret I kept close to my chest.

Most of my coworkers were new to the division and didn't know about my personal life. Those who did kept a respectable distance after Elle's funeral.

I smiled tightly, and took the hand Sasha extended to me.

"It's so great to meet you, Detective Lieutenant Tiernan." When Sasha spoke, it was in an eager, clipped tone, making me groan internally at her enthusiasm. "I've heard so much about you and your work. I even read some of the essays you published in American Psychology Today while I was still in the academy. They were suggested course reading, but I couldn't stop there. Your work is impressive." I half listened to her voice, focusing more on how the hell I could talk my way out of this one. Though she squeezed my hand in a professional way that asserted power, there was also something oddly comforting about this woman. Her skin was warm, gentle, and it eased some of the tension that always came to me with shaking hands. I swallowed hard and released her hand, curling mine into a fist to unconsciously save the feeling.

My cheeks flushed, and I quickly filled my empty hand with the case file, embarrassed at how much I immediately missed the contact of my new partner.

I kept my smile tight, unreadable. "Thank you." I winced at how stupid my thank you sounded. "How long have you been with the department?"

Her smile grew. "About five years as a patrol officer. I took the Detective test last month and almost beat your score." She shrugged innocently, still smiling. "Only missed it by five points."

I nodded. Her tone erased my mild embarrassment, allowing my irritation to grow and my patience wane, a deadly combination.

"Only five points." My tone came off cold, but I wasn't one for small social chatter, so I didn't care. I turned to Liam, glaring at him. "Please tell me this is just one case. Show the rookie the ropes and then I can go back to solo work. I don't have the time, nor the patience to be an FTO right now, Captain."

I could feel Garnier — and the air around her — tense up. I wasn't lying. I truly preferred to be alone as much as possible and learned over the years that following through with the Ice Queen image kept people away from me. I could focus on closing cases and do my work, my way.

Liam scowled at me. "This is an indefinite assignment, Detective Lieutenant Tiernan. You of all people should know how much this unit's caseload has increased over the last few months. The department is drowning, and we need more fresh detectives out on the streets. You're one of the best I have, and I need you to train others to be as good as you." He then nodded at Garnier. "She's proven herself to be one of the best patrol officers and came highly recommended by her shift supervisors."

Liam and I stared each other down, neither one giving an inch. I knew I wouldn't be able to negotiate out of this new partnership. I hung my head in silent defeat and sighed, standing up from the chair. "Alright, fine. But I won't promise you anything, Captain Jameson. You know my partners don't last long." I tucked the file under my arm and looked back at my new partner, clenching my jaw. "Let's go. We have work to do. This is day one of becoming a detective."

I stepped to the door, opened it and walked out, leaving Garnier to scramble, to grab her stuff and chase after me.

"Tiernan! Halt! Get back in here!" Liam was pissed with me and my flippant concession to taking on a partner.

I glanced at Garnier. "I'll be right back. Don't move an inch." I rolled my eyes when she nodded and stood straight as a board in her spot. Five years on the road, my ass. More like five days out of the academy.

I angrily walked back into Liam's office, closing the door behind me. He had his hands on his hips, softening his tone as he spoke. "Look, Emma, I know you hate having partners, and it's evident to everyone in the entire department you only work alone. But my hands are tied. I'm getting shit from the Alderman's and city officials about rising crime statistics. Garnier's file was put on my desk by the Superintendent as a favor to one of his cronies. If I can't push back, you can't." He paused, looking me over. "This might actually be good for you. You know they call you the Ice Queen around here? Having a partner might melt that opinion a bit." I saw he felt bad repeating the nickname. "Please, just try with this one, for me? Sasha has the street smarts and she'll become a good detective if you let her. Like I said, you're stuck with her. Don't try to make her quit or make her cry." He raised a knowing eyebrow at me. "Your tricks aren't that tricky, Emma."

I smiled, trying not to laugh. "That was one time, Liam, and you know it." It had been one time, and one time only, that I made a trainee cry, out on the road. It happened a handful of years ago. I wouldn't speak to the kid for hours on end in the unmarked car. Only giving him directions in-between pointing out everything he'd done wrong on the last traffic stop. I then spent hours criticizing him and how he could improve on everything, never really cutting him a break. The kid fell apart two weeks after I rewrote all his reports since they didn't meet my high standards. He quit the training program that night. Last I saw him, he was working as a night security guard over at Soldier Field.

Liam looked at me with that fatherly look I hated. "Please, Emma. I'm so close to retirement and it's my last wish to see you keep a partner for more than a week. Let me have that? The tiny little wish of a tired old man?"

I didn't hold back from laughing. "Okay, I'll give you one month. No more." I pointed at him with the case file. "And only because you're one of my dad's best friends." I winked at him and walked back out to Garnier, who stood exactly as I left her, waiting for my return. As soon as she saw me, she rushed to the elevator to hit the call button. She even smiled as I stopped next to her.

"What kind of case do we have, Detective Lieutenant Tiernan?" The eagerness in her voice grated on my ears and nerves like literal nails on a chalkboard. She was so full of excitement, eager to work on her first homicide. I also detected a tiny hint of her trying to impress me with a positive, proactive attitude. Further annoying me.

When the elevator doors opened, I walked to the back of the car. I leaned against the wall, gripping on to the silver handrails, and focused on the red digital floor display. I took a breath, mumbling. "Murder." I was already done with this new partner. It didn't help that I was beyond overloaded with cases and wasn't sleeping.

I had five open homicides, five more pending closure once I collected the final statements for the prosecutor. On top of those ten cases, I'd begun to do some consulting work with the State Troopers. I was working with them to assist in re-evaluating evidence processing techniques for cold cases, which would in turn help find new leads. It was interesting work, and I enjoyed it, but I was pushing the borderline of being burned out. I was not in the mood to deal with an eager rookie who asked stupid questions.

"What kind of murder?" Her voice dripped excitement around the second stupid question of the day. Worse than that, I could hear the smile in her voice.

"The kind of murder that leaves us with a dead body, Detective Garnier." I gave her a shitty look, before my eyes drifted on their own to her baby blue uniform shirt and how it fit a little too close around her chest.

The idle glance became an all-out stare as I focused on how the shirt curved around certain areas, making my throat dry. Garnier was gorgeous, even in that horrible polyester uniform.

I cleared my throat. This wasn't good. I was tired and lonely, and perving on my new partner wasn't the cure. I distracted myself by looking back at the grime covering the floor buttons. "You know you don't need to wear that uniform anymore."

Garnier smiled, shrugging. "They called me first thing this morning to tell me I was promoted. It's all I really had to wear on such short notice." She looked down at her uniform, fidgeting with her gear belt. The action drew my eyes back to her. I sighed. Even her gun looked sexy as it perched at an angle on her hip.

Once again, my new partner struggled to keep up with me the second the elevator doors opened. I shook my head. This was going to make for a difficult few months.

Looking through the open door to my office, I saw Aaron sitting in the spare chair, his feet up on my desk. The moment I walked in, I shoved his feet off my desk, making him sit up straight. "You know I hate when you put your feet on my desk."

He grinned back at me. "I know you do. That's exactly why I do it." He slouched back in the chair, tossing a file on my desk. "Here's the preliminary autopsy report. Oh, and where's your new partner?" He swung his head around dramatically.

"Right here." Garnier walked into the office, causing Aaron to give himself whiplash. He looked at Garnier, who stood straight as a pin in her tight-fitting uniform, then back at me and mouthed, *Oh my God*. I rolled my eyes as Garnier held out her hand.

"I'm Sasha Garnier. Emma's new partner."

Aaron took her hand, cringing as we both heard my first name roll past the rookie's lips. He looked at me warily, waiting for what was about to come next.

I didn't bother to look up from the file Aaron gave me. "Detective Garnier. Do not ever use my first name. You may only refer to me as Detective Lieutenant Tiernan, Lieutenant, or LT for short. Most everyone uses the latter." I looked up at her with a hard, biting stare. "Only those who I trust *implicitly* may use my first name."

I watched color rise fast into Garnier's cheeks. She nodded tightly, doing her best to hold back embarrassment or anger. It didn't matter to me which. I didn't trust her, I didn't need her, and the quicker she got pissed off at me, the quicker she'd quit.

The tension grew thickly in the room, as if a fog full of it had rolled in through the door. Aaron cleared his throat and attempted to ease it. "It's great to meet you, Sasha. I'm Detective Aaron Liang, but feel free to call me Aaron." He smiled that nauseating charming grin that'd broken many a secretary's heart. "Don't worry about the Lieutenant over here. It takes a minute or two to get used to her."

I glared at him, and watched the color fall from Garnier's face as a small smile appeared. Aaron had rescued her for the moment. She let out a slow breath. "Thank you, Aaron. I'm happy to be in the homicide unit. Even if some aren't." The last part she whispered, hoping I wouldn't hear it.

By the time their introductions drifted to idle chatter, I'd already looked over the entire file. I scribbled a few notes and names on the top sheet and handed it over to Garnier, not bothering to look at her as I spoke. "Detective Garnier, we have our victim's name. Will you go run him through the local database and pull any records we may have for him?"

Garnier took the paper I held out, excited to be finally doing something. "Where do I start?"

"The basement. That's where the main database computers are. The LEIN system only has current info, but I need everything. The records department has access to State and Federal databases." I reached for a pen, still ignoring the woman. "Ask for Paul. He may or may not be asleep down there. If he's awake, ask him about his days on the road. He'll warm up to you after a couple of stories and give you what you ask for faster. He'll also set you up with logins for everything you'll need up here."

Garnier smiled, nodding that she understood, and walked out of the office.

Aaron watched her walk out — less than innocently, as he tilted his head to get a better view of her walking away. I threw a paper clip at his face. "Don't make her key your car like that secretary from robbery did after one of your infamous one-night stands."

Aaron chuckled. "She's super hot, Emma. Like unbearably, out of control hot and that uniform, good lord! Can you imagine for a minute what's under there?" He shook his head in disbelief.

I clenched my jaw. I suddenly did want to imagine what that uniform was hiding, but I wasn't going to. My main goal in life now was to shake this Sasha Garnier loose as fast as possible. But Aaron was right. Garnier was beautiful and there was something about her that drew me in as much as it annoyed me.

Aaron threw his feet back up on the edge of my desk, "Oh, and dick move sending her to Pauly. You know he won't shut the hell up when she asks him about the whole two months he was on the road. That poor girl will be down there for hours, maybe even days. You could've just shown her how to log in from your computer, Lieutenant, with Lieutenant access."

I shrugged. "Call it a learning curve? I wanted to look over the preliminary report in silence before I get thrown into the second round of twenty questions from her." I looked back at the file. "Is there anything that stands out to you at the scene, Aaron? I didn't see anything out of the ordinary, other than the pages placed under the victim's head."

Aaron dropped his feet from the desk. Leaning forward, he flipped a page in the file as it sat in front of me, his finger jabbing at a paragraph. "Dr. Willows found what looked to be knife carvings in the victim's lower back."

I flipped to the autopsy pictures, grateful Liam had made the call for Dr. Willows to put a rush on the autopsy, since it wasn't the first body of the morning. With luck, I could look at the body by lunch.

I found the one photograph of the lower back. The left side was red and had definite knife wounds. Someone had roughly carved *'Ego te provoco'* into the poor man's skin.

I stared at the Latin, and wrote the phrase down, quickly translating it. My study of Latin had been part of my mother's attempt at a religious education, before she realized science was more important to me than a dead language.

I looked up at Aaron. "It reads, *I challenge you*. Someone must have a fucked up sense of humor." I handed him the file. "Other than that, the whole scene reads like a robbery gone bad. No personal belongings found on the guy, and the significant defensive wounds on the front of his forearms, tells me it was a fight to the end." I leaned back in the chair, rubbing at the bridge of my nose. This case was amplifying my exhaustion. I just wanted to go home and crawl into bed for a few days.

As Aaron sat quietly reading the reports, I stood and went to the corner window. I loved my view of the city and the river from this high up. The view was often the sole reason I did not file my early retirement paperwork. I could sit at my desk when I needed a moment away from a case and watch sailboats enjoy the first warm spring day, dotting the river and lake like small white paper boats. I couldn't help but smile as I watched a few move across the water with graceful ease. Not a care in the world other than catching a stiff wind.

I was taken out of my moment of Zen when something hit the top of my desk with a hard, angry slap. I turned and looked right in the flushed face of my new partner. Garnier's face was bright red as she stood in front of my desk. Her arms folded tight across her chest, accompanied by an evil, irritated look on her flawless features. "I get that you don't want me here, but you're stuck with me. I had to pry Pauly off his chair to get him to help me, then he wouldn't shut the hell up. When I finally got him to stop telling me about his first real traffic stop, he hit on me."

She glared at me. "I know I'm a rookie, and I have to go through the hazing process. But you need to understand, *Detective Lieutenant Tiernan*, I'm not going anywhere." My full title came out of her mouth dripping with venom.

I saw Aaron trying to not laugh out loud from his chair, covering his mouth with a fist. I shot him a look before addressing Garnier. "Well then, Detective Garnier, did you get what I asked for?" I was not about to let this woman, who was even more beautiful with the blush around her cheeks, get to me.

Garnier took a deep breath before she pointed angrily at the file. "That's the printout of our victim. David Harrow. Age twenty-nine with no real record aside from a few parking tickets. He was a medical student at Northwestern, about to enter his last semester before taking a residency at City Hospital." Her eyes never left mine as she rattled off the victim's basic facts with clear and crisp irritation hanging from every word.

I nodded. "Very good." I sat forward in my chair, flipping through the file Garnier had thrown in front of me. I wouldn't look at her, blatantly ignoring her presence, even if I could feel her eyes boring holes into me.

I blatantly ignored her, focusing on the file she threw on the desk, and it set her off.

She took a step closer to my desk, trying to get me to look up again, to acknowledge her. "Now I fully understand why they call you the Ice Queen." She spoke the two little words loudly, finally getting my attention.

I heard Aaron slightly choke as he stood. "Uh, I'm going to grab a cup of coffee." He made a quick exit, knowing it was best to leave before the hurricane hit.

I met Garnier's hard stare with one equally as hard. "Excuse me?"

Garnier chuckled lightly. "You heard me. Ice Queen. The entire department calls you that. Now I see why." She took a deep breath, obviously trying to reel in her temper as I continued to stare at her. "I was excited to be partnered with you. I've always heard amazing things about the great Detective Emma Tiernan. I was willing to leave the locker room gossip to just that, gossip. But now, I can agree with the rest of the department. You *are* the Ice Queen. You're incredibly rude and cold."

I stared at Garnier a moment longer. I didn't want to show her in any way that her words stung and stung deep. I was an Ice Queen, I knew it, but I wanted to keep people at a distance. Ever since I lost my true love, my one purpose to keep trying, I didn't want to connect with anyone anymore. It was easier to live my life in solitary silence.

I measured my words carefully before responding to Garnier's outburst. "All you need to do to succeed here is listen to me. Be quiet and ignore what others think of me. If you do that, you might actually learn something other than having unprofessional outbursts in front of my coworkers." I tossed her an empty file folder. "Now make yourself useful and start the formal case report."

Garnier was thrown off by the lack of emotional response to her little tirade. I knew she expected me to get red faced and passionate, to yell back or counter her with reasons why I wasn't the Ice Queen. But I didn't. I wasn't going to show the woman standing in front of me that she could inspire any sort of emotional reaction from me. It was bad enough her eyes shifted to a brighter coppery green when she was angry, drawing me further into them and the strange magnetism of her entire aura. Garnier was fierce, and I liked it. I liked it too much.

She glared at me for a minute before she sat on the chair Aaron vacated. As she began to fill out the paperwork, she spoke with a softer tone. "You don't have to be like this with me, Lieutenant. I'm not like the rest." She waited for any reaction from me. When I gave her none, she returned to the paperwork before her.

Garnier slid the file back to me a few minutes later, twirling the pen in her fingers. "All set. What's next?"

I kept my head down, my eyes on my own paperwork as I spoke. "You can go home for the day. Tomorrow we start again. Be here at eight, not a minute later." I glanced at her out of the corner of my eye, eager to see her reaction as I continued to find, and push, her buttons.

Garnier smirked, standing up. "Sounds good." Her rookie eagerness to solve the world's crimes was back in full effect. She stepped towards the door, turning to look over her shoulder. "Goodnight, Lieutenant." She smiled lightly, and I caught a glimpse of dimples hiding near the corners of her mouth.

I swallowed hard, trying to shake off the feeling those dimples stirred in my stomach. "Remember, you no longer have to wear that uniform." I waved my pen at her baby blue shirt and long, dark blue polyester pants.

Garnier nodded and smiled. "I wondered how long it would take you to ask me to take my uniform off." She tapped twice on the door frame, and before I could respond she walked out of my office towards the elevator, and disappeared behind the steel doors. I was left staring at the closed doors, asking myself if my rookie had just openly flirted with me.

Chapter 3

I shoved my front door open and added the newest pieces of mail to the massive pile on the side table. I dropped my keys into a bowl next to the stack, kicking the door closed behind me. My house was spotless and obsessively organized to a tee, except for my mail. My bills were all on auto pay. The rest was mostly junk mail and catalogues, all lying in a messy heap.

The only person to touch the ignored mail was my mother. She would come over every so often and sort through it for me, leaving the long-unopened sympathy cards in a separate stack that I'd cover up until they were shuffled back to the bottom. There they'd sit until my mother shuffled them back to the top on her next visit.

I opened my industrial-sized fridge and frowned at the only things staring back at me: an expired gallon of organic milk, a few sad pieces of fruit, and two bottles of beer. I grabbed a beer and opened it, taking a large swig as I wrote on the dry erase board stuck to the fridge door before heading to the living room. *Buy groceries, or you will starve.*

The massive mahogany brown leather chair in my living room had been a splurge purchase after we moved in. I sat facing the large picture window, looking out onto the lake.

My house sat in a quieter part of the city off Lakeshore Drive. It was fancier than my tastes and paycheck could handle, but I loved the fact I could sit in my old leather chair while I looked at the water for hours. It was what calmed me down after a shitty day at work.

Twirling the bottle in my hand, I thought about my new partner. Garnier was gorgeous and different. She was fierce, feisty and kind. As much as I hated having a partner, there was something about the woman that I welcomed. Maybe my heart was trying to tell me this life of isolation was killing the both of us, and Garnier could be a good place to start melting the ice. I sighed. I had to be careful about my thoughts on this particular matter and my burgeoning feelings for her. It'd been a long time since Elle, and I'd shut down that part of my heart and brain when I lost her. I never ever wanted to open it back up.

Finishing the beer, I stood. My head was now far too heavy with sad memories. I tossed the empty bottle into the recycling bin before heading upstairs to my bedroom.

I stripped out of my pantsuit, hanging it up in my closet, in perfect order with the many others before placing my gun in its holster on the bedside table. It was a cold reminder, and the only constant companion I had, along with work.

After throwing on an old Chicago Marathon shirt and a pair of sleep shorts, I sat down in the middle of my bed and tried to read over David Harrow's file.

David had been an average young man navigating through life in the Windy City. He'd been working through college to become a doctor in hopes of helping humanity. From his college transcripts and other work records, David had led a normal life. He had been a random target of a murderer, and that left a sinking feeling in my stomach.

Usually, I would've passed this run-of-the-mill murder off as a random mugging gone wrong, but the Latin phrase, *'Ego te provoco'* stuck out. It was very unusual to see something like Bible pages purposely placed under a victim. Someone had purposely taken the time to carve those words into David with care and precision, leading me to believe it was an attempt at leaving a signature. A common theme for serial killers when they start their killing games.

If my sinking feeling was right, I'd have a couple more bodies fall in my lap before long, with similar carvings or pages. I blew out a breath, grabbed my notepad and began scribbling out thoughts and keywords I'd found in David's file.

I sat with his file for a couple more hours, reading it over in its entirety twice, making a list of witnesses and acquaintances to interview in the coming days. I put one person, Katie Thompson, at the top of the list. David had her listed as the first contact for emergencies on his university forms. It was possible she was family or a girlfriend. She would be my first call in the morning.

I closed the file and tossed it on the floor as I stretched out cramped legs. I rolled onto the side of the bed, rubbing at my eyes and scanned the room. My bedroom was the largest room in the house and had been empty — aside from a bed and dresser — when Elle was alive, but over the last year, I'd begun to fill it with bookshelves. Turning one corner of the room into a small study for those sleepless nights on a case.

Like at my office, there were books on criminal psychology, forensic techniques, firearm analysis, interviewing strategies with a large section of medical texts stuffed onto the shelves. I roamed my eyes over the spines of all the titles I'd collected, shaking my head at how strangely obsessed I'd become with books to fill the emptiness, when they wandered across the photograph of Elle and me.

My heart tumbled into my twisting stomach at the sight of it, a simple color photograph in a plain mahogany frame.

In two breaths, I was up and holding the frame with a shaky hand. The photograph was of Elle and me on summer vacation in New York City. We did all the silly tourist things, but only took one photograph of us.

We stood together under the Brooklyn Bridge, the city skyline in the background. Elle was kissing my cheek and I was grinning like a kid on Christmas morning. My grin stretched from one corner to the other, to the point I'm sure my face hurt, I was that happy.

I ran a finger over Elle's face, tracing her cheek. I swallowed hard, whispering to no one but my books. "I miss you so much, Elle." I closed my eyes and pressed the frame against my heart, letting my memory drift back to when I first met her.

* * *

It was my fifth year in the department, back when I was a patrol officer still learning the ins and outs of the job. I loved that every day on the road was never the same, but at the same time my frustration was beginning to build. Every day I saw the same junkies, the same dipshits with outstanding warrants, and the same couples beating each other black and blue. Then there were the kids who were caught in the middle of it all, reminding me of my own listless childhood. The job was beginning to give me a bitter outlook on humanity even though I was doing my best to stay positive.

One weekend, my shift Sergeant volunteered me to represent the Chicago Police Department along with the local Police Athletic League chapter at the conference center. Evidently, it was a large conference for urban renewal contractors, developers, and architects. The place would be packed with the rich and wealthy, looking to do their part to continue revitalizing the downtrodden sections of the city.

The Captain at the time wanted to make sure the police department was represented, and by represented, he meant getting the rich out of towners to donate to PAL and the department. My Sergeant handpicked me because he said I looked like I came from money and could relate to being wealthy. I knew it was his politically correct way of saying I was one of the better-looking female officers and could persuade a few more dollars out of the wallets of old rich men. I wanted to tell the Captain to stick it up his ass, but I was still new and had a detective badge in my sights.

I sighed as I walked into the convention center, wearing my stiff dress uniform. I felt awkward as hell in the sea of cocktail dresses and suits that must have cost at least three months' worth of my measly cop paychecks.

Shaking my head at the sight before me, I hollered over my shoulder at the other officer I was stuck with for the night. I knew his last name was Donnelly from our days at the academy. The rest I didn't care to know. He ignored me shouting his name over and over as he talked up the few random women drinking at the front bar, leaving me alone to set up the meet and greet table.

When everything was perfect, I stood behind it, all perfect myself in a neat blue uniform, doing my best to engage with every passerby. I plastered a fake smile on my face and went to work swindling handfuls of money out of the masses of people intent on bringing new hope to the city.

Within a couple of hours, I grew tired of the false smiles and laughs. The sympathetic looks. So, I sat, alone, on the hard-plastic folding chair the conference center had provided, blindly uttering well-practiced lines to anyone who stopped at the table. After a handful of unsuccessful attempts, I stopped even looking up, just mumbled and hoped they'd leave a few bucks in the jar, then leave me alone.

I placed one of the criminal psychology textbooks I'd brought on my lap and out of view of any possible donors. I sighed as I leaned on my hand, reading over how the serial killer's mind worked, when I heard a soft, feminine voice.

"If I donate to the Police Athletic League, will it buy kids giant red rubber balls to throw at each other?"

I sucked in a breath, eyes still trailing along the paragraph about how inhibitors in the brain's chemistry could contribute to the development of deviant behavior and rattled off a practiced speech.

"Ma'am, if you do decide to donate, your donation will be put to appropriate use. It will purchase much needed sports equipment for the many of the city's youth sports teams. Giving kids a chance to participate in a team building activity that is fun and community oriented." I shook my head. Even *I* was bored by my own monotone voice.

"Well, that does sound fantastic, officer. But what I really want to know is, will my money go to buying kids dodgeballs? So, kids can pelt each other with rubber balls and learn how to compete to the death?"

I furrowed my brow and looked up at the person behind one of the most unusual questions of the night. What I saw made me stand up and straighten out my uniform jacket.

Before me stood a tall, elegant young woman. Her dark red hair was pulled back into a tight, classical hairstyle, giving me a clear view of her long neck and pale skin. When she smiled at me, the smile seemed to carry up into her dark sapphire blue eyes. My eyes drifted to the fire engine red dress this woman wore. It sat off the shoulder, went to the floor and showed off her shape just enough to be decent, but incredibly sexy. I cleared my throat. I knew I was staring and tried to stop myself, to make eye contact instead.

This woman was beautiful. Looking at her made me nervous, and my uniform suddenly felt very warm. "Yes ma'am. Your money will go to buying kids' sporting equipment."

The woman laughed. "I was just kidding, Officer..." She trailed off, her head tilting as she looked at my name tag.

I pointed at the name tag with an awkward motion, fumbling over my tongue as I spoke. "Officer Tiernan." I tapped on the tag, watching her eyes land on my finger where it pressed against the slim silver bar. I tried to recover and held my hand out. "Officer Emma Tiernan, ma'am."

She grinned and took my hand. I bit my lip at how warm her hand was and the tingle of electricity that swirled as our palms pressed together. "Officer Emma Tiernan, it's nice to meet you. My name is Elle Adair."

Her grin grew as I held on longer than was polite. I couldn't help it. I was mesmerized by this striking woman.

I quickly released her hand, wanting to jam mine into a pocket, but couldn't — it was against regulations to have your hands in your pockets while in the dress uniform. Instead, I filled my shaking hands with PAL pamphlets. "If you'd like to read more about the program, I have these." I frowned. Good lord, I was an awkward idiot.

Elle moved closer to the table. "I noticed you from across the room, looking extremely bored. I had to find out why." She nodded towards the front bar. "I saw your partner over there, talking to some of the Chicago Bears' cheerleaders and realized you were an abandoned police officer. I apologize if I caught you by surprise." Her eyes never left mine as she spoke.

Tugging at my clip-on tie, I tried to let some of the rising heat out. I was starting to overheat from embarrassment and instant attraction. "Donnelly never made it to the table. He abandoned me from the start."

"I can keep you company. I'm equally as bored. I'm only at this conference because my boss had tickets to the Bull's game, and I've long ago run out of patience for shop talk." Elle picked up a pamphlet, glancing over it. "I would love to hear some exciting police stories, and in trade I'll help you wiggle some more money out of these fat cats' wallets."

When she looked up at me, her smile drifting to a smirk, I felt my heart skip.

I shrugged, giving her a bashful smile. "I might have a couple of exciting stories to tell."

Elle came around the table and sat in the chair I'd set out for Donnelly. She grabbed my hand and pulled me down to sit next to her. "I would love to hear them, Officer." The large grin she gave me melted all my will to stay tough.

I sat with Elle for the rest of the night, sharing stories. I told her about when I chased a junkie down Michigan Avenue and how when I caught him, he stabbed me with an old school ruler he'd sharpened into a point. He later told me he was so high, he thought I was one of the nuns from his Catholic school days. I then told her about being the first officer on scene to a rollover accident on the highway. I'd lain on the hot concrete with the woman trapped inside, holding her hand and telling her bad jokes to keep her calm until they cut her free. She recovered fully from her injuries and every year on the date of the accident, I'd get a card from her with one terrible joke in it and a thank you.

Elle smiled at that story, placing her hand on my knee. Her touch filtered through the heavy polyester pants, and my heart bounced around in my chest like a rubber ball.

In between the cop stories, and manipulating rich developers out of a few more dollars, Elle told her own story. She was an architect for a large firm and had designed a few of the new buildings popping up around the city.

I smiled at how excited she was when she talked about her work, so passionate in the way she spoke with her hands and sparkling eyes. I found myself grinning. I was enjoying every minute of being with this woman.

An hour later, Donnelly ran over to us, interrupting a story Elle was telling me about her first design.

He banged on the table with his meaty fist. "Yo! Tiernan, wrap this shit up. It's time to go. I have a hot date!" He waggled a napkin with a number scribbled on it in pen. I couldn't decide whether I wanted to punch him in the throat for abandoning me, or for interrupting Elle.

He shot me a dirty look when I didn't immediately jump at his orders. "Seriously Tiernan, hurry your ass up. I'll be in the car. Leaving in ten minutes, with or without you." He strutted away from the table and back towards the bar where three cheerleaders were giggling and waving at him.

I clenched my jaw, running my hands over my thighs to prevent myself from getting up and chasing after Donnelly. I huffed and stood, gathering up the pamphlets and donation jar. "I'm sorry about that, Elle. Donnelly is my ride back and I certainly don't want to have to ride the bus in this." I motioned to my blue police uniform.

Elle stood up, reaching for some of the pamphlets, still smiling. I was starting to suspect the woman always had a smile on her face. "That big lug seems like a jerk."

I chuckled. "You have no idea." I dumped my stack of flyers and pamphlets in the box, and turned to Elle, reaching for the stack she held out, when our hands brushed against each other. I gasped like a silly teenager, and looked into her eyes. God, they were so blue. A shade of blue I didn't think could exist in the natural world.

I forced in a steadying breath, desperate to settle my racing heart. Elle had me teetering on the edge of smitten to full blown love at first sight. "Thank you. Thank you for sitting with me, keeping me company. It was really great to meet you." I drifted off, not knowing what else to say. I didn't want to leave this woman, but I'd no clue how to draw out the night. Especially since Donnelly was standing nearby, tapping his watch like the obnoxious ass he was.

Elle reached into my chest pocket, slowly pulling one of my pens out. "Let me give you my phone number. Call me the moment you ditch that jerk. Maybe we can have a drink and grab something to eat?" She glanced up as she scribbled her name and phone number on the box top. She then slowly slid the pen back in my pocket. Her eyes were so blue, blue like a thousand oceans and made my heart skip a thousand times with one look.

I couldn't wipe the smile off my face. Unable to utter a word, I was already beyond smitten for this woman.

Elle grabbed my hand, squeezing it as she grinned at me. "Till then, Officer Emma Tiernan." She tapped my name badge with her finger before walking away. Her red dress disappeared into the thick crowd of real estate developers.

It was my turn to run. I hustled Donnelly into the car and made him drive full lights and sirens back to the station. I threw the box of flyers into the storage closet, dropped the donation money with the desk sergeant and ran to the locker room. I changed in record time, and as I walked out of the station, I pulled out my phone and dialed the number my photographic memory had memorized.

I strode down familiar Chicago streets as the phone rang. It was early evening and the city felt alive. I fed off the energy around me.

The phone only rang twice before I heard Elle's voice. "Hello?"

"This is Officer Emma Tiernan. I'm calling to follow up on how your experience with the police department was today?" I cringed at how awkward I sounded, my joke falling flat.

"It was amazing. This beautiful lady cop kept me intrigued the whole night." She paused. "Hello, Emma." I felt her smile through the phone.

"Hi." I was ridiculously nervous. This woman already had quite an effect on me, and I was clueless as to what to say.

"Dinner or drinks? Or should we be adventurous and do both?" Elle's voice chased away the tension.

"Yes, to both. I'm starving and could use a drink." I stopped walking. "Where do you want to meet?"

"There's an outdoor restaurant at Millennium Park. Would you like to meet me there in say, a half hour?"

"I'll be there." I slipped my phone into a pocket and jogged the rest of the way, an eager grin stuck on my face.

The park was busy but not overwhelming. The evening, just cool enough for a light jacket, was perfect for a night outside. Tourists and locals were all enjoying the beginnings of a beautiful fall. I walked up the steps, looking for Elle. I expected to see her standing in her red dress, a beacon of beauty in the middle of the city. Instead, I found her at the top of the stairs, grinning, dressed down but still gorgeous in a white V-neck with a grey jacket over it, her hair gathered in a loose ponytail. My eyes scanned over her dark blue jeans to land on what made me smile the most: the worn grey Converse on her feet.

I walked up the steps to stop in front of her. "Hi." Without my uniform and sense of bravado it always offered me, I was just a shy woman in jeans and a button-down.

Elle smiled. "Officer. I'm glad you could make it." She motioned to the restaurant behind us. "Shall we?"

I nodded, following her to the table she'd reserved for us. We ate dinner, shared drinks and conversation. Elle was intelligent and funny, and she talked about her work with such passion; I was falling for her, little by little. I watched her eyes light up like tiny shards of sapphire as she talked about her work.

When it was my turn, I told her about how I fell into police work, taking a different route from being the doctor my mother wanted. I was drawn to helping people and I'd been entertaining returning to school and perhaps going into medicine in a few years if I didn't make detective, putting what I'd learned about the human mind on the streets and mixing it with medicine in hopes of helping more people.

I'd be eligible for an early retirement if I spent ten years as a detective and would only be in my early forties when I entered medical school. I also rambled on about some of my side projects in psychology and studying the human mind. Elle giggled and asked if I was a genius. I blushed, telling her I was just smarter than the average bear, but became a cop because each day provided me with a new puzzle to solve.

Her only remark to my comment was to reach across and take my hand, and tell me I was a very beautiful bear. Which, of course, made me blush.

The rest of the evening we people-watched and chatted. At the end of dinner, I offered to walk Elle home, since she was only a few blocks away from my own apartment. "I cannot let you walk home alone, Elle, without offering the best personal police protection." I smiled, wanting to draw out the evening as long as I could. I had a full-blown crush and reveled in the feeling of being with her.

Elle squinted, thinking for a moment. "I guess that's an offer I can't pass up, Officer."

"After you." I held my arm out for her to take. She laughed lightly, wrapping her hand around my elbow.

We walked through the city surging with life, radiating in our closeness. I couldn't stop smiling as I felt Elle pull closer into me, sliding her hand down into mine. She glanced at me to see if I would object. I grinned and squeezed her hand tighter, hearing her softly sigh.

We arrived at her house quicker than I hoped. I guided her up the front steps and when she opened the front door, I opened my mouth. "Um, thank you. This was lovely." I cringed. Why was this so hard? I was a cop who talked to people all day long. "You have my number if you want to hear some more cop stories or hear how your dodgeballs are doing." I was so awful at casual conversation.

Elle smiled, saying nothing as she stepped closer to me. She reached up with both of her hands and placed them on the sides of my face. My heart began to spin out of control.

She smiled as her deep blue eyes met mine. "I want to hear every one of them, Emma."

She closed the gap between us, and kissed me. Her lips were soft, and it took me a moment to react, but then I put my hands on her hips, pulling our bodies together.

I felt her smile against my mouth before pulling back. "Goodnight, Officer." She drew slow fingers down my jaw before letting her hand fall away. She winked at me before stepping inside and closing the door.

I stood there with a big dumb grin on my face, staring at her bright red door, taking in the moment, trying so hard not to run down the stairs in excitement.

After that first date, Elle and I became inseparable. Two years into our relationship, we bought the house facing the lake. Elle had found a cheap foreclosure and we renovated it to exactly what we wanted in a dream house. Elle tapped into her connections and her own design talent, turning the house into our home.

When the renovations were finished, we began to plan the rest of our lives together. She was finishing up a hospital contract and wanted to open her own firm with a coworker. I'd been promoted to the detective bureau a few months after that first date, and was preparing to leave the police department. I wanted to go back to school and become a doctor. I wanted a more stable lifestyle that wouldn't have me shot at every night and make her worry.

Everything in our lives was perfect and right on track.

One night, six months after we moved into the renovated home, I was knee-deep in a dumpster, looking at a dead prostitute dumped in there by her pimp, when Aaron ran up to me with a look I'd never seen on his face before.

"Emma, it's Elle." His voice trembled.

In those days, he never called me by my first name on the job. We were still figuring out our rhythm. We'd met when I was promoted and had become fast friends. He was like the brother I never had and he, in turn, became close with Elle. Elle would invite him to dinner, we'd double date, and we were becoming a small family.

When he called me by my first name, I knew something was wrong. "What is it?"

He handed me his phone. "It's your dad. He's at the hospital."

I swallowed a rising lump of panic and climbed out of the dumpster, grabbing the phone. "Dad? What's going on?"

"You need to come to the hospital. There's been an accident." My father's voice was raw, as if he'd been crying.

I threw the phone at Aaron, ran to a marked patrol car and drove to the hospital with full lights and sirens on.

I met my father as he stood in the waiting area of the emergency room. He said nothing as we walked me back to the trauma bay. He wrapped a hand around the edge of the curtain. "Elle was on her way home. A truck driver lost control when a car cut him off, and he slammed into her car. She rolled multiple times and it took them an hour to free her from the wreck."

"She's fine, right? She's going to be okay?" I swallowed hard, reaching for his hand.

He squeezed my shoulder. "I'll be out here if you need me." He opened the curtain, waiting for me to step past him.

What I saw before me brought me to my knees.

For days I never left her side, not until she quietly died in her sleep. The doctor tried to explain how extensive her internal injuries were, and that it would've been a harder life if she'd lived. He continued to give me specifics of her injuries. I stared at him blankly, and before he finished, I walked away and went home.

In the cold darkness of my bedroom, I fell apart. Uncontrollable sobbing, curling up in the middle of the bed. Crying until my stomach hurt and it was impossible to breathe. My heart literally felt like it had stopped beating in my chest. I pressed a hand against it. It was still in there, beating. I was still alive.

The day before the funeral, I was sorting through our closet, looking for the jewelry Elle's mom had requested for the viewing, when I found a small box with my name on it. I opened it to reveal two simple platinum bands nestled in the center. A small note was stuffed in the lid.

Emma, I know we were going to wait a little longer. But I can't. I love you and want to marry you in a pool of dodgeballs.

Heavy tears fell onto the note. I quickly wiped them away before they washed away the last little bit of Elle I had left.

I laid Elle to rest that week and proceeded to shut down and bury myself in work. I moved up the ladder to Lieutenant because of how fast I closed cases and became the Ice Queen of the department. I didn't care. I'd lost the one thing that kept me alive.

* * *

I sighed, setting the photograph back on the shelf, my stare lingering for a moment longer until the spine of a book caught my eye. I removed *Psychology Behind Hate Crimes* off the shelf. My gut feeling about the phrase that had been carved into the victim's stomach pointed towards a religious hate crime, but I needed to figure out the motive behind it. If there was a motive. I sat in bed as I sifted through chapter after chapter, hoping something would jump out. I finally found a section which stated most hate crimes were a result of an imagined need to protect oneself. A paragraph explained there is often a sense of panic when the target of the crime does not fit into the perpetrator's world vision. The victim is viewed as not being a part of the norm for one reason or another, and must be eliminated. This statement intrigued me, and I took notes. I'd have to talk to David's family, coworkers, and Katie, his emergency contact. This could've been a situation where David was the popular one who ignored his strange coworker and became a target. I made a note the perpetrator might have a mental illness.

After filling two pages of notes for Aaron, I shut off my light and tried to go to sleep. I laid in the bed, staring at the ceiling. My thoughts drifted away from case work and to other things, like my rookie. I'd not had feelings close to what I felt for Elle in the year and a half since she'd died, but when I looked at Garnier, I felt something. Whether it was lust or irritation, I'd yet to figure it out. I really didn't want to think about it with a fresh body on my mind, and willed my brain to shut up and move past it, until I fell asleep.

Chapter 4

I woke up earlier than I desired. Sleep escaped me each day the cases stacked up on my desk. I'd be lucky if I got a solid six hours of sleep every other night. I showered, dressed, and went into work, stopping for a triple espresso on the way.

It was four in the morning when I arrived, and the station was almost empty. I loved early mornings in the department. The midnight shift was busy at the start but slowed down right before shift change, bringing in the new day with an eerie peace. The midnight officers were very quiet and always smiled when I came in. They'd never gotten the Ice Queen memo and I was thankful for that.

I slipped into my office and went to work on the stack of files on my desk, signing off on the unit's currently closed cases. The only downfall to becoming Lieutenant was having to sign off on everything. It was interesting to read over the cases and how each detective worked them, but extremely frustrating to catch minor mistakes that drove my attention to detail to the brink. I yawned, glancing at the empty Styrofoam cup. I'd need another boost of caffeine by the time the sun rose.

Two hours later, Aaron walked out of the elevator, two paper coffee cups in hand.

"Morning, Emma. Another sleepless night?" He set a cup in front of me. "Hot green tea, no sweetener, with a splash of honey and two ice cubes." He winked as I smiled and wrapped my hands around the warm cup.

"It only took you a year to get my order right, but thank you, Aaron. How'd you know I'd be in this early?"

He sat down, placing his feet on the edge of my desk. "Don't praise me for my memory. The girl at the coffee shop has been making your drink for the last two years. She helped me make sure it was perfect." He leaned back, looking over my bookshelves. "I know you, Emma. You get stressed out. Then you stop sleeping from the stress, so you come to work and stress out some more." He raised his eyebrows. "You have patterns you never seem to break, only stick to harder. Are you sure you're not becoming a serial killer in waiting?"

I shook my head, smiling. "It's nice to see you actually have detective skills." I leaned forward in my chair. "Why are *you* here early? You usually don't come in for another four hours." I glanced at the clock over my door. It was still very early, almost six a.m. and yet it felt like midnight, the sun still hiding for a few more hours

He chuckled. "True. I'm due at the morgue in an hour. I picked up another body yesterday afternoon. It'll be my rookie's first time in the cooler." He waggled his eyebrows. "Want to make a barf bet?"

I sighed, rubbing at my temples. "Normally I would, especially with your rookie. I'm certain he pukes in the first ten minutes, and maybe if we're really lucky, he'll puke all over Willows' wingtips." I didn't want to admit it, but I had been lucky getting Garnier. Aaron's new partner was straight from the suburbs and knew an Alderman who'd pulled every string to get the kid a gold shield. He had minimal road experience and Aaron was struggling to keep his cool with the kid. "How about you? What kind of hell are you going to put your rookie through today? Make her hand file all the old fingerprint cards from the last twenty years, or maybe have her scrub your cruiser with a toothbrush?"

"I have an interview set up with the victim's emergency contact. Garnier pulled her name from his work file. I need to start somewhere since we have very little physical evidence." I sifted through some notes, running a hand through my hair.

Aaron dropped his feet. "You okay? You seem off your game lately."

"You know I hate having partners."

He shook his head. "Not that. I've been noticing this for a while now. Well, before Wonder Woman's twin became your partner." He let out a breath. "You need to investigate her situation if you get my drift. In time, someone else will and I hate when you get jealous."

I frowned. "Don't. Leave her be, Aaron. Leave at least one woman in this department untouched, and no, I do not need to investigate anything other than dead bodies." I sighed, rubbing my face. "I'm really tired, Aaron. Tired of the never-ending cases. Tired of having to train a new detective, and I've been thinking a lot about Elle."

Aaron reached across the desk, and poked my elbow, smiling softly. He got it. I didn't have to over explain what I was feeling. He'd been there when Elle died. He helped with funeral arrangements when I became overwhelmed. He held me up at the funeral when I couldn't stand and hold back the tears. He even sat with me as I stared out the window at the lake, trying to get me to talk.

When that didn't work, he sat with me in silence. He always seemed to know when I needed someone around me as I dealt with losing half of my heart. Even if we were both too busy with work, he checked on me or made me have dinner once a month. It was his way of keeping me moving. I loved him dearly for it and I knew Elle would be happy I'd kept one person close.

Aaron looked at his hands. "It's only been a year and a half. I know how much she meant to you. I loved her too, and I don't know how you stay so strong, Emma."

"I'm really not, Aaron. If you only knew." I gathered the files. The elevator dinged in the distance, but I paid little attention to it. I finished off my tea and threw the cup away. "I miss her every day and it's getting worse lately."

"Who do you miss?" Garnier's voice filtered into the office. She leaned against my door frame, holding two paper cups. Aaron looked at her with a warm smile. I quickly noticed she wasn't in the blue uniform. She'd upgraded to a black pantsuit that was almost as tight as her blues. A white button-down shirt hugged her chest, bordering on inappropriate, but not enough to call the shirt unprofessional. And not enough to hide her curves. Aaron was right, she could make anything look couture. Her brown hair was in a looser ponytail, and she wore a touch more makeup, bringing out her natural beauty. Even out of the chunky patrol boots, she was only an inch shorter than me. And, of course, she was smiling.

"Nothing that concerns you, Detective." My tone was beyond cold as I dropped my gaze back to the desk. Aaron took the change in temperature as a cue to leave. "Hey, Lieutenant, let's meet up for lunch, rookies in tow, and compare notes?" He was trying to ease the tension I was creating.

"Maybe. Depends on how far we get with the interview today."

He grinned at Garnier. "Nice to see you retired the horrible uniform for something a little nicer." Aaron was checking her out and it irritated me, which was probably why he made it so obvious. I squinted at him, and he smirked, saluting me with two fingers. If Garnier wasn't in the room, I would've thrown a stapler at him.

Garnier blushed. Aaron's flirting distracted her building rage at my cold demeanor. "Thanks Aaron, I bought it last night. I hope it's ok."

Aaron winked. "It's perfect." He gave her a toothy grin and walked out of my office. Garnier turned her focus towards me, still leaning against the door frame, but I ignored her. I found myself ignoring a lot about Garnier.

After a minute, I looked up. "You don't need to stand there, you can sit down. There are a few details we need to go over before we head out."

She gave me a tight smile and took the seat Aaron just vacated. She set down a cup next to the phone. "I made a quick stop for coffee. I'm not used to getting up this early! I hope you don't mind, I grabbed you something." Her smile was amazing, and I had to swallow hard to hold back the silly sigh that wanted to come out when her dimples deepened.

"I don't drink coffee." I looked away, reaching to turn on my computer. Now I was starting to lie to her, glancing at the garbage can with my empty, 4 a.m. Styrofoam cup staring up at me.

Garnier's smile faded. "Good thing it's not coffee, Lieutenant. It's green tea, no sweetener, a splash of honey and two ice cubes." The smile was gone, chasing those dimples back into hiding. "My patrol route was in the loop. I'd stop at the coffee shop two blocks from here every night to check on the girls working the late shift. I became friends with one of them and told her this morning I'd been promoted and was working with you. She told me the way to your good side was to order your favorite drink." Garnier's dimples returned as she chuckled. "You're very predictable. Green tea suits you." She was working way too hard to be friendly, hoping to break through the ice.

I took a steady breath. "Detective. Keep your focus on the case and not on my life. I'm a coworker, your teacher. I don't need apples to win me over. Just do your job and do it right." I felt bad being so hard on her. It was very nice and slightly adorable of Garnier to learn my drink. But I had to keep her at a distance. Work came first, friendships never.

At least in my eyes.

Garnier's smile had completely disappeared again, and a flush of anger covered her cheeks.

I held out the file. "This is who we're interviewing today, Katie Thompson. Read it over. We leave in a half hour to meet her. Have you ever done a field interview?"

Garnier was still upset, but kept it contained. "I have, mainly street scene interviews at an accident or a shooting. Nothing too formal."

I frowned. Perfect. I hated showing new officers and detectives the proper way to interview. It was a frustrating process to successfully teach if they didn't have a natural talent for it.

I stood. "Katie Thompson was listed on David's emergency contact list, and she's our first lead until the rest of the evidence is processed." I handed Garnier the file. "This will give you insight on the type of person she is and the direction to take with the interview."

Katie was very clean and a typical upstanding citizen. Only blemish on her record was a parking ticket three years ago. She worked at the University hospital as a trauma nurse and was just another face in the city. I had no suspicions or bad feelings about her. Now I wanted to see what Garnier's gut told her about Katie and how to go about interviewing the girl.

Grabbing my cell phone, I opened the bottom desk drawer and stared at the gun in the black holster before picking it up and sliding it onto my belt. Garnier was still reading as I walked past her and towards the elevator. It took her a minute to realize I was leaving, and she had to jog to catch up.

"You lack manners." Her jaw was tight as she spoke.

Smirking, I stepped to the side to let her in. "I have manners. I took etiquette classes until I was seventeen. I don't have time to cue you to move when I move." My tone was harsher than I'd intended. "Rule number one of homicide investigation: don't waste time." I reached past her in the elevator and hit the button for the parking garage, grazing her arm. As I pulled back, I shivered at the minimal contact, and swallowed hard, opting to stare at the fake wood grain on the doors. I caught Garnier's reflection in the chrome walls and smirked. Her jaw was clenched so tight, I thought it would shatter any second.

My smirk faded as I heard Aaron's voice in my head, telling me to be nicer to rookies. Especially this rookie. I was provoking her like I normally did with new partners. But with Garnier, there was something about her reaction that made me feel bad. I made a move to apologize, but as I opened my mouth the door chimed, opening to the dim, dank parking garage.

Garnier walked out first, clearing her throat when we reached my car. "I'll drive." It was a simple and polite offer.

I swept past her, opened the driver's side door, and sat behind the wheel. I waited for her to get in before I put the car into drive. The tension in the car built with every mile we drove closer to Katie Thompson's house.

I parked in front of an old townhouse on the east side of Wicker Park. The block looked clean and in the beginning stages of revitalization. I double checked the address and looked at Garnier, still tense. I softened my tone as I spoke. "I'll start the interview, so you can get an idea of how formal interviews work. It's like a chess game. You move when they move. Never give up too much information."

She nodded, refusing to look my way. "I got it, Lieutenant."

Garnier was on the verge of exploding on me. It was written all over her face. I stepped out of the car and waited for her to come to my side, so we could reach the front door together, old habits from the road never dying. Pressing the doorbell, my stomach twisted in knots as its dulcet tones rang through the house. I was always nervous before interviews because of the challenges they posed. Not one interview was ever the same or predictable.

I pressed the doorbell a second time and looked back at Garnier. She was wearing sunglasses, scanning the neighborhood like a road officer would. Survey your immediate surroundings for signs of a threat. I chuckled at the memory of doing the same thing when I was on the street. I smiled and found myself observing Garnier a little harder, my mind taking a detour. The morning sun hit her just right, making her brown hair shine like caramel.

What was going on? I never looked at a woman like this. Wondering if she would do that small half smile she did when she was listening to me with her full attention. Noticing how the sun soaked into her hair and thinking what color Garnier's eyes would be today under those sunglasses. Would they be a normal hazel, or a soft muddy green, the color of the lake after a storm? She was pissed, so I leaned towards the latter.

I would've stared longer, but I heard a girl's shout from inside the townhouse. "Coming! I'm coming down!"

Turning to the door, I smoothed out my shirt. I felt Garnier move closer behind me, her perfume floating past my nose. I shook my head. I didn't have time for an overactive libido. I had a dead body and a homicide to solve. I let out a slow, calming breath as the front door sprang open to reveal a smiling young girl. "How can I help you?"

I held up my badge and ID card. "I'm Detective Emma Tiernan and this is my partner, Detective Sasha Garnier. We're here to ask about David Harrow. Are you Katie Thompson?"

Katie's smile faded a little as she looked between me and Garnier. "Um yeah, I'm Katie." She paused, her face going pale with fear. "Did something happen to him?" Her knuckles were white where she clutched the doorframe.

I motioned to the door. "Do you mind if we come inside and talk?"

Katie stepped back, allowing us to enter. She directed us to a small living room. "Please, take a seat. Can I get you something? Water? Juice?"

"No, thank you." I smiled, taking a seat on the couch. Garnier sat down a little too close. Our legs brushed for a moment before Garnier readjusted herself, moving away. She was nervous and kept fidgeting with her hands.

"Katie, this is going to be difficult. You were listed as David's emergency contact at his work. You were the only one listed, no family contacts or anyone else." I paused, waiting for her to take a seat.

She slowly sank into the chair across from us. "Is he okay?"

I paused. It was always difficult to tell family and significant others about the loss of a loved one, the sole aspect of the job I despised. It took years to build up the necessary emotional toughness to issue the *sorry for your loss, but I need information* speech.

Garnier spoke up, startling me. "David was murdered two nights ago. We need to know as much as you can tell us about him and if he was acting unusual." Her words came out like rapid fire, exactly how a road officer would interview a street witness. I flinched at Katie's raw reaction. She gasped and started sobbing. I stood up, grabbing Garnier by the arm. "Take a minute, Katie."

Garnier's brow furrowed as she felt my less than gentle grip around her bicep, then looked in my eyes. Panic flooded her face as she realized her error. Garnier had just set the tone for the rest of the interview. I'd have to calm Katie down in hopes of getting the info we needed, and chances were, I'd get nothing outside of broken sobs and used tissues.

I shoved Garnier to the small foyer and moved inches away from her face. "You. Stand right here. Do not move, do not say anything. Just watch and listen. I think someone needs to teach *you* tact and manners." I rasped out in a hard whisper.

Garnier held my stare, her epic cockup sinking in. I dropped my hand and went back to Katie, sitting on the edge of the coffee table in front of her.

I took a breath, reaching for Katie and placing a gentle hand on her knee. "Katie, I apologize for my brash partner, but I need to ask you a few questions. Take a breath, I'll be ready when you are." I kept a soft tone, doing my best to comfort her.

Katie sniffled. "How did David die?"

"We think he was mugged and fought back." I couldn't give away too many details of his death, in case Katie ended up being the number one suspect. She nodded for me to continue, wiping her face. "David's file listed you as his emergency contact? Were you in a relationship? How long have you been together?"

She nodded. "He's my ex-boyfriend, and we dated for about three years. I met him at the hospital when we were both interns. We broke up a few months ago. The relationship ran its course… and he was consumed with finding his birth parents." Katie's smile was weak. The weight of

David's death seemed to be settling in. "He never told me he was adopted until recently. He'd found his birth mother, who turned out to be heavily addicted to drugs. The second he contacted her, she latched on. She saw a big fat paycheck in her soon to be doctor son. After finding her, David changed." She shrugged. "I understood his drive. He was always passionate about everything he did."

"Is there anything about David that would make anyone want to hurt him? Was he into drugs or anything like that?" I could see Garnier out of the corner of my eye, leaning into the room. I ignored her. She needed to learn, but I was still pissed at her lack of tact. She'd made this harder than necessary.

Katie shook her head. "Oh, God, no, David was all about clean living, through and through. Everyone at work and school loved him. He was so friendly and would give the shirt off his back to anyone." She choked back sobs. "He lived to help others, probably why he was adamant on saving his mother." Katie leaned forward, cradling her head in her hands as she fell apart. "I loved him so much. He was my family."

"Katie, what about David's family? His adoptive family?" I pressed a tissue into her hand.

She shook her head, tearing the tissue apart. "They were amazing. They took me in like one of their own when I met them. I lost my parents in a car accident years ago when we first started dating, so I grew close to David's. We're still close."

I swallowed hard as thoughts of Elle rushed in. I shook it off. I had to keep on track with the interview. My gut still told me this was more than a mugging gone south.

"Were there any bars or places David hung out that seemed unusual? Anyone that could've targeted him?" I dreaded asking the question, but it was key.

"The only place he would hang out at was a bar in Wrigleyville. The Black Kettle. It's a gay bar, but not exclusively gay. A lot of our classmates go there after games because of the cheap beer and welcoming atmosphere. David would go at least once a week for a study group meeting, and sometimes I'd go with him. But I never noticed anything weird. Everyone loved David and we all watched out for each other. Making sure everyone got home safe. The bar is like a little family." Katie drifted off as shock began to set in.

Nodding, I sat back. I'd gotten everything I could out of Katie. She was too emotional to continue. Handing Katie my card, I stood. "If you have any questions or think of anything else, please call me. My office number and cell number are on the front."

Katie took it and tried to smile through her heavy tears. "Thank you, Detective." She walked me to the door and even smiled at Garnier, who was standing in the corner like a statue.

Garnier exited first. She headed straight to the car without looking back.

"I promise I'll find whoever did this." I laid a hand on Katie's arm. "Call me if you need anything." She began to sob again, mumbling a thank you. As soon as I heard the door click shut behind me, I dropped the professional smile and glared at my partner as I approached the car.

She met my glare, frowning. "Hey, Lieutenant, I want to apologize..."

I cut her off, stepping inches away from her face as I carefully measured my words and anger. "You want to apologize for being a rude asshole? This isn't the street anymore, *Detective* Garnier. Get your head in the game. You have to talk to people like they're people, not street thugs. That poor girl just lost her best friend, and how did she find out? You blurting it out like it was last night's Cubs score."

Garnier's face flushed red. "You don't have to tell me I screwed up. I know I did." She swallowed hard. I said a silent prayer she wouldn't cry in front of me. I'd made more than one partner cry, and I didn't have the patience for her to start now.

I was angry, but kept my tone even and calm. "No, I don't have to, but I'm going to. If you want to keep your brand new gold shield, I suggest you keep your mouth in check until you learn how to talk to people properly. I promise you, if you do that again I will make sure you're put on meter maid duty for the rest of your career." I pushed past her, moving towards the driver's side door. "Get your head out of the streets and listen to what I'm trying to teach you."

It took a minute before Garnier got into the car. She was very quiet as she picked up the notepad I'd thrown onto the dash, tore the pages off and tucked them into the file. I took a deep breath before starting the car.

My phone rang as I pulled out into the street, Aaron's name flashing across the screen.

Leaning against the cool glass of the window at a red light, I answered. "You have something for me, Aaron?"

"Sadly no. I'm sitting here with my rookie watching him try to figure out how to use the NCIC database. It's like watching a monkey trying to peel a plastic banana." He sighed hard. "Anyway, the Medical Examiner's office called you, I took the call. Your body is ready to be viewed."

I rubbed my eye, exhaustion creeping in. Finally, Dr. Willows was doing his job. I could have a last clean look of the body before I read over the final autopsy report. "Okay, we'll head over now." I caught Garnier looking at me out of the corner of my eye.

Aaron dropped his voice. "How goes it with the sexy rookie?" I could feel his smirk through the phone.

"Let's talk about that later."

"Uh oh. I know that tone. You made her cry? Didn't you?"

I huffed. "Almost. I'll be back in the office in an hour or so. We can talk then." I hung up and tossed the phone into the middle console. I glanced at Garnier. "You ever been to the morgue?"

Still hesitant to speak after I tore into her, she shook her head no.

I sighed for the millionth time, navigating through rush hour traffic. My headache was growing by the minute. I started making silent bets of how long it would take before my new partner threw up from the sight of a body on the autopsy table.

Chapter 5

The drive to the Medical Examiner's office was quiet and awkward. Garnier fidgeted with the file on her lap. Neither of us said anything, even as we walked into the stale beige building. I led us to the basement, where the morgue and autopsy bays were located. It was as cold as a walk-in freezer and eerily quiet in the room, both of which encased us in a stiff chill that went straight to the bone. Autopsy rooms never bothered me. They did the opposite, often calming me down and helping me to refocus. The thick concrete walls shut out the outside world, offering perfect silence and stillness, something I'd been craving for months.

I wondered idly if I could transfer to the ME's office and file paperwork away in the cold caverns of death.

My mental reverie was broken by the sound of Garnier catching her breath as we walked into the room. Her eyes roamed over the bodies laid out on steel tables in various stages of autopsy and cold storage. The shade of green that crept around her cheeks told me she was less than three minutes away from puking. I half smirked when Garnier swallowed hard a few times, coughing to clear her throat.

I frowned as I walked towards Dr. Roger Willows' desk. Dr. Willows was the Chief Medical Examiner for the county and was the world's biggest pompous asshole. He cared very little about the police department and would often take his sweet time delivering results to the detectives he wasn't fond of. Lucky for me, I was on that list. All because I rejected his advances on my first crime scene with him. He was a greasy salesman who loved showing off his title to the ladies, constantly on the prowl for the perfect first lady to stand behind him in the mayor's office.

Dr. Willows spotted me and scowled. He waved at one of his lab techs and turned away from his desk, but when he saw Garnier a few steps behind, his mouth shifted into a wide grin. I sighed and grabbed Garnier's elbow, pulling her closer. "Dr. Willows is a good ME, but he's a dick if you get on his bad side. He tends to be flirty, so don't be afraid to reject his advances. I'll gladly help you fill out a complaint form if he gets out of hand."

Garnier nodded. She had turned a whiter shade of pale, her eyes darting around the room, stopping on tables with bulky white sheets draped over unmoving human forms.

I whispered, a wave of concern washing over me. "Are you okay?"

She cleared her throat. "Yes, Lieutenant. It's my first time down here. The smell is different." She swallowed a few more times with a tight smile.

"If you have to leave, you can. There's a small bathroom over to the left behind you. If you think you're going to lose it, let me know. But we have to look at the body." I squeezed her shoulder, confused by my sudden concern for the woman. As I looked in her eyes, I saw her distress at being in a room full of dead people. It was a feeling I had long forgotten. Something I shouldn't have ever forgotten.

I moved closer to Garnier, meeting her gaze to steady her. I'd never ever cared about a rookie in the morgue. If they wobbled, or threw up, so be it. It was the name of the game in homicide. Garnier was different. Something about her tapped into my soft side.

She cleared her throat once more, nodding and stepping away from my touch. "I'll be fine, thank you."

I held back another comment, spotting Dr. Willows walking towards us. He glared at me. "Detective Lieutenant Tiernan. I see you've made it on time." He then turned to Garnier, blasting his shitty grin her way. "Hello, I don't believe I've met you yet. Dr. Roger Willows." He shot out an over-manicured hand.

I half stepped in front of Garnier as protection. "This is my new partner, Detective Sasha Garnier." I kept my tone professional, giving Dr. Willows every indication his flirtation was not welcome. I watched as Dr. Willows' eyes roamed over Garnier's body, his grin widening. I felt a sudden pang of jealousy, but chased it away.

Dr. Willows still held his hand out to Garnier, ignoring that I was even in the same room with them. "It's nice to see some new faces in the homicide unit."

I swore, for a second, I saw him wink at Garnier, making my hand curl into a fist on its own volition. I had an overwhelming need to punch him.

I cleared my throat, pulling Willows' attention away from ogling my partner. "Do you have the autopsy report for David Harrow ready?"

Dr. Willows frowned and moved to a tray table across the room. He lifted a thin manila file folder and practically shoved it into my chest. I lifted my arm to grab it, but he pulled it away. "I completed it an hour ago. Rushed it per *your orders*. I found an unusual carving in his lower back near the kidneys. I've attached photos in the file, but I'm sure you won't trust my work."

God, I hated this man.

Dr. Willows pointed towards the second steel table off to my right. "He's over there. You may look at his body now. I'll be releasing it to the family within the next two hours." He then set the file on the farthest corner of the table. "My complete report."

I rasped out an annoyed thank you and grabbed the file. I glanced up in time to see Dr. Willows creeping closer to Garnier. "Detective Garnier, over here." My hard tone startled both of them. Dr. Willows took the hint and left us alone in the room.

Garnier almost bumped into me as I stopped next to David, stepping off to my right side as if she was trying to hide from Willows' prying eyes, in case he came back. I half smiled as she whispered out a quick sorry.

Handing her the file, I reached over to lift a corner of the white sheet, and pulled it back to reveal David. He'd been washed and looked far different from when I last saw him on the docks. The ever-present grey pallor of death had set in. A Y-incision had been neatly stitched, and his facial wounds were clear and visible in this sterile state. He looked nothing like the clean-cut kid, with brown eyes full of life, from his driver's license photograph.

I examined his face. The injuries were brutal and the clear cause of death, confirmed by Willows' report. The skull fracture had been so deep, and his brain so badly bruised, forming blood clots that slowly worked their way to his heart. Killing him within an hour. David endured a slow and painful death.

I pulled on a pair of nitrile gloves and handed a pair over to a very green Garnier. "I need your help."

She looked at me with wide eyes. "My help?"

I nodded. "I need to look at his back. Help me roll him on his side." I placed gloved hands on his shoulders and pointed to his hips. "Grab there and push gently towards me."

Garnier took a deep breath, placing her hands on the spots I pointed at, swallowing down a need to puke with fervor. I looked for the closest garbage can before giving her a three count, rolling David onto his side.

I laid a hand against his shoulder while I bent to look at the Latin carving on his back. It was clean, precise, and intentional. The skin wasn't torn. The edges were clean and made with a trained hand. *'Ego te provoco.'*

Something about the carving felt familiar to me, and a rush of déjà vu settled in. It took me by surprise, and I suddenly felt lightheaded. I gripped to the edge of the table with a free hand, my knuckles turning white as the room wobbled.

Garnier covered my other hand, the one still on David. "Are you okay, Lieutenant?" Her voice was soft, and it brought me out of the tailspin the déjà vu was causing.

"Yeah. I'm just very tired." I shook it off and focused back on the carving's clean edges.

It was evident that care and time had been put into forming the letters. The edges suggested a scalpel could've been used. The cuts were too intricate to be by anything large and blunt like a pocketknife.

I motioned to Garnier to roll David onto his back. I draped the sheet over his body, issuing a silent prayer before I stepped away and picked up the autopsy report. I was satisfied with what I saw. David could be laid to rest, and I could start chasing his killer.

I half shouted at Dr. Willows that we were all set and started walking towards the exit. If I didn't, Garnier would be caught in his clutches and then I would have to punch him.

We exited the building, the early afternoon sun hitting us with a welcomed warmth. I closed my eyes, letting the sun chase out the chill and smells of the frozen morgue. When I opened my eyes, I saw Garnier leaning against the side of the building. She was gasping for air, trying to bring a color other than varying shades of green back into her face. It was what every cop, detective, or citizen did after their first trip to the morgue. I smiled and chuckled at the memory of my first-time wobble, puking in the bushes right next to the front entrance.

Garnier pushed off the side of the building and strode right over to me. I watched as the color of anger replaced the green tint. She stopped hard in front of me. "What's so funny?"

I shrugged, a small smile on my face. "It's nothing." I stepped back from her, digging in my pocket for the car keys. "We should head back to the office. I want Aaron to look at the report and photos. He should have the trace evidence findings by now."

"You're clearly laughing at me! Why do you think this is so funny? That was the first time I've seen a dead body on the slab. Yeah, I had a hard time in there with all the bodies and that smell. I don't have a steel stomach, but that doesn't give you the goddamn right to laugh at me for showing I'm human. God knows you wouldn't know what that's like." Garnier didn't hesitate to spew her frustration out as fast as she could. It'd been building up. I'd been relentlessly pushing her buttons and saw the tea kettle was about to blow. But I was taken aback by her outburst, triggering my own paper-thin temper.

I spun around, stepping right back into her face. Garnier hit a nerve and I couldn't contain what spilled from my mouth, even if it was pieces of my past. "You're right, Detective. I don't know what it's like to be human. I only spent most of my childhood bouncing from foster home to foster home. I've been beaten, starved and forgotten. I still have nightmares about the abuse I endured from people who only wanted me for a monthly check from the state. I've lost the one person I've loved more than my own life and can't seem to shake her a year and a half after her death. I've been chastised for loving a woman when it's more acceptable to love a man. And every single day I wake up, I go to work and deal with the worst humans can do to each other." I huffed, bringing my voice down, realizing how much I just overshared. But Garnier drew it out of me. Something about her begged me to break down the walls even if I was furious at her. "You're right, I'm not human. You have to have a heart to be human and I lost that a long time ago. So good work, Detective Garnier, you're going to be one fucking amazing detective."

I didn't realize I was yelling so close to her face. Now, as my anger died, I took a good look in her eyes. She hadn't budged or flinched, and endured my outburst with professional silence.

She didn't give an inch and held my gaze so long, it made me feel awkward because it made my heart skip. Garnier was a strong, independent woman with an intensity that made me terribly attracted to her at that moment. I finally broke away from the stare down, stepping away to reach for the driver's door handle. My hand trembled as I opened the door, and a heavy silence followed us into the car. This was bad. I'd gone too far.

When I slid the key into the ignition, Garnier glanced over, speaking in a firm but gentle tone. "I'm not like everyone else, Lieutenant. Give me a chance and I'll show you."

I refused to look at her. I was still on an emotional high from our little verbal altercation and that I'd shared more with her than most, including Aaron. I turned to look out her window to check if traffic was clear before pulling out, and caught Garnier looking right at me. I saw a flicker of something that scared me shitless.

It reminded me of the first moment I met Elle over dodgeball donations, it was that same flicker. That same spark that promised something more.

My stomach dropped, and I turned away, busying myself with driving back to the station as fast as I could.

* * *

The painful silence followed us back and into the station. Garnier walked behind, letting me take the lead to my office. I frowned at the sight of Aaron sitting behind my desk with his feet up.

"Detective Liang." I half growled his name out.

He immediately stood, moving to the chairs in front of the desk. I tossed the autopsy results onto his lap. "Read this. I know you're technically not on the case anymore, but you were there first, and I could use your input." Aaron looked up and saw I was flustered. He then looked at Garnier taking the seat next to him. He looked between the two of us, slowly picking up the weird vibes between us.

He gave me a dirty look as he flipped it open. "So, Sasha, how was your first trip to the morgue?"

"Educational." She looked dead at me. "I learned a lot from the Lieutenant."

I dropped my gaze to the paper desk calendar, feeling my stomach turn at what was about to happen in the next few hours. Garnier would do exactly what the others before her did. She'd complain about me to Captain Jameson. I'd be reprimanded and probably sent to the anger management courses he'd threatened me with the last time a partner quit because of my pushy ways.

I pulled the gun off my belt and set it in a desk drawer. "Aaron, I think we may have a hate crime on our hands."

Aaron glanced over the top of the file. "Really? Why's that, Lieutenant?"

Garnier spoke before I did. "The victim, David, was adopted and just found his drug addict birth mother. The Latin carvings on his back point towards it possibly being a religious hate crime. The phrase has some sort of challenging connotation and might lead back to a section of the Bible about children born out of sin. Job 14:4 '*Who can make the clean out of the unclean. No one?*'" She shrugged, suddenly nervous both Aaron and I were staring at her. "Well, that's what I think it is. Some hard-core religious freaks have a grudge against adoption, thinking it's always sinful for women to give their children up."

Aaron grinned. "Look at the rookie here! I think you may be on to something, Sasha."

She smiled as the praise from Aaron eased the tension in the room. Garnier stood, nudging Aaron's shoulder. "I'd like to call the bar Katie told us about, try to get started on finding possible witnesses. Where can I use a phone?"

I stared at her, trying to hide that I was impressed by her theory and motivation. I still felt uneasy about what happened in front of the morgue, and showing more emotion might get me deeper into trouble with this woman. I pointed to the small desk right outside my office door, facing into the rest of the bullpen. "Your desk is right outside of my office."

Garnier looked at it and then back at me. "I have a desk?"

"All detectives have a desk."

She sighed, her jaw twitching. Her irritation raced back.

Garnier went to move to her desk when Aaron spoke. "Hey Sasha, when you're done making those calls, you want to grab bagels and coffee at the deli down the street? I'm starving, and my rookie won't be back for another hour." Aaron smirked. "The kid puked all over the morgue floor, getting splash back on his suit. You should've seen Dr. Willows. He was so pissed off, I thought he was going to make the kid clean the entire floor by hand."

Garnier grinned, and even I had to hold back a laugh. "I'm hungry now that the morgue is behind me. Give me a minute and we can go." Garnier rushed to her desk and sat down, reaching for the phone. I watched her for a minute and couldn't help but notice when she bent a certain way, her shirt held onto her curves. Her body was toned, and it was evident she worked out. When she moved to sit in her chair sideways, she caught me staring and cocked an eyebrow. I was definitely caught red-handed. She smirked as she spoke on the phone. I blushed and turned away, picking up random interoffice memos.

"You've been caught, Emma. Tsk, Tsk." I heard the grin in Aaron's mocking tone.

I sighed, focusing on mentally organizing my desktop. "Shut up, Aaron. Did the techs find any trace evidence?"

He leaned forward in the chair, poking the side of my hand with his pen. "Something happened at the morgue. The tension between you and your partner is thicker than shit. That's not the norm for you and rookies. What happened?"

I leaned back in my chair, turning it so I could look at anything other than the beautiful woman I'd lost my temper with. "There's something about this case that's way too familiar. I had a déjà vu moment while looking at the body. Then when Garnier and I left, I chuckled at her rookie wobble. She went off on me, and I quickly returned the favor." I cringed at the memory of us yelling at each other in the parking lot. "I said some things." I ran a hand through my hair, freeing it from the loose ponytail I kept it in. "She has a wicked temper that triggers mine." I paused, looking up at Aaron. "She told me I didn't have a heart."

"Oh shit." Aaron sighed, sitting back in his chair. He glanced over his shoulder at Garnier. "You think she'll go to the captain?"

I absently tapped a pen on the edge of my armrest. "Most likely. I haven't been very accommodating to her. I wasn't kind when she screwed up the interview this morning and I've been hammering her all day." I tossed the pen on the desk. "I need to retire, Aaron. It's getting harder and harder. I miss Elle so much lately it's starting to become unbearable."

Aaron sighed, smiling. "I know you miss her, but you know Elle would kick your ass for acting like this. Sasha is smart. She wants to be here, so cut her some slack." Aaron winked at me. "And I can tell you're crushing on her."

"Oh no, I'm not crushing on her or anyone. Hell no, Aaron you're crazy." I stared at him with wide eyes. "Have you been slipping whiskey into your morning lattes?"

Aaron stood up and handed the autopsy report back. "You're crushing. You have that look you get when you're giddy. It's the same look when you eat expensive ice cream or close a hard case. I saw it just now as you were eyeballing how lucky Sasha's white button-down is."

I sighed, shaking my head. "You're such a boy. I'm not crushing on her. She sometimes reminds me of…"

"Who do I remind you of?" Garnier's voice filtered around me and my stomach tumbled. I spun in my chair to face the window. I needed a full view of the lake to calm my racing heart.

I didn't turn to look at her. I knew the flush on my face would betray any lie I could tell. "No one."

Aaron grabbed Garnier before the tension between us reappeared. "Come on Sasha, let's get those bagels."

She grinned, tearing a piece of paper from her notepad. "Sounds good, Aaron." She held out the paper. "Here, Lieutenant. I contacted the bar owner. He claims nothing sticks out to him about that night. He said it was the usual crowd, no weirdos hanging around. He gave me a couple names of David's friends who are regulars. I left messages with all of them to call us back."

I swung my chair just enough to grab the paper from her hand. "Good work, Garnier."

It was her turn to blush and whisper a thank you. She left my office, stopping at her desk to grab her bag before telling Aaron she'd meet him at the elevator.

Aaron's mouth was open in mock shock. "You just complimented a rookie, Emma. I have to write this down in my scrapbook." He held up his hands. "Emma Tiernan. Lieutenant Ice Queen and resident hard ass, told her rookie they did a good job." He chuckled, squinting at me. "You totally have a crush on this one."

I threw a pen at Aaron, striking his arm. "Get out of here." I nodded at my partner standing at the elevator. "Find out if she's going to file a complaint against me. I think I'm close to the end of my rope with rookie complaints."

Aaron saluted me. "Yes, sir! I'll see what I can get out of Sasha over bagels and coffee." He turned on his heel and met Garnier at the elevator.

When I was alone again, I let out a heavy breath and leaned forward on the desk, my head in my hands. Something about Garnier conjured up far too many emotions. She made me so angry, irritated, and frustrated. She was nothing like Elle, but the feelings sneaking up out of nowhere, reminded me of my time with Elle. I felt guilty, both for losing Elle and for feeling whatever it was for Garnier.

I sighed hard, and rubbed my face. I needed to focus on the case, not emotions and mixed feelings. I opened one of my other drawers and lifted out a pile of witness statements, when I spotted the early retirement forms I'd filled out two years ago. I'd thrown them in the bottom of the drawer with the other random forms left by the previous owner of this office. It was a pipe dream I began when Elle was alive, and abandoned when she died.

I picked up the massive wad of paper and held it in my hands. I was more than eligible for an early retirement, only losing some of the benefits of a full retirement. I closed my eyes, then dropped the forms back in the bottom of the drawer and slammed it closed.

I swung my chair back to the window, to watch the parade of sailboats drift on the lake.

* * *

Aaron and Garnier returned just as I finished the initial report for Captain Jameson. There was nothing much to go on, but I had to keep a record of everything we did. Aaron set down an iced tea in front of me. "Sasha has the bagels." He glanced around, whispering. "She said nothing. Nothing about anything that may have happened outside the morgue. She raved about you. Blithering about how much she's learning from you. Only thing I picked up on is she kind of wishes you'd ease up on her and let her prove herself." He smiled, shoving a chunk of everything bagel into his mouth. "You need to stop being an asshole and let the girl work. She's smarter than you think."

Before I could comment, Garnier walked into the office setting a brown bag dotted with grease spots on the edge of the desk. "I didn't know what you liked, so I got a mix. Feel free to dig in."

Aaron took that as his cue to leave. "I saw my rookie down in the locker room. I'm going to go snatch Sir Barfs A Lot up and get to work. We're already behind on our case and his puking up blueberry waffles has set us way back." He stepped out, throwing Garnier a wink before trotting away.

I grabbed the iced tea, poking a straw into it. It had become very awkward in my office the moment Aaron left us alone.

Mid-sip, Garnier suddenly asked. "Who do I remind you of?"

I squeezed the plastic cup in my hand. "Someone I used to know." I reached for my keyboard, desperate for anything to fill my hands.

Garnier took a bite of a cinnamon raisin bagel. "Is it the woman you and Aaron always talk about?"

I remained silent, staring at my emails.

Garnier softly sighed. "I'm sorry, I didn't mean to pry. Your eyes dim whenever you two talk about her. Was she a case you never solved?" She took another bite. "You know what? Never mind. I'm prying, and I certainly don't need you going off on me again."

Her tone showed care and genuine concern. It was still there even as she dismissed her own questioning, out of nervous fear of my reaction.

I took a deep breath, starting at the drops of condensation on the iced tea. "Her name is Elle. She is, was, my girlfriend of almost three years." I paused. It was difficult to talk about Elle with Aaron, let alone a stranger chewing a bagel in front of me. And why was I telling her? Why was I constantly opening my mouth and letting things out? I groaned. Sharing my personal life leaned towards that maybe I did have a crush on her.

Garnier nodded, her voice much softer. "This job makes it hard to keep a solid relationship alive. I had bad luck as a road officer. The hours we keep aren't human."

I turned, meeting her bright eyes. "She died a little over a year ago, from injuries she received when a truck ran her off the road." I clenched my jaw again as my eyes filled with tears. Fuck. I'd just opened the door I always kept locked.

Garnier fell quiet and set her bagel down. "I'm sorry... I..." She paused.

I shrugged. I didn't expect her to have a wealth of words. Who really does when you tell them how you lost a loved one?

It was a quarter after one in the afternoon, and I was ready to leave. We had nothing scheduled for the rest of the day. Our next interview was with the owner of the Black Kettle, and that was scheduled for a few days from now. We were waiting for a few callbacks from David's friends and coworkers, but that could take weeks. "Let's call it an early day. Go home and get some rest. If any of the friends call back, we'll meet up here and head out for interviews, but I think we both could use the rest."

Garnier picked up her bagel with a tight smile.

I knew I'd made things even more awkward between us.

I reached for the file, finding the photographs of the pages found under David's head. I'd almost forgotten about them. I set them to the side while Garnier reached for the bag of bagels. "Did you want any of these, Lieutenant?"

I shook my head. "No, but thank you for offering." My gaze was stuck on the pages. There was something very familiar about them, and it had my gut going into overdrive.

Garnier silently left my office, taking the bagels with her. I watched her for a minute as she collected her things. She stopped to talk to a few of the detectives, and her face lit up. Her smile was big, and I felt a pang of jealousy as most of the male detectives flocked around her. I wanted to be in the middle of that flock. I wanted Sasha to smile at me without an undertone of irritation because I just lectured her about everything she was doing wrong.

I returned my focus to the photographs and after a few minutes I realized they were pages from a Latin Bible, like Garnier had pointed out. It was the only clue I had until the trace evidence reports came through, and it bothered me. My gut told me to pay attention to it, especially the section about sin and children born out of sin. I leaned on my hand. Whoever did this was making sure I paid attention to his message.

I made notes, hoping the lab could lift fingerprints from the blood-stained pages. I was now even more driven to solve this case. I didn't need a self-proclaimed God running the streets of Chicago, purging it of all its sinners.

Chapter 6

As I stood staring into the still-empty fridge, I regretted not taking the bagels. I was starving, having forgotten to eat all day. I was tired from the roller coaster of emotions I'd been on, and all I wanted to do was sit in my chair and eat. I moaned, but made the responsible decision to go grocery shopping after a shower.

I stripped out of my clothes and stood under the scalding hot water. The sting of the heat carried away the lingering feeling of the altercation with Garnier. The woman was a firecracker and I'd have to devise a new tactic to handle her or get her off my hands.

Stepping out of the shower, I caught myself in the mirror. I was thinner than I wanted and the bags under my eyes had deepened. I was two sleepless nights away from looking like a walking skeleton. True signs of working too hard and sleeping too little.

I scanned over my body, stopping at the multitude of scars dotting my skin. Many of them told the story of my life. The one over my right hip was from a car accident when I was eighteen. The lovely thin pink line along the inside of my left arm was a gift from a crackhead who shot at me as I chased him. Then there was the large, ragged scar that ran from just under my right breast to my belly button in a strange diagonal. It was an old scar, white from age and still bumpy from the lazy stitches of a rushed emergency room doctor.

I ran my fingers along the ridge, trying to remember how I got this one. It'd been a part of my life for as long as I could remember, but I had no idea how it came to be. My parents noticed it when they adopted me, but my memory was so spotty from blocking out my time in the foster homes, I couldn't tell them if it was a stupid accident, or something more. My father went through my files and found nothing. My mother played it off as a bicycle accident from when I lived in Detroit. I smiled and agreed, afraid to tell her I never learned how to ride a bike until I was a sophomore in high school, in Chicago.

I pulled on an old Detroit Pistons shirt, the soft material covering up the scars. I'd taken it upon myself when I first became a detective to investigate my foster records, but I also found very little. There wasn't a record of any accidents, let alone any medical records. I truly was just a number to the system.

I pulled on a pair of sweatpants, letting my hair air dry as I went downstairs to make my grocery list. I had too many other mysteries to pick apart. Mine could wait a little longer.

Leaning across the kitchen island, I scribbled the list on a notepad, doing my best to stick to healthy things and not the junk food I was craving. Despite looking like a starving skeleton, I was a stress eater, and the stress was definitely piling up on my shoulders.

I was finishing the list when the doorbell rang. I figured it was Aaron, since he was the only one who would dare to show up at my door unannounced. My mother always called right before she came over, making sure I was home, and my father preferred to wait until I came over to visit them. I rolled my eyes. It was probably Aaron, stopping by to give me hell for leaving early. It was something I rarely did, especially when I started a new case.

I shuffled to the front door and pulled it open. "Don't be jealous I took an early day, but being in command has its benefits." I looked up, my smirk quickly fading. "Oh sorry, I thought you were Aaron." I paused, staring at the visitor on my front step.

Garnier stood on my doorstep with a soft smile on her lips. She was dressed down, wearing a tight pair of black jeans and a deep red tank top with a battered leather jacket over it. Her hair was down, laying over her shoulders in light brown waves. I took a slow breath. With her hair down, Garnier was completely stunning. I cleared my throat, leaning on the door jamb. "Detective Garnier."

She tipped her head with a sheepish smile, her cheeks pinking at the sound of her brand-new title. "I hope I'm not bothering you, Lieutenant. I felt bad about how I handled the interview and wanted to apologize. I couldn't find you at the station. Aaron caught me on the way out and gave me your address. He mentioned something about you preferring face to face apologies."

I was going to kill Aaron. I knew what he was doing, and I was going to kick his ass all the way down Michigan Avenue and back. I hated face to face anything, in fact I hated being social outside of the office. Yes, I would kill him for this.

I nodded. "Ok. You apologized." I stepped back, readying to close the door and say goodnight even though it was still late afternoon. I sighed. Now I really did need to buy junk food.

Garnier slid her hands into her pockets. "I really am sorry for my behavior. It's taking me longer than I thought to shift gears. Patrol interviews were always so quick and to the point." Garnier sighed with a hint of frustration. I wasn't exactly receptive to her apology, or her standing on my doorstep waiting to be invited in like a friend. Frankly, I was caught off guard that someone I worked with wanted to apologize to me, let alone come to my doorstep and do it in person.

"I should leave." She looked down, making a move to turn and leave.

I took a breath. "You want a beer?" What the hell was I doing? Was I getting kinder in my old age?

Garnier paused her steps, a smile forming on her lips. "That sounds great."

I opened the door wider for her, waving her inside. As she brushed past me, a quick waft of her shampoo filled my nose. A mix of vanilla and lavender, a calming combination. I sighed and closed the door behind her, leaning my forehead against cool wood. Why was I doing this? My primary goals for the evening were grocery shopping and eating organic ice cream while reading my newest research book on psychological evidence collection. I didn't have time for a friendly beer with a partner I did *not* want to become friends with.

"Wow, your house is beautiful, Lieutenant." Garnier stood right inside the foyer.

I walked past her towards the kitchen. "Thank you, but I had very little to do with it. I inherited it." I opened the fridge, staring at the last two bottles of beer for a breath before grabbing them with a groan. This was a bad idea. I opened one and slid it across the kitchen island to Garnier. "It's all I have right now. I was about to go grocery shopping."

Garnier grinned and picked up the bottle. "Thank you, Lieutenant."

I frowned. It was strange having her call me by my rank in my own home, but I wasn't sure I could handle her using my first name. It was a big step letting her in my house, it would be a bigger one if she started calling me Emma. No one ever came over from work. Only Aaron and he always brought the beer.

I cleared my throat. "So, Garnier. What's the real reason you pilfered my address from Detective Liang?"

She chuckled, picking at the label on the bottle. "He gave it to me quite easily. I think he has a crush on me." She sipped her beer. "Please call me Sasha. We aren't in the office." She spun the bottle on the counter, looking up with a warm glance.

"You should be careful around Aaron, Garnier. He has a reputation with the ladies." The ease in her manner was making me anxious. "As for earlier. Water under the proverbial bridge." I moved around to her to walk to my living room couch, sitting down as she followed me.

Garnier walked into the living room and stopped at the front window. The early afternoon sun poured in, casting the entire living room and Garnier in a warm golden light that created a halo-like effect around her. I couldn't pull my eyes away.

Garnier seemed a little downtrodden that I'd stuck with using her last name. "I'm not worried about Aaron, he really isn't my type. Great guy though." She paused. "This view is incredible."

Garnier hesitated again, fiddling with the label. "I want to apologize, Lieutenant. For my behavior over the last few days." She faced me. "I have a temper and you have so many walls that are difficult to break through or understand. You kind of frustrate me. I usually have an easier time with partners." She tipped her head back to the bottle. "I shouldn't have gone off on you. It was rude of me."

I suddenly felt horrible for my outburst at the morgue. "I wasn't laughing at you, Garnier. I was laughing at the memory of when I puked after my first trip to the morgue. It's way different seeing bodies in a clean, quiet room. You're forced to acknowledge death instead of dismissing it in the name of looking for evidence." I ran a hand through my hair. "I still have a difficult time. Never grow too thick of a skin that you stop seeing the human under the evidence and violence."

Garnier sat on the edge of the coffee table across from me, eyebrows raised asking for silent permission. I waved her to go ahead. I hated the distressed wooden coffee table but kept it because Elle chose it.

"I need to admit something, Lieutenant." She looked up. "Can I call you Emma? It feels odd calling you Lieutenant outside of work."

I clenched my jaw. She was pushing too hard now. "I try to keep work and my personal life separate." Garnier held her gaze, those bright hazel eyes asking more of me. My heart skipped twice, telling me to open up to this woman. I sighed and bent to her request. "Fine, but never use my first name at work, or anywhere else." I knew it was petty, but it was the fine line I used to keep my sanity around my coworkers.

She smiled, her dimples in full force. "Emma, I asked to be assigned to you. I had the highest score on the detective's exam and the Superintendent let me pick any detective to be my training officer. I chose you." She stared hard at me, making my stomach do flips until I laid my hand on it, pressing down to get the flips to stop flopping. "I've followed your work since you made detective. I used to see you on crime scenes when I was assigned to maintain the perimeter. I always stood close enough to watch you work. You're amazing and impressive in the way you handle crime scenes." She sighed. "You're the reason I took the detective's test. I knew I could learn so much from you."

I broke her gaze to stare out the window. The intense look in her eyes hinted there was more behind her choosing me as a partner and trainer, but I couldn't place it. I didn't want to place it. This woman made me nervous and sweaty.

Garnier finished her beer and set the empty bottle on a coaster. "I wanted to come over and apologize in person for being a jerk and for prying. I heard rumors about you, but never wanted to believe them. I heard about Roberts." She let out a slow breath. "I wanted to give you a chance to prove me and everyone else wrong."

I furrowed my brow. The rumors. Those god damn rumors were started by my first partner in the homicide unit, John Roberts. Roberts made my life hell when he found out I was dating a woman. I'd dealt with his daily abuse about my relationship and my sexuality. He refused to work with me and bitched to the Captain every morning. He went so far as to screw up cases on purpose in hopes I'd be pushed out of the boys' club. He even started rumors about me being a dirty cop and a cold man hater.

One night while chasing a suspect through the streets I'd been blindsided by the suspect's friend and taken down, leaving me fighting for my life in a knock down street brawl. Roberts was nowhere to be found while I was getting my ass kicked. The beating was severe, but I finally managed to overtake my attacker, handcuff him, and call for backup with blood running down my face.

As I sat in the back of an ambulance getting patched up, Roberts showed and started making inappropriate jokes to the masses of cops who showed up to the officer in distress call. I'll always remember his last sentence. "Dumb dyke deserves it, chasing after a suspect like that. I taught her better than that, but I guess a man hater like her won't listen to me. Maybe I should visit her pretty little girlfriend and show her what a real man can do."

In two long strides, I covered the distance from the ambulance to Roberts, landing a vicious right hook. I dropped the piece of shit, stared at him, and said nothing as I walked back to the ambulance to be transported for broken ribs. Roberts rolled on the ground, crying like a baby while a few officers cheered me on.

Captain Jameson visited me in the hospital to check on my recovery. He'd heard what happened and about Roberts' harassment. He promised to take care of it. The last I saw of Roberts, he was doing parking lot security at the airport. After that, I opted out of partners for good and closed myself off from coworkers, keeping my distance but staying polite.

Until Elle died; then I stopped caring all together.

I met Garnier's eye. "John Roberts was a good detective, but an ignorant human. I never bothered to fight the rumors. It was pointless." I stood up, grabbing her empty beer bottle. I was agitated she'd brought up Roberts. I avoided looking back whenever I could. Anytime I did, it was nothing but pain and assholes. "Thank you for stopping by and clearing the air, but it wasn't necessary."

Garnier quickly stood up. "Emma, I just—" She sighed. "I'd like us to have a civil working relationship, maybe even become friends. But if we keep bickering back and forth and you keep treating me like you have, it's going to be difficult."

I set the empties in the sink. Leaning on the edge of the counter, I spoke in a soft tone. "I don't need friends, Garnier." I turned to look at her, her smile fading.

She sighed in defeat. "At least I can say I tried. I'm not going anywhere, so please stop with the petty things that worked on other rookies." She made direct eye contact. "I'm not leaving you."

The air suddenly grew thick, and I swallowed hard. Pushing off the edge of the sink, I walked to the front door and opened it. "I need to run a few errands before it gets too late." I was being rude, but Garnier had crossed an imaginary line and pushed another one of my buttons.

Garnier nodded, her smile tight. She moved towards the door. Before she stepped out, she held out her hand to me. "Well, Lieutenant, I'm not going to give up, so let's shake on at least being civil with each other while we work this case."

I looked at her for a minute, then took her hand in mine. I would agree to that. I didn't want to face any more parking lot outbursts by either of us.

When our hands met, my skin tingled. It was what romance novels called a spark. Her hand was warm in mine, and it caused a hitch in my breath. "I'll see you in the morning, Garnier." She squeezed my hand before I gently pulled mine back.

"Have a good night, Lieutenant." Garnier jogged down my steps and disappeared down the street.

I closed my door, leaning the back of my head against it. I'd work this one case with Garnier then ask for her to be reassigned. I didn't want to develop feelings for this woman. It was already apparent my mind and body saw something in her I didn't. Or didn't want to.

I groaned and grabbed my grocery list. I prayed the monotony of grocery shopping would chase away these unwanted feelings.

Tucking the list in my pocket, I was two steps from my car when a man approached me, waving. "Excuse me! Hello! Hi! Can you help me?" He half jogged over. "I'm completely lost." He unfurled a map of the city. "Can you point me in the direction of Millennium Park?"

He was clearly a lost tourist. The cargo shorts and cliche Windy City souvenir t-shirt gave him away. He shrugged sheepishly, pushing up large-framed glasses. His eyes were laser focused on mine.

"Sure. Take a left at the corner and head east for about four blocks. You'll see the top curve of the bean, follow that and you'll be there in about ten minutes." I clutched my keys, "But hurry up, you don't want to linger after dark." I looked up to catch him staring at my house.

"Is that your house? It's very clean." He cocked his head in an unusual manner, giving me goosebumps. Something about him was eerily familiar. I moved my hand to my concealed holster. "Like I said, it's not super safe for tourists after dark." I scanned his face, but the setting sun cast dusky shadows everywhere, covering his features in a rosy shadow.

He chuckled. "Oh, I think I'm staying for a while. I've found so many lovely things here." He turned to me. "It's a beautiful home, you must be doing very well for yourself."

My jaw twitched, and I stepped towards the car. "I'm a police officer. Please excuse me." I walked away, pointing over my shoulder. "Four blocks east."

The tourist winked. "Well, thank you for your help, Officer. I hope to see you around." He saluted me with two fingers and headed east. I waited until he was out of sight before I climbed in the car and drove off. I looked at the corner he turned down, and saw him walking towards the park. I sighed, my paranoia ebbing away. He was just a kooky tourist, one of the million I saw on the streets every day.

I had bigger things to worry about.

* * *

Three weeks later, David's case had come to a complete standstill. The lab had nothing for us. No DNA, no fibers, no solid leads on the paper found under his body. It was from a motel Bible that was produced in the millions and distributed to many parts of the country and sections of Canada. The pages were free of fingerprints and the analysis revealed only David's blood. They were working on the carvings. It was confirmed a scalpel had been used, but again, millions of scalpels were produced and distributed throughout the world. David's tox report came up clean. Not a drop of alcohol or drugs in his system, not even over-the-counter allergy meds.

His friends were dead ends. All upstanding citizens who fully cooperated when the police asked if of them.

So, I was facing a dead end and hated that I would have to either wait for another body to show up, or toss this case into the cold case files and move on.

Because of this lull in the case, I was forced to really train Garnier as a detective. Against my better judgement, I was building a rapport with her and found her to be charming, intelligent. She was a lot like Aaron, but without the stubble and brotherly bathroom jokes. We went out with Aaron on his last body, to observe. Well, Garnier observed as a trainee, and I observed her as the trainer.

Then this morning, we fell into the rotation and caught a fresh body, found under the freeway. The first on scene officer was calling it gang retaliation for last week's drive by in the next district. Looking at the dispatch notes, it felt pretty cut and dry. Jameson sent us against my protests that the vice unit could handle it, telling us we were doing nobody any good by sitting and waiting for David's killer to drop another body in our laps.

And so, here I was trapped in bumper-to-bumper traffic. A car accident two miles ahead had cocked up the freeway and turned it into a parking lot. Garnier twirled her phone. "Can't you throw on the lights and sirens?"

I shook my head. "At this point, it'll make things worse." I leaned back, digging in my bag. "People won't move for the lights." I smirked as my fingers latched onto a bag of Skittles. "I'm fine waiting in traffic. Means I won't be waiting at the scene for Willows to show up when he wants."

I tore open the bag and shoved a handful of candy in my mouth.

"Candy and coffee for breakfast?" Garnier gave me a look. "I thought you hated coffee." She gave me a dirty look, unraveling my lie from a few weeks ago when she caught Aaron and I at the coffee shop.

I nodded. "Yep." I shook out another handful. "Don't be jealous you didn't think to grab a snack when we stopped for gas." I chuckled. Even though we were on our way to a body, I was in a good mood. I'd slept a whole seven hours and felt like I'd been reborn. Never mind the bet I won with Aaron. He'd lost when his second rookie partner puked outside the morgue as soon as Aaron opened the door and the smell of death hit the kid's olfactory senses. I had a free fancy steak dinner in the near future.

"You constantly surprise me."

I raised an eyebrow. "I do?"

Garnier nodded. "You do." She shifted in her seat, trying to look around the lines of brake lights. "You're this cranky detective who is incredibly brilliant at her job. Then every so often I see you smile and realize you have a heart. Probably a really big one." She chuckled. "I saw you the other day with Betty's grandkids. They had you wrapped around their little finger."

I shrugged, shaking out more candy. "I like kids. They get me, and I get them. Kids don't put up with bullshit and only expect honesty." I tried to brush off the fact Garnier had seen me with Betty's grandkids. I loved those kids and turned into the biggest mush when they visited.

"Yeah, and the smile on your face. Well, it'd be nice to see it more." Garnier sat back, tossing her phone in the console. "As I was saying, you surprise me. You're a shifting enigma and I wish I could figure you out." She sighed.

I sat for a moment, thinking over the last three weeks. Our partnership had begun to level out. I wasn't being a complete hard ass to her. I'd realized it would be impossible to shake her loose, and she did show glimmers of being a great detective. I'd also noticed Garnier was trying to figure me out and in turn, I was growing to like her as a person. She was kind, funny, and did her best to make me smile, whether it was bringing my favorite drink every morning with a bagel, or doughnut, or making fun of Aaron to earn a small chuckle out of me. I secretly liked it when Garnier was on a mission to make me laugh or smile. It took the edge off the day and reminded me that being an Ice Queen wasn't who I really was.

I did sometimes catch her staring at me while we reviewed notes, or when I went off on a tangent about the forensic techniques the lab used to fingerprint impossible surfaces. She smiled and listened intently. Her eyes didn't glaze over like Aaron's — or anyone else's — when I spoke. If I was forced, I'd admit she was slowly melting my ice walls.

I emptied the bag, stress eating my thoughts away, and grabbed the second bag I'd bought. I tore it open as traffic moved an inch.

"Seriously? Two bags?" Garnier sipped her coffee.

"It's a bad habit from when I was a kid." I looked at her. "I'm sure you have one. Everyone has a bad habit they learned in their youth that carries over into adulthood." I paused, my gut telling me to go with it and share something personal with her. "I ran the streets as a kid before I was adopted and moved to Chicago. Candy was my comfort blanket. It made me happy when life sucked. And more often than not, it was the only food I could afford." I stared at the bag. "It's strange logic, but candy is my de-stressor. I'm eating two bags because I know in the next half hour when traffic clears, I'll have to endure a dead body. I'll be charged with picking apart their secrets and putting a puzzle together to bring their death to justice or peace. Then I'll have to watch Dr. Willows act like an egotistical asshole and flirt with you. That alone, I'll need the third bag I'm saving for the ride back."

"I didn't know you were adopted." Garnier's tone was soft. "Does it bother you when Dr. Willows flirts with me?"

My jaw twitched. I was afraid to truthfully answer her. "Not many in this world know I'm not a Tiernan by birthright." I palmed the bag of candy. "What about you? What's your bad habit?"

Garnier turned to face me. "Travel size toiletries. I always have to have shampoo, soap, toothpaste in tiny little bottles everywhere I go. Let's just say my mom wasn't too budget conscious and we constantly ran out of the basics." Garnier's face dropped. "I like feeling that I can get clean anytime, anywhere. That's my de-stressor." She picked at the lid of her coffee. "You know, this is the first time we've ever had a personal conversation without it breaking down into insults and yelling?"

I cleared my throat, "We've only worked together for about a month." I leaned forward as traffic started to clear.

"I like it. I like hearing about what makes the great Detective Lieutenant Tiernan tick. I like the woman behind the ice." Garnier's voice had a slight tremble, probably nervous I was about to lash out for getting too personal.

"Trust me, it's nothing impressive." I looked over, catching Garnier giving me that one look again. The one that sent my heart in overdrive. "We still have a slow drive to the scene. Tell me why you wanted to become a homicide detective."

Garnier grinned and began rambling about the first crime scene she'd worked perimeter on. She watched the detectives work the scene with such meticulous grace, she became hooked. She wanted to step behind the yellow tape, collect the clues and put them together herself. Garnier went off into detail about her first scene. It was a double homicide born out of a domestic situation. The wife was found half out of her car with a butcher knife in her back, gun in her hand. The husband ten feet away with two gunshots to the chest.

I listened, vividly recalling that particular crime scene. Aaron and I worked it two years ago and I vaguely remembered an officer who looked a lot like Garnier, working perimeter. I didn't look at her twice that night, too focused on the murder ahead of me and getting home to Elle.

My gut flickered. Maybe it was time to become that person Garnier was rambling about again. The kind detective who didn't treat her like crap because of rank. Maybe she was worth letting in.

* * *

The phone woke me from a dead, dreamless sleep. I picked it up and mumbled out a raspy hello.

"Wakey wakey, Emma. We caught another dead body up in Wicker Park." Aaron was far too cheery for a quarter to three in the morning.

I ran my hand through wild bedhead, grumbling as I squinted at the clock. "Why are you calling me? You take it. I'm not in the rotation today."

"I'd love to take it, but you need to come down here. The scene looks exactly like your Latin murder."

I rolled over onto my back, groaning. "Give me the address." After scribbling the directions down, I hung up and dialed Garnier. I heard her mumble when she picked up, along with another voice in the background, calling her name. "Hello?"

"Garnier, get dressed. I'm picking you up in twenty minutes. We picked up another body in Wicker Park. Aaron is waiting for us."

She cleared her throat at the sound of my voice. "Okay, yeah, I'll be ready. Do you need directions to my place?"

"No, Aaron gave me your address."

"Oh. Okay. Um, I'll be ready." I heard her rustle out of bed. The voice I'd heard in the background was asking her to come back to bed.

I felt a slow wave of jealousy creep in. "Good." I hung up the phone and rolled out of bed.

Garnier sat on the front steps of her large apartment building with her head down, talking on the phone. The look on her face told me it wasn't a pleasant conversation. I wondered if it had anything to do with the background voice I'd heard earlier. A voice that sounded a lot like a man's.

As soon as she saw me, she tucked the phone away, jogged to the car, and hopped in. She was dressed down, wearing a white button-down and black slacks. Her gun jutted out from her hip in a paddle holster, her gold badge tucked in next to it. As I pulled away, I caught her looking at me, then looking at her own clothes.

I'd dressed quickly and without formality, selecting a soft grey Detroit Pistons shirt with an old pair of jeans. My gun sat in its holster in the middle console. My hair was tied in a messy ponytail with loose chunks of hair framing my face. I'd been to a lot of middle of the night crime scenes and knew getting dirty was par for the course. We'd be digging around for evidence with little to no light.

Stopping at a red light, I glanced over and caught Garnier staring at me in a less than professional way. She turned away, looking out her window at the oncoming traffic. My rookie was checking me out. The tension had been building between us for a few weeks as our working relationship smoothed out. That day stuck in traffic had opened a door between us.

I tapped on the steering wheel, blushing from her gaze. "I hope I didn't disturb you."

Garnier shook her head, still looking out the window. "You didn't. I'm glad you called. I mean I'm not glad there's another body." She blew out a breath. "I wasn't sleeping well. It'll be good for me to get out of the apartment. Maybe working will tire me out and I can fall asleep."

I said nothing. If I did, I would ask about the voice I heard. If he was the reason Garnier was happy to be heading to a crime scene in the middle of the night.

I drove the rest of the way in silence, internally analyzing the phone call and trying to pick apart Garnier's personal life.

I sighed. I was getting too attached to Garnier. Maybe even crushing on her, if the strange jealousy I was stewing in was any indication of my feelings.

The flashing red and blue lights around the crime scene pulled my focus back to what was ahead. I parked the cruiser off to the side and got out as Aaron walked towards us. He saw Garnier and flashed his usual grin. "Good morning, Sasha. Got a hot one for you two." He held up the yellow tape for us to step under.

"What do we have?" Garnier asked as she dipped under the tape.

Aaron flipped his notepad open. "A white female who appears to be in her mid to late twenties. She has multiple stab wounds to the chest and abdomen. She also has severe blunt force trauma to her face as if she was beaten. The techs found a few pages under her head, just like David. No wallet or purse was found on the victim. We have no identification at this time." He lifted his head. "Call came in almost an hour ago. Late night dog walker found the body and called it in. I was next up on the rotation, but when I got here, I knew it was the work of your guy." Aaron stopped in front of a body lying at a strange angle, crime scene techs hovering around the edges.

I took a deep breath, kneeling next to the body. "Dr. Willows on his way?"

"Willows sent in his assistant, Eddie. He's waiting for you before he takes the body. The techs have been cleared to look for trace evidence, but I told them to wait for you."

I smiled. Aaron knew precisely how I worked. I looked over at Garnier. She was pale, with her eyes rigidly fixed on the crime scene ahead. "Garnier, if you think you might throw up, do it away from the scene." I kept my tone gentle, placing a hand on her shoulder. "Are you ready?"

She nodded and took a step forward. I grabbed the gloves Aaron held out for me and tossed her a pair. Stepping carefully around the body and pools of blood, I bent down to examine the victim.

The victim had definitely been beaten. Her face was unrecognizable and in far worse shape than David's. I would've picked blunt force trauma as her cause of death, but her shirt was covered in dark blood stains. I grabbed the edge of her shirt when I saw Eddie move closer to watch. Lifting her shirt, I saw at least a dozen lacerations from a knife or a scalpel across her chest and abdomen. They were random, made with an angry hand. I laid the shirt back down and scanned over the rest of the body. "Aaron, did you find any carvings?"

"We haven't moved the body."

I saw Garnier move to the head of the victim, then bend down, looking over the victim's mauled face. "Can I have a pair of tweezers and an evidence bag?" She motioned a tech over.

"You found something?"

She nodded as the tech handed her the items. Garnier slowly removed what looked like a matchbook and dropped it into the bag. She then removed two pages filled with Latin and placed them in bags. She stood, handing the evidence to me. "The match book looks like it was purposely placed under her neck. I don't think this murder was random. I think the killer knows we're looking for him and is starting to leave clues."

I held the matchbook in the light to get a better look. I couldn't read the logo; there was too much blood smearing the entire thing. I took the second bag and immediately recognized the Latin print as well as the same page numbers I saw on the pages from David's murder. I frowned, handing everything back to Garnier, then motioned for Eddie to come over. "Can we roll the body?"

Eddie smiled. He was a big man who had worked as an Assistant Medical Examiner for the last three years. His size gave people the impression he was dumb, but he was far from it. Eddie was smarter than anyone I knew, including his boss. I secretly hoped Eddie would take over for Willows when the time came. "Sure thing, Lieutenant." His voice was always soft and kind, no matter the horrors laid before us.

As he crouched down with me, I motioned Garnier to take the legs and the three of us rolled the body. Eddie and Garnier balanced it while I looked over the victim's back. It took a minute, but I found it. Carved into her lower back was the Latin phrase '*Ego te provoco.*' I examined the rest of the body and found nothing else, frustrating me. I hated when the evidence was deliberately thin.

We rolled the victim back and stood up. I kept my eyes on the body. "Aaron, this is our guy. I hate to guess, but I think more bodies are coming our way. I also think this might turn into a hate crime as we investigate the victim's background. The pages will tell us." I stepped back and walked out of the crime scene, leaving the techs to swarm in and collect evidence. I stopped next to Eddie as his team laid the body on a gurney. "Can you rush this one? At least get me an identification by lunchtime?"

Eddie nodded. "Of course."

I stripped off my bloody gloves and tossed them into a bio bag before walking towards the car. I was angry. Was there a serial killer on my hands? One with a religious agenda or motive? The fury of the stab wounds led me to believe that, along with the Bible pages and the carving.

I walked to the car and sat inside, staring at the red and blue lights that continued to illuminate the scene. I'd forgotten about Garnier until she opened the passenger door and sat down. "Are you okay, Lieutenant?"

I glanced at the genuine concern echoing in her eyes, then turned back to the window. "I'll meet you in the office when the sun rises. This guy is taunting us. He's growing bolder." I turned the car on and backed out of the crime scene.

"Do you think this guy is targeting so-called sinners?"

"I won't know for sure until we get an ID. I'll run her background, see if she was adopted or maybe gay. The Latin pages are the same from the first murder but included a section about homosexuality. I recognized the passage from my years in Catholic School. One nun was a huge homophobe, constantly reciting the passage, in hopes of shaping young, fragile minds. He's leaving us morbid clues through the Bible pages. If he is leaving clues for us, he'll ramp up soon, taunting us to come after him." My anger was starting to boil up. It'd been a long time since a case had made me angry. "I want you to hound the crime lab all afternoon. We need the matchbook and pages processed as soon as possible. Fingers crossed, the killer left DNA or a fingerprint. After we get an ID, we start knocking on doors. I want to get this guy before he leaves us with another body."

Garnier sat in silence, nodding as I issued instructions.

In a matter of minutes, I pulled up in front of her apartment building. She whispered a polite goodnight, but I missed it. I was too busy soaking in anger to acknowledge it. This case just got personal.

As Garnier was about to get out, I saw a shadow creep past her front door and dip into the alley. I swore the shadow moved with intent, like someone was waiting to grab her. Garnier was talking, but I ignored her. My gut instinct told me something was wrong. I grabbed my gun from the middle console and stepped out of the car, leaving Garnier talking to an empty seat.

I crept past the front steps and heard glass crunching under feet in the alley. I watched for a moment as the shadow moved when Garnier called after me. When her voice moved closer the shadow stepped out, revealing a hooded figure.

"Stop! Police! Let me see your hands!" I leveled my gun at their head.

The figure jumped, its hands shooting straight up into the night sky. I heard a loud crash as a glass bottle hit the sidewalk, shattering on impact. "Whoa! Whoa! I ain't no mugger!"

I flinched at the feminine voice but held the gun steady. "Why are you in the alley?"

The figure pulled down its hood, revealing a young girl with bleached blonde hair, streaked with a smattering of assorted colors. She took a cautious step into the light. Her eyes were wide and blue, the color of pure ice and soaked up the ambient streetlight.

I kept my stance until a hand fell to my back, making me flinch again.

"Oh shit, Lieutenant! Please put the gun down. That's my roommate, Morgan."

I glanced sideways at Garnier and back to the girl in front of me, who nodded with fervor. "Sasha's right, I'm her roommate! I locked myself out when I went to the liquor store for chips." She made a motion at the broken bottle on the ground. "And a late-night whiskey run. Oh, sweet amber liquid of the gods, I've failed you." She frowned at the broken bottle and liquid seeping into the concrete. I cleared my throat, slipping the gun back into its holster.

Morgan stared at me, still scared, and blurted out, "I've got my driver's license in my pocket." She pointed at the front pocket on her hooded sweatshirt.

I motioned her to give it to me. She dug in her front pockets and produced one of the best fake licenses I'd ever seen. But it had her name on it and the picture was hers. I handed it back as Garnier stepped next to her.

I sighed, crossing my arms. "If you live here, why are you creeping around the alley? You could get hurt."

Morgan shrugged as Garnier tugged on her sleeve, shoving her towards the front steps. "I didn't recognize your car. I grew up on the streets and learned that strange cars in your neighborhood mean trouble. So, I hid." She gave me a sheepish look.

Garnier turned, a slight smile on her face. "Morgan, this is my partner, Detective Lieutenant Emma Tiernan." Garnier took her keys out, shoving them into Morgan's chest. "Go inside, I'll be up in a minute."

"Oh, hell no! This is *the Ice Queen*?" Morgan saluted me with a smirk. "Nice to finally meet you in the flesh and see your flesh isn't ice."

She winked as Garnier shoved her. "Inside. Now."

Morgan ran up the front steps, unlocked the door and tossed the keys back to Garnier. "Check you bitches later." My last view of Morgan was her skipping up the interior staircase.

"I almost shot your roommate."

Garnier smiled, shoving her hands into her back pockets. "I'm glad you didn't. Morgan's unique, but she's my best friend. I met her while working on the road. She mugged a professional wrestler, and I took the call. After sorting her out and convincing the wrestler not to press charges, I took her under my wing." Garnier glanced at the building. "And she took me under hers."

I dropped my arms. "Just tell her not to hide in shadows or alleys. I thought she was waiting for you, and not to let her back in the apartment. You need to be careful in this neighborhood."

Garnier smiled. "Well, thank you for the police protection." She took a step and slid on the broken glass.

Garnier fell forward, and I reacted, catching her before she hit the edge of the curb. Her hands grabbed my upper arms as her face pressed against my shoulder.

"Are you ok?"

Garnier took a moment to find her footing. I felt her heart beating as she lightly squeezed my arms. She pulled back, her eyes locked on mine. They were dark, and sensual, making the butterflies in my stomach spin. Garnier focused on mouth as she bit her bottom lip and whispered. "Yeah, I just slipped."

Her hands slid down my arms to rest on my forearms, squeezing again. We were inches apart and my heart thundered. Garnier was warm, and the scent of her shampoo filled my senses. It melted a little bit of the ice surrounding my entire being.

Her breath lightly floated across my lips. My jaw twitched as the air thickened. She started to move closer, and I wasn't stopping her or making a move to prevent what I knew was about to happen.

I wanted her to kiss me.

"Sasha! The cable is out again! Come help me jiggle the shitty wires. I don't want to miss my shows." Morgan's screeching filled the night air as it carried down from the second-floor window she half hung out of.

Garnier closed her eyes, sighing with frustration as she slid out of my arms. "Thank you again, Lieutenant." She didn't look at me as she navigated the broken glass. "I'll see you in the morning."

I nodded, watching her run up the steps to her door. She pushed it open, looking back once before disappearing. I let out a shaky breath and unlocked the car.

After flopping into the driver's seat, I stared out the front windshield. My heart still pounded like the percussion section of a high school marching band.

I almost kissed my partner.

I wanted to kiss my partner.

I jammed the keys into the ignition and drove away as fast as I could. The look in her eyes burned into my thoughts.

Chapter 7

I couldn't sleep when I returned home. Instead, I lay in bed, staring at the ceiling. I counted the small cracks in the corner, saw an errant dust bunny lingering along the crown molding. I even mentally alphabetized the bookshelves, my version of counting sheep.

Both Garnier and the new body were on my mind. I tried desperately to separate Garnier out of the equation and stick to the crime scene, but failed. I thought about the scene, the blood and the Latin words crowding my mind, but it kept drifting back to Sasha.

I'd been inches away from kissing the woman, and God, did I want to kiss her. I wanted to know how she felt in my arms as I picked out the minute details of her face that could only be seen up close.

I didn't sleep for the rest of the night, and it got to me. I was crankier than usual when I walked into the office and sat down behind my desk. I held my head in my hands, as I stared at the preliminary autopsy report from Eddie. The victim died the same way as David, almost the exact cause of death.

I flipped the pages and turned to the victim's identification.

Alice Sirhan had been twenty-seven and a graduate student at Northwestern University in the anthropology program. Aaron managed to locate a few contacts at the university for us to interview. What made my heart break and my suspicions rise that this had been a hate crime, was when I saw the next of kin contact in her file. Her girlfriend, Caitlin.

I always hated being the one to talk to the family, but this time it hit home harder than any other time. I remembered what it was like to be on the other end, and I dreaded being the one to do it. I knew the pain and sadness first-hand, and with the inability to shed my professional face and hold the victim's loved one. Telling them it would be okay, and they'd heal, I'd put on a professional smile and comfort them, even though I was still far from okay after losing Elle. I knew it would take years, if not forever, to completely heal.

I sighed, and shoved the file away, rubbing at the bridge of my nose. It didn't help that sleep had abandoned me. A steaming paper cup appeared in front of me along with a small bag of Skittles. "Good morning, Lieutenant. I got you a hot tea and breakfast." Garnier grinned, sitting down across from the desk.

"You don't have to do that." My crankiness was at a full tilt.

She shrugged. "It's my small thank you for not shooting my roommate. Who, by the way, cannot stop talking about how she was almost blasted away by a cop." Garnier leaned forward, holding her own cup in both hands.

"I didn't almost *blast* her away." I pushed the cup away. My stomach was pissed at me for not getting any sleep and it mixed with the anxiety of contacting Alice's family. I was on track for having one fantastic day.

Garnier chuckled. "Morgan has a flair for the dramatic."

I cocked an eyebrow. "She has a flair for doing dumb things. She shouldn't be hiding in alleys or walking through that neighborhood in dark clothes." Garnier's neighborhood wasn't the best. A lot of muggers and drug dealers dressed in all black to make it harder to be seen during their business hours. "I don't want to see her get hurt over a bag of corn chips."

I wanted to change the subject. I knew we would continue talking about Morgan, and that would shift to the almost kiss. I scribbled Alice's girlfriend's name down and handed it to Garnier.

~ 98 ~

"Find her address and information. She's our first stop of the day."

She scrutinized the paper. "Is this our victim?"

I shook my head. "It's the girlfriend of our victim. We need to do the death notification and interview her. I'm still waiting for the evidence to be processed and the autopsy to be completed, but I'm not going to wait. I have to stop this guy before he grows bolder." I sighed, looking at Garnier. Her face changed. She wanted to say something about this case hitting me close, but only nodded. "I'll be back in a few with everything you need."

I was grateful Garnier had learned my moods over the last few weeks and seemed to know not to push when I was this cranky.

She stood to grab a pen from my desk, and I noticed she was wearing a light grey pantsuit with a pink button-down. The color combination made her natural beauty stand out. I groaned and became even crankier. My libido needed to relax. I covered my face until my partner left the office.

While Garnier ran Caitlin, I flipped through the scene photographs of the Latin pages and the carving on Alice's lower back. It was just like what we had found on David. I made a note for Dr. Willows to look at Alice more closely, to see if the carving had been made from the same hand with the same kind of tool.

I scribbled notes about what I wanted to ask Caitlin until Garnier returned and gently set down a piece of paper. "This is her address. I already called her to let her know we were on our way. Apparently, she filed a missing person's report on Alice when she didn't come home from working late in the Anthropology labs and none of her lab mates had seen her. It was just shy of the twenty-four hour norm, but patrol went with it when three other students called in, wanting to file a missing person's report as well. Adding to the suspicion, this wasn't Alice's usual behavior and worth a look. I checked, and Caitlin is home waiting for patrol officers to collect a photograph of Alice."

I closed my eyes, sighing. I couldn't get attached to this one. I not only had a tough time doing death notifications, I also had a hard time disconnecting myself from victims in the past and I knew this case was going to be difficult.

I huffed and snatched the paper. "Let's get this over with." My tone was harder than I intended, but my temper and patience were wearing thin. As I walked past Garnier, I handed her the car keys. "You can drive."

Garnier tried to hide her grin as she took the keys from my hand. I avoided looking at her, holding my head down as we entered the elevator. I breathed in Garnier's shampoo and a small hint of vanilla as she leaned past me to hit the floor button. I closed my eyes, allowing my mind to zone out and away from the woman who stood next to me, twirling the car keys.

Caitlin lived near Lincoln Park, in a small trendy neighborhood on the rise as young professionals moved in and began to rehab the area. We pulled up in front of a brownstone as Garnier craned her head down. "This is the place."

The building reminded me of the townhouse Elle lived in when I first met her. I stepped out of the car, tucking the file into the visor. I'd already memorized everything in it.

Garnier stood outside of the car, smoothing down her jacket. "Are you taking the lead on this one?"

I nodded once. "Yes. I'd normally give you a second chance to prove to me you can interview properly, but this one… this one I need to do." I sighed, my jaw twitched with anxiety as I walked up the front steps. I rang the doorbell and waited, emotionally preparing for what was to come next.

The door opened, and we were greeted by a young, dark-haired girl with a warm smile and hair up in a messy bun. "Hi! You must be the detectives? Detective Tiernan and Detective Garnier?" Her welcoming smile was equally measured with worry.

I nodded, holding out my identification and badge. "That's correct. Are you Caitlin Fisher?"

"That's me." Caitlin held the door as we walked in and continued talking as she directed us to a large living room with a couch straight from an Ikea catalog. "I filed a missing person's report on Alice this morning. I know she's been busy with school and her internship. But she always checked in with me, whether it's a short phone call or a quick text." Caitlin sat down across from us on a smaller couch, holding her arms close to her chest. "It was unlike her to not call during her afternoon break." She looked right at me. "Did you guys find her?"

I knew the look in her eyes. She already knew why we were here. I'd forgotten to ask Garnier what she had told Caitlin about our impending visit when she called her. I took a deep breath. "We did. Alice was found this morning in Wicker Park, at approximately three in the morning. It appears she was murdered."

I paused, as I always did to wait for the emotional reaction to come at me full bore. Caitlin covered her mouth with her hand as she fought back explosive sobs. Garnier moved beside me, one leg pressing against mine for a second as she reached into her pocket and pulled out tissues. "Here. Please, take your time."

Caitlin took the tissues and spoke through choked sobs. "How? How did she...?"

I went to open my mouth when Garnier spoke first.

"We don't have the specifics yet, but I can tell you she fought back." She gave Caitlin a comforting smile. "We have to ask you a few questions. Do you think you can answer them?" Garnier shocked me. I was amazed she'd taken note of my harsh criticism at our last interview and how well she'd adjusted her tactics.

She met my eyes, uncertainty washing over hers until I nodded for her to continue. She leaned towards Caitlin. "Can I ask you a few questions about Alice?" Caitlin nodded, sniffling. "Is there anyone in Alice's life who bothered her or did anything that made her feel uncomfortable? Whether it was at work, the grocery store, or a local coffee shop?"

"No, not that I know of. All her coworkers loved her. She rarely indulged in work drama." She swallowed hard, wiping her nose. "She was focused on her internship and graduating this summer. We were both busy with school and work, but it didn't affect our relationship. She was in the process of moving in with me." Caitlin looked up at the ceiling, tears streaming down her face. "We were going to get married in the fall."

Garnier was visibly struggling with the pain this line of questioning drew out, but kept at it. "Are there any places she hung out? Any bars, or restaurants she favored where she might have drawn attention?"

Caitlin shook her head. "Alice wasn't a drinker. The only bar she'd go to was the Black Kettle, and it'd be with me when I could actually drag her out of the house. Alice was all about her work, school, and me." Caitlin covered her mouth, sobbing again.

"Can you think of anyone who would target Alice for her relationship with you? For being gay? Any jealous ex-lovers or new romantic interests? Were you suspicious she may have been seeing someone else on the side?" Garnier's clipped tone came off less than accepting of Caitlin and Alice as a couple.

Caitlin scoffed, her sadness quickly melting into anger at the insensitive implication "Really? No. Alice and I loved each other, more than anything else in this world. I know there are gay stereotypes out there someone like you would believe to be true. That gay couples are swingers, cheaters, or promiscuous, but not Alice and I." Her anger fell away to tears. "We were going to marry each other. I know that's hard for you to accept. A gay couple wanting monogamy and the white picket fence." Caitlin closed her eyes tight, clutching to what little control she had left.

Garnier turned bright red and looked down.

I sighed. She'd done so well up to that point.

Sliding forward, I took over the interview. "Caitlin, you said you were moving in together? Did Alice still have her own place? An apartment or a house?"

"Apartment. She didn't finish moving out. That was for this weekend." She trailed off.

"Do you mind if we take a look at her apartment? I promise we won't disturb anything, but we need to look at everything we can." I laid a hand on her knee. "I promise I will catch whoever did this."

Caitlin saw I was being honest with her, despite the firm, neutral exterior I'd learned to project. She stood and walked to a small desk, where she scribbled on a notepad. She brought me a set of keys with the note wrapped around it.

"Thank you, Caitlin." I took the note from her.

Caitlin looked lost as she stood in the middle of the living room, hugging herself.

I nudged Garnier, signaling we were done. Smiling at Caitlin I stood and squeezed her shoulder. "Caitlin, if you think of anything later, please call me." I tucked a card in her hand. "My personal cell phone number is on there. My office will be contacting you soon about Alice, but if you need anything, call me." I paused. "I know what you're going through. I lost my girlfriend of three years in a car accident." Caitlin tried to smile for my comfort. "I'll make this right for the both of you." I walked away, nodding to Garnier to open the front door.

Outside, I walked past her, motioning for the car keys. I was frustrated at her for asking an insensitive question so quickly in the interview. Garnier handed over the keys in silence. We said nothing as I drove away.

The tension in the car was so thick it could've choked us both.

Alice's apartment was on the other side of town. Before parking the car, I glanced at Garnier. "Don't touch anything, wear gloves, and call the techs to meet us here."

"I'm sorry, Lieutenant. I screwed up. I don't know why I went that route with my questions." Garnier blushed, admitting her mistake.

"Learn from your mistakes or continue to fail." I cut her off. My crankiness had grown during the drive over. I kicked the car door open, moving to the trunk to dig in my gear bag for gloves. Garnier stood next to me. And I knew I'd struck a nerve with her. The anger radiated off her in hot waves.

Honestly, I didn't give a shit. I lacked sympathy for her today. Caitlin's tragedy hit too close to home and Garnier kept making mistakes, pissing me off. She took the lead on the interview and started well, but I had to step in and save her ass. Everything about this case was far too close to my heart, and I hated I was letting it get too close.

Shoving a pair of gloves in my pocket, I absently held another pair out to Garnier.

As I unlocked the front door to the apartment, I mumbled over my shoulder. "Take the kitchen and living room. I'll take the bedroom and the bathroom. Anything suspicious, leave it and come get me."

"Yes sir." Garnier grumbled, snapping on her gloves before brushing past me. I took a deep breath before moving to the bedroom.

The apartment was disorganized, with things half in and out of moving boxes. I poked around the bedroom and found nothing unusual. I walked past a large dresser and stopped as a picture frame caught my attention. It held a photograph taken during the holidays. Alice and Caitlin were smiling and laughing, both wearing Santa hats. Alice was a beautiful girl and almost unrecognizable from the body I'd seen lying on the street, bloodied and battered. I closed my eyes, taking another breath before searching through her drawers.

Everything in the bedroom was innately organized, telling me the couple were saving packing up the bedroom for last. Socks were folded neatly in descending color order, and the entire room was crisp and clean despite the empty moving boxes scattered throughout the apartment. It would've been easy to spot something out of place.

In the bathroom, I searched the medicine cabinet. There were a few half-empty prescription bottles. I noted the prescribing doctor and pharmacy, another possible lead. Poking around, I found matching toothbrushes, shampoo, and the usual grooming supplies. Nothing felt out of place or gave off a vibe that someone other than the girls had been in the apartment.

I walked down the hallway and met up with Garnier, who was searching a small office desk, pushed into a corner of the kitchen. I picked up a pile of local carry out menus. "Anything?"

"Nothing really. I found a bunch of gay rights material mixed in a handful of political pamphlets." She laughed flippantly. "They were definitely loud and proud, if you know what I mean." Garnier held up a flyer from last summer's Pride parade, and waved it around.

I closed my eyes with a sigh. She was pushing my buttons. "They have their rights. It should not detract from the fact Alice was murdered. Murdered because of the things she was involved with or just because she loved a woman. Don't be so Goddamned judgmental, Garnier." Her tone pissed me off.

Garnier shrugged, tossing the flyers on the desk. She was growing visibly agitated by my standoffish tone. "Well, whatever. I didn't find anything outside of the flyers and gay marriage information. I can't get into the computer because it's password protected. I'll need a warrant for that even if Caitlin gave us permission to enter the apartment." Garnier looked around. "Other than that, it looks like these ladies lived a very humble almost-married life."

Garnier had an air about her that screamed she was disgusted about having to sift through their unacceptable lifestyle.

My temper spiked. "No, Garnier, not whatever. You need to take this seriously. Put your personal feelings and judgements aside. Bottom line, Alice was murdered. David was murdered. And you're now tasked with being their representative, so to speak, in finding the killer and bringing them to justice. Gay or not, Alice was loved."

Garnier's eyes held a strange intensity. "I'm not judging their lifestyle or them. I'm saying I haven't found anything here. I have respect for the two victims, their loved ones, and I intend to do better than my best for them."

"Your attitude is telling a whole different story. You better keep yourself in check." I bit my cheek to refrain from calling her a fucking homophobe.

Garnier strode around the desk, her face flushed. Frowning, I knew what was coming, I'd pushed her buttons and was about to face her rage.

"My attitude? Look who's talking, Lieutenant. Maybe I'm learning my piss-poor attitude from you, since it's the only thing you seem to teach me. I'm sorry I'm not letting this case get too close to me and under my skin, just like you taught me to avoid in your first few lectures." She blew out a sarcastic laugh. "Funny, Teacher won't follow her own lessons." Garnier's face turned a deeper shade of red as her voice rose.

I rubbed my temple, trying to control the outburst screaming to the tip of my tongue. "This case has become too personal, so forgive me for that. I guess a homophobe wouldn't understand how hate crimes like this hit home. Especially being gay and investigating them." I waved a hand at her, turning to walk away. I didn't have the energy to fight an ignorant bigot.

"What did you call me?"

I continued walking, desperate to get outside and into the fresh air. My anger was about to spill out. She'd pushed me to a dangerous place. "I said, you're a fucking homophobe." I struggled to keep my tone even, professional.

The second I hit the sidewalk, Garnier bounced down the steps after me. It was admirable that she was willing to take this round to the streets. I kept my back to her, digging for the car keys.

She grabbed my shoulder, turning me to face her. "Say it to my face."

Garnier was inches away from me, staring with such an intensity that it scared me and made my heart race at the same time. Garnier was angry. Angrier than I'd ever seen her.

"I said, say it to *my face*. What did you call me?" She was half yelling.

I took a deep breath, readying myself for what I knew was going to be one hell of a fallout. I lowered my voice, lifting my head to meet stormy hazel eyes. "I said you were a fucking homophobe." I squinted at her, my anger speaking for me. "Or maybe I should say a closet case? You do show the signs of being one." I winced at my words as her eyes lit up with pure fire. I'd definitely hit a nerve.

Garnier kept my gaze, laughing. "Really? A homophobic closet case? You honestly get that impression from me?"

"Yes. I do." My mind raced through all the signs of Garnier being at least bisexual. I catalogued them, ready to throw them in her face if she wanted to take this fight a full three rounds. If I was lucky, she'd quit by the end of the day.

Garnier bit her top lip. "Would a homophobic closet case do this?" She grabbed my face with both hands and kissed me hard, pushing the both of us into the rear door of the car. The intensity of the kiss caught me off guard.

Her tongue ran along my bottom lip, asking for more. Gut instinct took over, and I let her have it. Her left hand slid from my face, down to my waist, and pressed our hips together. I gasped at how perfectly we fit.

Her touch drove me crazy in an instant and forced me to react. I kissed her back, and found my hands running up her back as I tried to take as much of the kiss as possible.

I wanted more.

I pushed off the car, but Garnier pushed harder, trapping me between her hips and the car. A wave of guilt washed over me as I felt how warm she was, and I broke the kiss, shoving Garnier away.

"Stop."

Garnier took a quick step back, panic crossing her features. "Oh my God! I'm so sorry! I couldn't help it." She looked up with a flushed face, running a hand over her hair. "I've been wanting to do that since the first day I met you. I didn't mean for it to happen like this... you... my temper got the best of me. You challenged me, and I wanted to prove you wrong. I told you I'm not like everyone else."

I remained silent. The slow wave of guilt continued to consume me. I felt guilty for kissing her back. She was my partner and Elle was still on my mind. Yet, I was full of indescribable desire for this woman who had lunged at me in broad daylight, shoving me against one of Chicago's finest cruisers and pinning me with hips that made me ache. I just stared at Garnier, unable to speak.

Garnier didn't take the silence well. "Will you say something? Jesus, I'm sorry. I didn't mean to come off as rude in there. It's my short temper. I'm sorry I kissed you, Emma." She grabbed my wrist. "Please say something." She stared at me with those big hazel eyes that had snagged me from day one. I felt my heart skip, amplified by the urge to grab her and kiss her again.

I said nothing as I walked to the driver's side door and got in. Before I closed the door, I nodded at her, ignoring her visible panic. "Call Aaron. He'll give you a ride home." I drove away, leaving Garnier standing on the street, confused and lost.

She wasn't the only one.

***

I didn't go home. I didn't go back to the station. I went straight to Millennium Park and walked to the edge of the lake, taking slow steps along the dock, where nothing but the water surrounded me. I was overwhelmed with emotions. There was now a bigger situation on my hands than dead bodies and being stuck with a new partner, a situation I wasn't skilled to deal with. I was beginning to fall for Garnier.

My logical thinking fought with my heart, but my body — and the feelings I got simply from being around her — said otherwise. My heart wanted Garnier to come in and clear out the darkness. I closed my eyes as water lapped around me.

It felt so strange to kiss Garnier. It'd been more than a year since I'd lost Elle, and I knew she would want me to move on, but Elle was the only person I'd ever loved with my whole heart. She'd been the first person I let my guard down for. When I lost her, I lost pieces of myself.

I watched people walk by as I sat on the edge of the concrete stairs that led down to the water, my feet dangling over the edge. My phone had rung incessantly the second I was a block away from where I ditched Garnier. Aaron and Garnier were calling and sending messages, one after the other. I set the phone next to me, letting it vibrate until the sun dipped into dusk and I shivered at the chilly air slipping around me. I stood up, grabbing the phone as it vibrated, Aaron's name taunting me in bright white letters on the screen.

"What do you want, Aaron?"

"Jesus Christ, Emma! It's about time you answered the damn phone." He was upset with me, which meant he was also worried. It was out of character for me to abandon anyone, let alone a partner.

"I was called to another scene." Walking back to the car, I groaned as the dinner crowd thickened.

"You're so full of shit." He huffed. "Why did I have to pick up Sasha on the side of the road? She wouldn't tell me anything, just kept repeating she needed to talk to you. Did you chew her out again? She looked pale, just like the last time you tore her a new one."

"Nothing happened. I had to take a supervisor call at another scene." My tone was clipped. I was terrible at lying, especially to Aaron.

He sighed. "Emma. Something happened."

It was my turn to sigh. "I'll tell you later. I need to go home. I'll see you in the morning." I hung up and drove home. I did want to tell Aaron what happened between me and Garnier, but in the morning I'd most likely be dragged into Captain Jameson's office. I'd have to endure whatever punishment for leaving my rookie on the street, never mind the fact I kissed her.

It was late by the time I got home, and all I wanted to do was crawl into bed and sleep off my feelings. My stomach twisted at the sight of thirteen missed calls from Garnier, plus a handful of texts I refused to read. I trudged upstairs to my bedroom and changed clothes before moving to the office next to my bedroom.

As I went over the interview notes, the bar stood out as the only reliable link between the victims. The Black Kettle. That was my solid link to connect David and Alice. I made a note to check it out in the morning, to interview the staff. I was certain these two victims had been targeted at the bar, but had to make sure. I needed more, since there was absolutely no trace evidence. The killer had been smart and cleaned up after himself.

Staring at the bookshelf across the room, I couldn't shake the feeling of déjà vu I'd felt in the morgue. There was something awfully familiar about the carvings, almost as if they were connected to the one on my stomach. I sighed and picked up the phone.

My father answered in two rings. "Well, if it isn't my favorite daughter! How are you?"

I smiled at his lame joke. "Dad, I'm your only daughter."

"But you're still my favorite. You haven't called in a week. What's up? I heard from Liam you have a new partner."

"I did. She's fresh off patrol. Very green to investigating homicides." I rubbed my forehead. "Dad, you know how much I despise having partners."

"Oh boy, do I, but Liam tells me this new girl is just as good as you."

I swallowed hard. I didn't want to talk about Garnier in detail. My dad would pick up the tension in my voice. "She's learning. But I wouldn't be surprised if she transferred out."

"Emma, not again. What did you do?" My father knew my history with partners. He had tried giving me the father/daughter, cop to cop talk, but I wouldn't listen. After I was promoted, and he retired, he joked I was way above his pay grade. I secretly knew he wanted me to shake the icy persona. He was still in the gossip loop of the department, thanks to his weekly golf games with my boss.

But how in the hell could I tell my father that Garnier had kissed me, and I kissed her back, outside of a witness' house, before driving off like a petrified teenager? I had a quick flashback of when I came out to my parents. I'd been caught kissing the goalie of the girls' soccer team under the bleachers. What made things worse was that I was in Catholic school, and the head mother caught us. As we drove home from the emergency parent-teacher conference, my father looked in the rearview mirror.

"Emma, I don't ever want to have to sit in that office again with that creepy thing staring down at me."

I blushed. "I'm sorry dad, I didn't mean it. Sister Jude's massive Jesus statue is really creepy."

He laughed. "Oh, I wasn't talking about the statue. I meant Sister Jude. She was a beast back when I went there."

My mother turned in her seat. "He's right, she gave me a hard time when I started dating your dad." She took my hand. "But I hope you know your dad and I are happy with whatever and whomever you decide to love."

Their hearts broke just as much as mine did when Elle died, but they moved on more quickly. My mother was still setting me up on blind dates here and there, playing matchmaker.

"Nothing happened, Dad. I've been a little too hard on her, that's all." I swiftly changed the subject, "Dad, I have a few questions about my foster records."

"Shoot, kiddo."

"Is there any way I can get the sealed records from Detroit?" My father had been great in getting me information when I started digging in my past, but much of my life was sealed and well outside his jurisdiction. I managed to get public records but nothing else. My gut told me I needed to dig deeper. I ran a hand over my stomach scar.

"Of course, kiddo. I know someone who owes me a favor and her rank is higher than both of ours." I heard my mother's voice in the background, hollering for my father to give her the phone. "Your mom wants to talk to you, hold on."

I grinned. I adored my mother. When I first met her, she'd been stern, as I adjusted to rules that never existed in the foster homes. Margaret Tiernan was a former prosecuting attorney and did not budge an inch with my wild ways. I loved her and my father dearly, and as I grew up, she became a best friend. She was tenacious and unbending when it came to keeping me on the right track. She was still stern with me. Even though I was in my mid-thirties, I'd always be her little girl.

"Emma Tiernan. Please don't tell me you're too busy to pick up the phone and call."

I chuckled at her comment. I called home at least once or twice a week even though my parents lived ten minutes outside of the city. "Mom, I've been busy. I have a weird case and I'm sure Dad told you I have a new partner."

"He did. I also heard this new partner is very attractive?" Her tone told me she was about to put on her matchmaker hat.

I groaned. "I've really not paid any attention to her."

She snickered. "When you say that, it means you've paid plenty of attention. I know my daughter. Are you interested in this one?"

"I... I don't know, Mom." I really didn't know. I could barely handle the growing feelings for my partner, let alone define them to my mother.

"Emma, you have to let your heart breathe. You can't keep it locked up forever. You know she wouldn't want that for you."

I bit the inside of my cheek. My mother was right. I'd shut my entire life down after Elle. I worked, slept, and worked some more. On the rare times I went out with Aaron, I'd been asked out by men and women. I always turned them down or threw out their numbers. I wasn't ready for anything romantic. I wasn't sure if I ever would be.

I whispered. "I know, Mom."

My mother picked up my tone, changing the subject to random neighborhood gossip. She made a point to schedule dinner in the next week, to physically check up on me and sort through my mail. After a few more minutes of idle chatter, I hung up. The tension in my shoulders had eased, so I went to make dinner. I pushed past the organic salad in my fridge for the leftover fried chicken.

I devoured the cold chicken as I walked to the table of junk mail. Pushing a few magazines to the side, I grabbed my cell phone to take back upstairs.

There were a few more messages from Garnier. I took a deep breath and scrolled through them. Many of the messages were apologies and *please call me, I need to explain.* I groaned, methodically deleting them before pausing at the last message she sent.

-*Yo Ice Queen, call this number. It's Sasha's roommate. I need help with her.*-

I squeezed my phone, groaning with irritation. I had a difficult time refusing calls for help. It was one of my weaknesses, and the reason I became a cop. I dialed Garnier's number and Morgan answered, talking a mile a minute.

"I didn't know what to do. Sasha doesn't really have any friends. Well, any good ones. We're down at O'Malley's. She's drunk as shit and I can't get her to leave."

"Morgan, this better not be a ploy to get me to talk to her."

"What the hell are you talking about, Tiernan? A ploy? Can you turn off the Cagney and Lacey schtick for a second?" I heard Garnier's slurred voice in the background.

"How drunk is she?" I rubbed the bridge of my nose. Why was I entertaining this phone call? I should hang up and eat more cold fried chicken. Not go out on a late-night rescue.

"I pretended to throw her car keys down the toilet." A loud voice in the background drowned Morgan out. "She trusts you and I can't wrangle her when she's this drunk. Sasha is stronger than she looks. She's like a Goddamned ant."

I stared at the ceiling, then at the half-eaten drumstick in my hand. I sighed, tossing it in the trash. "Fine. I'll be there in fifteen minutes."

* * *

O'Malley's Irish Pub was on the other side of the city. It was a total cop and firefighter bar, packed to the gills with my coworkers, old and new. They gave me curt glances as I pushed through, tossing out snide comments as I passed. Not altogether unexpected, since my reputation as the Ice Queen was department-wide.

Morgan was tucked into a booth near the back of the bar, trapping a drunk Garnier in the corner. She lit up when she saw me. "Hey hey! I owe you huge for this."

I folded my arms and looked at Garnier, whose face was flush and sweaty. She still wore her pantsuit from earlier, but it was now wrinkled with wet spots down the front. It didn't take a detective to see she'd been drinking for a while. Morgan was trying to get her to drink water, but Garnier kept pushing it away, mumbling about wanting to drink away the feeling.

I stood next to Morgan, assessing the situation. "Let's get her outside. The fresh air will sober her up, then we'll figure out the rest."

Morgan climbed over the back of the booth to the other side of Garnier, pushing her out. "Come on, Sasha, Detective Hottie is here. Time to get you home."

Garnier mumbled. "Hottie? Who?" She looked up, saw it was me through her booze-soaked eyes and groaned. "You. Great. Super."

I shook my head and gently grabbed her elbow, holding on as she tried to pull away. I took a deep breath and bent down to hoist her up. "Come on Garnier. It's time to go home."

The eyes in the bar were on us as Garnier mumbled louder. My appearance in the bar was already drawing attention, but now, as I wrangled a very strong Garnier, the looks became intense. I needed to get the hell out of here.

Morgan and I got Garnier up and out of the booth. She leaned on me as I took most of her weight and Morgan propped her up as best as she could. The whiskey was heavy on her breath and oozed from her pores. I huffed, knowing I was responsible for her getting this hammered.

The three of us pushed through the crowd and out of the bar. When the cold air hit Garnier, she glared at me. "The great Lieutenant, coming to save the day after ruining it."

She tried to pull away from me, but I grabbed her side and held on, trying to fight the feeling of her warm body against mine. I yelled over my shoulder to Morgan. "My car is parked around the corner. Grab it and bring it here. She's getting too heavy to carry like this."

I tossed the keys to the smaller girl, and watched her jog to the corner where I'd left the car. Now that I was alone with Garnier, her penetrating stare made me uncomfortable. I had to turn away and look across the street to avoid her gaze.

Garnier's hand brushed my chin, pulling it up so I would look at her. "You don't like looking at me. You'd rather steal looks when you think I'm not paying attention." Her fingertips were electric against my skin. I lifted my chin, letting her hand drunkenly drop to her side.

"You're very drunk, Garnier."

She squirmed against me. "What's a girl to do after being rejected?" She tried to step away. "You left me."

I held Garnier tighter. "We can talk about it later." I cursed Morgan silently to hurry the fuck up, so I could get away from Garnier's body. It melded with mine as she continued to lean on me for support.

"There's no talking to you, Emma. You just crawl up in your ice castle and hide when shit gets too tough to handle." Garnier's words were slurred, but bit deep.

I cringed, struggling not to sling hurt back at Garnier, when Morgan drove my car half up on the curb. She hopped out, shaking her head at the both of us like a disappointed parent.

I buckled Garnier into the passenger seat and closed the door as she pressed her forehead against the glass. She was two breaths away from passing out.

"I'll drive her back to your apartment and help you get her inside. Just meet me there."

Morgan nodded and took off down the street to wherever she came from. I took a deep breath before sitting in the driver's seat. I groaned when I noticed Garnier had taken off her seat belt. I leaned over to buckle her back in and made gentle contact with her thigh. Garnier rolled her head, her breath floating across my cheek. "Why are you doing this, Lieutenant? Just leave me, like you did earlier."

I stared out the front windshield, and started the car. My knuckles turned white as I tried to control myself. "Because." I left it at that and pulled out into traffic. Garnier was quiet during the ride back to her apartment, staring at me with unfocused, hazy eyes, as if she could unlock all of my secrets.

At a red light that was longer than necessary, Garnier spoke. "I don't regret doing it." I shot her a sideways look. "I don't regret kissing you, Emma."

My first name, rolling off her tongue, added more tension. I focused on the traffic, my heart trapped in my throat. Waiting for the cross traffic to stop, I felt Garnier's hand on my arm. "I mean it, Emma. I think you're beautiful and amazing. I wish you'd let me in." Her hand fell away.

I peeked over at her, my heart skipping in my chest from her words. I wanted to say something, but Garnier had passed out. Her chin tucked into her chest as she snored.

I sat in front of her building with a snoring Garnier for ten minutes before Morgan showed up. It took both of us to drag the unusually heavy, passed-out woman into her apartment building. As Morgan ran to grab a bucket and water, I put Garnier to bed.

I took off her boots, looking around the room. Garnier's room was sparse, not packed with books like mine. A large bed took up most of the floor. Dark burgundy sheets were exposed as I laid her on the unmade bed. There were no pictures, just a dresser, some candles, and random pieces of clothes strewn on the floor. My partner was not one for organization, and it showed. I swung her legs into the bed and covered her with a blanket. I stared for a moment as she groaned and rolled over. She was incredibly beautiful, even this intoxicated.

Her brown hair fell over her face, and I instinctively reached out to brush it back. My fingertips grazed soft, warm skin and I let out an uncontrollable sigh that caught me by surprise. I drew my hand back as if I was stung.

As I turned to leave, she grabbed my hand, startling me. "You can stay." Garnier's eyes held such intensity, it creeped into my stomach and knotted there. Her fingers wound in mine and squeezed. A moment passed where we both stared at each other. I fought an immense urge. The feeling of her fingers mixed with mine felt too good.

I closed my eyes as Morgan came in and set down an orange bucket. "Barf bucket at your service." I pulled my hand away from Garnier's and stuffed it into my pocket.

I stepped away, Garnier's eyes still on me. "I should go." I pushed out of the room, staring at the floor until I reached the front door. Morgan hollered a thank you as I closed the door.

Choking a deep breath down, I let out the overflowing feelings through a steady sigh. This wasn't good. This was distracting, but deep down, I liked it.

But feelings always led to trouble.

Chapter 8

I arrived at the office at a painfully early hour. Sleep hadn't been an option after dropping Garnier off. I was beginning to realize this might become a trend while I worked this case and dealt with my new partner. My mind was working in overdrive, closer to burn out every day.

It was close to four in the morning when I sat down at my desk. I half smiled to see the full autopsy report waiting on my desk. Dr. Willows had even provided close-up photographs of the carving on Alice's back. It perfectly matched with David's carving. I'd be able to confirm with hard proof it was the same killer in both cases and maybe link their evidence together.

Alice's cause of death was blunt force trauma to the head. The tox screen came up negative for drugs and alcohol. Her defensive wounds were clear of any trace evidence. Even her fingernails were spotless.

I had nothing. No fibers, no DNA, not even a dust molecule to trace back to the killer. I was dealing with a meticulous pro.

I set the report to the side, and embarked on the progress report for Captain Jameson. I had to tie the two cases together in order to request more resources and manpower. I sat typing, my mind finally starting to focus on the task at hand, and I lost myself in clear and concise report writing. Three hours passed in a blink. I didn't notice until Aaron barged into my office, flopping into his usual spot, kicking his legs up onto the desk.

"Spill it. I only came in this early to hear the truth." He cocked a condescending eyebrow.

I looked over my computer monitor and spoke. "She kissed me yesterday." I continued typing.

Aaron grinned, dropping his feet from my desk. "Shut. Up." He leaned on a hand, grinning. "She kissed you! So that means she's on Team Emma?" He waggled his eyebrows like a giddy teenager.

I frowned at his poor wordplay. "I don't honestly know. We fought again after searching the latest victim's house. She said things that pissed me off. I went off on her and walked away. She chased me, cornered me, and next thing I know..." I lifted my shoulders, trying to shrug away the memory of how soft her lips were against mine.

Aaron laughed. "And next thing you know you're leaving her on the curb, making her call me to pick her up on the other side of the city. Are you sixteen again? Do I have to teach you how to handle the ladies, Emma?"

"I will punch you, *hard*." I sighed. "I panicked. I haven't been kissed in a long time. I felt guilty, weird. I shut down and ran." I leaned forward, holding my head in my hands. "Shit. This is a mess."

Aaron poked my arm. "Hey, it's okay. I mean, I can't blame the girl, your Ice Queen ways are a bit of a turn on. I saw from day two your rookie was starting to develop a crush on you." He threw his feet back up, ignoring my glare. "Have you talked to her?"

I cringed. "Sort of. I picked her up from the bar last night. She was drunk, and her roommate called for help."

Aaron grinned like the cat who ate the mouse. "And did you...?"

I threw a pen at him, hitting him square in the forehead. Bullseye. "I took her home. Helped her roommate put her to bed and left." I huffed. "You know I'm weak when someone asks for help. Garnier was super drunk. I doubt she'll remember anything."

Aaron's tone turned a little more serious as his grin faded. "You like her."

I said nothing. I didn't have to. Aaron was the only person in my life who knew me better than I knew myself.

"Well, stop being a dick and give her a chance." He pointed at my chest. "Give that long-forgotten organ in your chest a chance to feel something again."

The desk phone ringing broke the moment. It was the crime lab, calling to let me know the preliminary reports on the pages and matchbook Garnier found were ready. I hung up.

"I'm going to the lab. If my partner shows up, tell her to sit tight."

Aaron winked, following me out of the office. "Will do, Lieutenant. Oh, we have to talk about my rookie later. He apparently resigned his position yesterday and quit the force altogether. Homicide and dead bodies are not his gig."

I frowned. "Why did you get lucky?"

He shrugged. "Why did you get the good one? I guess we'll never know, but good news is Captain is putting me on the Latin murders with you and Sasha. He wants to close this case as much as you."

I grinned. Aaron was an amazing detective and the more eyes and ears I had, the faster I would close this case. He'd also distract me from my thoughts about Garnier. I motioned to my office. "Everything's on my desk. Read over it and get updated."

Aaron saluted me as I entered the elevator. I just rolled my eyes and sighed.

* * *

I spent two hours in the crime lab, looking over evidence with the techs. They were amazing at providing me with exactly what I needed, forgoing the detailed explanations they gave other detectives. I was handed thorough reports and explicit photographs, and I looked them over as the elevator carried me back to my office, but there was still nothing to give me a lead. No fingerprints on the matchbook or Bible pages. The only evidence was left by the victims.

I walked through the bullpen and saw Aaron sitting in my chair, his feet propped up on the desk.

I slapped his feet off. "You can sit in my office but not in my chair."

Aaron moved. "I read the reports. Our next step is to surveil the bar."

I nodded. "Already on it, I plan to interview some of the regulars." I handed over the evidence report. "Fresh from the lab." As he took it, I asked. "Any signs of my rookie?"

He waved to the desks behind him. "At her desk. I think she's still breathing."

I leaned forward, looking around Aaron to see Garnier at her desk, head down and asleep, by the gentle rise and fall of her chest. I smirked and quietly made my way out. I crouched down next to her, nudging her chair. Garnier was dead to the world.

Removing a pencil from the holder on her desk, I began to poke just under her ear with the eraser. "Dammit Aaron, stop it! I told you to wake me up when Tiernan got here."

I chuckled and whispered in her ear. "Maybe you should wake up, because I'm here."

Garnier's head shot up, blinking like a cartoon.

Batting my eyelashes, I put on a cheery tone. "Good morning, Detective." It was out of character for me, but so was her behavior last night.

Garnier groaned, covering her face. The woman looked rough around the edges. I dropped the pencil back into the cup holder. "Get your things together. We're going to the bar."

She cringed and stood up to slip her jacket on. I motioned to her hip, reminding her to grab her gun. I watched as she fumbled in her bag, then struggled to get the gun in a comfortable spot on her hip. I shook my head. Maybe it'd be better if she left it here. Her massive hangover was making her slow and sloppy.

I rolled my eyes at Aaron, who was trying not to laugh. "Garnier and I are going to the Black Kettle to interview whoever is willing to talk. Can you stay here? Meet with the UC unit about finding an officer interested in becoming a barfly for a couple weeks? I think we need to start monitoring the place inside and out."

Aaron nodded, jotting down notes. "You got it." Before he walked out of the office he leaned over to whisper in my ear. "Take it easy on her. She might barf on you." He threw Garnier a flashy grin and trotted away. I walked out to find her still struggling to get her gear situated. "Are you going to be okay?"

She nodded, and followed me in silence to the car. She fell into the passenger seat with a grunt, shoving sunglasses on her face. I sighed for the hundredth time and grabbed a bottle of water from the gear bag I kept in the trunk. I tossed the bottle in her lap as I climbed into the car. "Here, drink this."

She tried not to chug it all in one sip.

We drove two blocks before Garnier broke the awkward silence. "Hey, thanks for taking me home. Morgan told me what happened."

I winced as I faced her and again took in her rough appearance. I'd go easy on her today, especially since she looked like death warmed over. Death warmed over twice. "Thank Morgan. It was her call that pulled me away from cold fried chicken."

Garnier winced at the mention of food and pressed her head against the window. "No food talk, please. I still might throw up."

"Good thing our first stop of the day is a bar. We can get you some hair of the dog."

Garnier frowned. "Hair of the dog? Who still says that?" She was trying to hide a smile and small laugh.

"I do, but then again I've not gotten as drunk as you since I was in college." My tone came off condescending.

"Yeah, because you're always perfect and amazing. You don't ever need a drink here and there to take the edge off life." Garnier huffed, leaning her head against the window.

Her words hit hard and true. I did give the impression everything in my life was perfect and I didn't need friends. Truth was, my life was far from perfect. It was a rebuild I gave up on a long time ago, leaving a crumbling foundation that would give out with the next heavy blow I took.

I swallowed my hurt as we pulled into the parking lot of the Black Kettle. It looked like any small hole-in-the-wall bar smashed in between two large apartment buildings. Garnier sighed with relief as we entered the dark interior. She took off her sunglasses, squinting. "Place is half empty."

It was a quarter after noon. The few random customers sat spread out in booths. The bar opened for the lunch hour, and the manager told me this would be the best time to mingle with the regulars and meet employees.

The bar décor was full of the typical posters, band flyers, and couches placed here and there. Nothing about the bar stood out from the countless others I'd been to in my lifetime as a police officer. I motioned to Garnier to take a walk around while I approached a young man behind the bar.

I chose a bar stool and sat down, holding my wallet open for the bartender to see the badge. "Detective Tiernan, Chicago Police. Is Johnny here? He told me to ask for him."

The bartender bent closer to the badge and ID card. "Sweetie, you're way too cute to be a cop. Johnny's in the back. You want a drink while I grab him?"

"Just water for me and my partner." I waved to Garnier, who sat next to me.

The bartender batted his eyelashes at her. "Aren't you gorgeous." He flicked his hand between us. "Are you two? You know?" He winked at the blush covering my cheeks.

"No, not all. We just work together." I cleared my throat. The room was getting very warm.

The bartender clicked his tongue, setting two waters in front of us. "That's what they all say, honey. I'll be right back." I took a large sip as he disappeared into the back room. Garnier snatched her glass, downing it in a handful of sips. I looked at her as she gasped for air like a fish out of water. She frowned at my stare and set the empty glass down.

The bartender came back with a shorter, older man, who wore his salt and pepper hair in a crew cut. He was very attractive, even next to the strapping young bartender. I got the impression the attractive staff was what brought people in. The older man offered his hand to me. "Detective Tiernan, good to meet you. Johnny Rand. I'm the manager." I smiled at how strong and firm his handshake was.

"I wish I was here under better circumstances, but I think my partner glossed over the details of why we're here."

Johnny nodded and leaned back against the bar. "She didn't explain much aside from needing to speak with me. I read about David in the newspaper, how can I help you?"

I dug in my pocket for pictures of David and Alice, and slid them across the bar. "Have you ever seen these two in your bar?" I asked the vague question, even after Johnny confirmed knew David. A truth-seeking tactic.

Johnny picked up the photos, sighing at David's. "David was a regular. In here two or three times a week. The girl looks familiar, but I see so many faces, especially on ladies' night. It's hard to remember just one girl."

I nodded. "Has there been anyone in the bar over the last few weeks that made you feel suspicious? Any creeps hanging around?"

Johnny furrowed his brow, "Not really. We have security here to keep the riff raff out, but none of the guys have brought anything to my attention. Our customers are like family, and they come here because I run a safe, clean bar. So, no, there's not been anyone that piqued any interest. We get the occasional wrong-turn college kid, but they make a quick exit as soon as they realize it's a friendly gay bar." He grinned.

I smiled back. "Would you be okay if I placed an undercover officer in here for a few nights to sit and observe?"

Johnny paused. "I guess that would be fine. As long as the officer blends in appropriately with the crowd. I don't want a sore thumb sticking out and chasing away customers."

"Of course, extreme discretion will be used." I shuffled up the pictures and handed Johnny a card. "This is my information. If you could, please keep it quiet about having an undercover officer in here."

Johnny tucked the card into his pocket. I stood up as he spoke. "I remember your face. You used to come in here years ago with that gorgeous redhead, and sit at the back table. You two were always glowing."

I tipped my head down. Elle and I had come to the Black Kettle a lot when we first started dating. "That was a long time ago." I motioned to Garnier, who had been quiet the whole time, trying not to vomit. "Detective, let's go."

Garnier slipped off the stool and followed me out. She groaned as the bright Chicago sun slapped her across the face. "Never, ever again. I hate whiskey."

* * *

Garnier napped for the drive back to the station. I let her, calling it my good deed for the day. I did, however, wake her up by slamming the driver's side door, jolting her awake. It was mean, but I wanted her to remember why getting wasted on a weeknight was a terrible idea. Garnier shuffled behind me as we entered the bullpen.

I paused at Aaron's desk. "Aaron?"

He was on the phone, waving he'd meet us in my office. Garnier trailed a few steps behind. She was very ineffectual today. It irritated me.

I felt like I was dragging the boss's kid around for bring your kid to work day. I sat down, waiting for Garnier to sit across from me.

"Do you think you might sober up at some point and get some work done?"

She mumbled. "I really don't need one of your lectures today. I made a mistake in not calling off today, but you would've lectured me about calling in sick when I was working a case."

"I do not lecture you."

Garnier laughed weakly. "Oh, yes, you do. You lecture me every day about every little thing I do that doesn't meet the impeccable standards of the great Detective Lieutenant Tiernan." She sighed, shaking her head. "I'll be fine after I eat. Let's just forget last night and my hangover."

My heart jumped when she mentioned forgetting last night. I didn't think I'd ever forget that moment in her bedroom, the intensity in her eyes.

I was about to say something when Aaron bustled in, dropping a white wax paper-covered, greasy burger in front of Garnier. "Here, champ, eat this. You're struggling and that's my magic cure for hangovers."

She poked at the greasy wax paper, hesitant to open it. When she peeled back the wax paper, the contents smelled incredible.

I pouted at Aaron. "No worries, Lieutenant. Your lunch is coming. I ordered us salads from that weird hipster cafe you love." He patted his stomach. "I need to watch my figure, I've got a date tonight."

I sighed as Garnier took a bite of the greasy, drippy, cheeseburger, moaning in delight as each bite soaked up the remaining booze in her stomach. "This is amazing, Aaron, thank you."

Aaron winked, throwing her a smirk. "No problem, Sasha." He turned to me. "You get anything at the bar?"

I shrugged, still eyeballing the cheeseburger. "Not much to go on. The manager agreed to us putting an undercover officer in there for a few nights. Hopefully we can pick up on someone or something."

Aaron jotted down notes. "Who do you have in mind? The UC unit has a bunch of new guys. Fresh faces might work in our favor."

"Try Bobby. He moved from traffic and did some undercover work for me in the past. He'll fit in the bar perfectly. He's calm, and very observant." I dug around in my desk for overtime forms. "Tell his sergeant I'm approving the overtime on our budget and to have Bobby in first thing tomorrow for a briefing."

"Roger dodger." Aaron leaned forward, slapping his notebook on the desk. "Man, we really have shit-all to go on, don't we?"

I pushed the files around. "It frustrates me as much as it frustrates you." I watched Garnier wipe grease off her face. "What about you, Garnier. Do you have anything to add?"

"We need to do a tool comparison on the carvings on the back of the victims. It looked like a scalpel was used, with a precise hand behind it. Maybe if we figure out what kind of scalpel was used, we could trace it back to a hospital or a doctor's office. I know it's casting a wide net, but sometimes you have to use a big net to catch small fish."

Aaron nodded in agreement. "I think it's a good idea."

I couldn't disagree. It was a good idea. I was shocked my bumbling rookie thought of it. "Sounds good, Garnier, you can take the lead on it. The lab is on the second floor." I tossed her the autopsy report with photos of the carvings. "See what you can come up with."

Garnier grinned as she stood. Aaron's burger had worked, and the woman was back in the right frame of mind. "Thanks, Lieutenant." She bounced out of the office, turning back at the last second. "If you need me, call?"

I said nothing as she disappeared into the elevator.

Aaron and I poured over witness statements, interview notes and both of us read the autopsy and evidence reports. We were stuck. There was very little, aside from small cryptic clues the killer left for us.

I sighed, unsatisfied, as I threw out my empty salad container. I closed the files and swiveled the chair around to stare out the window.

My friends, the sailboats floating in the water, might reset my brain. The only sound was Aaron tapping a pen on the edge of the desk.

The incessant staccato wore on my nerves. I swung around to yell at him, when my eye caught a tall, elegant, woman walking through the bullpen towards my office. Aaron followed my gaze, his attention drawn in the same direction.

The woman lightly knocked on my door frame. "Detective Lieutenant Emma Tiernan?"

She had clear green eyes, and her blonde hair was lighter than mine, pulled up into a high bun. She wore a professional form-fitting black pantsuit that screamed federal or district attorney.

"That, um, that's me. How can I help you?"

The woman grinned, and held out her hand. "Special Agent Rachel Fisher, FBI."

The handshake was brief and very federal. Rachel released my hand to dig into her briefcase. "I'm a friend of your father's. He mentioned you were looking for this." She held up a thick stack of manila envelopes and handed it over. I hesitated before taking it, recognizing the seal for Michigan's child protective services stamped on the front.

I looked at the agent. "Is this...?" I drifted off, anxious. I possibly held my entire childhood.

She smiled, glancing at Aaron, who stared at her like a broken robot. "It's what you've been looking for. All the questions you have, the answers are in there." Rachel grabbed her briefcase in both hands. "I owed your father a favor, so when he called, I had these sent to my office."

I set the stack down with trembling hands. "Thank you. I, um..."

"You're welcome, Emma." Rachel removed a card from her jacket pocket and set it on top of the files. "If you have more questions, call me. Tell your father thank you. I still owe him more than I can ever repay." Rachel walked out of the office as quietly as she had come in.

Aaron almost fell out of his chair. "Holy. Shit. Emma, you're a hot chick magnet." He squinted. "Do you think your dad and her...?" He wiggled his eyebrows in a suggestive manner.

"Stop now, before I have to hurt you." I sat down, eyes locked on the files.

"Is that a critical break in the case? The FBI are helping us out already?"

I shook my head. "It's a critical break in my life." I picked up the stack and shoved it into my bag. I'd look at the files when I got home, not at my desk where prying eyes prevailed. "If I'm correct, these are my birth records and every file from every foster home I lived in."

I let out a shaky breath, nervous about what was in those plain brown file folders. Aaron fell silent. He knew about my past. He was the only one who knew, outside of my family. He smiled to ease the tension radiating off me.

"Agent Fisher's visit has me thinking. I think we should file a VICAP report and open it up to the federal agencies. Our killer might have more bodies under his belt. This will open up more resources for us to tap into." I glanced at the clock. It was close to six in the evening, the day clearly getting away from me as I avoided my feelings. "Let's call it a day, Aaron." I wanted to rush home and dive into my past.

He yawned, stretching his arms over his head. "I'll work on the VICAP form in the morning. That thing takes hours to fill out." Aaron smirked as he adjusted his shirt. "You want to grab a drink at O'Malley's? The grumpy desk sergeant on midnights is retiring. We're sending him out in style. Dollar beers and two-dollar shots."

I groaned. "Aaron."

"Aaron what?" Garnier walked in, looking much better than she had hours ago. She set a few files on the desk along with a small bag of Skittles. She gave me a soft smile as I grabbed the bag before Aaron spotted it. "He's my hero. I hope you weren't lecturing him." She gave me a shy smirk. This woman knew all my buttons and constantly pushed them. The good ones, and the bad ones.

"No, no lecture for me." He draped an arm around Garnier. "But you can help me out. I'm trying to get the good Lieutenant to come and have drinks with us to celebrate grumpy Chapmans retirement."

Garnier laughed. "Old Chapman is finally retiring? I dealt with him far too many times on midnights." She tilted her head. "Have one drink? So I know you might be human?" When she grinned, her dimples appeared again, and I cursed under my breath. I was a sucker for dimples. Her dimples.

Giving the two dirty looks, I conceded defeat. "One drink, then home. I have too much work to do."

Aaron fist pumped the air. "Oh my God! Finally!" He scooped Garnier in a hug, "This is a rare moment, the great Tiernan venturing out of her reclusive natural habitat."

"I'll meet you both at O'Malley's." I left without another word. I wanted to make up an excuse and go straight home, not have drinks with my coworkers.

Chapter 9

The loud, packed bar made me regret coming. O'Malley's was fuller than it had been when I picked Garnier up the night before. Aaron smiled, shoving a beer in my hand. "For a second, I was sure you were going to bail."

"I almost did, but you'd never let it go." I looked around the room, trying to spot Garnier. Aaron caught my wandering eyes. "She's up front, rubbing elbows with her old unit." He motioned towards a cluster of blue uniforms.

It wasn't hard to pick Garnier out in a crowd. Her infectious laugh and bright smile ignited a room. I watched as she hugged her former coworkers, joking with them as they poked fun at her new pantsuit look. Garnier was charismatic as much as she was infuriating. It was the combination that attracted me to her. She'd fight me tooth and nail one second, then turn around the next and try to win my heart over with the small gesture of bringing me a bag of Skittles to feed my secret addiction.

I couldn't take my eyes off her, and she eventually caught me staring. Our eyes locked and a slow smile crept across her face. She raised her glass in acknowledgement. I grinned, lifting mine.

"I hope you invite me to the wedding." Aaron slapped my back, chuckling.

I tore my eyes from Garnier's. "Never going to happen. She's my rookie, nothing more."

"Sure, say it all you want, but I don't stare at my rookies like you do Garnier, and my rookies certainly never stare at me like that." He nudged me. "Speaking of stares, she's laser-locked on you, and coming this way."

Before I could protest Garnier appeared. "Can I buy you a drink, Lieutenant?"

I looked down at the half-drunk beer in my hand and slid it to Aaron. "Sure."

Garnier laughed. "Let's go to the bar." She raised her glass of water. "I'm keeping it clean tonight. That hangover was terrible, and I don't want a repeat."

I followed her as she pushed people out of the way, many of them stopping to say hearty hellos to her and issue wicked glares my way. I wasn't a part of the popular crowd, and it showed.

Garnier leaned across the bar top, grabbing the bartender to bring us a fresh beer and a diet soda.

She handed me the beer. "I'm glad you came, Lieutenant. It's nice to see you out of the office, especially when I can remember it."

"It happens here and there." I shrugged, opening my mouth to ask about her coworkers, when I was interrupted.

"Hey ladies! Do you mind if I take your picture for the wall of honor?" The young bartender grinned, his bright blue eyes wide with the adrenaline of working a busy bar. His t-shirt and hat bore the O'Malley's logo. The kid must be new. I'd never seen him behind the bar before, and his shirt was too clean to be a veteran of cop retirement parties. Before I could politely decline, Garnier's hand slid around my side, pulling me closer. "Smile for the camera, Tiernan."

I turned to come face to face with the Polaroid camera in the kid's hands and as I met his eyes, another déjà vu hit hard. I squinted, searching my expansive memory. Something about him was extremely familiar.

Before my mind could filter through its catalog of faces, Garnier's hand slid further down to rest at my waist, squeezing.

I forgot everything, even to smile, as the young man took our picture and moved to the other officers. I was too busy looking at the side of Garnier's face.

Her hand quickly left my waist, leaving me trying to hide my disappointment at losing contact.

I took a few more sips of beer, and checked my watch. I'd been at the bar for an hour and a half. That was long enough. I could leave without Aaron berating me for the rest of the week. His date showed up, pulling all of his attention. Giving me the perfect escape.

I fumbled in my pocket for money. I wanted to leave a nice tip, so the staff wouldn't talk more shit about me when I left.

"I got this round." Garnier's hand covered mine. It was warm, and yet made me shiver. It was the same shiver I had felt when her hand was on my waist. Her grin took my breath away and the intensity from last night reappeared in her eyes, petrifying me.

I smiled, dropping a few bills on the bar top as I gently removed my hand. "I should go." I pushed my hand into my jacket pocket, taking a step back. "I'll see you in the morning."

Garnier placed a hand on my elbow. "Bright and early. I wouldn't miss it for the world."

I gave her one last smile before cutting through the expanding crowd, grateful when I finally made it out. I had to suck in a deep breath of the night air to settle the tremors running through my body.

* * *

Piles of papers were scattered across my bed. I'd raced home and torn open the envelope Agent Fisher had given me. It was everything I'd been searching for, like she said. My birth records, my complete foster records, and the police report of my parents' murder.

I sat in the paper swamp, holding my head in one hand as I rubbed my eyes. I'd only made it through my birth record and the police report before I stopped. It was all so overwhelming. Finally learning who I was, who I came from, and who I could've become if it was for my adoptive parents.

I was born in Detroit, Michigan, to drug addicted parents. When I was three years old, my parents had been brutally murdered in a drug deal gone south. The responding officers found me in my crib three days later, silent and in shock. Neither of my parents had any family willing to claim me, and I was swiftly thrown into the system.

I'd poured over graphic details of gruesome murders in my life, but I'd never let it affect me. But reading this murder, I could barely look at the crime scene photos of my parents before I had to set them aside, my stomach turning. Their murderer was cruel, determined to ensure they didn't survive. He was never caught, disappearing into the underground like so many other drug dealers. My heart broke as I read through the details, as I stared at my birth mother's driver license photo.

I looked exactly like her.

I cried, tears falling on the pages of my life. I had no reason right now to suck it up and be the strong, cool detective. These were the hard facts I'd been searching for as long as I could remember. This was my life, and it hurt. It hurt like hell.

Tossing the files to the end of the bed, I leaned back on a pillow. I'd call my father later and find out how he knew Special Agent Rachel Fisher, how she got my files.

The low pitch of my doorbell carried upstairs. I frowned. I wasn't expecting anyone. My mother wasn't coming over until the end of the week, and when I left O'Malley's Aaron had been consumed by his date at the bar.

I rolled off the bed and grabbed my gun before walking downstairs. It was late and there was no reason for anyone to be at my door.

With the gun tucked behind my back, I looked through the peephole before opening the door in confusion. "Sasha?" It was the first time I ever uttered her first name.

She caught the slip and grinned. "I know it's late."

"Come inside before someone gets an idea." I sighed, letting the gun drop to my side.

Garnier moved past me as I set the gun down on a side table. She'd changed since the bar, forgoing her pantsuit for a pair of loose-fitting dark blue jeans and a baggy light blue sweater over a white V-neck.

I locked the door, motioning her towards the kitchen. "Before I ask why you're knocking on my door at this hour, would you like anything? Water? Coffee?"

"Do you have any whiskey?"

I raised my eyebrows in silent criticism.

Garnier held a hand up. "I'm kidding, water will be fine."

I slid a glass of water across the kitchen island, and leaned against the sink. "What brings you to my door, Garnier?"

"Please call me Sasha." Her look sent shivers through my body. I looked at the marble countertop, fidgeting with my glass.

She huffed. The woman was easily frustrated by my lack of engagement. "Emma, I'm here because I don't want to keep playing back and forth with you."

I flinched at the sound of my first name wrapped in her voice. I went to correct her when she held up her hand.

"Let me finish, then you can lecture me. I like you, I like you a lot. I also get the feeling you may like me more than you want to admit. I catch you staring and sneaking glances. I see through the tough icy exterior you hide behind and see a warm, incredible woman. I get it, I do, but I can't avoid the attraction hovering around us. You frustrate me unlike anyone I've ever met, but you intrigue me, unlike anyone I've ever met." Garnier wrapped her hands around the glass. "I don't like playing games, especially when it's with someone I care for."

She winced at her words, then looked me dead in the eyes, pausing to make sure she had my full attention. "I like you, Emma, and I can't keep skirting around it when all I want to do is grab you and kiss you."

I stood silent, while my heart pounded like a jackhammer. I couldn't pull my eyes away from her. I finally tipped my head down, the marble counter becoming awfully intriguing. "Garnier, I appreciate your honesty." I froze, with no clue what to say next. I wasn't good with feelings. I wasn't good at feeling things.

I pushed off the edge of the sink, moving towards the foyer. I needed Garnier to leave before I did something stupid. "I have work to do." Good God, I was repetitive in my dismissal of her. Cold, vague.

"You kissed me back, outside Alice's apartment." She moved around the island.

"I didn't mean it. It was an accident." I was a lying sack of shit and beginning to sweat.

"Bullshit Emma, you meant it." Garnier stood right next to me, bending her head to get me to look at her. "You mean everything you do. It's who you are. Every look you give me, every rude comment or criticism you throw my way. Every soft smile and touch to steady me, you mean it all." She reached out, grabbing my arm. "It's because you're afraid. You're afraid of your feelings for me. Is that it?"

I squeezed my eyes shut. She was pushing buttons better left alone. I was angry. Angry at the files lying on my bed, and the beautiful woman calling me out on my bullshit. The bullshit I thought I hid so well until those piercing hazel eyes came into my life.

I withdrew my arm. "I think you should go." It came out a firm, but shaky whisper.

"Look at me, Emma, look at me and say it to my face." Garnier held onto my arm, not giving an inch.

I clenched my jaw and turned to face her, but said nothing as I shoved past her to open the front door I was about to kick her out of. I didn't get two steps before I felt her strong hand on mine, yanking me to a stop. I spun around to yell but suddenly she was cradling the sides of my face, her mouth crashing into mine in a hard kiss. I stumbled, my back slamming against a wall.

Garnier pulled away when I groaned on impact. She was breathless, searching my face with glassy eyes. "Emma..."

"Shut up, Sasha." I cut her off and bent forward, closing the gap between us, kissing her back. I gave up at that moment. I wanted her.

It took a moment for her to respond to my kiss. It was a gentler kiss than the one she had just attacked me with, but it wasn't any less passionate or needy. She moaned as my tongue glided across her bottom lip. Sasha eagerly opened her mouth, sliding her hands to my waist. Squeezing my hips and pressing me harder into the wall. I ran my hands down her back to the edge of her sweater, and lifted it over her head, nearly ripping it off her. I reached around to the front edge of her t-shirt and pulled that off just as quick. She shivered under my touch as cold air hit her bare skin.

Sasha broke the kiss, pressing her forehead against mine. "Touch me, Emma."

I honored her request by sliding my hands under the last remaining cloth barrier, pushing her jeans down with her underwear. Her breasts were soft, making me crave even more. Sasha pushed into my touch as I ran delicate fingers over her nipples. She kissed my neck, running her hands down my side, one finger trailing to the front of my pajama pants. Sasha abruptly pulled away to strip off her bra. I gasped as I took in the sight of my naked partner. Sasha was breathtaking. Her tight-fitting shirts had been hiding far more than they showed.

She smirked, watching me take in her naked body. She grabbed my hand, lifted it to her lips and kissed my fingers before placing it back on her breast. I closed my eyes. I was so close to losing it just on the sight and soft touches of this woman.

Sasha pressed her body against mine, her hand returning to the front of my pajama pants. "I've dreamt about this, about you, for a long time." Her whispers were hot against my skin.

Her fingers grazed the edge of my waistband, then pushed them down with my underwear. I leaned instinctively into her as her fingers found my desire, gliding inside with ease. I felt my heart stop at her touch. The slow movements of her fingers and her hot kisses on my collarbone drove me insane.

I couldn't hold back. I came as she moaned how wet I was. I fell forward, taking deep breaths, my forehead tucked in the crook of her neck. My heart started again, pounding like never before. I was embarrassed at how little it had taken, and went to push away, but found my legs were made of rubber. "Sasha, I…"

She giggled, pressing a kiss against my heated skin. "Don't. I'll take it as a compliment." She leaned back, placing a hand on my cheek. "At least I know for sure you like me."

I gave her a weak smile. Good lord, I was a pile of jelly in her arms. I swallowed a few times, licking my lips. "More than you know, Sasha." I bent and kissed her softly as my hands fumbled with her jeans. I shoved them down to the floor, and my desire for Sasha surged as she stood naked in front of me.

I lifted Sasha up, her legs wrapping around my waist as I carried her to the kitchen island and set her down, the cold marble against her bare skin pulling a gasp from her lips. We kissed hungrily, my hands running over her body, desperate to touch every inch of her. Sasha's body reacted to my touch. She pushed hard against me when I ignored the one place she wanted me.

I bit my lip. I wanted to savor this.

I ripped off my own shirt, so I could feel her skin against mine. I kissed her hard as her hands explored my breasts. I dipped my hand between us, finding the place she desired me the most, taking her breath away with the movement of my fingers. Each time I thrusted my fingers, Sasha raked her fingernails down my back, pushing her hips harder into my hand. She was desperate to match my rhythm. I watched her, marveling how it could even be possible for her to be so beautiful, and mine.

Sasha was right on the edge, crying out my name. I kissed her, my own need building again rapidly. It was going to be a long, exhausting night.

I was engulfed in the woman when my cell phone rang. I ignored it. If it was important, they'd leave a voicemail.

Then the landline rang.

I paused mid stroke. It was Aaron.

We had a code when a new body fell into our laps. If I didn't answer my cell, he'd call the house, let it ring once then wait three minutes before calling again. I turned away from Sasha, glaring at the phone and debating internally if I could ignore that another homicide had fallen into my lap.

"Emma, don't stop. Whoever it is can leave a voicemail." Sasha panted, kissing and nipping my neck.

My cell rang again, and I looked at Sasha, flushed and so close. She was right. He could leave a message. He probably just wanted me to go out for beers and hot dogs.

Then the house phone rang. I closed my eyes. "Fuck. Fucking fuck me."

"I know, I want to." Sasha pushed hard against my hand. She met my eyes and saw the concern.

I whispered. "It's Aaron. There's another body."

I pulled my hand gently from her body, and it was enough. Sasha gasped hard as I felt her contract against my fingers.

She leaned her head against mine, flush from her orgasm. "Not exactly how I wanted it, but I'll take it." She kissed the corner of my mouth. "You're incredible, Emma." Sasha wrapped her arms around me, pulling me in for a searing kiss.

I was beginning to forget about Aaron when it rang again. Clearly this homicide was urgent, or Aaron would've given up on the second call. "I'm sorry." I leaned around Sasha, grabbing the phone and answering it. "Aaron."

"Emma, we've got another body. Lincoln Park, under the EL stop outside of Diversey." Aaron sounded tired. "It's our guy."

I ran a hand through my hair, tugging the ends to focus. "Okay. I'll meet you there in twenty minutes."

"Sounds good. Call your partner. She isn't answering her phone."

I glanced at Sasha, who had slid off the island and was picking up her strewn clothing, pulling it on as I stared at her. "I'll uh, pick her up and bring her to the scene."

"You good, Emma? You sound out of breath, and you normally answer on the first call."

I swallowed hard, watching Sasha pull on her sweater, frowning as her bare skin disappeared under soft material. "I left my phone downstairs and was passed out, cold." I hung up quickly as Sasha walked over, my shirt dangling from her fingers. I took it from her and pulled it on. "That was Aaron. We have another body. Lincoln Park this time."

She gave me a tight smile, reality crashing around us. "Let's get to work then." She brushed past me to grab her bag, check her phone. "Shit." She showed me the five missed calls from Aaron.

I moved towards her, fighting the urge to touch her. "You don't need to call him back. I told him I'd pick you up."

"I think you already did." Sasha winked with a chuckle.

I blushed, and went to get dressed. I paused mid-step and turned back to Sasha. "We should talk after we clear the scene. There are a few things I need to tell you. Things I want to tell you."

Sasha leaned forward, softly kissing me as she ran a hand down my cheek. "You have my full attention."

I smiled and kissed her back before I ran upstairs. I wanted to be ready to let someone in. I wanted to let Sasha in.

Chapter 10

Sasha and I forced our way through the sea of uniformed officers and onlookers, surrounding the crime scene. It was as Aaron said, right under the train stop and in a very public place. The body was discovered by a group of late-night drunks going home. One had tripped over the body. Panic ensued, and now the uniforms were holding back the public from gawking and taking pictures.

Aaron waved us over to a handful of officers that held tarps to cover the scene. He tossed us a pair of gloves. "This one is messier than the other two, but I know it's our guy. Check out the message he left for us."

I crouched under the tarp to examine the body. It was a mess. There was blood everywhere. The body lay as it had fallen, twisted and broken. I bent for a closer look. It was a male. His face had been beaten beyond recognition and his wrists were slit, which would have ended the fight quickly. In the middle of the victim's chest sat a matchbook.

I motioned for Sasha to grab an evidence bag. I had a tech take a photo before I collected the matchbook. It was from the Black Kettle and had been purposely placed on the chest, postmortem. There wasn't a spot of blood on the entire thing.

I dropped it into the bag, looking at Aaron. "Any identification? Wallet?"

Aaron pointed at evidence bags next to the body. "The kid's wallet and ID were set cleanly next to him. The techs already bagged and tagged it." Aaron flipped open his notebook. "The victim is Stephen Amos, twenty-four and a political science student at Northwestern. He worked as an overnight security guard in the arena lots. Looks like he was on his way home from the Bears practice game. He has a receipt in his wallet from the Black Kettle, check out time was about an hour and a half ago. This body is fresh as fresh can get." Aaron flipped his notebook shut.

I reached out, placing a gloved hand on Stephen's leg. It was still warm. I took a deep breath. "Any carvings?" I already knew the answer.

Aaron went quiet. His face was white as the sheet covering Stephen's legs. "Under his shirt."

I lifted it up. *'Mistakes Happen'* was carved in English into his chest. I stopped, noticing a long gash along Stephen's side. I ran my hand over the same scar under my shirt. I didn't like where my mind was heading.

Aaron whispered. "There's one more thing. Follow me." The look in his eyes told me that I was to come alone.

I waved at Sasha. "Take a look around and tell me what you see."

She nodded, hunching over the body as I followed Aaron out of the tarps and to the crime scene tech van. Aaron signaled a tech over. "Ted, hand me the bag I told you to hide." The tech dug in a box full of evidence bags, handing Aaron a bag with a piece of bloody paper. "This caught my eye as soon as I saw the body. I made the techs process it immediately." He let out a steady breath. "I think this might mean something to you."

I took the bag, confused. "Me?" I used the interior light of the tech van to get a better look.

The item was a page torn from an old road map. The giant road atlas every grandparent had shoved in their glove box. It was crudely torn and matted with blood but it didn't take much to recognize the unique mitten shape of Michigan. A large black circle was drawn around the city of Detroit with small dashes drawn in a line leading straight to Chicago. Another black circle was drawn around the city, *'x marks the spot where I found you'* written above it.

My heart dropped straight to the pit of my stomach and my pulse quickened. Aaron leaned against the back of the van, constantly looking over his shoulder. "It's a huge guess on my part, but this doesn't feel like an accident. Not many people know where you were born, and half raised, Emma. Only your parents, Elle, and me. As far as the rest of the world knows, you were born in Chicago and raised by Eddie and Maggie Tiernan."

I covered my mouth with my hand, fighting waves of nausea. I shoved the bag into Aaron's chest. "No one can see this. No one." I looked back at Sasha pushing through the tarp. "Not even Sasha."

Sasha rounded the corner. "I couldn't find anything else on the body. I've asked the Assistant Medical Examiner to take clear photographs of the wrists and chest when they wash the body. I ran the victim for next of kin. Whenever you are ready, Lieutenant, I got a hit and have an address for the next of kin."

I didn't hear a damn word Sasha said. "Aaron can you… take this? I need to look into that federal file." My mind spun. I had to get back to the files spread all over my bedroom floor. My instincts were screaming that I'd find answers there.

"Sure thing, Lieutenant." He patted my shoulder, acknowledging he understood my vagueness.

I mumbled a thanks midstride. I didn't hear Sasha call after me until her hand was on my elbow, "Emma, are you okay?"

"I, um, Aaron will go with you to notify the family. I need to take care of something." I refused to look at her.

"Emma, something is wrong. You never bail on a scene like this."

I clenched my jaw. "Garnier, go with Aaron. That's an order." I was getting irritated. My anxiety — from the evidence and the desperate need to dig through the files — was overwhelming. I was struggling with the idea that I could've been the reason why people died. A killer keen on playing a game with me. Pushing buttons, digging in my past.

Sasha held onto my arm, dropping her voice. "Don't do this Emma. I know we're at work, but you're putting up walls." She stepped closer.

"After what just happened between us, you can trust me. You don't need to shove orders on me." I stared at her, my jaw tightening as my irritation grew. Sasha moved to stand in front of me, both of her hands now on my arms. "You're really worrying me."

I took a deep breath, but my defense mechanisms had already taken over. I didn't want anyone close to me if I was a target. I had to find answers before more bodies fell on my doorstep. I had to put distance between Sasha and me before she became the next target.

I sucked in a breath, hating myself for what I was about to do. "I said, go with Aaron now." I pulled my arms free. "Just because we had sex doesn't mean you're above my direct orders."

It was a blatant cold lie and a colder slap across Sasha's face. I saw the hurt wash over her as I turned and walked away.

I didn't look back, even when I heard a soft sob. I ignored it and kept on to my car. I drove away without a second glance.

* * *

I tore through my foster home records like a maniac. I dug until I found a record from the second to last home I was at before my father found me. It'd been the one place I lived the longest, and contained a police report attached to a hospital intake form.

I scanned the reports, my memories slowly coming back. I lived in this foster home for five years with a clean record, until I started having problems with another kid who lived there. A boy a year older than me.

Evan Carpenter.

Evan and I became close. He took advantage of my shyness and made me his lackey. I didn't remember much about him aside from being very controlling and odd.

I flipped pages, stopping on an entry written by my case worker. A caretaker had walked during a bed check and found Evan on top of me, cutting into my stomach with an Army knife. I was rushed to the hospital and Evan was taken into custody by the caretaker. The doctors examined me and stitched up, leaving me with a long scar on my stomach.

A psychologist's review of the incident determined I was being physically and mentally abused by Evan, but I said nothing to confirm their suspicions, too scared of Evan. I was diagnosed with Stockholm Syndrome and a mild form of PTSD long before it was commonplace. I bit my lip, wanting to cry over reading the cold facts about my life.

The next pages were about Evan and our criminal activity. The petty theft and vandalism. I was never charged, just remanded back to caretakers to be dealt with. Evan was ticketed a few times, but also shoved to the side. The last page of the police report was a rundown of a vandalism charge resulting in Evan's arrest and our separation for good. The responding officer took notice of the strange hold Evan had over me and asked me about it. I broke down and told the kind officer everything. Everything Evan did to me and how he scared me into silence with violence.

The police report stated that, as Evan was taken away, he told me to keep quiet and to remember how shiny it is. How it cuts. How it makes me bleed.

I dropped the file. The rest I remembered. I was placed in protective care until I was cleared and moved to the new foster home. Two weeks later I mugged my father and changed my life.

I held back the nausea and tears, struggling to understand it all. I grabbed the phone, digging in my bag for Rachel Fisher's card. Dialing her number with shaky hands.

"Hello?" Her voice was thick with sleep.

"Agent Fisher? This is Detective Lieutenant Emma Tiernan from Chicago. I know it's late, but you said if I had questions to call."

I heard a rustle and a small yawn. "Of course, how can I help you, Emma?"

"I need to ask a huge favor, Agent Fisher. Can you please get me information on the Evan Carpenter housed with me in the foster home on the eastside of Detroit? St. Mary Francis House of Hope?"

"I can check. When I opened your sealed files, it gave me access to everything. Is there anything in particular you're looking for?"

"I need to know what happened to him after his arrest. I was placed in protective custody, and I don't remember anything from those years. I have a sinking feeling he may be a suspect in an ongoing case." I chewed on a thumbnail, anxious to get my hands on anything.

"I should have something in a few hours." I heard the tip tap of a keyboard in the background.

I let out a slow breath. "It's okay, I know I woke you up, please take your time."

"Emma, it's fine. I'm a workaholic insomniac."

I smiled in my empty room. "Thank you, Agent Fisher. I owe you."

She chuckled. "Please call me Rachel. As I said in your office, it's a favor to your father. One of many I have left to repay."

I noted the tone in her voice again and wondered how she came to owe my father so much, frowning when Aaron's stupid theory popped in my head. My father would never step outside of his marriage, at very least for the simple fact my mother would kill him and ask me to help hide the body.

After giving Rachel my private email address, I sat against the edge of my bed and picked up the phone again. In a quick call to my father, I asked him to be extra vigilant, only explaining I had a case hit too close to home. I didn't dare tell him I might be a target for a serial killer. He balked, asking for more before giving up. Knowing I wouldn't tell him anything more that could jeopardize a case. He just asked me to be careful and not to tell my mother.

The moment I hung up, I knew he'd call Liam and have the entire department on my doorstep, but I begged him to let me handle it. It would be better if he kept my mother safe and away from the city. He sighed, promising to drive them up north to their cabin for a week-long vacation.

I held my head in my hands as I began to cry. The last thing I ever wanted was for anyone to be a target to gain my attention. I'd have to shut down to protect the ones I loved, including Sasha.

I couldn't lose her.

Crawling across the bed to my bedside table, I removed the extra handgun from the drawer and set it next to me on my pillow. I fell asleep staring at it, fearful of what the day would bring.

* * *

Later in the morning, I woke to find an email from Rachel providing me with everything I'd asked for and more. Evan's files were extensive and detailed. He spent most of his adolescent years in and out of juvenile detention for assault and battery with a dangerous weapon, most of the time, a large knife. At eighteen, he was remanded to a state mental institution where a psychologist evaluated him to have sociopathic tendencies with an intense lack of empathy. He showed four of the five main characteristics of a murderer. But nothing was done. He'd had no treatment, just observation from clinical staff.

Evan had been released at twenty-five, establishing a police record for himself in a matter of days. More assaults and robberies, eventually branching out into arson. He had dropped off the face of the earth in the last two years after he'd failed to appear for a court date for stabbing a woman leaving a bar in Detroit. Rachel included a note with her email. She had reinstated the Detroit Police's BOLO that had been put out on Evan after he skipped his court date, hoping she could pick up his trail.

I devoured the file and threw on some clothes. I had to get to the station, to show Aaron what Rachel found. Aaron met me the second I stepped out of the elevator, and followed me to my office. I closed and locked my door behind him. "Anything from the family?"

"Yeah, one big clue that makes the chest carving clear. Stephen wasn't gay or adopted. He worked part time at the Black Kettle, bar backing.

The kid was in the wrong place at the wrong time. You know, mistakes happen." Aaron wasn't smiling. He never smiled when he was worried. "What did you find in your files?"

I removed the large printout from my bag. "This is for your eyes only until further notice."

Aaron nodded as he took it. He read through my unedited childhood and reports on Evan, cringing a few times when he read about my abuse.

I paced the length of my desk, gnawing on a raw thumb. "I think our guy is a kid from my past. Some sadistic little bastard who cut me and abused me when we lived in Detroit." I paused, beginning to shake again. "I don't know what happened to him after we were arrested on a vandalism charge. I barely remember anything during that time. I blocked shit out when I moved to Chicago. Special Agent Fisher found Evan Carpenter's files and sent them last night. He sounds like our guy and is the only person I could connect to the map left at the scene. He would know I left Detroit for Chicago." I swallowed a thick lump in my throat. "He had complete control over me when we were kids."

I leaned forward on my desk, gripping the edge to settle the tremors. "That's all I have. The rest of it, I have no idea. This is the only concrete lead I've got. I think he's trying to get my attention. Sending a message. The victims have been gay or adopted. All graduated or spent time as students at Northwestern, my alma mater."

Aaron tossed the printout onto the desk. "Fuck, Emma. It's too much of a coincidence not to ignore. This kid seems like a real piece of work. But why now? After all these years, why come after you?"

"I took away his control and because of me he was placed under the scrutiny of psychologists. Because of me, he went to jail and the mental institution, they took away his freedom to carry on as he saw fit. I think he wants revenge." I let go of the desk, clenching my fists. "I can't say for certain until we find him. I'll meet with the Captain in the morning and fill him in. I might even ask to have Agent Fisher brought in to officially assist with the case."

Aaron stood, adjusting the gun on his hip. "What do you need me to do?"

"Keep quiet until Agent Fisher picks up Evan's trail. Meanwhile, we go to the bar tonight with the UC. I'm nervous another body will show up sooner than we want. He made a mistake and he'll want to fix it by finding a proper victim that fits his agenda, that relays the correct message."

"You want to bring Sasha in on this?"

Before I could give him an answer my desk phone rang. "Lieutenant Tiernan."

"Jesus H. Christ Tiernan, you did it again. I hope you're happy." Captain Jameson hollered in my ear.

"Excuse me sir?" I met Aaron's questioning stare.

"Your new partner's transfer request is sitting on my desk. Detective Garnier submitted her paperwork first thing this morning. She's requested a new division and district on the opposite side of the city." He huffed. "What the hell did you do?"

I swallowed hard, chewing on my bottom lip. "Garnier? Garnier is transferring out of my... our unit?" Aaron eyes widened, giving me a *what the fuck* look.

"Sure, as shit did, and I have to honor it. There's nothing I can do but bitch and tell you this is the last time. She was a good detective. We needed her here." Jameson was three seconds from losing his shit. I could hear him taking deep breaths to try to keep it professional.

I squeezed my eyes shut. "Where did she transfer to?"

"The 6th district, Southside. They took her with open arms. They've been overwhelmed with cases and need the extra detective." Jameson groaned. "So did we, Emma, so did we."

As soon as the phone hit the cradle, Aaron pounced. "What the hell was that all about? Did I hear Jameson say Sasha transferred?"

I bit the inside of my lip to stay calm. "Yes. She filed the paperwork first thing. Jameson chewed out my ass, since this is my fault." I blinked a few times, fighting a wave of tears. "This is all my fault."

"I thought you two finally figured your shit out. What happened last night? She seemed extra quiet during the family interview. She almost cried a few times in the car, but I played it off as her dealing with her first death notification." Then it hit him. The lightbulb flickered, and he squinted at me. "Wait. You two. Did you?"

I fell into my chair, swiveling it towards the window. The sailboats waved hello with their giant white sails. "Yes, we did. Right before you called. She came over to confront me then laid out her feelings. I tried to tell her how I felt about her. One thing led to another, and things happened."

I drifted off at the memory of what happened between us on my kitchen island, knowing it was more than just sex. I was falling in love with her and wanted to tell her, but then the new clues came into play. The risk and fear of Sasha becoming a target overwhelmed any feelings I had for her.

"Holy shit, Emma! You slept with your rookie? Is that why she bolted?" He threw his hands up in the air. "And you get on my ass about Jonesy." He ran his hands through his hair, shaking his head like a disappointed parent.

"Aaron, it's not that simple. I said things to push her away when she chased me down last night. I have to push her away. If my hunch is right and this is who I think it is, she needs to be far away from me, or he'll come after her next." I rubbed my temples to ease the raging headache. I had to call Sasha. I had to tell her why I did what I did. I had to protect her.

Aaron fell silent, his eyes boring into my head. "You love her, don't you?"

I grimaced, a tear escaping faster than I could wipe it away. "I think I'm falling for her. Hard." I covered my face with both hands. "I have to protect her, Aaron." The mantra repeated in my head over and over.

A soft knock on the door was followed by Bobby's voice. The officer I pulled in to be our undercover at the Black Kettle. "Hey Lieutenant, let me know when you're ready to start the briefing."

I collected the printout, jamming it into my bag before locking it up in a bottom desk drawer. I wiped my face, trying to collect myself. "Aaron, can you start the briefing? I need to make a call."

Without question, he opened the door and directed Bobby to a side interview room.

I dialed Sasha's number, closing my eyes as it rang, no clue what to say if she answered.

After three rings, she answered. "Hello." Her tone gave me the shivers.

"Sasha, it's Emma."

"Let me guess. Captain Jameson told you I'm transferring." She fired off the words like a shotgun blast. She was pissed, and not handling me with kid gloves.

"He did." I cleared my throat. "He told me you submitted your request first thing this morning." I was secretly glad she was leaving, but it still hurt more than I wanted to admit.

"Emma, I'm not playing games with you. Your words hurt last night. I get you're still in mourning and scared, but I don't deserve it. What we did was more than just sex, but if that's how you want to look at it, fine. You win. I can't come into work every day, sit across from you, work side by side with you and maybe wait for the one day you realize I was falling in…" She paused. "Never mind, Emma. This isn't worth it. Good luck with your new partner. They'll need it."

Sasha hung up before I could utter another word. My heart hurt, and a slow wave of regret washed over me. I was very much in love with Sasha but realized it too late. She was gone, moved on, and had done exactly what I had pushed her to do.

Leave me alone.

Chapter 11

I dove into work over the next week. Bobby immersed himself at the Black Kettle as a new regular, making friends and establishing himself as a willing target. He reported back every morning with minor observations but had yet to single out anyone suspicious. Rachel was coming up empty on Evan's whereabouts.

My days were filled with briefings, pounding the pavement and sitting with Aaron as we picked apart evidence for the hundredth time. The case was growing cold. In another week, I'd have to shut down the surveillance. Bobby was needed for an ongoing mafia investigation on the Gold Coast. Behind closed doors, I was secretly hoping the killer had grown bored and moved on, or Evan had been picked up somewhere and locked away on one of his many outstanding warrants, which would give me a chance to interview him and maybe tie him to the killings.

I never heard from Sasha.

Aaron did. She called him to ask questions and indulge in casual chit chat. I wanted to ask about her but didn't want to put him in the middle of my mess.

I missed her but vowed to keep the distance between us until I knew it was safe to chase her down, spill my heart out, and pray she would forgive me.

Everything fell into place the last Saturday night we had Bobby in the bar. I'd stayed late in the office, reviewing other backlogged cases, when Aaron burst into my office. "Get your shit. Bobby has something." He tapped the small radio in his hands. "He called dispatch five minutes ago, dropped the code phrase."

I grabbed my gun, leaving my vest on top of a file cabinet, and rushed after Aaron. "Fill me in."

"The unit keeping watch on Bobby as backup got a text from him. Some guy's been walking around the bar all night looking for a date. Kept asking a few guys if they studied Latin and if they knew what *ego te prevoco* meant. Bobby managed to snag the suspect's attention and keep him interested. The secondary unit is following them and currently has them on foot near the Corn Cob towers."

"Aaron, grab a couple more uniforms and head in from the east. Tell the secondary unit to hang back and keep eyes on Bobby. I'll meet up with them and we'll go from there. This might not be our guy, but let's not waste the opportunity." Adrenaline surged through my veins as we rode the elevator down. The towers were about ten minutes away, less at this hour with no traffic.

Aaron ran to the first floor to snag patrol officers as I raced to my car. On the way, the secondary unit called me, letting me know Bobby and the suspect were heading towards the underground parking garage at the towers. I gave them quick instruction to stay back and wait for Aaron's signal. I parked inside the garage, choosing an angle where I could see all entrances without being noticed.

Ten more minutes passed before Bobby appeared in the rearview mirror, followed closely by another male. I couldn't make out the man's face. His Cubs hat was pulled low over his eyes. I cracked my window, listening as they moved closer.

"Wow, I've never been to the towers! It's so exciting you live here! I bet the view is incredible!" I smiled to myself. Bobby was doing a great job playing it cool.

The suspect replied in a calm tone. "It's only going to get more exciting for you. I promise."

As they passed, I pretended to be on my phone, and waited until they were out of sight before I messaged Aaron we should take the guy while he was still with Bobby.

Bobby's screams snaked in through the cracked window. I flew out of the car, gun drawn, and ran towards his voice, calling for backup to make my location. As I rounded the corner, I found Bobby on the ground. The suspect straddled the squirming undercover officer while throwing hard punches at his face.

I pointed the gun at the suspect's chest. "Stop! Police! Show me your hands!"

The suspect didn't flinch. He hit Bobby once more, knocking him out. My hands shook; I needed backup before I moved. Deadly force wasn't an option.

As blood dripped off his knuckles, the suspect licked his lips. "I thought you would've stopped us as soon as we left the bar, but you didn't. It took you longer than I planned." He patted Bobby's cheek, sat back on his heels, and reached for a knife that lay on the ground next to him. He curled bloodied fingers around it as he stood up. "Nonetheless, I'm glad you made it."

"Drop the knife and back away from him!" I screamed, my finger moving to the trigger. Adrenaline raced through my veins, sending my heart into overdrive. I was so amped, I could've lifted a car off a baby.

The suspect looked at me from under the brim of his hat, raising his hands up slowly, purposefully. His mouth stretched into a sadistic grin. "I'll move away, but I will not set the knife down." He stepped over Bobby's unconscious body.

"If you don't put the knife down, I'll shoot!" I gripped the gun tighter.

"No, no, you won't shoot. You don't have it in you, Emma."

My name, from his lips, struck like a hard right across the face from Tyson, shocking me. I blew out a steadying breath as the suspect removed his hat, dramatically tossing it to the ground.

He grinned, smoothing his hair down, dead blue eyes locking on mine. "You won't shoot me. I did all of this for you!" He flicked his wrist. "I wanted you to come to me. Stephen was a mistake, but he did what I wanted. He gained your attention and forced you to look deeper into your past." I squinted, familiarity poking at my mind. I knew this man from somewhere, but couldn't place it as adrenaline continued to collide with fear.

A hearty sigh left his lungs as he shook his head. "I feel bad about him, the first one. He was a lovely boy. Offered to walk me home since I was too drunk to walk on my own power. He fought back until I cut him." Another sigh. "I was nervous you'd lose interest when you figured out Stephen wasn't gay or adopted. Then I made that little art collage for you. Did you like it, Emma? I thought it was very creative of me."

He looked at the overhead lights. "That's why I chose the gay and unwanted ones. David and Alice. They reminded me of you, and I needed that. I needed you to become personally invested and not pass my work on to others." He dropped his chin, and his grin shifted into an easy smile as he pointed at me with the knife. "I always had a feeling you were different from the rest of us."

I listened to his intricate details and sickening logic. I didn't respond. I wasn't about to feed his ego, but his words didn't make sense.

I kept my gun trained on his chest and wondered where the hell Aaron and my backup were. "Put the knife down and you won't get hurt!"

He rolled his eyes. "Nothing Emma? Really? That's not the reaction I hoped for. I've done all of this for you!!" He paused, glancing at Bobby and covered his mouth and gasped. "Wait, are you worried about your friend here?" He nudged Bobby with the toe of his boot. Bobby moved like a limp rag doll, sending shivers of fear down my spine. "Don't be, he'll be fine. I have no intention of killing him. I knew he was a cop from the moment I walked into the bar. I smelled you all over him. I knew he'd bring you to me." He spread his arms out as if I would walk right into them and thank him for his gifts.

My hands began to shake. "Why? Why did you choose me?"

"Emma, oh sweet ignorant Emma! You're the start of it all. Time has made your memories very dusty. I've been looking for you for years! I need to finish what I started so long ago." He shook his head, laughing.

I stared at him, confusion mixed with fear. I fought to think straight. I was wasting time. I had to pull the trigger sooner than later to end his pompous tirade. But I was stuck, stuck with fear.

He saw the confusion all over my face. "Aw, have you forgotten me? Let me help jumpstart your memories." He took a step closer, clasping his hands in front. "The scar on your side? My gift to you." He bowed slightly. "My name is Evan. Evan Carpenter. We're old childhood friends, Emma." When he looked right at me, the memories rushed back. Sleepless nights of him taunting me with his knife, whispering in my ear how useless I was. Screaming in my face I was nothing more than a toy for him to jab his knives in. I was staring at the face of the demon who ruled my childhood.

Everything around me began to move in slow motion. The memories surged forth and I clearly remembered the day I was arrested with Evan.

The vague lines of a police report turned into vivid memories, long lost memories I had shoved into tiny boxes the second I came home to Chicago. I remembered how hard I begged the officer to take me away from him, tears streaming down a dirty face. I remembered the night Evan sat on top of me while I slept, covering my mouth as he dug the knife into my skin. Whispering that God hated me and was punishing me for my sins, murmuring incoherently in broken Latin.

The Evan standing in front of me looked nothing like the baby-faced teenager who had tormented me. I would've never recognized if he stood in front of me in broad daylight, like he had outside my home weeks ago. Asking for directions to Millennium Park, or hanging a polaroid on the wall of heroes at O'Malley's.

Evan spoke again. "You were incredibly hard to find. I had no idea you were taken out of Detroit by that nice police officer — Ed? Yes,

Edward Tiernan — until last year." He huffed, shaking his head. "So, I packed my bags for the Windy City. I thought it would take some time to track you down, but a brilliant detective like you isn't hard to find. I went this route since knocking on your door wouldn't properly grab your attention. And here I am!" Evan stepped around Bobby, moving closer. "Shall we pick up where we left off? I do owe you. I ended up in a hospital for disturbed children, and let me tell you, those shock treatments everyone raves about do very little. They *do* make a man very determined to seek revenge." He tilted the knife, the blade glinting as the light caught its edge. "Do you remember how shiny it is?"

I finally found my voice, stumbling over the sobs trapped in my throat as I spoke. "Fuck you, fuck you for everything! You're going to rot in hell for what you did!" I was scared shitless. My fear muddled with adrenaline as my trigger finger trembled. I wanted to shoot, but couldn't. My whole body shook as I prayed for Aaron to arrive with backup.

Evan frowned, anger flickering across his eyes. "You shouldn't talk to old friends like that, Emma. I have to finish what I started."

We were at a standoff. I knew any minute Aaron would come flying around the corner. I just had to hold out for a few more seconds, keep Evan calm and away from me. A noise off to the right startled me, and I made the mistake of turning to look.

It gave Evan the second he needed, and he made his move. He bolted forward, spearing me in the chest and taking us both to the ground. I landed hard on the concrete but managed to hold onto the gun. Evan grabbed my right hand, pinning it and the gun to the ground. He hit me with a hard right across the face, the hilt of the knife curled in his hand like a roll of quarters. The punch would've knocked me out if I wasn't flooded with adrenaline.

I came back with a left hook, just as hard, to his jaw. It did nothing but make him angry. I tried wiggling my gun hand free, but his grip was too strong.

Evan raised his fist to strike again and I thrust a knee up between his legs. He fell back onto my legs, clutching his groin, groaning.

It knocked the wind out of him for a second and he released my right hand. I swung the gun up to empty the magazine into his chest, but as I squeezed the trigger, a flash of silver blinded me, then a burning sensation lit up my right forearm. I dropped the gun and grabbed my wrist as the blood poured out. Evan had sliced deep, cutting through muscle and vein. My hand was numb and useless, the rush of blood making things slippery as hell.

I tried to ignore the intense pain in my arm as Evan rolled off me, giving me a chance to scramble to my feet, to go for my gun. I still had my left hand. I could still shoot him.

Evan suddenly landed on my back, with a punch to the kidneys that drove me back to the ground. I smacked into the floor as the fingers of my left hand brushed the bottom of the gun. I could still — Evan slammed the hilt of his knife down onto the back of my left hand, and the loud crack of impact echoed in the air. The incredible pain distracted me from my mission.

Evan pinned me to the ground, slamming my forehead into the concrete. Blood filled my mouth and I began to choke on it as I struggled to breathe. He straddled my lower back, laughing with pure excitement. His weight shoved out what little air I had left in my lungs.

The fight began to feel hopeless, but I wasn't giving up. I couldn't give up. I'd made it this far, survived this long.

I wheezed, my body now overwhelmed with pain and blood loss.

I watched as he slowly reached over to pick up my gun. He bent down to whisper in my ear. "I'll finish this. You have a few minutes before you bleed out. Just do me one favor, Emma, and lay still."

I tried to wiggle free, but kept slipping in the blood pooling underneath me. The edges of my vision darkened, and I struggled to keep my eyes open.

Evan pulled up my shirt. The cool night air scraped along my skin, the cold tip of the knife dug into my back. Pulling a weak whimper from me.

I gasped for air, yelling at myself to fight him, to not let him do this again.

I couldn't think straight. I couldn't focus. There was no way out and I was about to give up when Evan paused. "Wait, I want you to look at me when I do this. For old times' sake." He roughly rolled me onto my back. The world was fading to black, and I welcomed it.

The knife fell to my skin again. I hardly felt it slice into my stomach. My body was shutting down, about to let it all go.

A tiny voice in my head begged me to fight.

Fight him.

I rolled my head and saw my bloody wrist. It was my last chance. I sucked in a rattling breath, and with what little strength I had left, swung my arm at Evan's face. Hitting him on the forehead, I dragged my wrist down, smearing blood in his eyes.

"You bitch!" Evan shrieked, desperately pawing at the blood in his eyes.

I tried to grab his knife with my swollen left hand, fat fingers fumbling over the hilt like rubbery worms. Evan caught my arm, twisting it. "Smart girl. You're different now, Emma, stronger and smarter. But it's too late." He bent close to my ear, his breath against it. "You're always too late."

I met his eyes and blinked, my vision blurring. The last few moves had taken everything I had left. I lay in my own blood, gasping for air. Dying.

I regretted not calling Sasha and telling her what she meant to me. Admitting I was in love with her and too chickenshit to say it to her face. Now I was going to die alone like I always imagined I would.

I tried to come to terms with everything I'd done in my life as I lay on the garage floor, bleeding out, slipping away with every shallow breath I took. If Sister Jude could see me now.

"Drop the gun and the knife before I blow you away, motherfucker!" Aaron's booming voice burst into the garage, tugging me from the edge of darkness. I rolled my head to Aaron. His gun pointed at Evan as he ran towards us.

Evan didn't move. He shook his head with a dramatic sigh. "I can't do that, Detective Liang."

"Drop the Goddamn weapons!"

I rolled back, to stare dead in Evan's eyes. He smiled and winked. "I'm sorry I have to end this in such a brutish way. You deserve a classier death, but alas, your partner dictates otherwise." He bent down, kissing my forehead. "Apologies, Emma, but it *was* good to see you again."

I managed to croak out. "Fuck you."

I grabbed at his arm with slippery, bloody fingers, groaning out Aaron's name.

Evan laughed as the world blurred. Aaron was distracted by his name weakly falling into the air. He didn't react fast enough as Evan threw the knife. Aaron fell to one knee, the knife lodged into his thigh.

Aaron's screams were overshadowed by a single gunshot thundering through the air. Something hot slammed into my chest and everything went black but the sound. I heard more gunshots, footsteps running away, then Aaron screaming for help.

* * *

It might have been an out-of-body experience, but I'll never be sure. I opened my eyes to see my battered body, Aaron hobbling over, stripping his shirt off, wrapping my wrist, before trying to plug my chest wound with his bare hands.

He was screaming into his cell phone that an officer was down, and he needed an ambulance.

I was covered in blood, lying in a growing dark red lake of it. My face was swollen and red, eyes were sealed shut and my chest was motionless. I wasn't breathing.

I heard Aaron talking nonstop, but it sounded like I was under water. Everything was muted and distant.

"Jesus, Emma. Don't let go. The paramedics will be here shortly, stay with me. Fucking stay with me. Oh, oh God don't let go, Emma. Please, stay here." His voice was tangled in broken sobs.

Then there was nothing but darkness and silence.

Chapter 12

I woke up in a white room. For a moment, I thought I was in heaven, until a stout nurse appeared out of thin air. She stood next to the bed holding a clipboard. I rolled my head to look at her, groaning. She flinched when she saw I was awake. "Oh! I'll get the doctor."

I blinked a few times. Well, my left eye blinked. The other refused to do anything I asked of it. I stared at the off-white ceiling tiles until a face, belonging to a thin doctor, hovered over my bed. He flashed a light in my eyes.

I wanted to yell at him, but couldn't. Someone had shoved a tube down my throat, making it impossible to do anything other than breathe. I tried to lift an arm when the doctor mumbled my name, but hot pain shot through my body and I passed out.

When I woke up again, the tube was gone. I was still lying in a white room. I managed to roll my head to one side, and saw an obnoxious amount of flower bouquets mixed in with a few terrible shiny metal balloons with happy animals and well wishes on them.

The pain was still there, but it was muted. A series of IV bags hung over my head, tiny tubes twisting and turning until they met in the crook of my elbow.

These had to be some heavy drugs. I couldn't feel a damn thing, and could swear I was floating off the bed and up into the sterile white ceiling.

Blinking a few times, I noticed my right eye was out of commission. I moved my gaze back to the ceiling, desperate to remember anything about how I got here.

It didn't take much to figure out I was in the hospital, but the rest was a blur. I was tired, beyond tired. I was exhausted, or dead. I heard the television from across the room and someone coughing underneath it. The sounds ticked back into my ears one at a time, almost overwhelming my senses. I squinted my one good eye, scanning the room.

Aaron sat, hunched over in an uncomfortable ball, the hard plastic hospital chair biting him with every move he made.

I swallowed down a dry throat and spoke. "Sleeping on the job?" My voice came out a harsh, rough whisper, and hurt. Aaron squinted at the television as if my whisper had come from it. He ran a hand through his hair, yawning, and then shifted his glance my way, almost jumping out of his chair when he saw I was staring at him. "Holy shit, Emma! You're awake!"

I nodded once and winced. It hurt too much to look in his direction. Aaron sat down on the edge of the bed, his eyes watery as he smiled.

"How long was my nap?" My voice sounded like I had eaten glass, then swallowed a hive of bees.

Aaron looked down, tugging on my blanket. "This is the first time you've been awake for more than a handful of minutes in a week and a half." He grabbed my hand. His smile was tight and forced.

"What happened?" I didn't remember anything other than that strange nurse hovering over me the last time I woke up.

"Later. We'll talk about that later." He clutched my hand. "You're awake now, that's all that matters."

I tried to lift my right arm again, but it was stiff and wrapped in gauze, the pain muted from the bag of heaven attached to my arm, killing any ounce of feeling in my body. A nurse walked in, and grinned as she approached the side of the bed. "Ms. Tiernan, it's nice to see you awake! How are you feeling?"

"I feel like a mummy." I motioned to my arm, wincing as a slow burning sensation lit up my limbs. I glared at the IV bag above me, silently cursing it a traitor.

"It's understandable. I need to check your vitals and then I'll get the doctor." The nurse looked at Aaron. "I hate to kick you out, but visiting hours are almost over. You know the drill."

Aaron chuckled. "Not a problem, Ally." He leaned forward, and kissed my temple. "I'll be back tomorrow." He swallowed a few times, struggling to hold back his emotions. Aaron never held back from me, that's why I loved him so much. But him holding back told me something wasn't right, something had gone terribly wrong. "It's so Goddamned good to see you awake." He scooted off the edge of the bed and grabbed his jacket, smiling one more time before limping out of the room. I swallowed hard at the sight of his awkward gait. He was hurt and hiding it. Aaron, who would cry if he got a papercut and begged me for a band-aid. I took a deep breath, my heart racing and smashing against burning ribs. I looked at the nurse, opened my mouth to ask for her to pour more drugs into my IV.

The nurse took over, untangling IV lines and adjusting blankets. "He's a nice guy. He's visited you every day since you were admitted. He even sat with your parents while you were in surgery." She helped me to sit up.

I felt woozy from the pain edging its way back in, but was able to get a better view of the room and my current state.

My right arm was wrapped from fingertips to elbow, my left was swollen, but I could still feel my fingers. Bruises covered my arms in a morbid rainbow of purple, black, and yellow. When the nurse pulled down the blanket and lifted my gown, I winced at the large dressing covering my chest.

A young man wearing a baggy white doctor's coat walked in. The kid barely looked old enough to drive, let alone be a doctor. He leaned on the edge of the bed. "Ms. Tiernan, welcome back. I'm Dr. Bettis. How are you feeling?" He gave me a condescending grin, the one all surgeons gave patients after saving their lives.

"Weird, I feel weird." My mouth was full of cotton, making it tough to speak. I glanced at the nurse. "Can I get some water?"

"Ally, can you grab her some ice chips? See how those go down and we'll try a cup of water." Dr. Bettis nodded at the nurse and moved to my right side. He spoke as he pulled on gloves. "That's to be expected, considering the pain medications you're on. Hopefully they're keeping you comfortable." He peeled back the bandage on my chest in a way that I couldn't see what was underneath.

The nurse distracted me with idle chit chat as Dr. Bettis replaced the bandage. He rechecked my vitals, flashed a light in my good eye and scrutinized the rest of my injuries before peeling off his gloves. He nodded with approval as he scribbled in my chart. "You're healing nicely, Emma. In a few more days, we can seriously consider releasing you." He handed the chart to the nurse, slipping his hands into his pockets. "How do you feel about maybe getting up and moving around this week?"

I took a deep breath. This doctor was just like me, enthusiastic to get back on the horse. "I can try." But I still had the urge to tell him to fuck off.

Dr. Bettis smiled. "That's all I can ask for." He patted my foot, but I scarcely felt it. "I'll be back later if you have any questions. I'm glad to have you back with us." He disappeared in a blur of white.

The nurse covered me, added a few more pillows, then left to get me a sippy cup of water.

I waited for a count of three, then let my curiosity get the better of me. I pushed down the blankets, wincing at the pain, and lifted my gown. I wanted to see what was under the bandage and picked at the edge until I caught a corner and peeled it back.

There was a neat half-dollar-sized hole under my sternum. It wasn't closed with stitches or staples, just packed with gauze. I stared at it, trying to remember something, anything, but nothing came. I covered the wound, reaching for the blankets when I heard the nurse's squeaky shoes coming around the corner. I was exhausted, sore, from the minimal movements, barely able to reach for the water next to me.

I fell asleep five minutes later with my sippy cup in hand, staring at plastic women on the television.

* * *

I woke up in a panic. The room was dark and the hallway outside the open door was dimly lit. It took a second to get my bearings and remember I was still in the hospital.

The pain was less, and I wanted to look at the damage again. I'd seen the way the nurse flinched when she changed my gown and checked the bandages.

Scooting to the edge of the bed, I pulled Aaron's chair close and used it as a walker, dragging all of my tubes and wires along as I shuffled to the bathroom.

It took what felt like three days to move my stiff limbs all the way to the bathroom. I closed the door and steadied myself on the steel handrail and took a deep breath before looking in the mirror.

I gasped at my reflection.

My face and neck were covered in bruises. Blacks, blues, and purples were painted across my cheeks and eyes. My right eye was swollen shut like a prize fighter had used it as practice, and my bottom lip and cheeks were riddled with cuts. Tugging the front of my gown open, I saw the bruising continued down my body. Specifically, on my hips and across my chest and arms. The bandage under my sternum was chased by a smaller one on my stomach and laid next to my old scar. I tried to lift my bandaged arm up, but the pain was enormous, and forced me to lean forward, clutching the edge of the sink with my left hand. My right throbbed with pain.

I started to sob and before I knew it, I'd thrown up in the sink. Suddenly very lightheaded and dizzy, I let go of the edge of the sink and began to fall, preparing myself for a hard hit on the tile floor.

I never hit the floor. Strong arms stopped the fall, holding me against a warm body. The arms circled around me, cautiously avoiding my sore spots. A hand reached to fix the gown, protecting my modesty. My vision blurred as I looked around to look at my savior, the arms dragging me gently back to the edge of the bed.

"Jesus, Emma. Why are you trying to run before you can walk?" It took me a moment to place the voice behind the tender whisper.

"Sasha?" Tears welled up as I looked at her.

"Why were you out of bed?" Her voice shook as she reached for blankets.

I lay flat on my back, watching her as she fidgeted with my IV lines and wires, untangling them. She was wearing an old ratty Cubs t-shirt under her black leather jacket and was quite possibly the most beautiful thing I'd seen in weeks. I whispered. "I wanted to know how bad it was."

Sasha lifted her head and our eyes met, a flood of emotions flickering across hers. She sat on the edge of the bed, looking towards the bathroom door.

"Don't worry about it. Your doctor said you should make a complete recovery." She bit her bottom lip, still staring at the bathroom door. "It's a miracle you woke up." Her words came out in a whisper and I barely caught it. Sasha sighed, turning to me with a half-smile. "I guess it was a good thing I decided to sneak in here and check on you." She reached for my left hand, linking her fingers in mine as silence fell between us.

I flat out stared at her as if it was the first time, I'd ever seen her. The last time we spoke, it was to fight about her transferring away from me. I squeezed her hand. "Sasha, I'm sorry..."

She shook her head. "It's okay Emma. I know why you did it." Tears were on the cusp of spilling down her face. "We don't need to talk about it now. You should get some rest." She went to pull her hand from mine. With the little strength I had, I held on to her, refusing to let go.

A nurse leaned into the room. "Hey Sasha, everything cool here? I heard something fall while changing Mrs. Joaquin's saline bag."

Sasha glanced over her shoulder at the nurse. "Yeah, we're good, Wendy."

"Sweet. Same deal again tonight? You want me to wake you up an hour before Aaron gets here?"

Sasha's face turned bright pink. "I might leave soon. I'll let you know." She untangled her hand from mine, tucking it in her pocket.

The nurse tapped on the doorframe, smiled at both of us and disappeared.

"You should go back to sleep." Sasha's smile faded. "Try not to go anywhere without help. I'll let Wendy know you're determined to move on your own."

She moved to leave, but I caught the edge of her jacket with my fingers, pulling as best as I could. The drugs in my system made everything weak and fuzzy. "Sasha, will you stay with me?" My heart raced in my numb chest.

Tears rolled down my face. I honestly never expected to see her again after she transferred. And, with how Aaron looked at me, I knew I almost didn't survive whatever had happened. Sasha squeezed her eyes shut, bit her lip, debating if she should. She sighed, opening her eyes and frowned. "Let me get a chair."

"I meant in the bed. I need a hug." I gave her a weak smile. My feeble joke was an attempt to hide how much I wanted her close, feel her, and maybe the bruises would disappear, the pain. It was the only thing I wanted more than to pee without a nurse holding me up on the toilet.

Sasha grinned, cocking an eyebrow. "The Ice Queen wants a hug? That's a first I thought I'd never see." She walked to the other side of the bed. I heard her shoes hit the floor as she swung her legs up, trying to position herself close to me without sitting on me or the IV lines strung everywhere. I was drawn to her warmth, inching closer for more. My trip to the bathroom had expended all my precious energy, all my body heat.

Sasha let out a soft sigh, her tell that she was very nervous. She stared straight at the TV, her hair covering most of her face like a curtain. I tried to hold her hand with mine, but the gauze made it difficult to do anything other than grab the tips of her fingers. "Relax, you won't break me. I can't feel anything on these drugs." My voice was smoothing out from the harsh rasp, but it was still a struggle to speak. She smiled, and tucked her hair behind an ear. She appeared visibly conflicted about being in the bed next to me.

I dropped my head. "I don't remember anything. I don't know what happened to me, why it happened. My memories are fuzzy, and the last one is of the horrible things I said to you." I squeezed her hand tighter. "I wish…"

Sasha let out a hard sigh. "Emma, stop. You don't need to explain. I was mad at you, livid and heartbroken at the shitty things you said. I transferred to be the furthest away from you. I wanted to forget you and move on. I had to leave you in your self-imposed prison of misery." She turned to look at me, her eyes soft and glassy. "I was working on an assault and battery when the call came over the radio. I recognized Aaron's voice, heard the panic and knew it was you. I arrived at the hospital just as they rushed you into surgery. The on-scene officers confirmed it was you. They then told me who was involved and how it happened."

Sasha paused before she spoke again. "When I saw Aaron with your family, I felt I didn't belong in that moment because of your last words, you pushing me away." She sniffled, wiping her face with the back of her hand. "I couldn't avoid you for long. I've been sneaking in every night after hours to sit with you. Wendy, the night nurse, is an old high school friend of mine. She wakes me up an hour before Aaron comes in for his morning visit. I sneak in and out before anyone sees me."

Sasha smiled, wiping tears from my cheeks with her thumb, being gentle not to press too hard. "As much as I try, I can't shake you, Emma Tiernan."

I licked dry lips. "What happened to me?"

Her smile faded. "Later. We'll talk about that later. You need to rest." Sasha lifted my hand to her lips, kissing the knuckles. She then moved to snuggle up against my side, laying an arm gently across my stomach, avoiding stitches and sore spots. "Here's your hug. Now will you go to sleep?"

I nodded, warmed by her vast body heat. Sleep came quickly, as Sasha held her hand against my cheek, stroking the one area where I wasn't bruised.

Chapter 13

I woke, briefly, to an empty bed, but felt more rested and clearer than I had the day before. Sasha's perfume lingered on my pillow and I drifted back into an easy sleep.

Ally, the day nurse, woke me up in the afternoon. Informing me I'd missed Aaron and a few other visitors.

I was somewhat thankful I'd missed them. I wasn't ready to play pretend with people, to lie about how great I felt. I mentioned to Ally I wanted to try walking after my liquid lunch. She grinned and got me a fancy silver walker with tennis balls on the bottom. Giving it a critical glare, I motioned to Ally. "I hope you didn't steal this from a retirement home. I'm sure there's an Ethel out there who needs this more than I do." The nurse shook her head, laughing as she held out her hand.

It took most of my strength to stand up. I fought through the pain, my sheer will and stubborn determination allowed me to forget everything hurt. I was bruised, battered and down to one swollen hand. Completely useless. Once I got moving, I shuffled to the nurse's station right outside my room and back with Ally right behind me. Those six feet took a lot out of me and I was eager to crawl back into bed.

Dinner was another liquid one, just like my lunch and breakfast. They were using the liquid diet to monitor minor stomach tears from the bullet shrapnel. I tried to ask Ally if she knew what happened, but she only smiled, and told me to drink more of the green sludge she'd set on the tray table.

My parents visited in the late afternoon. Both hugged me through tears but soon fell into their usual chatter. My mother filled me in on the neighborhood gossip and Dad went over the latest Bears scores. Aaron stopped by right at the end of visiting hours and hugged me, too.

All these hugs showed me how lucky I had been to survive. No one hugged me unless it was around the holidays, and I was forced into it.

And no one was talking about my incident, which infuriated me. I was hurt, not broken. Dr. Bettis explained mild amnesia was normal for such extensive injuries, and in time I'd snap out of it. My memories would either trickle back or hit me all at once. In the meantime, I was supposed to focus on healing and walking.

Sasha came back that night. She grinned at me as I flipped through channels. "You should be asleep, young lady."

"I should, but I heard there's been a beautiful woman sneaking into my room at night while I sleep." I bit my bottom lip to hold back a grin, very thankful I'd bribed Wendy into waking me up ten minutes before Sasha came in my room.

She dropped her bag before sitting on the edge of the bed, laying a hand on my thigh. "You sound better today. You don't have that old raspy smoker's voice." She paused. Her eyes ran over my face, stopping on stitches and bruises. "How are you feeling?"

"Better? I made it to there and back today." I pointed out the door towards the nurse's station. "Tomorrow, Ally and I are going to the end and back." I huffed, frustrated I couldn't move faster and farther. I wanted to be back to normal already, but my body was telling me I'd been through a lot. The buffet of pain meds masked everything, made me feel like I could run a marathon in the morning, when I could barely use the bathroom by myself.

"Emma, for once in your life, take it easy." Sasha slid off the bed, dragged a chair over and sat down. I hid my disappointment she didn't crawl in with me like the night before, but I'd been a total asshole to her.

My right eye had opened to some extent overnight, making me look more like a stoner and less like Tyson's punching bag, allowing a better chance to stare at Sasha as she drew her eyes to the television. She looked exhausted. "Have you been sleeping?"

She shrugged, eyes still on the TV. "Here and there. I work during the day and my nights have been busy." She drifted off.

"You don't have to keep coming in every night now that I'm awake."

"I know I don't have to, but I want to." She turned from the TV, shrugging again. "It's become a routine."

I took a shaky breath, my mind shifting to the last thing I'd said as we left for Alice's crime scene. That's when the fuzzy pieces of the crime scene came trickling back, and what I had said to her. Why I said it to her, what my past held and why I didn't tell her what I should've when she was in my arms on the kitchen island.

I closed my eyes. It hadn't been just sex between us. It was more than that. It was love. I loved Sasha and I'd allowed my past to wrench her from me. Evidently, I'd barely escaped death, and it was time I stopped wasting time. My years with Elle were something I'd never forget, but it was time to let Sasha in.

Struggling to sit up, I swung my legs to the edge of the bed and slid my bare feet to the cold floor. Sasha stood, reaching for me. "Do you need to go to the bathroom?"

I shook my head, grabbing her hand. She steadied me as I stood on weak legs. "I want to say this to your face."

Sasha's hands slid under my elbows for extra support. "Emma, you should lay back down. Your legs aren't strong enough."

"I love you, Sasha." I met her gaze, "I'm tired of ignoring it. I'm done pushing you away day after day because of my past, and a messy childhood riddled with secrets." Sasha's jaw clenched, but I kept on. "I said those shitty things to make you walk away from me. I did it to protect you from my past." I took a slow breath, and my legs almost buckled. "The truth is, I love you. I love you so much it scares me. I lied when I implied what we did in my kitchen was nothing." I closed my eyes to power through a wave of dizziness. "I was in deep trouble the instant I laid eyes on you in your blues."

I blinked my eyes open to find Sasha was still there, her face unreadable, her eyes glassy with tears or anger. I looked away. "I might be too late, because I'm a stubborn idiot, but I love you."

I wobbled and stepped out of her grasp, reaching back for the edge of the bed. When I went to open my mouth to apologize, soft lips pressed against mine.

Sasha's hand fell to my cheek as she gently kissed me. I kissed her back, ignoring the pain of split lips and stitches.

Sasha broke the kiss, whispering. "You said I love you four times." A tear rolled down her cheek.

"I did?" I raised a shaky hand, wiping her cheek.

She laughed. "You did. You never repeat yourself, Emma." She bent forward, kissing the corner of my mouth, catching a sore spot. I flinched, and Sasha stepped back, "Oh God, I'm sorry!"

"I'll suffer through it." I smiled, brushing hair from her face with my good hand when another wave of dizziness struck. I grabbed her hand to slow down the spin. "Help me back to bed?"

Sasha eased me back onto the mattress and followed, curling into my side. She kissed the edge of my jaw. "I love you too, Emma. I have for a very long time."

"How long have you been creeping on me?" I glanced at her, curious at her words. I'd had plenty of stalkers, but they were criminals, not pretty rookie detectives.

She chuckled, gently picking up my hand. "I've always had a long-distance crush on you, but then I met you and saw through the bullshit you hand out. You're intelligent, strong, beautiful, sassy, stubborn and have a heart bigger than you want to show. It was hard *not* to fall for you."

I let out a slow breath and laid back in the pillows. "There's so much I need to tell you." I pulled her close, ignoring the sore spots her body pressed against. "I'm about to pass out. Will you be back tomorrow?"

Sasha snuggled into my chest. "Wouldn't miss it for the world."

* * *

Over the next week, my mobility improved. My bruises faded to soft yellows and I felt almost normal. Dr. Bettis continued to encourage me, telling me one more day and he would consider sending me home. I smiled at his positive attitude. It was working. I soon walked at a slow pace around the floor with little assistance, Ally now walking next to me instead of behind me. I'd even upgraded to solid foods, and was excited when Aaron brought me a cheeseburger for lunch, which I threw up five minutes after I ate it.

Aaron laughed, stealing the rest of my fries. "Sorry, Emma. I figured you could use the grease and fat. You're looking a little bony lately."

I sat on the bed and glared at him as I sipped water. My memory was slowly returning, but there were large gaps where everything was a mystery.

My right arm was the only major hurdle left. Whenever I tried to move or flex it, I was met with dull pain and stiffness. It was still wrapped up like a mummy and I was desperate to yank the gauze off to look at the damage.

I watched Aaron finish his own greasy burger, jealous when he didn't throw it up. We were watching some silly cop movie, picking apart the Hollywood cops and horrible procedures. I laughed even as I started to miss work, a sure sign I was healing.

As Aaron and I laughed at the car chase scene, Captain Jameson entered the room with a fruit basket. "Emma! It's great to see you awake!"

I smiled, frantically trying to smooth out my tangled hair. "Captain."

Jameson set the fruit basket down. "I was pleased to hear you were awake and moving around. I apologize for not visiting sooner. I wanted to make sure your family got first dibs."

My dad told me Jameson had visited every day while I was in the coma. The days he couldn't make it, he'd call my parents for updates. "Captain, I hope to return to work in a week or so, if it's okay with you."

Jameson sighed. "Please take the time, Emma. Aaron is picking up the slack and the Lieutenant from the ninth is running things until you return." He chuckled at the blank look on my face. "Don't worry, no one is using your office." Jameson glanced at the wires and tubes surrounding me. "But you're more than welcome to come back as soon as your doctor clears you."

"Thank you, Captain." The grin on my face hurt, but I couldn't contain it. I was desperate to get back to the job.

Another light knock landed on the doorframe. The three of us turned to see Agent Rachel Fisher walking in, well, gliding in with her perfect suit and flawless beauty. I smiled as Jameson and Aaron immediately straightened up, putting on their best manners.

She took notice with a smirk. "Pardon me, gentlemen, but I was wondering if I could have a moment with Lieutenant Tiernan?"

Jameson nodded, and Aaron looked at me for approval. I waved him off. "It's okay, Aaron. I think my stomach's settled down. But could you bring me back a smoothie and maybe a salad?"

Aaron winked with a grin. "Anything for you, boss."

Jameson and Aaron issued polite goodbyes to Rachel. She closed the door behind them and sat down in Aaron's empty chair. "How are you feeling, Emma?"

"I'm getting there. But I hate when people ask me that. It reminds me of how much farther I have to go. I clearly don't have the patience to wait for my body to catch up to my mind." I smiled. "Maybe you can help me out. My friends and family have been skirting the edge and refuse to talk about my incident. My doctor said I have temporary amnesia from my injuries. But I'm frustrated. No one thinks I can handle the truth."

Rachel sighed, clasping elegant hands in her lap. "It's understandable. I'm surprised no one has told you. Your doctor said it was okay to start discussing it, in hopes it would trigger your brain into letting go of the hidden trauma." She paused. "I'm actually here because of what happened." She leaned forward. "What is the last thing you remember?"

I leaned against a pillow, studying the ceiling. "I went home, read through the foster records and slowly put the pieces together that Evan Carpenter was our suspect. Aaron called because our undercover officer picked someone up at the bar. Then everything fades away until I woke up in the hospital, feeling like a truck ran over me."

Rachel reached into her briefcase, setting a large file folder on her lap. "I'm going to tell you what happened. I reviewed your progress with Dr. Bettis before I came in here and he's certain you've recovered enough mentally. He doesn't believe you'll have any setbacks, but I've been advised to stop at any sign of distress." She smiled, opening the folder. "I think your amazing support group has everything to do with how fast you're recovering."

I smiled in agreement. For an Ice Queen, I did have a lot of friends.

Rachel raised an eyebrow. "Would you like to proceed?" Her professional tone threw me off. This wasn't a friendly visit. This was an official FBI interview.

I bit the inside of my cheek, nervous as I shifted in the bed, trying to find a comfortable position. "Was it Evan? Did he do this to me?"

"Yes." Rachel tipped her head down, reading the file in her lap. "Evan has been tracking you for the last year. You put the pieces together on your own, with the help of your foster files and the clues he left you. We had a vague idea who he was and that you might be his target when I first met with you. He purposely led you and the officers to the towers, making sure you were the one to confront him. It was a very elaborate plan." She paused, looking up.

My jaw was clenched so tight, I could hear my teeth creak under the pressure. I gave a short nod for her to continue. "You had a showdown that quickly became a brutal fight for survival. Detective Liang arrived as Evan was leaving his mark on you."

Rachel handed me the official report, sheet by sheet. I skimmed the thick federal speak, only stopping when key words stood out. I caught a quick glimpse of the crime scene photos in Rachel's lap. As I winced at the image of a large lake of blood on the garage floor, my memories started trickling in.

"Detective Liang received a stab wound to his left thigh. Shots were exchanged, but Evan escaped and disappeared into the night. The investigators found a blood trail leading to the river, but no body." Rachel paused once more, looking for signs of stress on my face. "You barely survived the injuries inflicted." She handed me another page, my ER intake form. "When you woke up, your memory was spotty. Dr. Bettis suggested to your family and friends they avoid discussing the incident until you were stabilized. He was worried any sudden trauma would hinder your rehabilitation and cause more setbacks."

I listened as I read over the graphic details of the attack. Aaron's eyewitness statement broke my heart, but my memories grew more vivid the further I read. Evan's face flashed behind my eyes. Him straddling me, the knife glinting in the low light before it dug into my skin. I ran a hand over the thick bandages on my arm.

"He told me he killed the three victims to garner my attention. I was his first test subject, and he never forgot me."

"I'm sorry, Emma." Rachel's eyes betrayed her professional exterior.

I held out the report, done reading the gruesome details. "Any leads on where he could've gone?" Evan was a cockroach, always surviving the inevitable.

"He was severely wounded. Detective Liang swore he shot him in center mass, giving Evan a debilitating wound. We tested the blood found at the scene leading to the river and confirmed it wasn't yours. The labs are running a DNA profile in hopes of proving Evan was there and tracing his whereabouts if he isn't found in the river. We've yet to find a body, or evidence he's still alive." Rachel moved closer to me. "You're safe, Emma. There's a protective detail outside of your room and at your home. I have agents watching over your loved ones. If Evan tries anything, we'll catch him." The sound in the room filtered away, leaving an awkward hum of machines.

There was no body. No solid proof Evan was dead. He was still out there — I felt it in my bones. He was still out there, waiting for me.

She collected the pages, setting them in her bag. "I need your help. When your father asked me to pull your files, something fell onto my radar. I think Evan is responsible for more than just the three homicides here. I know it's a little insensitive to ask this, but I need your help. You know Evan better than any of us, you know his work. Would you be willing to help me connect the dots in some cold cases?"

I sighed hard and laid back. "How do you know my dad? And what exactly do you do for the FBI?"

Rachel smiled. "Ask your father about me. He tells the story better than I ever could. As for what I do, I work for the Behavioral Science Unit, the BSU. I profile and catch serial killers."

I went silent as everything Rachel told me began to sink in. The feelings came back, the original ones I had when I singled out Evan as my prime suspect. Fear, mixed with determination to stop him. The moment on the garage floor replayed over and over in my mind, even as I half listened to Rachel explain the BSU's mission.

I'd barely survived.

Those three words circled in my mind, and my chest felt heavy with guilt. I vividly remembered not being able to pull the trigger to stop him. I'd frozen when the time came, scared shitless of the man who had terrorized me as a child and reappeared like a ghost. If only I'd pulled the trigger the second he took one step towards me, everything would be different. I wouldn't have to worry about a madman coming after me. After the people I loved.

"I hope you don't mind. I grabbed your food from Aaron and told him I wanted a moment alone with you." Sasha walked in the room, carrying a brown paper bag. She paused when she saw Rachel sitting next to me. "Oh, sorry. Aaron didn't tell me you had a visitor." She set the food down, smiling as she held out a hand to Rachel. "Hi, Detective Sasha Garnier. Lieutenant Tiernan's old partner." I chuckled at Sasha's strained professional tone.

Sasha held onto Rachel's hand a minute longer than appropriate, offering a look that could kill an entire army. The jealousy poured off her in waves.

"Special Agent Rachel Fisher, FBI. I was checking on the Lieutenant here. Her father and I are old friends."

I cleared my throat to cut the tension. "Sasha, Rachel is the agent who acquired my birth records and foster files. She also helped me put the pieces together with Evan."

Sasha's eyes lit up, easing away the unmitigated jealousy. "Nice to meet you, Agent Fisher."

Rachel smiled. She must have sensed it was time to leave the room, before the tension thickened again. "I'll be back in a few days, perhaps we can discuss further details then." She whispered goodbye to Sasha and left as quietly as she'd come in.

Sasha sat on the edge of the bed, opening the brown bag. I grabbed her arm, stilling her. "She told me what happened. I understand why none of you wanted to tell me when I woke up."

She stopped fidgeting with the food, her face a whiter shade of pale. "Emma, it was bad. I didn't think I'd ever see you again."

"That's the rumor around here. I see how the doctors and nurses look at me like I'm a damn miracle." I squeezed her arm until she looked at me. "Now we focus on finding him." I marveled at how calm I was about this situation. I'd almost died at the hands of a serial killer, and he was still on the loose. Maybe it was the secret security detail watching over me. Maybe it was because I had survived the impossible and felt invincible. Either way, I was determined to heal and get back to work.

I tugged Sasha closer, lacing our fingers together. Now was the time, I had nothing to lose, and everything to gain. Sasha deserved it from me. "Did you know I was born in Detroit?"

She grinned, leaning into my side. "No, but it explains a lot."

I poked her side with a finger. "I have so much to tell you about my past. I need to tell you everything, so I can protect you. If Evan is alive, he'll come back for me."

"How can you be so calm? If it was me, I'd be looking for a way into the witness protection program." She gave me a critical glare. "Are you sure you're human? Not made of ice like everyone says?" Sasha kissed me on the forehead. "Evan's probably dead by now, floating in the river. Aaron shot him in the chest. The crime scene techs found a blood trail."

"But no body." I leaned against her shoulder. "I love you, Sasha. You need to know everything. Because if he's still alive, he'll come after you. He knows you're important to me. And he loves destroying the things people love." I let out a slow breath. "I'm determined to end this. To stop him like I couldn't in the garage."

Sasha gathered me in a half hug. "You said it twice." Grinning, she kissed the space between my jaw and ear. "I love you, Emma." She raised an eyebrow, "So Detroit, huh? Is that where you learned your hard-ass ways?"

That night, I forced Sasha to go home. She'd spent too many nights by my side sleeping in a cramped hospital bed, or in a small chair. I wanted her to get a real night of rest and stop worrying so much.

Falling asleep was a futile activity. My brain wouldn't shut down and I was antsy, desperate to get up and go to the station. The television was on, but I couldn't focus on the stupid movie I'd chosen. Rachel's visit had made me anxious on top of antsy. A terrible combination for a workaholic.

I slipped out of bed and shuffled to the bathroom, smirking in victory that I didn't need the walker. I washed my face and spent a handful of minutes looking over fading bruises. My arm was another story. It still hurt, a dull burning ache. "Thank God for modern medicine." I whispered as I picked at the IV port. My arm moved like it was made from lead. I had a vague memory of the damage done to it, and had an urge to see it.

Picking along the edge, I started to unravel the gauze, shivering when cool air hit raw flesh. A thin line of stitches ran from my thumb to the middle of my forearm, tying together angry red skin. It was easy to see an expert had closed the large laceration, and the tiny stitches wouldn't leave me with such a gruesome scar.

Flexing my arm and wrist, I found it to be painful, just as painful as the memory of when it happened. I decided the cool air felt good on my arm. I tossed the bandage into the trash and returned to bed.

Wendy came in to check on me the moment I laid down. She noticed the lack of bandages around my arm and gave me a dirty look. I shrugged, flipping through channels as she went to work wrapping it back up. "I'll tell Dr. Bettis you want the bandage off. I think you can manage without it while you're still admitted."

"How much longer will I be here?" I wanted to go home, lay in my own bed and eat something other than bland hospital goop.

"Not my call, kiddo." Wendy patted my shoulder, leaving me with promises of returning with more delicious goop for dinner. I groaned, collapsing in pillows as I flicked through endless channels.

I passed out while watching an old black and white movie, dreaming about my bed at home, when a warm hand shaking my leg woke me. I squinted, blinking a few times at a person-shaped shadow hovering over my face.

"Emma, wake up." Aaron kept his voice low, but there was urgency in his tone.

"Hey." I pushed to sit up. "It's late." I rubbed my eyes, trying to focus on the gold badge swinging from his neck. These painkillers made waking up difficult. I was pretty sure the bull on his Chicago Bulls shirt was winking at me.

Aaron sighed. "They didn't want to get you involved, but it's important you know." He hesitated. "They found another body up on the Gold Coast, in Sasha's district."

A surge of panic hit. "I'm going to assume it's not a normal homicide."

Aaron shook his head. "Sasha was the lead detective." He paused, holding up a hand to stop me before I started. "She's okay, a little shaken, but okay." He then held up a file folder. "They haven't pulled her off the case. No one knows she's romantically involved with you, just that you were partners and you kicked her to the curb."

I took the file from his hands and looked at the photographs. The victim was female and was positioned just like Alice and David had been. She was nude from the waist up, showcasing a long laceration that ran from her hip to the middle of her stomach. It mirrored mine. I placed a hand over my own scar, wincing.

A crude carving of words sat off to the side of the laceration. I cringed, looking up. "Aaron, did the specifics of my attack ever get out, specifically, how I'm connected to Evan?"

"Only a select few within the department and Agent Fisher know the truth. The media and the department only know your attack was a shitshow that's currently being investigated by internal affairs. Jameson takes the credit for that one. He wanted to keep things quiet the second the FBI showed up."

I tossed the photographs to the edge of the bed. The carving mocked me. I let out a shaky breath. "He's a sick bastard, Aaron. I knew when I saw *Detroit is for Lovers*, that it's Evan. Did they find any trace evidence?

Anything to lead us to where he may be? Or could this be a copycat murder?"

"It's not a copycat." He removed an evidence bag from his pocket. "Sasha found this under the victim's head and hid it away before anyone saw it."

I grabbed the bag with a Polaroid stuck to the thin plastic and my heart dropped.

It was the photo taken of me and Sasha at O'Malley's.

I closed my eyes and the face of the young man who took it flashed. The blue eyes that stared at us as he asked for a hero picture were the same blue eyes that had stared down as Evan pinned me to the ground before cutting into my skin.

"We need to get Sasha into protective custody and I need to get the fuck out of here." I went to get up, when Aaron put a hand on my shoulder.

"I put a unit on her the second she called, but she refused any sort of protection. She's stubborn like you; and you, you need to stay here and finish healing." He pushed me back into bed.

The stare down lasted thirty seconds before I gave in. "Fine. But come back in the morning with more details. I want to stay involved in this case. I'll reach out to Agent Fisher and ask for more resources."

Aaron clutched the file. "Will do. I placed a few guys in hospital security uniforms to keep an eye on you. They have orders to act like bored security guards." He smiled, squeezing my shoulder. "I'll call if anything changes."

I waited about ten solid minutes to make sure Aaron was gone, then rolled out of bed and went to the bathroom. I grabbed the Patient Belongings bag from the closet and dumped everything out. I frowned at my wallet, badge, broken cellphone, keys and an old blood-stained t-shirt that had to have been Aaron's.

I sighed, looking down at the grey and pink flannel pajamas my mother had brought last week with the excuse she was tired of my ass hanging out for the world to see. I would be noticeable in the pajamas, and wouldn't get very far before a nurse stopped me.

I slipped out into the hallway and mumbled to a nurse who was checking supplies that I was taking a short walk to tire myself out.

The second she dipped her head back into the boxes of band-aids, I limped to the doctors on-call room and pilfered a pair of scrubs. I shoved them up my shirt and shuffled back to my room.

I changed in the bathroom. Since I knew Wendy's schedule from sleepless nights, I knew I had about fifteen minutes before she started her rounds. I shoved my wallet and badge into a pocket and made my escape.

I shuffled to the nurse's station in the slippers my mother brought with the pajamas and found a self-release form. I filled it out, leaving it on Wendy's computer. No need for her to get in trouble for my itchy feet and my escape.

I snuck down the hall and took the elevator on the opposite end of the floor. Weaved in and out of rooms to sneak past the real cops walking the floors and looking in every room they passed.

One of the real hospital security guards smiled at me as I stumbled out of another on-call room, and as he entered the men's restroom. I waved back, stepping to the rear of the elevator as it opened, trying my best to hide in a corner. I hit the lobby button and looked down at my feet, chuckling that the guard hadn't noticed my pink fuzzy slippers.

Chapter 14

The cold air hit me like a brick wall. Somehow, in the time I was asleep, fall had hit Chicago and brought with it the cold winds. I folded my arms, shivering as I hailed a cab. The driver kept looking back at me in the rearview mirror, at the bruises covering my face. He pulled in front of my house twenty minutes later. I tossed him a few dollars and whispered, "I ran into a door."

The cab driver's eyes widened in disbelief. "Lady, you should call the police if your boyfriend is hitting you like that."

I grinned. "You should see what I did to him." I shuffled into the house, fumbling for a few minutes with getting the key into the lock. Kicking the door closed, and tossing my keys on the side table, I relished in the feeling of being back in my own house.

The pile of mail on the table was sorted, letting me know my mother had been in the house. I walked around, checking windows and doors. I was relieved when it was apparent that only family had been in the house.

In my bedroom, I grabbed the extra gun I kept under the bed in a holster. It was still loaded and ready. I took it into the bathroom as I took the longest, hottest shower I could stand with plastic wrap covering my bandaged arm and the wound on my stomach. The hot water stung on the scrapes and cuts littered over my body, but the need to feel clean outweighed the pain.

I redressed my stomach wound, balancing a towel around my chest as I tried not to drip water everywhere. The nurses had taken out the packing days ago, issuing strict instructions to keep it clean and dry. I left Evan's failed attempt to carve his opus into me, uncovered. It was healing on its own and looked nothing more than a series of scratches.

I carefully pulled on a sweatshirt and my favorite pair of pajama pants. Sitting on the edge of the bed, I sighed at how tired I felt from even the minimal exertion of getting dressed. I wanted to curl under the blankets and sleep for days. Instead, I reached for my phone, turning it on for the first time in weeks. I was surprised it still worked, having been tossed around and soaked in blood. The thing blew up with missed calls and texts. I ignored them and dialed my father.

"Emma? Are you okay?" His voice was steady and authoritative.

"I checked myself out of the hospital about an hour ago." I mumbled, nervous at the ass chewing I was about to receive.

"Why did you do that? Your mother is going to have a fit when she finds out." He dropped to a whisper. "What's going on?"

I ran a hand through my damp hair, tugging on a few tangles. "Another body was found tonight. Evan's still alive and sent me a message. If I stayed in the hospital, I'd be an easy target. I think he may be after my friend." I hated using the word 'friend,' but Sasha and I had just sorted out our feelings for each other. I wasn't ready to shout to the world that a serial killer was after my girlfriend, the woman I loved.

My father scoffed. "Well, being home isn't exactly safer. Do you have your sidearm?"

"I do, the extra .45 you bought for my academy graduation." I leaned forward, cradling my head. "Dad, I called to ask you about Agent Fisher."

His slow, steady intake of air worried me. Was Fisher a *friend*-friend, or a *federal* friend? "Rachel mentioned she visited you and asked for your help. What do you want to know?"

"Who is she, and how does she know you? Why does she seem to think she owes you? Owes you enough to access my records? I'm having a hard time trusting anyone outside of my family, Dad."

"Rachel was doing a sting for the FBI a handful of years ago, around the time you were a brand-new road officer and I was pushing paperwork with Sergeant stripes. She was a rookie agent attached to the vice unit to run surveillance on a Russian mafia human trafficking ring operating around the meat packing district. One night, I was her backup as she went in to negotiate a buy for the next order coming in from Russia. Rachel slipped, and they pinned her as a cop. They tried to teach her a lesson with fists. I interceded right before they beat her to death." He drifted off. "I saved her life and the three assholes who were using her as a punching bag never quite made it to trial. I helped her with the bosses, and she was transferred to a different division. We've kept in contact over the years."

It was hard to picture my father doing anything other than smiling and helping people, but he had the same protective streak I did when it came to protecting good people. "Thanks, Dad. I didn't know if she could be trusted. This situation with Evan isn't going to end easily." I took a breath to tell him my plan, and the doorbell rang.

My heart stopped, and I reached for my gun. I asked my father to tell no one I'd left the hospital and slid the cell phone into my pocket. I grabbed the .45 as best as I could with my right hand.

The doorbell rang twice more. There was no reason for anyone to be at my door. I just left the hospital. Neither Aaron nor Sasha would know I self-discharged until morning when they arrived for their daily visit.

Tremors threatened to take over my entire body, and blood pounded in my ears with every step.

Wrapping a hand around the doorknob, I took a few steady breaths as I tried to get a solid grip on the gun. My right hand refused to flex and properly take on the gun's weight. I counted to three and ripped open the door, pointing a wobbling gun in the face of whoever stood behind it. "I won't make the same mistake twice!" The words hissed out, adrenaline surging hard.

"Holy shit, Emma, put the gun down!" I expected a male voice to come out of the darkness of my front step. Instead, it was a soft, feminine one. My fear didn't give in even as I saw Sasha duck to the side and reach for her own gun.

I blinked a few times before recognizing it was Sasha crouching out of the way. Not Evan.

I flicked on the porch light, squinting in the bright white light. Sasha holstered her gun, holding up empty hands. "Emma, it's ok, it's me." She blew out a slow breath. "You have a peephole. You could've used that instead of opening the door, guns blazing."

I sagged against the wall. A bone-chilling pain took the place of the adrenaline that had pushed my broken body parts too hard. I dropped the gun on the table, my right hand giving up on me. I slid down the wall to sit on the floor as Sasha stepped into the house, closing the door behind her.

She knelt next to me, running a hand through my hair. "I went to stay with you at the hospital. Why did you check yourself out?"

"You know why."

She met my eyes. "Aaron told you."

"I can't sit in the hospital waiting for him. He knows I'm still alive and he knows about you." I grasped the side table to pull myself up. I cringed from the pain radiating through my body.

Sasha whispered. "Let me help."

She wrapped strong arms around my waist, lifting as I held onto the table. I whimpered at the feel of her. Although she'd been staying with me every night, and her warmth and softness had been a welcome reprieve from the cold hospital room, it had been hard for us to relax in the cramped hospital bed.

Her hand squeezed my side. "Let's get you to bed." I blushed at the idea as Sasha carried my weight up the stairs.

Sasha sat me on the edge of the bed, chuckling at the book collection spilling from overstuffed shelves and desk covered in file folders and work. "Hard to believe you chose to be a cop when it's clear you're smarter than the average police officer."

I tucked the gun under my pillow, earning a smirk from Sasha. I wanted it close even if I was wrapped in gauze like a mummy. "I was accepted to medical school almost two years ago. I was six months out from an early retirement and debated becoming a freshman at thirty-four."

Sasha's eyes widened. "You're going to retire?"

"This job was getting to me back then. I was about to start my life with El..." I paused. It was strange talking about Elle after revealing my feelings for Sasha. "Anyway, the job was becoming too much. It still is. I found the early retirement packet in the bottom of my desk two days after David Harrow's death. I think after this is done, I should leave the job." I sighed, pushing at blankets. "I need to keep you close. He will come after you."

Sasha sat, laying a warm hand on my thigh. "I'll be fine. I can protect myself." She scanned over the bandages and bruises littering my body. "I think you need someone to watch over you."

"I can move you in with my parents, or Agent Fisher can put you in temporary witness protection if I ask her." I was going into protective mode, thinking I could prevent something from happening this time.

"Emma, no. We have no proof Evan dumped this last body, and the Polaroid? Anyone could have gotten it from the bar. A copycat wannabe who knows your face from the news, looking for his thirty seconds of fame." Sasha folded her arms, her infamous temper about to make its appearance. "No one knows we're together." Irritation soaked her voice. The last thing I needed was to fight with her.

"It *is* him." I made direct eye contact. "*Detroit is for lovers* is from the red neon freeway sign that hung right outside my window at the foster home Evan and I grew up in. The red light burned across my bed day after day, making it impossible to sleep. Evan had loved it, said the color reminded him of blood."

I closed my eyes. The neon sign was a reminder that finding anyone to love us was a hopeless cause. Detroit wasn't for lovers if you were a forgotten kid.

Sasha's face flushed red. "I can protect myself. I always have, always will."

"I have to keep you safe. I couldn't bear it if I lost you."

"Like Elle? That was an accident! You have to stop beating yourself over something you couldn't control. You've lived in *that moment* for the last two years."

I cut her off. "Stop! This is different."

Sasha scoffed, giving me an indignant smirk. "I told Aaron not to tell you about the body, because I was worried you'd push yourself too hard and want to do this exact thing. Gain control, put up walls." She took a step towards the door. "Your past is the only thing you live for, Emma." The anger soaked her every word.

She was right. From the moment I met her, my past was always there. I kept my emotions close to my chest and pushed people away to control every situation. This time, when I pushed her away, it was to keep her safe. I never wanted Evan to come near her or use her as bait.

But her words bit deep and stung, igniting my equally short temper. "You don't understand, Sasha."

Striking a nerve, Sasha spun around. "I don't understand? Really? I understand you haven't had the greatest childhood, but you've come out the other side remarkably well. You don't get to push it on me like that and make me join your pity party. I *do* understand, Emma." She was on a roll, the words spilling forth. "I was raised by a single mother, an alcoholic single mother who dumped me with creepy neighbors whenever she got the chance to make money by stripping or hooking. Strange men came to my house every night, sleeping in her bed and trying to be my father in the morning. I raised myself, learned how to fight off men with grabby hands and ignored the kids who picked on me for the ragged hand me downs I wore. I grew up thinking this was my life. Booze and bullshit. Until a female cop came into my class for career day. I latched onto her and she became my Big Sister. Showing me there was more to life than living in the past, where the future can be changed in an instant."

Sasha was yelling, her eyes glassy as she emptied her heart. "I became a police officer to help others change their future. I know it's cliché, but Morgan was the first of many." I watched as memories flooded her eyes.

She paused, letting out a controlled breath, trying to harness her temper. "I may not understand the pain you went through, but you have to stop living in the past before it eats you alive. When I met you, it gave me hope when I started falling in love with you. I thought my love would break through the walls and no matter what, I loved you for everything you are and aren't. For a split second, you let me in, and it was amazing." Sasha shrugged, a tear slipping free. "I love you, Emma. Simple as that, but I will not keep going back and forth with you every time something wants to pull us apart."

She moved away, backing out of the bedroom as I sat in silence, digesting her words. She had hit the nail on the head. Shattered the goddamned nail, and sent the shards straight through my heart.

Sasha whispered a soft good night and left.

I'd be a real shit if I let her leave like this. I'd gaped at her like an idiot as she professed unconditional love, then left her hanging. I rolled off the bed and shuffled down the steps as fast as my legs would let me. I half fell down the last few, calling out, "Sasha, wait."

The front door was open, and she had one foot out, her head tilted down. "What now, Emma? Are you going to tell me something else I don't understand about you or waste more time telling me how I should feel?"

I stood behind her, close enough to feel her body heat flowing backwards to seep into my skin. I moved an inch, to press a hand on the door, shutting it and holding it closed. I leaned forward, my lips brushing against the shell of her ear. "You're right, I do live in the past. Always have. And I hate that I do. I've never had a reason to change." My hand dropped from the door to land on her forearm. "Until you. I'm so damn afraid to lose you."

Sasha kept her back to me. "Then don't lose me, just trust me." I heard the faint click of the lock as she turned to face me. A thick silence fell between us as our eyes met and my heart leapt into my throat.

She lifted a hand, gliding it across my cheek and held it there. She bent forward, closing the millimeter between us, kissing me. It was a slow, delicate kiss I pushed into, wanting more. Sasha whispered against my mouth. "You should be sleeping."

I swallowed hard. "I should." Who cared that my body was still light years behind the thoughts I was having at that moment? I needed to solidify that I was putting my trust in Sasha. All of it.

I grabbed her with my good hand, pulling her hip to hip as I bent down and kissed her hard. Sasha whimpered, her hands falling to my hips, her thumbs digging into my skin.

I broke the kiss, licking my lips. "It was never just sex. You know that? I love you."

Sasha captured my lips again, less gentle than the first time. I felt her hand slip to the small of my back. She pulled me closer, and her tongue glided along my bottom lip. Her fingers drew down my side, stopping at the waist of my pajama pants.

She grinned with eyes full of desire. "Why are you always in pajamas when we do this?"

"Always prepared?"

Sasha shook her head as her other hand slipped under my sweatshirt. I gasped when her fingertips grazed the bottom of my breast. She placed slow, wet kisses along my neck and I moaned at the feeling of her soft lips against my skin. I pulled back to catch my breath and grabbed her wrist, directing her to move back to the bedroom.

Sasha slid her arms around my waist from behind the moment we entered the room, kissing my neck as her hands tugged off my shirt. She pressed her front against my back, palming my breasts, and I groaned at the intimate touch. Kisses dotted my bare shoulder, and I felt her smile against my skin. I wanted to turn in her arms, but Sasha held me in place, her fingers running slow circles around my nipples.

I almost buckled at the knees as one of her hands slowly slid down to the waist of my pajama pants, pausing for a moment before she pushed the thin fabric out of the way.

Sasha swore as her fingers found how much I craved her. She had to hold me tighter when I pushed against her hand.

She took me to the edge and I was about to come, but Sasha stopped and pulled her hand free. Leaving me breathless and frustrated. I turned in her arms, and found her smiling as she grabbed my hips, pushing me gently to the edge of the bed. She laid me down, scanning over my flushed body, eyes pausing at the bruises and bandages. A flicker of worry crossed her hazel eyes.

I reached out for her arm, pulling her to me, and our mouths met in urgency. It had been too long since our first kiss, and the tension between us was thick. I moaned as Sasha nipped at my bottom lip. The feel of her cotton button-down shirt against my naked skin drove me insane.

I pushed my hands between us, yanking at the buttons, trying to unbutton them with my fumbling, stiff fingers. Sasha grabbed my hands and pulled them to her lips, kissing them. She then guided my hands down with hers to unbutton the shirt together.

After throwing her shirt across the room, she gently laid beside me. Sasha kissed me as her fingers drew soft, heated lines down my chest, over the swell of my breast and down to my stomach, careful to avoid the bandages. She followed the trail her fingers left with wet kisses, then settled between my legs. She kissed around my belly button as she slid my pajama pants down. She paused, looking up at me and I knew what she was asking. I ran a hand through her hair. "Don't hold back, Sasha."

A wicked smirk was her answer before she kissed my stomach again, moving further down. The feeling of a soft kiss between my legs had me arching off the bed. The sudden movement pulled a moan of both desire and pain from me. My weakened muscles were not used to this, but I didn't care as each movement of Sasha's tongue made me forget. I clung to the bed sheets as waves of ecstasy hit me hard and rode through my body. I collapsed against the pillow, breathless and totally numb.

Sasha moved back up my body, kissing me deeply. I wrapped my arms around her, running my hands over her bare skin. She whispered, her hand on my chest just under the collarbone, "I hope that wasn't too much."

With a stupid grin, I kissed her. "Whatever pain I feel in the morning is worth it." I looked down at her pants, looping a finger into the waistband. "Those need to come off."

She laughed, shifting to lift herself off my hips before practically ripping her pants off. She sat above me as I stared at the woman in admiration. I took her hand and sat up with her, our legs wrapped around each other. Hooking a hand around her neck, I drew her closer, our mouths meeting in a renewed desire as I made it clear I wanted to keep going. I held Sasha with my bandaged arm as my left hand ran over her body and between us. She gasped as my fingers teased before slowly pushing in.

I smiled as Sasha began to move with my hand, setting the rhythm. I took one of her breasts in my mouth, making her moan and thrust harder against me. Before I knew it, her hand had pushed between us and quick fingers slipped inside of me. I gasped as she had, still sensitive from my last orgasm, but I couldn't hold back.

We moved together, our hearts racing in sync.

Both of us were breathless, panting for air. I moved my hand from Sasha, watching as she shuddered when my fingers grazed very sensitive spots.

She opened her eyes, grinning. "Not bad for one hand."

Kissing her sweaty skin, I mumbled against her neck. "I may have pulled something." I winced as I lay back onto the bed, while Sasha slid to the side to snuggle against me. She laid her head on my shoulder and looked at me, her gaze turning solemn. "I meant it when I said I love you, Emma."

I studied her, running a hand over her hair before letting it settle against her jaw. "I feel the same. I love you, too. More than I thought possible." I bent and kissed her forehead, "I know that sounds very cold, Queen-like."

Sasha giggled. "It does, but I understand." She slid an arm across my waist. "We're a work in progress, but I like it when we fight." She nipped my collarbone. "It results in amazing makeup sex."

It was my turn to giggle. "Let's just hope I can move in the morning. Thank you to the painkillers still in my system." I let out a slow breath. My body was numb, and I wasn't sure if it was from the painkillers or from Sasha ravishing me.

"I guess I should take full advantage of your current state." Before I could object, her hand slid down my stomach, disappearing under the sheet covering my waist. She smiled as her hand drew through my folds. I covered her hand with mine, guiding her to continue.

I suddenly wished I'd filled those prescriptions instead of throwing them out in the trash at the hospital each time Dr. Bettis left them on my tray.

It was going to be a long night.

Chapter 15

I yawned, cringing. I was so incredibly sore, but the memories of why kept me from falling into a bad mood. I rolled over to find Sasha's bare back. I ran my eyes over her smooth skin, memorizing each freckle, down to where the blankets around her waist cut off my view.

I scooted closer, pressing against her and laying a hand on her hip. She grabbed my hand and weaved our fingers together.

I pressed a kiss against her shoulder. "Morning."

She leaned back with a grin. "We went a little overboard last night. You should go back to sleep."

I buried my face in the crook of her neck. "Maybe."

Sasha rolled over, her eyes widening at the clock. "Shit! I need to get ready for work." She jumped out of bed, snatching strewn clothing off the floor. I watched her walk to the bathroom naked. She left the door open as she showered, a silent invitation to join her. I tried to get up, but my body was now void of painkillers and pissed off from our night of physical activity.

Sasha came out a few moments later, still naked. I pouted as she dressed and I couldn't touch her. She leaned over, kissed me on the cheek and pushed away my grabby hands. "I'll call you when I get to work. I'll try to come over for lunch." Her seductive smirk left my entire body blushing.

"Please be careful." I caught her hand.

She crawled across the bed to give me a lingering kiss. "I promise you." She stood, slipping her holster on, another somber reminder of what she was walking into every day she went to work.

Before Sasha left, she sat on the edge of the bed. "Call if you need anything. If I don't make lunch, I'll be here for dinner." She took a breath and whispered. "I love you."

Grinning like an idiot, I whispered back. "I love you, too, Detective Garnier."

Sasha laughed, rolled her eyes, gave me one more kiss and ran down the stairs.

Rolling over to her side, I ran a hand over where she'd just been. The bed was still warm, and the soft scent of her shampoo was everywhere. I fell back asleep with a grin on my face.

Aaron's annoying ringtone drew me out of a lovely dream. I reached blindly for my phone and saw his name in bright white letters. I set the phone back down.

Seconds later it rang again. "Aaron. I know. You're going to chew me out for leaving the hospital. I couldn't stay there and wait for him to come to me."

"Oh, I'm fucking pissed you blew out of the hospital like an idiot. Dr. Bettis said you should've stayed at least one more week. Your idiocy is beside the point. Have you heard from Sasha?"

"Um, yeah, this morning. She left about two hours ago for work. Why?" I ran a hand through tangled hair.

"I took a call from her Sergeant. She hasn't shown up to work and isn't answering her phone. Even her roommate can't get a hold of her."

I felt my stomach drop. "Did you have a detail on her?"

"We did. They last saw her leaving work around nine p.m. and then she went home. No one saw her leave her house or yours." Aaron was frustrated. "God dammit, I *shouldn't* have used patrol officers to keep an eye on her."

~ 204 ~

My stomach churned. "Call Agent Fisher. Ask if her detail saw anything." Aaron paused. I knew he wanted to question me. I repeated he needed to call Rachel and hung up.

I forced myself out of bed and pulled on a sweatshirt as I dialed Sasha. It went to voicemail three times. On the fourth time, as my heart was about to explode out of my chest, she picked up. I held back the panic in my voice. "Sasha, where are you? Everyone's looking for you."

"Ahh! I knew you would call! I waited four times, to match the times you told your lovely girlfriend you loved her. Brave of you to admit your feelings so soon, Emma."

Rage surged through my veins as I clutched the phone in my left hand. "Evan."

"Aw! You recognize my voice. It's lovely to see you still remember me after our street fight." Evan sighed. "I'm sure by now your mind is racing. Why am I answering the phone of the lovely Detective Garnier? Let me ruin your fun. I have her, Emma, and before you say you don't believe me, have a listen."

Muffled footsteps mixed with quiet whimpers. I strained to hear what Evan was saying when Sasha yelled for him get the fuck away before she killed him. I gripped the phone so hard I heard the case crack. "Your lover has quite a temper! I will beat it out of her. I learned from the best while in 'therapy' at the institute. It's a very effective process. Once you beat the resilience out of someone, they become very compliant."

"You touch her, and I *will* make sure your death is slow and painful." I hissed, limping towards the stairs.

Evan laughed. "I look forward to it, Emma. In the meantime, you better start looking for us. I will get bored soon and kill her." He huffed. "I'll give you the first clue. Listen carefully." Evan pulled the phone away. Industrial machine sounds and boat horns filled the background. I closed my eyes as I tried to search my mental maps of the city.

"Hurry, hurry, hurry!" Evan disconnected with a morbid laugh.

I called Aaron to come get me as I stumbled around, fighting the panic as I waited for him. I was running out of time.

I ripped the bandage off my arm to have a better range of motion in my right hand. I picked up my gun, begging my fingers to work with me, to wrap properly around the grip. Angry muscles and tired tendons fought back, filling my body with pain. Pain I shoved into little boxes, fear taking its place.

Aaron pounded on the door as the phone rang. I looked at the unknown number and answered. "I'm playing your fucking game, Evan. I'm coming." I whipped the door open, waving Aaron inside.

"Whoa, Detective Ice. It's Morgan, Sasha's roommate. I got back to our apartment and found something weird in her bedroom. You need to see it." Her voice trembled.

"What is it, Morgan?" I didn't have time to be sidetracked.

"I can't explain over the phone. This shit's too weird, like serial killer weird."

I looked at Aaron, his jaw clenched. "Alright, we'll be there in a minute."

"What the hell is going on, Emma?" Aaron took my elbow, steadying me as I half fell over trying to get my boots on. "You make me nervous when you're vague. And I haven't pissed you off in weeks."

I clutched the gun, wincing at the shooting pain. "Evan has Sasha. I have no idea how he did it. How he got her." I closed my eyes, trying to calm down. "He gave me a clue but I haven't pinpointed where we need to go. We need to go to Sasha's apartment first. That was her roommate, Morgan— Evan left something for me in Sasha's bedroom." I looked at my friend. "I'm trapped in another one of his stupid fucking games."

I pushed past Aaron and limped to his car as fast as I could. He glanced at my right hand, white-knuckled around the gun. "Emma, I can call for backup."

"I have to do this. He wants me."

I called Rachel, telling her to meet us at Sasha's apartment. I wanted her input on the clues Evan was doling out. She would have access to Evan's previous crimes and have an idea where to find him. She knew his patterns. She knew his MO.

* * *

Aaron barely had the car in park before I kicked the door open and hobbled out. Morgan sat on her front steps, her face whiter than normal. She stood. "Hey." She sighed hard as we went inside the apartment building. "Is my best friend okay?"

I didn't want to frighten the girl with the truth. "She will be." I smiled, gently pushing Morgan forward. I had to get into the apartment, not fuck around with light conversation and false promises.

She unlocked the door, letting Aaron and I enter first, guns up and ready. We cleared the apartment before waving Morgan over. "Show me what you found."

Morgan led me to the bedroom. "I was all over the city today, calling old friends to see if they could track Sasha down. The girl never disappears without calling. We have a routine and when she broke it, I knew something was wrong. I came home to take a nap and saw her bedroom door open. When I looked in her room..." The girl drifted off as we stopped in the doorway. She pointed towards the bed. "I saw that."

The entire bed was covered in neatly arranged pictures and news clippings. Aaron appeared behind me. "What the hell *is* all that, Emma?"

I stood at the edge of the bed and scanned over the clippings. The clippings were my major headlines from over the years. Every one of my cases that made the news was neatly cut out and placed in chronological order. From when I was injured on duty the first time, my first big homicide case, to my promotions, and to the most recent article about the night I almost died in the garage.

My department issued photograph stared back at me with the morose headline.

Detective falls at the hands of the Latin Killer

The photographs around the clippings were of all of me on the job, taken as if I were being followed by a surveillance unit. Crystal clear photographs of me at crime scenes, walking into the station, and laughing with Aaron over coffee in the park.

In the middle of the bed sat a large picture of Sasha walking out of my apartment a few hours ago. I laid a hand over my stomach, fighting the urge to vomit, to break down. Evan had been watching me for months, waiting for his moment to strike.

A cartoon bubble drawn around Sasha's head caught my eye. "**Call me! Clue number two is waiting!**"

I reached for the photograph with a shaky hand, but Aaron stopped me. "Evidence, Emma." He nodded towards the cartoon bubble. "Call me? What does it mean?"

"It means Evan's playing a game and I have to play along to keep Sasha alive." I dialed her number as Aaron tried to arrange a trace on Sasha's phone.

"You're right on time, Emma! You're actually a few minutes early!" Evan used a giddy tone that made me feel even sicker.

"Where is she?" I didn't want to play his games.

"Oh! You didn't like my little art project? It took me a long time to make. I had to slip out the window when the roommate came home sooner than I expected."

Aaron held up a finger letting me know the trace was locked and to keep Evan talking. "Why are you doing this? Why her?"

"Because she's important to you. She's someone you care about. I want to ruin the feeling you have every time you think about her. Every time you look at her, I want you to feel pain, regret. She loves you so much!

I watched her sit with you in the hospital and pray to her God to have more time with you. It warmed my dead heart to watch you curl up in bed together and snuggle like baby kittens. I decided then I had to have her, not because I want her in the same ways you do. I want to watch you watch her die." Evan's voice dropped.

I closed my eyes, struggling for control. "I'll kill you, Evan, before you can lay a finger on her."

Evan laughed. "That's so brave of you, Emma. But time is running out! I'm getting bored." He pulled the phone away then came back. "I forgot— your second and final clue is David." Then the line went dead.

"Fuck! Not long enough to get an accurate position. The closest we have is a ping off a cell tower, and that's not reliable. This city has fifty million cell towers." Aaron yelled in frustration.

"He gave me another clue. David." I ran a hand through my hair, my mind searching everything about David's scene.

"David? That's it?" Aaron paced, hands on his hips.

"David was Evan's first victim in this city. He could be referring to where you found his body." I turned and found Rachel standing in the doorway, her eyes falling to the bed. She continued. "He rarely breaks his pattern. Evan loves coming full circle."

"What makes you think that, Agent?" I glared at her, frustrated that we were standing around dissecting stupid clues.

"I've been tracking Evan for years, since I moved into the BSU. I can't go into details right now, but you and I, Emma, have a lot more in common than I initially thought." Her deep blue eyes were intense. "Evan killed someone I loved because I got too close." She glanced at Aaron, who was staring at us. "We don't have the time for stories. I'll explain everything when the time is right."

Rachel turned to walk out of the room. "Emma, do you remember the address where you found the first victim?"

"I do." I was about to follow Rachel out, when Aaron grabbed my arm.

"I don't know how I feel about this," he hissed. "Something is fishy with the good Agent."

"If she's right, it gets me one step closer to saving Sasha and taking Evan out of this world. It's a risk I'm willing to take." I covered his hand, smiling grimly. "Call for backup and meet us at the first crime scene, same signal as always."

Aaron sighed. "I don't like this, Emma. But I got your back and I'm not going to wait like last time. Last time I almost lost my partner."

I left the apartment building, leaving Aaron to arrange backup and interview Morgan.

I climbed into Rachel's governmental sedan, implicitly putting my trust in her. "Drive to the docks. That's where we found David. That's where we'll find Evan."

She nodded as she drove away from Sasha's apartment. Deep down, I knew this wasn't going to end well, but Evan had me cornered. I couldn't run away this time. I couldn't freeze up. If I did, Sasha would die.

Chapter 16

Rachel stepped out of the car, scanning the docks. I frowned at the remnants of crime scene tape and blood stains that the fire department had missed in their haste to clean it up. Rachel drew her gun and looked over the roof of the car. "Stay close to me." She motioned to my right arm. "How's your hand?"

I looked down at my arm, where blood was seeping out of the stitches. I absently swiped it away. "It'll work if I make it."

She paused, staring at the wound. "Fine, but stay close."

We navigated through the rows of warehouses sitting on the semi-abandoned docks. I whispered to Rachel, "Should be one of these buildings. Over there is where we found David."

Rachel nodded and crept to the closest building. She pushed open the side door of a dilapidated warehouse that looked like it had fallen straight out of a horror movie. Its eerie creaking sent shivers down my spine. Rachel and I stood on each side of the doorframe, looking in. The interior was dimly lit and had the iron smell of a rusty river.

She entered first. I stayed close on her heels in a covering position, pausing when I heard something fall to the hard concrete floor behind me.

Looking in the direction of the noise, I motioned to Rachel to hold. I focused and heard footsteps, and the sound of something being dragged. Then it abruptly stopped. I followed my gut and walked towards the opposite side of the warehouse, pausing at another door. Rachel came up quietly, signaling a three count. On three, she shoved the door open and went to the left, gun raised.

The interior of the second warehouse was brightly lit, but still carried an eerie feeling. I looked around at the empty shipping crates, long-forgotten piles of rope and tools dotting the interior. I smelled the same mixture of rust and water, but something else filled my nose.

I swallowed hard when I recognized the smell of blood. Fresh blood.

Rachel cursed behind me, staying out of clear sight like I should've. I'd taken a few steps into the middle of the room when I heard his voice.

"Maybe the clues were too easy to figure out. It doesn't matter, you're here now!" Evan's voice floated around us. The echo ricocheted off thick walls, making it hard to pinpoint where he was. "I can't say I'm not excited! It's always a pleasure seeing you, Emma. But I should apologize. I got bored and started without you." A few hard footsteps trailed along with his voice.

"If you hurt her in any way, I will destroy you piece by piece!" I shouted, my voice echoing.

Evan laughed, the sound bouncing around the empty room. "I didn't hurt her. Well, I mean she won't feel the pain for much longer. With each passing second, she feels less and less. It happens when your life is slowly draining out of you."

Fighting a surge of panic, I tried to convince myself Evan was lying. He wanted me to lose control and focus. Throw me off guard.

"Let her go! This is between me and you! Fucking come out in the open and show me she's alive. Let her go and you can have whatever you want." I criticized myself for negotiating with this madman, but I had to save Sasha.

No matter the cost.

I spun in a circle, hoping to spot Evan. It was impossible in the spacious warehouse. Rachel stood off to the far right, motioning to a ladder leading up to the second level. She ran and climbed up.

"Evan! Come out and show yourself." I was growing impatient.

A loud thump came from behind me and I whirled to look over my shoulder. Rachel had fallen to the ground, landing on a pile of old rope. She was unconscious, blood ran down her forehead. I ran to her out of pure gut instinct.

That was my mistake.

As I crouched next to her to check for a pulse, the air behind me moved. Before I could spin around, a hand wrapped around my right forearm, fingers digging deep into the stitches. I shrieked in pain and dropped the gun as another arm came around, slapping a piece of duct tape over my mouth.

"Shhhh, Emma, try not to wake the neighbors." Evan's breath was hot on my skin as he hugged me close against his body. I tried to fight out of his grip, but every move I made, fingers dug deeper in my wound. "If you stop, I'll let you see her." I fell limp, the pain starting to overwhelm any conscious thought. "Good girl."

He seized my left arm and held it behind my back to handcuff me. He shifted to stand next to me, his hand never leaving my right arm. "I'm glad you brought Agent Fisher with you. I haven't seen her in a very long time. I had fun with her for a few years, but like everything else, I grew bored after I killed her wife." Evan looked at me with cold dead eyes, a slow smile creeping across his face. "Then I found you." He kissed my cheek, laughing. "Two birds, one stone, as my momma used to say. This will be enjoyable for me."

He dragged me by the arm through the warehouse to a side room where the smell of blood was thicker. He kicked the door open and threw me to the ground.

My eyes fell upon Sasha, who was bent over a table at an odd angle, her arms stretched across the tabletop with her hands tied to the legs.

She was unconscious, still wearing the clothes from this morning, now soaked in blood.

Her face was covered in cuts and bruises, and duct tape covered her mouth. I scrambled to my feet when I saw the pool of blood under her, but Evan yanked me back on my ass. "Not yet."

I tried to jerk away. "I told you. Not. Yet." A hard punch struck the side of my head, knocking me out.

* * *

I woke to the shock of cold water being dumped over my head. Choking out a few gasps, relieved I could breathe through my mouth. The tape was gone, leaving my lips chapped with the taste of blood. Reality rushed back, and I tried to stand as soon as I saw Sasha on the table, but the cold steel of the handcuffs cut into my wrists. I looked down, assessing my predicament. I was handcuffed to an old steel chair, barely able to move more than an inch as the handcuffs pinched my skin as I wriggled against them.

"I'll kill you!" I screamed, fighting as the metal cut deeper into my wrists.

Evan threw the bucket to one side with an echoing clang as he moved to stand in front of me, bending down to my eye level. "Should've done that a long time ago, Emma." He ran a hand over my hair. I flinched away from his touch, and he grabbed a fistful of my hair to wrench me closer. "This is my parting gift to you. You should *never* be rude when someone gives you a gift." Evan flung my head back and stepped away, giving me a clear view of Sasha. Tears streamed down my face. She was still breathing.

Barely.

"You motherfucking fucker! I'll make you regret the day you ever met me!" I screamed through tear-ridden sobs.

Evan's hysterical laughter moved around, settling behind me. "Of course you will." His voice came from the left side.

I turned to see Evan drag Rachel's limp body across the floor. The woman was unconscious, her hands and feet tied together in a fetal position. He threw her to the concrete floor like she was a rag doll and wiped his bloody hands on her shirt. "You've enriched my life more than you can understand, Emma." He waved his hands around the room. "Look at all the lovely women you've brought for me!"

He grabbed another bucket, dumping its contents over Sasha. Shocking her awake.

"Ah! Sleeping beauty awakens!" Evan clapped as he moved around the table and grabbed a chair. He sat down next to her, and pulled a large hunting knife from his waistband. Sasha's eyes found mine and she whimpered behind the tape, struggling against the rope that bound her hands.

Evan bent closer to Sasha, tapping her cheek with the knife blade. "Is there something you would like to say to your lover, Detective Garnier? Any last words or sentiments? Or perhaps a confession?"

Sasha glared as he peeled back the tape. She was weak, but hissed at Evan. "I hope she kills you slowly, you fucking piece of shit."

Evan giggled and clapped his hands. "Still so feisty! Even as your life is about to end! I admire that, and see why the lovely Emma fell for you." Evan turned to me. "All glowing with happy smiles from your night together, she was oblivious until I had her in my arms. She fought admirably when I snatched her off your doorstep."

"Fuck you, you psychopath." Sasha spat out the words as she tried to lunge at Evan.

Evan's smile faded. Sasha had hit a nerve.

He jumped to his feet, grabbed her arm and cut the rope that bound it. He twisted her wrist at a strange angle, pulling a yelp from her lips. He waited until he had my full attention, then dug the tip of the knife into her wrist and drew it down.

I screamed as her blood poured out. Evan slammed Sasha's arm back down onto the table and tied it with the rope again, then quickly repeated the action with her other arm.

She tried to fight, but the more she moved, the more she bled.

I was sobbing. "Sasha, stop fighting it. I'll save you, I promise. Save your strength... please." I wiggled in the handcuffs, hoping to slip out of them.

Sasha was losing strength. She laid her head back down on the table. "Emma, don't make a promise you can't keep."

Her eyes grew heavy, more void of life as more of her blood spilled onto the floor.

"Sasha! I'll get you out, just wait for me! Wait for me!" Blood pooled around my wrists as the handcuffs bit deeper into my skin.

She shook her head. She knew better than I did. This was hopeless. "I love you, Emma," she whispered as her eyes drifted shut, her breathing slowing.

Evan waited for the final rise and fall of Sasha's chest before putting his knife away and replacing the tape over her mouth. Sighing loudly, he turned to me with a mournful look. "That took longer than I expected. She truly was waiting to say her goodbyes to you." Evan put a hand over his heart in a mocking way. "It's really very touching. She really loved you."

I didn't hear him. My focus was on Sasha, searching for any signs of life. I saw nothing. She wasn't breathing and the pulse in her neck had long faded away.

I closed my eyes, the anger surging harder as I pulled at the handcuffs. She couldn't be gone. There was no way. I looked again. Nothing. Pure rage bellowed out of my throat as I twisted my wrists. I'd break them if I had to.

Evan stepped towards me, wincing at my screams. "Are you done? I want to get this over with. I'm thrilled to have some fun with the lovely

Agent Fisher, too. I owe her far more than I owe you." He went to cover my mouth again with tape.

A rush of hatred filled my entire being, an all-consuming, desperate hatred. There was nothing left to lose. I was going to take Evan to hell with me.

As Evan reached up with both hands with a new piece of tape, I swung my head down, smashing his nose. Bones connected with bones with a loud crack and Evan stepped back, grabbing his face, screaming in pain.

I took advantage of the moment and kicked him hard in the stomach. He dropped to his knees with a grunt.

I ripped my right hand out of its handcuff, using my blood as a lubricant, breaking my pinky finger in the process. When my hand was free, I wrenched my arm out through the spines of the chair. I rushed Evan as he groaned, stumbling towards the desk.

When I was a few steps away, Evan saw me, and dodged to the side at the last second. I slid into the desk, knocking the wind out of myself, and crumpled to the ground, gasping for air like a fish out of water.

Evan clutched his stomach, blood pouring out of his nose. "Why do you make this so hard for yourself? It makes me want to cut deeper." Evan reached to the back of his waistband for his knife. The light caught its edges, and it glinted like a piece of morbid jewelry.

I tried to slide away, but Sasha's blood made the floor slippery, it was impossible for me to get away. Evan grabbed my leg, dragging me towards him.

He seized my right arm, roughly hauling me to my feet. His face was inches from mine as he growled. "No more fighting, Emma. This ends now."

I gasped in a breath before spitting blood in his face.

Evan backhanded me, splitting open my lip. "I'm done being nice. You will feel this. I promise." He lifted the knife up and just as he was about to slice across my throat, a loud pop filled the air and something hot grazed across my right shoulder.

Evan froze, tilting his head down at the blood pooling in a small lake on his shirt. He released me, and clutched a hand to his upper chest, frantically trying to stop the bleeding.

I staggered. Falling to the floor hard, my head smacked the concrete, and the room went blurry. Everything was hazy, and I heard another shot smack into Evan. He was dazed, and I saw him turn and stumble out of the room.

I fell into darkness to the sounds of more gun shots, followed by sirens, shrieking like angry birds.

Chapter 17

The whirring sound felt like a bee buzzing next to my ear, waking me from a dreamless sleep. I opened my eyes slowly, squinting to focus. The bee was a janitor, cleaning the floors outside my room. I groaned when it dawned on me. I was once again in the hospital.

I dropped my gaze to my right arm and saw it wrapped up from fingers to my shoulder in thick gauze. An IV line poked out of my left arm, snaking up to a bag full of painkillers. Still squinting, I made out the word morphine printed on the label.

Ah, that's why I couldn't feel anything.

The room was dark save an overhead light, illuminating the machines attached to my body. The clock on the wall stared down, obnoxious black hands pointing out the time. Four a.m.

The clock and I stared at each other like dueling cowboys as I pushed through the morphine haze to remember how I got here this time. I fumbled with thick fingers, mashing at the call button. A nurse I vaguely recognized rushed into my room. "Ms. Tiernan, is there anything you need?"

I fought through the cotton fields in my mouth. "My cell phone. I want it."

The nurse smiled and shook her head. "I can't let you have a phone in the ICU." Before I could issue a handful of profanities, Rachel appeared behind the nurse, and whispered something to her. The nurse gave me a look, nodded, and left the room.

Rachel moved to the foot of the bed. Her face was bruised. She sported a black eye and tiny stitches along the top of her forehead. She looked like hell, yet she was still smiling.

"Did you shoot me?" I rubbed my eyes. The world was enveloped in a weird pink haze.

Rachel blushed. "You moved right as I pulled the trigger. I grazed your shoulder." She looked at my bandaged arm.

I fidgeted, tried to sit up, and gave up when the pink haze began to spin. "You were knocked out and tied up."

"And he took my gun, but your father taught me to carry a backup after the Russians. I had a spare in an ankle holster." Rachel took a breath, folding her arms across her chest. "While Evan was occupied with his little game, I came to. Slid out of the rope and shot him before he could kill you."

I glanced at her wrists. The rope burns were still raw and red. "Is he dead?"

"He ran after the first two shots hit home. I followed the blood trail to the edge of the docks. His body wasn't found right away, but I just got word that harbor patrol pulled a body from the river this morning, with two gunshots to the chest. I'm waiting for final identification." Rachel pursed her lips.

I let out a sigh and leaned back. My stomach twisted at what I had to ask. "Sasha?"

Rachel's eyes softened. "Detective Garnier? She... we..." She paused, searching for words.

I held up a hand to stop her. I didn't want to hear it. I knew what I saw, and it was more than enough. Sasha couldn't have survived her injuries. "No, I don't want to know."

"Why don't you want to know?" Her tone was soaked with confusion.

"I was there, I saw everything. There's nothing more I want to know." Before Rachel could reply I hit the morphine drip, delivered as much as possible into my veins.

Rachel furrowed her brow, mumbling something that sounded like, *She's safe, Emma. Sasha's safe.*

But the drugs had hit, and her voice fell underwater, becoming a low hum. The world went deep purple and I passed out. Not hearing a damn thing Rachel said.

Four days later, I sat on my bed, waiting for my mother to bring me my discharge papers.

Aaron had visited, sharing the details of the warehouse scene. He'd become lead on Evan's body, processing it on our end before it was handed over to the FBI. The DNA tests were pending on the body. When it was pulled out of the river, it was already unrecognizable from decay and fish and had to be sent to the lab for testing. Aaron was upbeat until I growled at him for bringing me some of his mother's herbal tea. Shouting that no ancient Chinese medicine would heal me this time. He flipped me off, kissed me on the forehead and left.

Rachel tried to contact me to talk about Sasha, but I was so angry and miserable, I cut her off and told her to never bring it up again. Eventually, I'd pissed her off so much she completely gave up on me and left me alone.

I was angry, jaded, the entire time in the hospital. Shitty and rude to whoever was around. In time, fewer and fewer visitors came. I didn't care. I didn't want to hear their sympathy bullshit or heartfelt condolences.

I knew Sasha couldn't have survived the warehouse, and I didn't want to be treated like a grieving fucking widow.

I told Aaron to fuck off more than once, and resisted the urge to throw my jello at the therapist who worked on my shoulder. Her daily doses of positivity made me sick. She finally gave up when I told her she could shove her Hallmark phrases up her ass and just focus on getting my shoulder to the point where I could wipe my *own* ass. She ran out of the room with a red face. I'm glad I made her cry.

The doctor diagnosed me with post-traumatic stress disorder. My response to his very observant diagnosis was. "No shit, Sherlock. One would have that after being shot by a serial killer. Twice." He prescribed a mood enhancer and sent me on my way.

I'm pretty sure I made him cry, too.

The only thing that kept me somewhat sane was the St. Michael's medal my mother had given me on her last visit to the hospital. She explained I clearly needed extra eyes watching over me. I was beginning to think she was right. I needed something to focus on other than misery and pain.

I signed the discharge papers, only half listening to the post-care instructions and ignoring everyone as a nurse wheeled me out. My mother picked me up, since she was the only one who could deal with my bullshit.

During the ride back to my house, she started in with motherly advice. "I understand what you've been through, but it's time to shut down the pity party, Emma. You're pushing everyone away."

"It doesn't fucking matter. I want to be left alone. Plus, how can you understand what I'm feeling? You didn't see what I saw. Her lying there." I dropped off, not wanting to cry in front of her.

My mother slammed on the brakes, almost choking me with the seat belt, and glared at me. "Watch your fucking mouth around me. I do understand! You're my daughter and I almost had to plan a funeral twice. So, don't tell me what I do and do not understand. As for this." She poked me hard in the chest. "Leave some room in there for her. Regardless of what you saw, she needs to be in there."

I stared at my mother like she was crazy or had stolen some of my prescriptions. "Why? What's the point?" I didn't understand my mother's cryptic advice. Why was she telling me to hold on to another lost love?

My mother sighed, shaking her head. "When you're done being the Ice Queen, you'll figure it out. Ask and you shall receive." She threw the car into gear, and we drove the rest of the way home in silence.

* * *

At my house, my mother helped me in. She'd cleaned the entire house, stocked the fridge and made my bed. She stood over me like a protective mother hawk as I slipped under the covers, then tucked me in.

Her mood had softened from our pissing match in the car and she looked as if she had something to tell me but didn't know how to say it.

Settling into the soft pillows, I yawned. "Thanks, Mom. I'm sorry for being awful in the car. I'm just tired." I reached for her.

She patted the heavy gauze wrapped around my hand. "I know, Emma. I hate your job, but I love you so much. Both your father and I love you." She leaned over, kissing me on the forehead. "Don't be afraid to call if you need anything. Don't worry about safety. Liam sent a few officers to sit outside the house in unmarked cars." Her eyes watered, and she squeezed my arm before rushing out of the room. I heard her leave and lock the front door.

A thought sprang into my mind. I reached under my bed and found my extra gun, back in its holster. I smiled. I'd have to thank Aaron later and apologize for being an asshole.

Sleep evaded me, and I spent hours in bed staring at the wall. I grew restless, and decided to check my email. After twenty minutes of slow shuffling, I was out of bed and painfully sitting at my computer. I logged on to loads of well wishes from friends and co-workers. One from Captain Jameson informing me I was on a two-month medical leave from work. Seems word of my horrible behavior got back to him and his polite suggestion was that the time off would allow me to completely heal. He added a side note.

Take the time, Emma. It's a paid vacation. Do me a favor and stay the hell away from the office before I have more transfers to sign.

I cleared out the inbox, and moved onto the junk mail, when I scrolled across an email from Sasha. Dated the night she left my house. The night Evan found her. It was a random forwarded joke, but I opened it and read it. I stared at her name and the silly smiley face she added at the end, and broke down.

I sobbed. Why her? Why did he take her? Why didn't I fight harder?

I was angry at myself for not saving her. Not having the strength to fight him, and for letting her leave the house when I knew he would follow her.

It was my fault she was in that warehouse. Evan took her because I loved her. If I'd kept her at a distance, she would be going to work right now with her new partner, solving homicides on the Southside.

Pressing my head down on the desk, sobbing, I felt the St. Michael medal swinging around my neck. I opened my eyes and stared at it for a second, then sat up in the chair, grabbing it in my left hand. The medal sat in my palm, silently judging me for failing as a protector. I balled it into my fist, ripped it off my neck, and threw it across the room. "Useless piece of shit!"

I lost it. I grabbed the empty glass next to my laptop and threw it against the wall. I pulled books off shelves and threw them as hard as I could, screaming. I destroyed the office, smashing anything I could get my hands on. After running out of things to smash, I collapsed in the middle of the room on a pile of books, sobbing. My eyes fell on the back of the office door I'd tried to slam off its hinges, and saw Sasha's jacket hanging off the doorknob. She'd left it there in a hurry to get to work.

I stumbled to my feet, tripping over the mess, and slowly pulled it from the door. I buried my face in the material. It still smelled like her. I clutched it to my chest and cried harder, wondering what I could have done to save her. Overthinking my actions for the millionth time since I woke up in the hospital.

I crawled back to bed with her jacket tucked in my arms.

* * *

I was in a deep depression, stayed in bed for two weeks. I did nothing more than sleep and pick at my bandages. I stopped answering phone calls. I ignored the front door when the doorbell rang and let the mail pile up until it blocked the slot and the mailman couldn't shove more in.

One day, my mother appeared next to my bed. Her arms crossed over her chest and she shook her head in disappointment, at me, at my messy bed, at Sasha's jacket, which was now lying on the other pillow; it still held a hint of her scent. "You're better than this, Emma. Time to get up and live."

I shrugged and rolled deeper into the filthy blankets, watching her move around the room, trying to pick up pieces in the minefield of messes I'd left. She opened the office door, took one look, made a small noise and closed it. She pointed a finger my way. "That's all on you. You don't pay me enough to clean that big of a mess." She continued cleaning, filling the air with nonsense chatter.

I didn't listen too hard, and when I didn't respond, she huffed. Her hands fell to her hips, signaling I was about to get a motherly lecture. "The boys downstairs tell me you haven't gone outside since I brought you home. For Christ's sake, Emma, wallowing in whatever you're wallowing in isn't going to help you. I repeat, *you are better than this*. Get up. Move forward." She gave me her fiercest mom look.

I flushed with embarrassment. I hated disappointing my mother, and her words sunk deep. She chuckled at my red cheeks and shrugged. "Clean the mess up and you'll start to heal." She turned to walk out but stopped. "Call Aaron — he needs to talk to you. Try not to be rude. He's a good guy and it's his mother's egg drop soup you've been eating for the last week. He brought gallons of it over before you were discharged to make sure you didn't wither away. The man doesn't deserve your ridiculous rage. Love you!" She left before I could strike back with my own sass.

My mother was right, but I couldn't bring myself to care. I'd lost someone I loved, again, and I was tapped out. I'd go back to my closed off ways and maybe look at buying a bunch of rescue dogs.

I reached over and grabbed the phone to call Aaron. He needed an explanation, and a warning the ice storm was coming back into town.

Four rings later I got his voicemail. "It's Emma. Mom said you had something to tell me. Call me back, please. I turned the phone back on."

I was about to hang up when my heart begged me to ask where she was. I had to know where Sasha was, so I could say goodbye. I don't know why the urge struck me at that moment. Maybe it was my mother's guilt trip or the fact that every morning I woke up looking at the piece of her that lay on the edge of my bed. "And can you tell me where Sasha is buried? I need to say goodbye." I hung up before I started crying.

Putting the phone back on the side table, I took a deep breath. It was time to face the world. It would take me a day or two to slip the mask back on, but I would. I needed to go back to work.

After washing two weeks of filth off, I looked over my body in the mirror. The first gunshot was almost healed, now just a pink, puckered scar. The new scars under my old ones were almost invisible, thin pale pink lines. My right arm was still wrapped in gauze, but I could almost wipe my ass with it.

I dressed for the first time since I got home. In an attempt to clean the office I had destroyed, I opened the door, but after one look at the mess, I closed it again.

Maybe not today.

I left the house to walk outside along the lake and get some fresh air. My mother was right. I needed to get up and move around before my limbs rotted off.

Her exact words.

I had grabbed the phone and my gun before I left, forever paranoid because of Evan. Outside, I immediately spotted the two officers sitting on the other side of the street in an unmarked car. I nodded to them and walked down to the beach. It was warm, with a cool breeze as summer was moving to allow fall its turn.

Thankfully, the beach was empty; it was the middle of the day in the middle of the week. The lake and the sand were all mine. I walked, staring at the water, going over everything. I craved for someone to stop me and sit me down, to explain what was wrong with me, why I couldn't save the ones I loved.

I rolled my eyes at the silly internal pity party. I was better than this. I'd allow myself one day to be a pitiful human, and then that was it. No more.

As I sat in the sand, watching seagulls chase the waves, the phone rang. I answered without looking. "Hey Aaron."

"About damn time you called, Emma. Two weeks and I haven't heard shit from you."

"I know." I struggled. There was nothing to say. I just wanted to hear about Evan's body, and find out where Sasha was. "Did you get my message?"

"Not yet. Saw you called and called right back." Aaron took a breath, sounding relieved.

"Thank you for the soup." I cleared my throat. "Mom said you wanted to talk? And I want to ask you about something."

"Yeah, I wanted to let you know we closed the case on Evan and the Latin murders. The heavily decomposed body the harbor patrol pulled from the water is his. It floated about four miles away from where he fell in. Got stuck on a buoy and the fish had a field day, leaving us with very little until we checked dental records and made a match. Evan is dead. He's lying in the morgue with two gunshots to the chest. It's over, Emma."

I let out a sigh of relief, my eyes welling up. "Finally."

"I promise you, *it is him*. Agent Fisher will be out in a few days to double check the records. I'll forward you the autopsy report and dental records to see for yourself. He won't bother you ever again, Emma."

My mind went blank.

It was over.

I could stop looking over my shoulder, stop sleeping with a loaded gun under my pillow.

The bastard was dead.

"Thanks, Aaron, I should go." I choked on the words.

Aaron stopped me from hanging up. "Wait, what did you want to ask me?"

"Nothing. Never mind."

My life was mine again, but I had nowhere to go.

The woman I'd fallen in love with was dead. The man who took her from me was dead. I had nothing to push me. I was free, but lost.

I sat on the beach, dazed, unsure of where to go next. Aaron called two more times, but I didn't answer. He was calling to let me know where she was. He could leave a message and when I was ready, I'd listen to it.

Standing up, I dusted myself off and walked home. I waved at the officers and saw relief in their faces. They must have gotten the same call I did. They could go home to their families and eat like civilized humans. Stop babysitting me.

Aaron had left a message. I hit my voicemail button as I walked into the house, kicking aside mail before I climbed the stairs to the bedroom.

"Hey Emma, I'm confused. Why are you asking where she's buried?"

It wasn't that hard to figure out, Aaron. I huffed at the top of the stairs, about to call him when I noticed the bedroom door was closed. I'd left it open when I left the house.

I stared at it for a second as Aaron's message continued. "She's not buried anywhere, Emma. Sasha was released from Northwestern this morning. Shit, those must be some good drugs you're on." I toed the door open, looked up and dropped the phone.

Sasha sat on the edge of the bed, smiling.

"What are you doing here?" My voice was a raspy whisper.

"I forgot my jacket." She pointed at the jacket lying across my bed. "Aaron gave me a key this morning. Said I should stop by and get it."

"You're...?" It was like staring at a ghost. A very beautiful ghost I wanted to hold in my arms, but I was afraid she was a figment of my imagination.

"I'm right here, Emma." Sasha slowly stood up from the bed.

I dug the heels of my palms into my eyes and kept them closed. I was hallucinating from the pain pills and didn't trust anything. "No."

She grabbed my upper arms. "Yes, Emma. Look at me. I'm very real." Her hands slid to the sides of my face, tipping it up. "Look at me."

I swallowed hard and opened my eyes to lock on watery hazel eyes. Sasha smiled as I released a small sob. "I'm right here, Emma. Holding you."

My heart sat like a lead lump in my throat. I couldn't breathe. "I watched you..."

Sasha's smile faded as she cut me off. "I blacked out from shock and blood loss. The paramedics told me I stopped breathing for less than a minute before Rachel began CPR. I don't know what happened after I passed out." She winced and looked away.

I choked back a sob, tears running down my face. "It's my fault. I'm sorry. I should've made you stay with me. I should've forced my hands out of the handcuffs faster."

Sasha wiped away the tears, shaking her head. "It's not your fault. If we're playing the should've game, I should've stayed in bed with you like my heart begged me." She kissed my cheek. "It's over now, and I'm here."

I broke down, crying harder than I ever had before. All I could do was pull her close and wrap my arms around her. She was warm and alive.

Sasha's fingers dug into my shoulders, her tears soaking my shirt. I held her for a moment before leaning back to look at her, running shaky hands over her hair and face. She smiled through the tears, leaning into my touch.

"Why didn't they tell me you were in the hospital?"

Sasha sighed. "I was in the ICU for a few days and Rachel wanted to keep me in protective custody until the final word came down that Evan was dead." She grabbed my hand. "They released me this morning." She raised an eyebrow. "Rachel told me she told you I was safe, but she thinks the morphine you soaked yourself in made you forgetful. I've also heard you've been quite the handful? I believe Aaron's exact words were, you've been a frozen asshole."

I laughed, nodding in agreement. "I've been awful. Even I started to hate myself." I pulled her hand up to rest over my heart, trying to convince the last pieces of my mind Sasha was here with me. "I love you, Sasha. It's only been a couple of months, and I'm not one to rush into things." I met her eyes as she smirked at the joke. "But there is nothing in this world that will stop me from loving you."

Sasha sniffled, pressing her forehead against mine. "We're both finally letting go of the past and believing in love at first sight." She leaned forward and kissed the corner of my mouth as she whispered, "I love you too, just as much and maybe a little bit more."

Chapter 18

The next morning, I woke up with Sasha asleep on my chest. I brushed my fingers down her face to make sure this wasn't a dream. I watched her sleep for a few minutes before deciding to attack the mess that was my house. Starting downstairs, I grabbed the stack of mail I'd ignored for the last few years, silently cursing the postal system. Sitting at the kitchen island with a bowl of kids' cereal I'd found in the cupboard, I sorted through the mail, debating throwing it all out.

At the bottom of the stack was a white envelope with a return address of somewhere in D.C. As I unfolded the letter, the giant blue logo at the top made me pause.

It was the ubiquitous logo of the Federal Bureau of Investigation.

My initial reaction was to throw it out with the Voltaire lingerie catalogues but thought better of it.

Detective Lieutenant Emma Tiernan,
I'm sorry I've not been able to see you since your release from the hospital, but I had to return to Washington. I'll be back in Chicago in a week and would like to go over the casework you and your two partners did on Evan Carpenter and the Latin murders. As I mentioned during our last meeting, I believe Evan may be responsible for multiple murders throughout the country and possibly parts of Canada.

I know things are still fresh and healing, but I would appreciate it if we could sit down and go over the files. I examined the dental records Detective Liang sent to my office and found them to be a positive match. It appears Evan finally met his end.

I flipped to the envelope — the letter was dated almost ten days ago. I sighed, hating how fast federal agents get their hands on test results. I, the lowly detective in the lowly city, always had to wait through a backlog or bribe clerks with free coffee and pastries. I turned back to the letter.

Since you were the closest link to Evan and understood his motives, I believe you're the best resource to help me and the FBI put more puzzle pieces together and close some cold cases.

I will be in touch as soon as I arrive in Chicago. I also apologize for the strange formality of this letter, but it's part of the process of asking for your professional assistance.

I hope you are doing well.

Regards,
SAC Rachel Fisher.
BSU Quantico, Virginia

I held the letter in my hand, staring at the obnoxious logo. I'd been horrible to Rachel when I last saw her. I owed her some professional courtesy and a response to her request. At the same time, the last thing I wanted to do was sit in an office surrounded by stuck up federal agents, and go through stacks of Evan's madness.

After sticking the letter to the fridge using Aaron's hot dog magnet, I sorted the rest of my mail and finished another bowl of cereal, before cleaning the rest of the downstairs. I was half tempted to call my mother, tell her I'd pay her to clean the house however she saw fit.

I took a deep breath as I looked around the living room, smiling at a picture of me and Elle. I'd taken most of them down to the basement but had kept one up here. I didn't have to forget my past. I just had to remind myself to keep an open heart.

Upstairs, Sasha wasn't in bed like I hoped. She'd moved to the office and was rummaging through the mayhem I left in my rage. She was dutifully organizing the books I'd thrown on the floor, back onto shelves in alphabetical order. I stood in the doorway, watching her pick up book after book. She looked like a basketball player in a pair of my old running shorts and a marathon t-shirt I got for *almost* finishing the Chicago marathon four years ago. Even the bandages on her arms looked like sweat bands from the seventies.

My smile faded when I remembered what they hid from me.

Pushing off the doorframe, I walked into the room and bent to grab three psychology books. "Make sure they go in descending order by size, or you'll have to start over."

I startled her. "Jesus, Emma! Don't sneak up on me like that! I could've shot you!" She snatched the books out of my hands. "And if you want them in order by size, I suggest you do it. This is one hell of a mess. What happened here? Did the shelves collapse?"

She was right. I'd done quite the demolition job. "I fell."

Sasha gave me a dirty look and went back to cleaning. I reached over to lay a hand on her arm. "You don't have to do this. I can clean it up later. You need to rest. We need to rest."

"I can't. If I sit still too long, I think too much. I have to keep busy." She squinted at the spine of a forensic chemistry book.

I smirked. "I believe there are other things we can do to keep you busy."

She tossed the book to the floor as I tugged her closer for a kiss.

* * *

I stood in the bathroom, mentally digesting Rachel's letter while Sasha was in the shower. I hoped it would distract me from going in there to wash her back. Again. "So, something interesting came in the mail today."

She poked her head around the shower curtain. "What was it? An IKEA catalogue? Or another one of those Voltaire lingerie catalogues Aaron loves?"

I tossed a towel at her. "No, it was a letter from the Behavioral Science Unit at the FBI."

She stepped out of the shower, the towel now wrapped around her chest, and came up from behind to wrap her arms around my waist while I brushed my teeth. She murmured against my neck, her lips brushing over the skin. "Hmm. What do they want with you?"

I rinsed off my toothbrush, and held her arms in place as she laid her chin on my shoulder. I looked at her reflection in the mirror, debating telling her. I sighed, leaning back into her. "They want help with the cold cases Evan might have been linked to."

"You do know him better than anyone." I saw in her eyes she wasn't on board with the idea. "Do you want to help them?"

"I don't know yet. I'm not sure I want to look in the face of darkness again after barely surviving it. After *we* barely survived it." I laced my fingers in hers, glancing at the thin lines of stitches on her wrists. Tightening my jaw as flashbacks of that night struck. I held her closer. "I don't know what I want to do anymore." I traced the edge of her right wrist with a finger.

Sasha gently pulled her arms away, but not before grazing my breasts, and moved to the medicine cabinet. She reached for the first aid kit and smiled. "Help me wrap them? Since you're the doctor in the house."

"I haven't made a decision about that either. I'm leaning towards quitting everything and becoming a museum tour guide in Scotland." I held Sasha's wrist delicately as I began to wrap it. She flinched a few times when I grazed too close to the stitches. "Does it still hurt?"

She nodded once and became distant. She stepped away then, taking the gauze from my hands, continuing to wrap them herself.

"Sasha, are you okay?"

She sighed and closed her eyes. "I think so? Every time I close my eyes, he's there. Taunting me."

"He can't hurt you now. You're safe." It felt like a lie. The same fear struck in my heart every time I closed my eyes. Evan standing over me, his knife catching the light and blinding me with fear.

"I only feel safe with you, Emma. Call me cheesy, but it's the truth." She smiled with glassy eyes.

Kissing her on the forehead, I murmured against her skin. "I'll always be here."

Truth was, I felt helpless, no idea what to say or do. We both had gone through so much in the short time we had known each other, strengthening our bond. I held her close. Our bond hadn't been born out of trauma like many would suggest. It was a bond that existed from the moment we met in the Captain's office and was forged in the fires of hell.

We just happened to fall in love along the way.

* * *

I left Sasha in the bathroom and went to make some coffee. When I grabbed the cream out of the fridge, the FBI letter fluttered. I frowned. I'd call the Chicago office later and talk to Rachel. Maybe if I could help someone, I wouldn't feel so helpless in the world. Then again, maybe extensive therapy would be the next step. I couldn't expect either of us to wake up one day and be perfectly fine.

I ripped the letter off the fridge and brought it back upstairs to the half-organized office. I slid in, stepping over the stacks of books waiting to be reshelved and closed the door. I quickly called Rachel's Chicago office. Sasha was still in the bedroom getting dressed, and I didn't want her to hear me.

As the phone rang, a sinking feeling swirled in my stomach. Aaron was right. No matter what happened, I could never stay away from the job for too long. The retirement request had been filled out in its entirety years ago, but I'd never filed it. The paperwork still sat in the bottom drawer of my desk, waiting for Captain Jameson's elegant signature. I was literally a handful of letters away from changing my life, but had never followed through. I was addicted to the job, with no reason to quit now. Not with cold cases on my mind.

The phone rang twice before a high-pitched voice answered. "SAC Fisher's office. How may I assist you?"

"This is Detective Lieutenant Emma Tiernan, from the Chicago Police Department, Homicide Division. I believe Agent Fisher is expecting a call from me?"

"Please hold."

I doodled on a desk calendar while elevator music drifted through the phone. I hummed along with an instrumental version of the Magnum P.I. theme when the phone clicked.

"Hello, Emma, how have you been?" Rachel's voice was soft.

"Better than the last time you saw me." I paused. "I should apologize for my behavior. I'd thought Sasha, um, my old partner had suffered worse injuries." I cringed. I'd been such an idiot to immediately assume Sasha had perished in the warehouse.

I heard the smile in Rachel's calming voice. "I accept your apology, but I should apologize to you. It was my decision to keep her in protective custody and keep you in the dark until we had proof Evan was dead. I was afraid Evan had nine lives and would use every advantage to finish what he started." Papers shuffled in the background. "I'm taking this phone call as a sign you received the letter? I also assume you read it and aren't interested in my offer."

"I just found it buried under neglected junk mail. I've been distracted." I looked up to see Sasha walking into the office in a t-shirt and tiny underwear. She smiled over her shoulder as she continued to put books back on shelves.

"Understandable. I do hope this call is to tell me you'll help out with the cold cases?" The tone in Rachel's voice told me she was hopeful I was joining the team.

I thought for a moment. Why was I calling her? I'd just begun to close the chapter on Evan and the hell he brought with him. Now I was looking to dive back into it all, digging even deeper into the mind of a monster.

My silence must have been longer than polite pauses dictated, and I heard Rachel say my name. "Emma, I understand if you don't want to do this. You've been through a lot, but you are the closest link we have to Evan. You have the knowledge necessary to solve a handful of cases that have stumped the BSU for years. All I'm asking is for you, and possibly Detective Garnier, to come down to the FBI headquarters and sift through case files with me. I'm curious to see what you see in the files. I know it's been a short time, but the fresher a case is in someone's head, the faster clues come together. I'd like to get a few other families some closure."

I frowned at her words. Now I had to help. Rachel had asked, and I hated when I couldn't bring peace to the loved ones left behind. I was tasked with delivering justice for them. I took a deep breath. "What do we have to do? And where do we need to go?"

Sasha glanced over her shoulder, throwing me a confused look.

Rachel's tone now held a touch of excitement. "We can start here, in Chicago, or if you would like to wait a week, we can meet in D.C. My office there is far more private and away from prying eyes. I can do a quick briefing with you and Detective Garnier, then get you started on the cases. I'll have a courier deliver a detailed package with your travel arrangements in the next day or so. That is, if you're willing to come to me, Emma?"

I smiled at Sasha as she sat on the edge of the desk, her shirt riding up to expose more thigh. "Yes, I'll come. It'll be a nice change of scenery. How long do you need me for?"

"That's completely up to you and how much time you want to dedicate. You can leave at any point and end your agreement with me. It's not an official contract that will bind you to the FBI for years."

"Alright." I leaned forward, rubbing my temple. A fierce headache was brewing, and Sasha's naked thigh was doing very little to help me concentrate.

"Do you have any more questions, Emma?"

"I don't think so, no." I smiled at Sasha as she looked down at me, obviously curious about my conversation.

"Fantastic! The courier will deliver by the end of the day today or first thing in the morning. Thank you again. I hope we can make something good come out of Evan's evil." Rachel hung up after a polite goodbye.

Sasha scooted off the desk onto my lap. Her legs straddled my waist. "So, who was that?"

I wrapped my arms around her, slipping my hands under her shirt and pressing my palms against her warm skin. "That was Agent Fisher. I told her I'd help with some loose ends left by Evan. She asked you to come along since you also dealt with him."

Sasha gave me a tight smile. "I don't remember much, but I guess if it helps, I'll go with you. I don't want to let you out of my sight. Every time I do…" She sighed, running her hands along my shoulders. "Promise me if it gets too tough, we walk away. I love you far too much to watch you get sucked back in."

"I promise." Hearing her say I love you made my heart race.

She grinned, kissing me as I gripped her waist. We'd made love after I'd scared her, cleaning my office, but it'd been rushed and full of a need to feel something.

I kissed her now, ardently, and Sasha pressed into me, moaning as my fingers found the edge of her shirt. My hand lay flat against her back as goosebumps dotted her skin. Her hands fell to the sides of my face as she pulled me closer, biting my bottom lip.

I felt her desire grow as she sat on my lap. I moved a hand back to her front, my fingers running across the soft skin of her stomach. I moved my kisses to her chin and then to her shoulder, nipping. Sasha buried her face in my neck as I pushed past the thin cotton panties she wore.

She rasped against the shell of my ear. "Please."

I bit her shoulder as I slid two fingers inside of her. Sasha's back arched, lifting her hips to start a slow rhythm. I kissed her pulse as it raced with every moment of my fingers. She made eye contact, moving faster and faster against my fingers before moaning out my name, throwing her head back, riding out the waves of her orgasm.

I couldn't resist the sight of the flushed woman. I drew my hand from her and stood, holding Sasha as she recovered.

I kissed her again, but with an intense sense of need I'd never experienced before, catching her off guard. She grabbed the back of my head, holding me against her mouth. Our teeth bumped and bit at swollen lips.

I grabbed her hand, guiding it to where I needed her. Sasha took over, pushing past my pants. She didn't hesitate, and her fingers roughly entered me. I squeezed my eyes shut to keep from losing it as soon as I felt her inside.

She grinned against my lips. "God, Emma, I never knew the Ice Queen had it in her." She pushed up with her fingers before I could respond. Forcing me from her mouth to bury my face in her soft hair. She leaned forward, placing hot kisses between my neck and shoulder. I couldn't resist; she was taking her sweet time, giving me what I needed. My fingers found her still ready for me, and I slipped back into a very sensitive area. Smirking when she cried out against my skin.

Our hands moved in unison until both of us collapsed onto the desk, our skin tingling with electricity. Sasha wrapped strong arms around me as I laid on top of her, catching my breath. I whispered, kissing a flushed cheek. "I don't think I'll ever look at this desk with the same respect again."

She laughed, blushing. "Me neither." She covered her face with a hand, giggling. "At this rate, we'll never get your office organized."

Propping my chin on her chest, I shrugged. "I'm totally fine with that." I sat up, pulling Sasha with me. "You need to get dressed. I want to take you out for hot dogs."

"Hot dogs? Is this our first date?" Sasha slid off the desk, struggling to stand on rubbery legs.

"Yep. Hot dogs on the first date, pizza on the second, and if you're lucky, tacos on the third."

Sasha chuckled, smoothing out her shirt. "I could make a joke about tacos, but I'm not Aaron." She kissed my cheek, winking as she left the office.

"Thank God for that."

* * *

We flew into the nation's capital two days later. A government sedan driven by an agency intern picked us up at the airport and took us straight to the FBI building. We were dropped off with instructions to call the intern when we were ready to go to the hotel. The FBI was giving us the full red-carpet treatment. I was pretty sure the kid would've unpacked our bags if I'd asked him to. He handed me an envelope as he held my door open, explaining Rachel was waiting for us. The sense of urgency from the kid told me Rachel was eager to get started.

Inside the lobby, we were greeted by a lovely middle-aged woman wearing a well-fitting business suit and a genuine smile. A rarity with federal agents. She moved with a sense of purpose and when she greeted us, her firm handshake told me she meant business.

"Detective Lieutenant Tiernan and Detective Garnier, nice to meet you both. I'm Susan Clark, SAC Fisher's administrative clerk. She's tied up in a meeting right now and asked me to get you settled in." When Susan looked at Sasha, I thought I saw a flicker of recognition float across her eyes, but dismissed it when she motioned towards the elevators. "Please, if you'd like to follow me."

Susan walked two steps ahead of us, chatting about the building and where to get coffee. She took us to a security room where Sasha and I were photographed and fingerprinted. A moment later, we were clipping on shiny new visitor badges and given a large manual highlighting the rules of being a professional visitor to the FBI.

Susan chuckled at the massive document in my hands. "Don't worry about memorizing it. It's standard protocol to issue a copy to all professional visitors and consultants. It makes a great doorstop or fly swatter."

Susan led us through a side entrance, into an elevator, then punched in a code, sharing fun facts about the FBI in a chatty tone. I ignored her, but found it curious there was no digital floor counter. The elevator was just a steel box controlled by this chipper woman. The doors opened, and Susan stepped out first. She kept a brisk pace and it was hard to keep up with her. Sasha was a step behind me and had been quiet from the moment the intern dropped us off.

I slowed, tapping her arm. "You okay?"

She looked distant and wary. "Yeah, it's just... very intimidating. I'm only a street cop turned rookie detective. I'm not used to this level of law enforcement."

I smiled. "Do you remember your first day as my partner? I think that was far worse than this."

Sasha's cheeks turned a soft pink. "It was one of the worst first days on the job I've ever had, but totally worth it."

My cheeks warmed with a tinge of guilt, and I turned back to Susan, who was now a good three feet ahead of us. We had to jog to catch up as she weaved her way through a maze of hallways. I had opened my mouth to make a comment about her efficiency, when she suddenly stopped in front of a large black steel door.

She swiped her badge, then input a five-digit code on the keypad. Shoving the door open with both hands, Susan used her body to hold it open for Sasha and me to step through. I'd taken note of these strange details and wondered what I had gotten us into. I wanted to solve cold cases, not creep around the hallowed tombs of the FBI. Something felt off. I didn't like it.

The office was of a clean modern design and oddly soothing. Off to the right sat a large desk with a computer and phone I assumed were Susan's.

She closed the door behind us and smoothed out her jacket. "If you'll follow me again, I'll take you to SAC Fisher's office. She's on her way down now."

Susan made another efficient motion that made me think she was quite possibly half robot, and turned to walk down a hallway past her desk. She rounded another corner and opened a large, frosted glass door with *SAC R. Fisher* painted on it in black.

Susan kindly pointed to the two chairs that sat in front of a stainless-steel desk. Multiple monitors lined its edge, and the back wall was full of large black filing cabinets with digital locks on them. The setup was just like a spy movie. It pulled a smile from me as I imagined the Bond-like secrets they held.

Susan stood off to the side, hands clasped together in front. "Please have a seat. It'll only be a few more minutes. Would either of you like some coffee? Water?"

I continued to look around the massive office, ignoring the beverage request, leaving Sasha to speak for the both of us. "No, thank you, we're fine."

Susan smiled and stepped out of the office, closing the door behind her. Sasha sat down while I walked around the office marveling at the endless sea of filing cabinets. My imagination was replaced with a reality of what those filing cabinets held. It sent shivers of fear through my veins.

I had similar cabinets in my corner office. Drawers upon drawers filled with monsters, was the only way I could explain it. I leaned over to get a closer look at the digital lock. What was in there, and why were they locked with such fortification?

"The locks are temperature sensitive and calibrated to my ambient body temperature. If they detect one or two degrees of difference, this wing goes into lockdown." Rachel's voice was soothing, yet soaked in authority.

I immediately straightened up, turning to where Rachel stood in the open doorway. She gave a professional smile and stepped into the office, briefcase in hand. She extended the same polite smile to Sasha. "Detective Garnier, it's nice to see you again." As Rachel moved to sit behind her desk, I took a harder look at her. She was dressed in the standard federal government dark grey pantsuit, and as she looked at me, I saw she commanded respect from anyone she encountered. "I'm glad you decided to join us. I need all the help I can get."

Sasha nodded, looking down at her hands. "Not a problem, whatever I can do to help." Sasha was nervous, and it had me curious as to why. I'd only asked her to come along and help; the focus would be on me and my dealings with Evan.

Rachel tucked her briefcase away and gave me a direct look. One that said I needed to sit down and pay attention.

I took the hint and sat next to Sasha. "Sorry about being nosy. I've never seen a setup like this." I motioned to the wall of filing cabinets.

Rachel looked away, shuffling a stack of papers. "Curiosity killed the cat." I caught an edge to her tone, adding to my gut feeling there was more to this meeting than digging into the mind of a killer. "I wanted to brief you as soon as you landed. We've wasted too much time with these cold cases. I'd like you to brief me on your experiences — past and present — with Evan Carpenter, and get the ball rolling."

Sasha spoke first. "What can we do to get started? I'd also like to get the ball rolling, for the sole purpose of putting this all behind me, us."

Rachel's polite smile grew stale. "What I need, from the both of you, is a new, individual statement of exactly what happened. I know you gave statements at the hospital, but I want to be able to gather clean statements from the both of you. Emotion often corrupts memories." Rachel looked between Sasha and me, and I grew uncomfortable. "Detective Garnier, I'll need as much detail as you can provide about your time in Evan's custody."

She then turned to me. "As for you, Lieutenant, I need everything you can remember about growing up with Evan and the recent encounters. I believe you're our best chance at creating a timeline and MO."

I shrugged. "You probably know more than I do, but I'll try. I did my best to forget my life in Detroit."

Rachel turned back to Sasha. "Detective Garnier, you will be interviewed by another agent to preserve your statement. Later on, I'll be interviewing you and the Lieutenant together. Do you mind if we start right now?"

Sasha swallowed hard. "That's fine with me."

Rachel picked up the phone and pushed a button. "Susan, please escort Detective Garnier to Interview Room Five. Call Agent Markus and have him meet you there. He'll be conducting Detective Garnier's interview." Susan confirmed her instructions and disconnected. Rachel's stale smile never wavered as she engaged Sasha again. "You'll be working with Agent Steven Markus. He's been brought in by my boss to be the second in charge on this project and will treat you right. Please, tell him everything you know."

Sasha looked to me for support, and I reached for her hand when Susan opened the door.

"Detective Garnier, please follow me."

"Of course." Sasha stood up, and as she walked by, I grabbed her fingers and whispered. "I'm here if you need me." She squeezed back, then let go to follow Susan out of the room.

As the door clicked shut, I leaned forward. "So, which agent do I get?" I cocked an eyebrow, starting to get unsettled and agitated.

"Me." Rachel turned stoic. "Considering the extent of your involvement with Evan, I can't trust anyone else to properly gather information." She sat back. "Call me anal, but I want to make sure this isn't screwed up. I've been chasing Evan for decades."

Even though she was polite, agonizingly polite, Rachel's tone was irritating. She was treating me with a clinical approach, like I was a case study, and not a person. I saw through her façade. It was the same approach I'd learned in my forensic psychology courses. The words and tone used were cold and meticulous.

"You know, you can talk to me like a person and not a lab rat." I said it without attitude. She'd been an ally in this entire debacle, but I didn't like the vibe she was giving off. It almost reminded me of Evan.

"Understandable, but it comes with the territory. I must maintain an unbiased outlook. You should know that, being a homicide detective." Her words softened.

I nodded in agreement. This was not a social call. I had to follow her protocol just as anyone else would do for me in my own interview rooms back in Chicago. "Can we please get started then? What do you want to know?"

Rachel didn't answer. She stood and walked to one of the many filing cabinets surrounding her desk. She tapped a five-digit code and yanked the drawer open, then flicked through files before pulling out a thick stack. She walked to the side of the desk, holding the files out. "Read over these again, please."

"What are these?"

"These are your juvenile records, your foster home records, as well as your parents' homicide file, along with the unedited report from the responding officer who was the catalyst for your escape from Evan and foster home life." Rachel perched on the desk. "They are complete and accurate records. I know you read over them in haste, trying to find a lead, but I need you to read them again, carefully. They could trigger a memory about Evan." She raised an eyebrow. "I've found in past cases that allowing a person to fill in the gaps of who they are will open up old memories. You remembering your time with Evan as a teenager might tell me something from the past that carried through to his adult life. Patterns. I'm looking for patterns."

I flipped through the records. They were the exact same ones Rachel had given me in Chicago. I slid these to the bottom of the stack, not wanting to review my youthful embarrassments.

"You should read those. Like I said, complete and accurate." I looked back up at Rachel and was met with authoritative blue eyes. God, she was a pushy woman.

"I'll get to them." I opted to start with the case report of my parents' murder. I'd known they died in a gruesome manner but could never get my hands on the full, unedited report. The Detroit Police claimed they lost it, and hadn't bothered to look for it. I knew it was them trying to cover up that they'd made no effort to look into the murder of two junkies — collateral damage of underfunded police department.

My parents had been full blown heroin addicts. Neither had held a steady job, and any state aid money they got was spent on drugs as quickly as they cashed the checks. According to the report, the night they died was the result of a drug deal gone bad. My father took a dirty hit and attacked the dealer with a syringe, stabbing him in the eye. I cringed again as I read what happened next. The dealer shot my father ten times, then emptied a magazine into my mother, who at the time was lying in the bathroom with a needle still in her arm. She had been on the verge of an overdose. The dealer just sped up her demise.

The rest of the file went over the ballistics and evidence collected at the scene. I couldn't bear to look at the scene photographs again. It now felt too personal, not a hunt for answers, evidence. I flipped through them quickly. Blood was everywhere in the house, and my stomach twisted with long-forgotten memories. Memories I knew I'd retained from an extraordinarily young age, memories therapy would soon pull out of the darkness.

The lead homicide detective had found me in a crib next to the bathroom, sitting quietly as if nothing had happened. He'd written in the report that I didn't cry, and never asked for my parents. I was taken to the children's hospital to check for injuries, and not once did I cry. I remained silent and compliant, an easy child, as noted by the nurses.

Three days later, I was placed in my first foster home.

I struggled, scanning through the file. Even though I had completely disconnected from that part of my life, it was difficult to read. I closed the file and set it on Fisher's desk.

"Why did you want me to read that?"

"I want you to understand your lack of sensitivity towards homicides is not your fault. I wanted you to know why you latched onto Evan when you were younger, why it was easy for him to manipulate you. You lack the sensitivity to cry, express fear and exhibit other positive emotions. You're high on the apathy scale. It could be the initial shock of watching your parents' murder that recoded your brain."

Caught off guard by her words, I glared at the woman. "I don't quite understand. Lack of sensitivity towards cases? I'm not cold-hearted."

"That's not what I mean. You have an ability to look past emotion and focus on the facts. You also need to know why you sometimes feel distant from everyone."

Rachel's unsolicited psychoanalysis pissed me off. "Please stop. You're trying to analyze me, and that's not what I came down here for. I pay a therapist weekly to do that, and she has softer chairs. I'm here to help you solve cold cases. So, stop trying to pick my brain. You know from my record I have a Master's in psychology. I see through your bullshit."

Rachel showed no reaction. She picked up my parents' file and my juvenile records, then walked back to the filing cabinet, locking them away. She sat again, pressing her hands against the desk. "I apologize if you misinterpret my motives. I'm trying to lay down a foundation of your psyche. It is basic psychology, but I need to understand you to understand Evan." Rachel grabbed a notepad. "Basic psychology questions are protocol for any BSU interview. It's a requirement to ask questions that will pull a reaction out of a subject, especially in the nature of this case, where more than one party is involved with the murders."

I was embarrassed that my cold, frigid persona had popped its head out, and sighed. Maybe I should start taking the mood enhancers the doctor prescribed. They might keep my mouth shut when I couldn't.

Rachel continued. "As for your educational background, yes, I did already know. I know all about you, including your personal relationship with Detective Garnier."

I flinched but held my tongue, moving the subject away from Sasha. "What do you mean, the nature of these murders? Is there more than one party involved?"

Rachel smirked. "Nice deflection, but be warned, I'll be asking about your relationship with your partner. Again, it's just protocol. As for what I said about more than one party involved, we have a deep suspicion that Evan may have had a partner — or partners — assisting him."

I shook my head. "No, Evan was a selfish bastard, always was when we were growing up. He only liked having someone around he could abuse. That's what he did to me. I was the rag doll he threw around whenever he craved control."

"Fair enough. But have you heard of Stockholm syndrome?"

"Of course, that's basic psychology 101." I glared at Rachel as I said it.

"Evan might have been selfish, but at the same time, he also liked having a one-person audience. As you were when you were teenagers. He had a rapt audience and abused you to stay tuned, so to speak."

I leaned forward in the chair, digging fingers into my temples. All this psychobabble was driving me nuts. I was worried about Sasha and what they were asking her. I wanted to leave.

I looked up. "I think I'm done for the day. Where is Detective Garnier?" I wanted to maintain some sort of professionalism regarding Sasha until I established how much Rachel wanted to push at our relationship.

"She's in good hands. Trust me, no one will hurt her. I know how important she is to you." Rachel's tone warmed ever so slightly, but it was still far from friendly.

"I'll wait for her outside — or can I go see her now?" I stood from the chair and walked towards the door.

Rachel quickly stood, holding a hand up. "Wait, I'll walk you to her."

I paused midstep, waiting for Rachel to come up behind me. She opened the door and led me down a maze of hallways to another large office where Sasha was being interviewed. Rachel opened an unmarked glass door and entered a nondescript concrete room. The door closed behind her before I could get a look inside.

When Sasha walked out of the interview room, Rachel was right behind her. She looked haggard and beaten down. She walked right into my arms, and buried her face in my neck. "I can't do this."

I whispered back. "It's okay. They're just trying to get information out of you. It wasn't fun for me either." My eyes met Rachel's as she watched our interaction, and I squeezed Sasha closer. "Can we leave now?"

Rachel nodded and silently led us down into a basement garage, where a car was waiting. Before I got into the back with Sasha, Rachel grabbed my arm. "I apologize if I was too hard earlier. You do understand, though, why I must stay distant when I ask these questions. Will you come back tomorrow?" The look in her eyes poured sincerity.

"I'll be back, but keep the psychobabble to a minimum." She smiled and nodded, yet I didn't believe her.

The second I sat in the car, Sasha laid her head on my shoulder and sighed. As the car pulled away, I asked. "What did you tell them?" I kept my voice low, so the driver wouldn't overhear everything.

"They questioned me about when Evan kidnapped me. Random weird questions of what he said to me, what exactly he did to me. It was hard, Emma, I broke down."

"I'm sorry." I brushed a hand across her cheek.

"They asked about you and about us. I told them the truth about our relationship." Her voice trembled.

I closed my eyes, hating I'd brought us here. I lived a relatively private life, and everything was being pried apart. All because of my past coming back with a desire to kill me. A past that was being revealed as my future was being placed in the spotlight. All because of some monster with a knife.

For the first time in my career, I was thankful for selfish reasons a criminal was dead.

Back at the hotel, Sasha crawled into bed and passed out from exhaustion. Walking around the darkened room, I stared out at the capital city, illuminated by streetlights, the world a blur of dots of light. I needed to call my father and find out more about Rachel. I wanted the upper hand when she went full profiler on me.

I stood at the end of the bed, watching Sasha sleep. For a moment, I wondered if our life could ever be normal. I wanted to wake her up and run to the airport, grab a flight to anywhere or nowhere, and live a quiet life where neither of us would have to look back into the darkness.

I sighed, and told myself to stop dreaming the impossible. Instead, I climbed into bed next to Sasha, wrapping my body around her, promising I'd never let her go.

* * *

The next morning, they separated Sasha and I again. She was taken to the interview room with Agent Markus and I was left in Rachel's office, alone. With each passing minute of waiting for her to leave another meeting, I grew more frustrated with everything. She was sweating me, like a suspect waiting to be interviewed. I leaned back in the chair, putting my feet up on her desk, and closed my eyes.

I must've drifted off. I woke to Fisher tapping my feet.

"You're late." I straightened up, yawning.

"A last-minute meeting ran longer than I hoped." She removed a file from her briefcase and set it in front of her. "What exactly is the nature of your relationship with Detective Garnier?"

No hesitation with that shot to the gut. "Why does it matter? I'm not here to be interrogated or to reveal aspects of my personal life to the FBI. I'm here to go over case files and evidence."

"This is true, but in a way Detective Garnier is evidence. I do ask these questions for a reason. I need to know why Evan chose her as a target and if it goes beyond random selection."

I was furious that Rachel referred to Sasha as a piece of evidence. "He chose her because she's close to me. We were partners and coworkers, and to an extent, friends. He wanted any advantage to get to me, and she was one. She's not evidence. Next question."

Rachel ignored my outburst. "What exactly is the nature of your relationship with Detective Garnier?"

I held firm, glaring at Rachel. She did not waver, nor did she flinch. She was a pro. There was no way I'd break past her steel walls or get under her skin, no matter how much I deflected her questions or tried to reroute her psychology with my own skills.

I admired this for a second. She was as stubborn as I was, maybe worse.

Biting my bottom lip, I funneled out some anger. "Detective Garnier and I are close friends."

"How close, and do you trust her?"

"We're very close. That's it. I'm still lost as to why you're asking these personal questions."

Rachel repeated herself. I laughed and ignored her.

Then I said something I shouldn't have.

"No wonder you didn't make it as an undercover agent. You lack heart and tact. Good thing my dad had your back." I cringed as it came out, but she'd pushed my buttons like Sasha had in the first few days of her FTO. Once those were pushed, there were no holds barred.

Rachel flinched for a second, but quickly recovered. She took a deep, calming breath. It was obvious I'd hit a little too close to home. I grinned at the small victory, and leaned back in my chair.

Rachel flipped through her notes, speaking without looking at me. "I believe Evan had an accomplice. The characteristics of the Latin murders suggest it. The evidence does not match up to it being a singular perpetrator, and I need to explore all possibilities. It appears Evan had someone on the inside."

I cut her off. "Are you suggesting I helped him?"

"Not exactly. But he managed to get to you way too easily, and looking at the reports, he had been following you for some time." Rachel flipped through more pages. The sound of paper against paper infuriated me.

"Not exactly? That sounds like a Goddamned accusation to me. Why the fuck would I put myself through that? Did you read in your little file what he did to me? The damage he's done to me, physically and emotionally? Fuck!" I threw my hands up at her, fighting the urge to stand up, walk out the door, and fly back to Chicago.

Rachel sat, waiting for the outburst to pass. "I'm not suggesting nor implying it was you. What *I am* suggesting is someone close to you could've been helping him collect the necessary information to get to you. Whether it's a coworker, a family member, or even a significant other, there's a hidden connection."

The light bulb clicked into place. And shattered. "Wait, you're asking these questions about Sasha because you suspect she's been helping the man who tried to kill me? And almost killed her? You're out of your mind, Rachel."

I was livid, leaning forward in my chair, yelling at her. "You want to know the true nature of our relationship?! Fine, Sasha and I are lovers. I love her more than an insensitive bitch like you could ever understand. She saved me, and I know deep in my heart she'd never betray me. She'd never be Evan's pawn." I slumped in the chair, panting.

Rachel again waited for me to stop, cocking her head silently, asking if I was done. I rolled my eyes.

She closed the file with slow purpose. "I think we're done for the day. I'll escort you to the waiting room. Detective Garnier has a few more hours to go, but there are some lovely magazines to read."

She had an edge to her tone. I knew I had overstepped — more than once — but didn't care. I'd made the decision to leave for Chicago as soon as I could grab Sasha and walk out the door. I sat, staring at Rachel, wondering what my father saw in her to save her, all those years ago.

Rachel grabbed the files and placed them in her briefcase. She opened a side drawer and removed a small black box.

She placed the simple band on her left ring finger, looking directly at me. Rachel saw the question in my eyes. "I don't wear it during interviews. It reveals too much. Ultimately distracting subjects from the purpose of the interview."

She was using psychology again. I raised an eyebrow, throwing my own psychological warfare in the mix. "You said Evan killed your wife. Why do you continue to wear a wedding ring? You poke at my mind, chastise me for trying to keep my private life close to my heart, but here you flaunt yours. Asking for questions to be asked, a story begging to be told."

Rachel tilted her head. "He did kill my wife, and this is what I have left. A memory to remind me why I'm putting someone like you through this. It's cliché, but I want to make sure no one else loses what I have, and what you almost did."

I sighed hard. Rachel was speaking as Rachel again, not the cold FBI agent who sought answers. "I'm not coming back. I don't want to continue this project of yours. Evan is dead, and I want to be done with this. I want to retire and find a life with someone I love."

"I know. Your emotional outbursts have given me enough to go on, along with what Detective Garnier has provided us with." Rachel spun the ring on her finger.

"My *emotional outbursts*? Are you telling me I'm a suspect?"

She sighed. "No, Emma. Your emotional outbursts show me you've outgrown the weak mind you had when you were a teenager. There is no way Evan could manipulate you now. You're too passionate about remaining independent and in control of your life." Rachel tried to smile to make her words land a bit softer. She was still picking my brain apart, trying to create an open dialogue, in hopes I'd reveal my secrets to her, give her more than I really wanted to. I knew this game and wouldn't feed into it. I had underestimated her. Rachel was a professional manipulator.

I stood, folding my arms across my chest. "Can I leave?" I was frustrated with this turn of character in Rachel. I'd made a mistake in trusting her. I was just another step on the ladder of SAC Rachel Fisher's steady ascent inside the FBI.

"Yes. Let's." Rachel escorted me to the elevator. As we stood in silence, I'd caught myself looking at her ring finger, intrigued why she held onto a wedding ring when her wife had been murdered. What a horrible, constant reminder. One of the many reasons why I never wore the rings I found in Elle's closet. They'd remind me every day of what I'd lost.

I was tempted to poke and prod at Rachel. There was something curious about the woman. Suspicious, and curious. She was cold, rude like most federal agents, but her dedication to picking me apart went past common interest in finding answers. I left it, my desire to peel her apart, and stared at her reflection in the elevator doors and wondered why my father had saved her.

When the doors opened, Rachel led me to the waiting room, a very drab room with a couch and television that looped the Bloomberg report.

Rachel turned and extended her hand. "It was nice to work with you, Detective Lieutenant Tiernan. I'm sorry it didn't work out. You're a brilliant detective. I wish we could've come to an understanding."

I took her hand. "We would've if you'd left the psychology at home. I wish you luck, Rachel."

She held my hand for a second as she met my eyes, then let go. "I wish you the best, you and Detective Garnier. I hope you can put this behind you and live again."

Her words were full of sincerity. Rachel had seen right through me. She could see the ocean of pain I'd been treading in for decades.

I smiled as I watched her walk away. For a moment, I wanted to run after her, to stop her and follow her back into the windowless room, and scream more. It occurred to me that she had pushed my buttons on purpose, forcing me to release everything I held in. Attempting to clear my mind so I could focus again.

I sighed, sat on the couch, and made a mental note to call my therapist in the morning.

* * *

I sat in the waiting room for hours. I read all the magazines, memorized the afternoon's stock outlooks and counted every crack in the concrete floor. Right as I was about to lose my mind and search out Susan to get me a coffee, Sasha appeared, her head down and huddled into herself. I stood up as she stumbled into my arms, sniffling against my chest.

"Take me home, Emma."

Chapter 19

Sasha was silent during the ride back to the hotel. She said very little in the room, took a shower and went to bed. I stayed up to make the arrangements for our trip home in the morning. I would not put Sasha through anymore. If her ordeal had been anything like I'd experienced with Rachel, I understood why she was broken down. She didn't have the thick walls I did.

I sat in the small chair near the window, watching Sasha sleep. I'd sell the house in Chicago and take her out to California or to the Pacific Northwest. I needed to go somewhere far from the memories of my life. If I didn't, I'd soon lose the both of us.

I dozed off, not realizing it until my phone vibrated in my pocket. I squinted at the number. A local D.C. area code. I assumed it was either Rachel or Susan. Slipping into the bathroom so I wouldn't wake Sasha, I closed the door.

"Hello." I answered with a bitter tone, ready to tell them to please kiss my ass.

"Did I have a funeral, Emma? Was it nice? Or did you just keep my *'body'* in the morgue until the evidence was collected and you could hold your hands up in victory, shouting case closed?"

My entire body seized. I grabbed the bathroom counter to prevent myself from falling over.

"Oh, the silent treatment again? You need to work on your social skills, especially for a police detective like you. You have to learn how to talk to people." His nasty chuckle buzzed against my ear.

"How." The word puffed out in a shallow breath.

"How? How could I still be alive? Excellent question! You have a body and proof of death!" Evan was excited, but coughed between every other word. "Falsifying dental records really isn't hard these days. The difficult part is keeping the original owner alive long enough for you to utilize them. You must keep them fed, watered, and contained in a dark place where no one would ever think to look. But I had a hunch you and your crack crime-fighting team had wised up. That this time, they wouldn't waste their time charging down the doors to rescue you."

My heart raced as if it was going to explode. I swallowed a few times to force it back down into my chest. "Agent Fisher shot you twice. I saw the bullet go through you."

"She did shoot me twice! Agent Fisher is quite the marksman. But with the combination of you bleeding on the floor, and your love dead on the table, chasing me became a second thought." Evan paused for obvious effect. "Do you want to know how I did it?"

I couldn't speak, but squeezed hard, crushing the phone in my hand. I wished I could reach through it and crush his throat.

"No? Really? That makes me sad, Emma, I really thought we were friends. Some could say we were family." He let out a sad sigh. "I'm going to tell you anyway. I kept the dental records in the trunk of my car, riding around with me as I scooped up the lovely Sasha. I removed him after my escape and took him to the river, where I did the best to recreate your federal agents' marksmanship. Then all it took was a little push, and splash!" Evan broke into a coughing fit, gasping for air. "You and your love gave me enough time to escape. An Officer Down call takes all focus off the criminal, so sad. But that's beside the point! The dental records matched because they were switched along with the DNA samples. It helps to have an extra set of hands inside the cookie jar."

I panicked at his words. Evan was admitting he'd had help. Rachel was right. She'd been right all along, and I'd thrown it in her face like a petulant child.

"I will find you, Evan and I will kill you for what you did to Sasha and me. Then I'll find your partner and kill him too. I promise. *I. Will. Find. You.*"

Evan laughed a little, then coughed. "You won't have to look for me, Emma. I'll come to you when the time is right, like I have before and will again. It won't be anytime soon, because I need to heal. I can't let you have any advantage over me. It wouldn't be a fair fight. As for my partner, you shouldn't have to look far. She's been with you the entire time. Helping you the way I first directed her to, before she decided to think for herself."

My mind raced. "You're a monster, Evan. Stop playing games — it won't get you anywhere with me."

"I'm not playing any games, Emma. I'm simply telling you what the lovely FBI agent has been trying to get you to listen to. I'm disappointed in myself. I should've never chosen to work with family. They always make things so much worse."

Shivers ran down my spine. Rachel had hinted someone close to me was involved. Maybe Evan was just feeding my paranoia, trying to manipulate me again.

"You are a fucking liar."

"Emma, you should know by now, I have no reason to lie. I can get to you whenever I want. But it's time the secrets are revealed. I suggest you ask hard questions when questions are asked of you. You might well be intrigued at the answers. It truly is the last time I work with a partner, let alone family. She got in the way more than she helped, especially after

I found her after so many years. She ran from me like you did. When I found her again, I punished her by killing her wife." I heard his deep sigh on the phone. "Significant others always get in the way of family."

"What do you mean family? You fucking monster." I hissed through a clenched jaw.

"Ha-ha! I love it when you call me a monster! It's kind of cute and reminds me of how afraid you were of the monster in the closet as a child. Anyway, we can reminisce later. What was I saying? Oh yes, I think you should ask Catherine about her family, oops! I mean Rachel. Look in her eyes, and ask yourself if you see anything familiar in them. Rachel played along for a few years after I tracked her down. It helped that she had such a fancy job, access to all sorts of records and secrets. Then her heart got in the way, her guilt became too much. Betraying a lover, betraying her love was too much for her to bear." Evan paused, irritation rising in his tone. "I must be off. I have a bus to catch. Goodbye, Emma. I'll see you soon!" He hung up as the last syllable passed his lips.

I threw the phone into the sink. My head ached as I tried to rewind what Evan had said. I shook my head. "No, it can't be." Everything was clicking into place.

I heard a light knock on the bathroom door. "Emma? Are you okay?"

My body tightened, and I rubbed my face to shake off the shivers. "I couldn't sleep." My mind was processing what Evan had just dropped in my lap, and whether or not I should believe him. I knew he would say and do anything to get under my skin, to continue his game.

Sasha slid inside the bathroom behind me. "Are you sure? Who were you talking to?"

I kept a strong grip on the bathroom counter, my heart pounding. "Evan is alive."

I watched in the mirror as she turned completely white. "How?" She grabbed my hand. Sasha was tough, but it wasn't a wonder she'd still be scared after the events of the last few weeks.

"He tricked us, again."

She covered her mouth with her hand, leaning against the wall. Shaking.

"He has someone helping him. That's how he found me. That's how he kidnapped you and set everything up so perfectly, so I'd always be one step behind him."

Sasha's eyes turned glassy with tears. "Oh my God, Emma, what are we going to do?"

"I don't know." I turned, and pulled her into a tight hug, still stuck on Evan's cryptic words. He had been crystal clear in who he'd named, but I couldn't trust it. I wasn't going to scare Sasha or inspire her to go after Rachel unless I had hard proof.

I held her until a heavy knock on the outer door bellowed into the bathroom.

I let go of Sasha, and slipped out of the bathroom, stopping at my bag to grab a gun. I motioned for Sasha to get hers and to stand on the opposite side of the door.

Looking through the peephole, I saw Rachel standing at the door with an object under her arm. I took a deep breath, relaxing my grip on the gun and opened the door. "Rachel, it's a little late. We were about to go to bed."

Rachel stepped into the room. Sasha moved from her spot, setting her gun on top of her suitcase. She smiled at Rachel and sat on the small couch across from us.

"I know, I apologize, but I wanted to drop off a few files and ask you to look at them. I know you severed our ties, but I'd appreciate it if you took a look." She held up a thin stack of blue folders.

"What are they?"

"Open murder cases that reek of Evan's MO." Rachel sighed, and I looked up.

That's when I saw it. I was staring at the same clear bright blue eyes that stared at me as he lowered the knife down into my skin. I took a steady breath, and gripped my gun tighter. "Thank you, Catherine."

I watched Rachel's jaw clench as she looked down. "Catherine? Who's Catherine?" She tried to maintain her cover, but I'd had enough psychology and body language training to know better.

There was panic in her eyes.

Sasha stood, looking between Rachel and me, silently asking the same question. The more I stared at the woman, the more I picked up on the physical similarities between her and Evan. They had the same eyes, the same jawline... even their smile was identical. They were siblings, and I'd been so stupid not to see it before now.

"I think you know, Agent Fisher." I wasn't backing down until I followed through on this hunch.

Rachel smiled, blowing out a laugh. "I think you know? Okay, that makes perfect sense, Emma." She rolled her eyes, shaking her head. "Maybe Agent Markus was right. Your paranoia is beginning to rear its ugly head."

She took a step towards me, holding out empty hands. "No, I don't know. I apologize if I disturbed you with my line of questioning today."

I took a step back, trying to grip the gun in my stiff right hand. "Please, stop right there." I raised the gun a little higher. "Just tell me the truth. Do I keep calling you Rachel or do you prefer Catherine?" I paused. "Evan told me everything."

She continued forward, shaking her head, maintaining her trademark stoic smile. "Emma, I think you need to rest. It's been a very long day for you." Rachel looked to Sasha. "Help me get her to bed. I think she's stuck in an old memory and her PTSD is coming to the forefront." Rachel laid a hand on my arm.

I yanked my arm away and stepped back. Sasha tried to move between the two of us.

Rachel saw her in her peripheral. She turned to Sasha, speaking right at her, trying to turn Sasha against me. "Emma has suffered years of psychological trauma and it's broken her down." She put a hand on Sasha's arm, but she pulled back.

"What the fuck is going on?" Sasha glanced at the gun in my hand I'd slowly raised to low ready. "Emma?"

"I think that's the question of the day, right, Catherine?" I kept my eyes on Rachel.

Sasha yelled at us. "Who the fuck is Catherine?"

I took my eyes off Rachel for a split second. I wanted to tell Sasha to move behind me, to get her gun. Rachel lunged and backhanded her across the face. Sasha fell to the ground with a grunt, catching her forehead on the edge of the chair. She went limp.

I rushed Rachel, grabbing both of her arms to trap her against the wall, and shouted in her face. "Who the fuck are you? Tell me now! Tell me the truth!"

"I can't! If I do, he'll kill me!" She screamed back, looking at Sasha. "I'm sorry for that, but the less witnesses, the better."

Rachel tried to push me back, but I pushed harder. "Tell me the fucking truth! Who are you?"

Rachel broke. Her face turned red, and tears streamed down her cheeks. "*I am no one.*"

Her words pissed me off. I lost all sense and let go. I pointed my gun at her as I bent to check on Sasha. She was alive, thank God, murmuring incoherently. Before I stood, I heard Rachel rasp out. "He would've killed me if I didn't do it. He killed the love of my life because I wouldn't help him." Her voice was quiet, almost childlike. She moved closer, her hands out, palms up.

My finger slid to the trigger. "Don't." I saw Sasha move in my peripheral vision but didn't look. "He told me your name is Catherine."

She took a deep breath. "It was. My adoptive parents changed my name when I went to live with them. Even after they changed my name, he was the only one who ever called me Catherine." Rachel looked at the ceiling. "I was immediately placed with a family after our parents mysteriously died, but Evan had a hard time because he was so different and so much older. Even from birth he was odd, and I now know he carries the prime characteristics of a serial killer. I never saw him after that day I was adopted. Not until about a year ago, when he found me looking for you. I don't know how he did it, but he appeared on my doorstep. I was excited at first, then it all began to fall into place who he really was, and the crimes he committed, especially after he began asking about you. He told me you were his foster sister and he wanted to reconnect with you. I realized you were Eddie's daughter and the murders you were working on were Evan's doing. He slipped up, revealing clues never given to the press. I tried to stop him, to turn him in. That's when he killed my wife three years ago. He disappeared until we found him at the warehouse."

I wanted to vomit. I wanted to run out of the room and never stop till my legs gave out. I wanted to run away from these monsters.

"You're full of shit. You're an FBI Agent. You had a million ways to escape him." I held my gun up, my hand shaking from overextending torn muscles.

Rachel closed her eyes. "You're right, I did have a million ways out." She opened her eyes, locking on mine. "But I wanted my own revenge." Rachel took a step. "I used you and your girlfriend to get closer to Evan. I may have also blindly helped him get closer to you. He was so fixated on you, I knew you'd be the perfect bait." She turned to Sasha, who was starting to wake up. "You have to understand. This woman, Sasha. You love her completely and I'm sure you'd kill for her?"

Rachel began to spin the wedding ring on her finger. "He forced me to watch my wife die in a field in the middle of Virginia farmland. Evan tied me to a broken chair amongst the wheat, my wife across from me. I watched as he slit her wrists. She bled out before I could escape my bindings. It took hours to break free. By then Evan was long gone, my wife long past saving."

She made a move towards me. I raised my gun, pointing it at her chest. "Don't. Don't move any closer."

Rachel was crying, but still held her stale smile. She was losing it in front of me. Her mask was slipping. "Everything changed that day. No one could stop me from getting to Evan and killing him. Even you and Sasha. I did use you, I apologize for that, but I see now my brother and I share similar genetic traits when it comes to focusing on things. We become easily obsessed."

"Your brother. He was my foster brother too, but I didn't chase after him into the fires of hell." The question spat out like rotten food.

Rachel nodded. "Evan and I are biological brother and sister."

Even though I'd suspected it, it was a shock to hear the truth.

"I'm not lying. When you return to your Chicago office, there will be a package waiting for you. Everything you need to know about my brother and me is in there. I had a feeling after you left, you'd put some of the pieces together. Using my birth name, I know Evan has survived and started his game all over again." Rachel let out a shaky breath, her strong exterior starting to dissolve. "I don't want to play his game anymore. I couldn't kill him when I had the chance. He's my brother and..." Rachel drifted off, her tears falling harder.

With my gun still pointed at her, years of training usurped my desire to pull the trigger. I moved to the hotel phone, keeping my eyes and gun trained on Rachel and dialed 911.

"This is Detective Lieutenant Emma Tiernan of the Chicago Police Department. Badge number twenty twenty-one. I need the police over at the Grandview Hotel on Ninth Street, room one seventy-nine. I have a possible murder suspect in custody." I hung up, never looking away from Rachel. "I trusted you with my life and Sasha's life."

At the sound of her name, Sasha opened her eyes, grabbing the back of her head and groaning.

My jaw twitched. "You brought a monster straight into my life and he almost killed us. You should've stopped him, ended him when you had the chance."

Rachel laughed through tears. "Why didn't you when *you* had the chance?" She took another step forward.

"Don't move!" My finger twitched, taking up the slack on the trigger. I was a breath away from shooting her.

She kept walking towards me, ignoring my warnings, until she stood right in front of the gun. She reached up with both hands and pulled the gun into her chest. "Do it, Emma. Please do it. I have nothing to live for anymore. I've destroyed too many lives and he'll never leave me alone." I tried to tug the gun away, but her grip was too strong. "Emma. Please."

My finger shook as it sat on the trigger, as panic edged up my spine.

She sniffled, her blue eyes boring into mine. "I'm sorry."

Tears slid down my face as sirens screamed outside. The entire D.C. police department was descending on the hotel.

Flashing lights reflected off the window, distracting me. I squinted as red and blue lights flooded the room. "Let go of the gun, Catherine. Let go and we'll walk out together." I tried to pull it free of her hands, but my right hand wasn't strong enough.

She shook her head, leaning forward to press her forehead against mine. "This isn't your fault. Don't hold the guilt forever. Tell them I came at you."

Her finger slipped into mine and pulled the trigger.

The shot was deafening, and I jumped back like lightning had struck the ground between us.

She stumbled, clutching the wound on her stomach as blood soaked through her shirt and pooled around her fingers. She looked down, then up at me with a small, relieved smile.

Sasha scrambled to catch Rachel as she fell, screaming for me to help her.

Pushing out of her arms, Rachel stumbled and collapsed onto the floor with a heavy grunt. Sasha yelled for help.

I threw the gun on the bed and dropped to my knees, pressing my hands on hers, desperate to stop the blood, as Sasha ran to grab towels from the bathroom.

"No, oh shit, they're almost here. You'll be okay, oh God, Rachel, why did you do this?"

Her face was pale as she licked dry lips. "It's the only way out. My death takes away his advantage." She coughed, blood sliding out the corner of her mouth.

"We can figure this out, Rachel. We can tell them he held you hostage and forced you to do all of this. He manipulated you." I was rambling,

Sasha shoved towels into my hands. "I'll get the cops. I can hear them coming down the hall."

I nodded as she ran out of the room, yelling for someone to follow her.

Rachel shook her head, pulling my hands away from her wound. "It's over. Find him, kill him for me." She was losing strength and her blood covered my hands. I looked over my shoulder, praying for the paramedics to hurry up. Rachel didn't deserve to die like this. She was twisted but could be saved. I wasn't going to let Evan win one more round. "They're almost here. Fuck, Rachel, stay awake."

Police officers burst into the hotel room guns drawn, screaming for me to get against the wall as I was ripped off Rachel in a fury. They slammed me against a wall and handcuffed me. I was in a blurry daze of shock, unable to explain who I was as they yanked me out of the hotel room to let the paramedics in.

I was dragged down the hall between two officers, covered in Rachel's blood and my tears, when a familiar voice bellowed at the officers. "What the hell are you doing? Let her go right now! Goddamned idiots!"

"Who the hell do you think you are? This asshole just shot that woman." The officer on my right scowled.

I turned to see Sasha thrusting her badge in the face of the smart-mouthed officer. "I'm Detective Sasha Garnier of the Chicago Police Department. That *asshole* you're dragging around in handcuffs is my partner, Detective Lieutenant Emma Tiernan, the woman who called you for help." She stepped hard into the officer's face. "I suggest you release her and apologize. Now."

He glared at her in shock. When she didn't back down, he grumbled a rude comment under his breath and roughly removed the handcuffs from my wrists.

I fell backward and slid down the wall, cradling my head in my hands. Sasha knelt next to me. "What happened in there?" She placed her hands on the sides of my face, lifting it up.

I shook my head, closing my eyes. The hallway spun around me. "Save her, please."

Sasha turned to the two officers standing near us. "Are the paramedics in there?"

"Yes, ma'am, they're working on the shooting victim. Doesn't look good, though." The one who handcuffed me rolled his eyes, mumbling something to his partner.

"Then I suggest you go help them and make it look good. Understand?" Sasha's voice was strong and commanding, a far cry from the bumbling rookie I thought I was taking on, the kind woman I loved.

With a grumble, the two officers rushed down the hall.

I drew away from Sasha, curling into a ball on the floor as shock began its vicious hold. I couldn't control my shivering.

Sasha grabbed my biceps, hauling me up to my feet. "I need to get you out of here." She hoisted me onto her shoulder, walking towards the elevator and away from the scene of chaos behind us.

The world around me became muter and hazier with every step.

Chapter 20

A dog, barking in the distance, woke me from a dreamless sleep. I seemed to be in a comfortable bed in a dark hotel room, in a different hotel, wearing clothes that weren't mine. I rolled out of bed and took slow steps to the window. Drawing back the heavy curtains, I looked down into a governmental-looking concrete compound that surrounded the building.

I pressed my head against the cool window. It ached, and felt like it was made of stone.

A moment later, a hand fell onto my shoulder. Sasha stood close behind me, holding a small cup of coffee. I frowned at the thin line of stitches across the top of her forehead.

She smiled. "The view isn't great, but it's what we have for now."

"Where are we?" I cringed when my voice came out raspy.

"We're in the protective custody of the FBI. They're not too happy you shot one of their agents." Sasha ran a hand down my back. "They stopped us just outside of the hotel driveway, and took us here until everything is sorted out." She gave me a concerned look. "I keep asking, but Emma, what happened? What the fuck was that back there? I know I missed bits when Rachel hit me, but what was that?"

I took a deep breath, and leaned my heavy, throbbing head against the glass again. "Evan had a hand on the inside. Rachel."

Sasha made no move, nor did she react. She just stood there and, when I looked at her, she raised her eyebrows for me to continue.

"I was talking to Evan in the bathroom. He survived the warehouse. He confessed to everything. How he escaped us, how he planted the body and dental records. If you look at my cell phone, he's the last incoming call. But don't bother tracing it, it'll go nowhere." I cleared my throat, wincing at how dry it was. "He told me who was helping him on the inside. His sister." I drifted off, the urge to break down washing over me. I was tired, beaten down and barely holding my shit together.

Sasha sat on the edge of the bed. "His real sister? Did he tell you that?"

I shook my head. "Rachel did — or Catherine, as Evan knows her. She's his biological sister. Rachel told me everything when she showed up at our room. She explained how he had found her, then used her to find me. He killed her wife because she was an inconvenience in his master plan. Rachel became so consumed with her own rage and need for revenge that she used both of us to draw Evan out. That's why I had my gun out. I was trying to protect us."

Sasha began to fidget, looking down at her bandaged wrists.

I refused to look at her, instead focusing on the lone tree in the middle of the courtyard below. "I called 911 and Rachel advanced on me. She walked into my gun, begging me to shoot her. Ranting over and over it was her fault Evan found me. I tried fighting her off, but my hand is still weak. She forced the shot. She pulled the trigger. I didn't... I didn't want to shoot her."

Tears ran down my face. I was still in shock and nowhere near in control of any emotions. I'd shot people before, but this was something different. Rachel was someone I knew, someone I trusted.

Sasha was silent for a moment, then spoke. "I'll give them a statement of what I saw. You won't be blamed for this. I saw bits and pieces, but when she backhanded me, things got fuzzy."

I moved away from the window, and climbed back into bed, tugging at Sasha to lie down with me.

I'd shot someone and probably killed them. My mind was stuck on that, and it weighed heavy on my heart along with everything Rachel told me. It all collided in my head, creating a tangled mess.

I passed out from exhaustion in Sasha's arms, praying the room would stop spinning when I woke up.

I woke up, hours later, soaked in a cold sweat. I reached for Sasha, but only found cold sheets. Panicked, I sat up, but the door creaked open, and Sasha appeared with a bag of food in her hand.

"Good morning, you." She sat down next to me. "I scrounged up some egg sandwiches. You should eat." She dug into the paper bag. "I ran into one of the agents in the cafeteria. You've been cleared of all charges. The crime lab found Rachel's fingerprints on the gun. The ballistics and physics match up to your story. They're dropping the case against you, calling it an attempted suicide by cop." She'd overheard that Rachel was alive but comatose. The whole incident was the hot topic and would probably be on the news later today.

I sighed at the harsh term, and took a deep breath. "Okay."

Sasha laid her hand on my thigh, gently squeezing it. "Do you need to talk?"

I did.

I wanted to sit and rant. I wanted to let everything pour out, to talk until I ran out of air and the heaviness in my chest lifted away.

But I was tired and didn't have the energy to hold it together if I started.

I met Sasha's gaze and shook my head.

She leaned into my side. "I love you, Emma. I'm here if you need to let it all out."

Picking at the greasy sandwich wrapper, I sighed. "Did the agent tell you when we can go home?"

"As soon as you're ready we can be on the next flight back to Chicago. The Chicago field office will do our debriefing and interviews." Sasha shook her head, glaring at her sandwich. "Maybe they'll go a little easier on us."

I nodded in silent agreement but knew what was to come. I'd be interviewed again, pressured to tell them everything about Rachel. They'd put together a case file, place it in one of those high-tech filing cabinets, and I would return to my desk in Chicago. Sasha would return to her unit. And that would be that.

I grabbed Sasha's hand. "I want to see her before we leave."

"Rachel? Are you sure? I mean, after everything?" She was still bottling up her own emotions from what happened in the hotel room and bitter from finding out Rachel was Evan's accomplice.

"I think I need to. I can't explain why, but I think it's something I should do?" I glanced at the food in my hand. "Nothing makes sense and I need something tangible to hold on to, aside from you." I smiled.

She let out a breath. "I don't like it, but I'll go with you."

* * *

Sasha leaned against the steering wheel of the rental, and turned to me. "Are you sure you want to do this?"

I nodded, focusing on the map of the hospital map displayed next to the parking deck's elevator. Sasha had been quiet the entire drive over — her tell she was very much against this but would keep it to herself. I opened the car door and got out quickly, before I talked myself out of this crazy idea.

The ride up the elevator to the ICU ward was a long, silent one. Sasha stared straight ahead, holding my hand as we watched the floor numbers flick by.

When the elevator stopped at the ICU, Sasha went to step out first. I hesitated for a second. Bad memories came rushing back. The stark whiteness of the hospital and the antiseptic smell reminded me of the last two times I wasn't just a visitor, but a patient.

Sasha squeezed my hand. "Are you okay?"

I pushed away from the back of the elevator, letting go of her hand and forced myself out. My feet were heavy with nerves. I followed Sasha to the nurse's station where she was being told visitors' hours were two hours away. She asked to speak to the head nurse.

I smiled at this new, take-charge version of Sasha. Taking care of me and ignoring the fact I had to have control in every situation.

After a moment, an elegant woman floated around the corner in scrubs. Sasha raised her eyes from the visitation sheet she was scanning. "How can I help you?"

Sasha did most of the talking. "My name is Detective Garnier, and this is Detective Lieutenant Tiernan. We're close friends and coworkers of Agent Rachel Fisher. I know we're a little early, but we've been working on Agent Fisher's case and we'd really like to check on her." She played up the sadness and the elegant nurse fell for it hook, line and sinker.

The head nurse flipped through the pages on a metallic clipboard, furrowing her brow. "I'm sorry, but you can't see Ms. Fisher."

Sasha cut the nurse off with a firm authoritative tone. "Yes, we can. All of the necessary paperwork has been filed and we were told we would have open visitation rights. You can call the Chief Resident of the ICU ward, Dr. Corpus. He signed off on it. If that doesn't suit you, call my boss, Section Chief Harold Shaya." She was threatening the nurse with the age-old tactic of name dropping. Big names she'd obviously pulled from the visitation sign in sheets she'd been staring at.

The nurse fought back with her own authoritative tone. "I understand you have open visitation. I have all the copies of the waivers and memos right here on my board, but if you'd let me finish, I'd have explained why you won't be able to see Ms. Fisher. She's been transferred to another hospital. Three hours ago."

Sasha glanced at me, as confused as I was, then turned back to the nurse. "Transferred? That's not possible. She's under protective FBI custody until she comes out of her coma. Who authorized the transfer?" I was amazed at Sasha's ability to latch onto key components of a conversation she'd overheard in the cafeteria.

The nurse flipped through pages. "It's all right here. Special Agent in Charge James Cookson, FBI. He gave the night shift nurse the transfer papers, and had an EMS crew with him ready to transport Ms. Fisher."

She held out the transfer sheet. Sasha snatched it out of her hands. Her face turned a bright red as she read it. "I need to use your phone now. I also highly suggest you contact the night nurse and get her down here."

Sasha reached for the phone, her jaw twitching. She met my eyes as she spoke. "Aaron, it's Sasha. Do me a favor, run a quick check for an SAC James Cookson. Yeah, I know you haven't heard from us for a week, but now is not a good time." Sasha lowered her voice as the nurse kept her glare on me. I was frozen. A sinking feeling flooded my gut and I couldn't bring myself to speak.

Sasha turned back to the head nurse, covering the receiver. "Do you have cameras on this unit?"

"Yes, of course. We use them to monitor critical patients."

"Where is the control room?"

"The camera room is right over there." She pointed over her shoulder, and I noticed her shaking hands. Sasha could be extremely intimidating when she wanted to be.

Sasha slammed the phone down and started moving towards the room. "Show me."

The nurse let her in and showed us which recordings were the most recent.

I followed her, fearing the worst, and quietly asked for Rachel's room. The nurse pulled it up on a monitor and stood back.

Sasha and I sat reviewing the footage. Something felt off. Rachel was a high profile patient, a possible suspect, and yet she slipped out of the hospital like a load of dirty laundry.

Sasha looked at the nurse, who still anxiously hovered behind us. "Did you get a hold of the night shift nurse?"

The head nurse shook her head, and took that as her cue to leave us alone.

When the door shut behind her, I finally broke my self-imposed silence. "I have a bad feeling."

"Me, too."

Sasha rewound through the footage, stopping at the approximate time Rachel would have been transferred. She hit play and we sat in silence, eyes locked on the monitor. I clenched my jaw at the sight of Rachel in her bed, tubes tangled around her. I couldn't look for long, instead turning to focus on the wall of screens that monitored the other patients in the ICU.

"Fuck." Sasha muttered, grabbing my knee.

I turned back to the monitor.

A man in a dark suit limped into Rachel's room and bent down close to her face. Soon, the night nurse entered and began to remove IV lines and pull back blankets, readying Rachel for transport. Three paramedics came into the room with a stretcher, directed by a nurse.

I leaned forward to catch the man's face, but the camera was too far away. I watched in pain as they hoisted Rachel's limp body from the bed to the stretcher, and plugged her into portable life support units. It only took them a minute to wheel her out. The man in the dark suit stood with his back to the camera, speaking with the nurse for a moment. When she left, the man turned to follow her.

He took two steps then stopped and looked straight at the camera, his whole face in full view. He grinned and gave a small salute with a wink.

"Evan." I choked on his name. The room grew silent, blood rushing in my ears as I fought the need to vomit.

Sasha glanced at me then quickly rewound the tape, pausing when Evan looked at the camera. She took a closer look. "Are you sure? It's blurry, and his face is covered in shadows."

"I won't ever forget that monster or his eyes." I turned away from the monitor, wiping errant tears away. I was shaking. He would never let this end.

"Son of a bitch. Why would he take her?" Sasha had an edge to her voice, bordering on frantic.

"He doesn't leave things behind. He always cleans up his messes. He had to take her. Evan didn't want me to have the last word with her. Everything he does is to hurt me." I turned to Sasha. "Even if it means using his own family."

I walked out of the monitoring room into a sea of panicking uniforms and white lab coats. Sasha followed me, and ran to the closest police officer.

I moved through everyone without stopping, ignoring all the panic, and headed towards the elevator.

I didn't know where to go, so I just hit random buttons, ending up in the maternity ward. Walking past the newborn rooms, where the new inhabitants of this messy world slept, dreaming of what was to come.

I found the chapel for grieving mothers and walked in quietly, picking a seat at the back, staring at the stained-glass window of Jesus holding a lost lamb. Even the familiarity of the best parts of my youth couldn't chase away the crushing dread. Evan was alive, he would come for me. Again and again, and even God couldn't save me from an evil like him.

I stared at it until the image burned into the back of my mind. Completely numb, I laid down in the pew and closed my eyes, praying this was all a bad dream.

"Ma'am? Ma'am? Are you alright? Do you want me to call the priest?" I was shaken awake by a smiling orderly.

I squinted up into the older man's gentle eyes. "No. I just want to lay here. Is that okay?"

"Oh, I don't have a problem with that, ma'am, but there are some policemen walking around the floors. They might come in here and bother you. You want me to tell them to stay out?"

"That's okay. I think they're looking for me."

He took a step back, defensively. I smiled at him and sat up slowly, holding up my badge and ID card. "Don't worry, I didn't do anything. I just disappeared. Can you tell me if one of them is a good-looking woman, with long, light brown hair?"

The orderly looked around the chapel, obviously thinking harder than was necessary. "Yeah. I just walked by her. She's talking to a bunch of nurses at the nurse's station. You want me to go get her?"

I smiled and nodded. He smiled back and quick-stepped it out of the chapel on a mission. I took a deep breath and let it out, leaning forward on my knees. It wasn't a dream.

I didn't hear Sasha come into the chapel, only felt her sit next to me.

"I was a little worried. You disappeared." She leaned into me, taking my hand in hers.

"I wish I could."

"Do you want to know any of it?" Sasha stared ahead, her eyes fixed on the stained-glass window.

"What more is there to know? Evan took Rachel. Took her out of the damn hospital just as easy as taking a book out of the library."

"He left this for you." She handed me an evidence bag with a note inside. I stared at it for a moment before taking it from her, pulling the plastic taut so I could read it.

Emma,
She is in good hands with me. I couldn't let you have her. The victory of killing her before I could doesn't seem right. Call me selfish.
Don't worry, we will have a reunion soon enough.
-Love, your brother.

I laid the bag back in Sasha's hands, lifting my head to the ceiling.

"The FBI have begun to trace the ambulance company he used. They should be able to track where he took her. He has to go to a hospital with an ICU to keep her alive. He'll slip up, and then we'll get him."

I turned my gaze back to the lost lamb. "Why bother, Sasha? We won't find him. He finds us."

She pulled my hand into her lap. "I promise, we'll find him. I'll make sure he never hurts you again." I looked into her eyes. Their intensity told me she would spend the rest of her life tracking him down if I asked it of her.

"Don't waste your energy. It's over. It's done. I can't keep fighting like this." I ran my other hand through my hair, tugging at the ends to feel something.

"Emma, don't think like that. We'll win this one." She pressed my hand harder against hers.

I snapped at her. "Win what? There isn't anything to win. I have nothing left to give him, or anything I want to keep risking. I think it's time I walked away."

Sasha sat in silence, taken aback by my outburst.

"I want to go home." I slumped back in the pew.

"We can leave today. I'll call Aaron." She whispered, her voice shaky.

I stood to leave the chapel. As I stepped out into the hallway, I spoke to Sasha, with my back facing her. "We have to let it go. I'm done living in fear. He'll come for me, for us. Until then, I want to live, not let him continue to have a hold over me and the ones I love."

I left the chapel, and I never looked back.

Chapter 21

Sasha and I were released from FBI custody later that day. On the flight home, I thought about our relationship. My obsessive mind kept filing over what happened to us. Sasha had stuck by my side through it all.

I'd been completely cleared of any formal charges for the hotel incident and the FBI applauded me for my quick thinking and action.

Even with the accolades, I felt like I'd been through a war and the only person who understood was Sasha. She'd seen the darkness and faced it, but I was left with guilt that I'd been partly responsible for everything that had happened to both of us. I wondered if we could overcome the pain when the dust settled.

I was relieved to open my front door and set our bags down. Sasha followed behind me, grabbing the bag I'd just dropped.

"I'll take these upstairs." She spoke softly, her smile tired. There was tension between us, rightfully so.

I removed my jacket, tossing it on the couch before heading straight to my leather chair. The sun was setting on the lake. I fell into the chair and took a deep breath, watching the water. The sunlight reflected off the small waves, welcoming me home, asking me to relax and stop for a moment. Even the lake looked different, felt different.

Sasha came back down and stood next to the chair. "I'm going to run to my apartment. I need to check on Morgan and a few other things." I looked up and saw how tired she was. I couldn't blame her for wanting to go home. It had been a long couple of weeks.

"Will you be coming back?"

She sighed. "If you want me to." When her eyes met mine, I saw she wanted to talk, but if it was with me, I wasn't sure.

Standing up, I slipped my arms around her waist and squeezed. "I want you to come back." I held her as I reached for the extra key in the side table drawer, pressing it into her palm. "Come home when you've checked your mail and watered your plants."

She grinned, pocketing the key before kissing me. "I won't be long." She stepped out onto the porch and turned around. "I'll bring us some dinner and we can talk after."

"I'll be waiting. Use the key in case I fall asleep." I closed the door and locked it behind her, immediately returning to the chair and the lake. I sat, gazing at the view for what felt like an hour, until I heard a knock at my door, then saw Aaron's face appear in the large front window.

I chuckled as I let him in. He uncharacteristically swooped me into a brotherly hug. "Holy shit, Emma, what's going on? I read the briefings that came over the wire."

He dropped me and headed to the couch, as I went to the fridge for beer. Aaron held up the large manila folder I'd asked him to bring when we landed.

"Here's that thing you asked for. It was sitting on the middle of your desk like you said." He threw it on the coffee table in exchange for the beer I offered. I handed him a beer and sat down beside him. The folder stared at me. Rachel's handwriting scrawled across its front, and I dreaded reading what was inside.

"Evan is still alive. Hiding in the shadows and I don't know what to do." I looked at Aaron, holding his beer bottle in mid-sip.

"Evan is still alive? How? Agent Fisher shot him, and we have a body."

I sighed. "Agent Fisher is Evan's sister. His biological sister. Evan used a decoy body to throw us off and is still out there. He left me a note, but the FBI took it for evidence." I closed my eyes, leaning back into the couch. "I need to quit this job."

Aaron was confused when he spoke. "I, uh, you have to explain everything real slow. You lost me at biological sister and decoy bodies."

I took a deep breath and told Aaron the short version of everything that happened in D.C. When I was done, he gave me a blank stare.

"Holy shit, Emma. That's all I can really say." He set the bottle down, leaning elbows on his knees. "Where's Sasha? How is she doing?"

"She's at her apartment, taking care of a few things." I groaned, rubbing my hands across my face. "We're both exhausted. Things have been awkward between us and our conversations feel forced. I just don't want to fight anymore and play Evan's game and I think it frustrates her. For the first time in my life, I've no idea what I want to do with my life." I shrugged, reaching for my beer.

"You love Sasha, right?"

A dopey grin covered my face.

He smiled. "And she loves you?"

I nodded. "Yes, she does. She stuck with me through it all. Even after her experience with Evan, she's still here. At least I hope she wants to be here with me." I took a sip of beer.

I needed to prepare myself. I half expected Sasha to not come back. Like everyone else in my life after Elle, she would fade away, find a stable life without serial killers chasing her or having to endure my emotional crankiness.

Aaron slugged me. "All that matters is she loves you, you love her. You've been talking about leaving this job for years now. Every day, you zone out and stare at the lake. I call it your retirement stare. So, I think you need to start a new life like you should've after Elle." Aaron smiled. "I love you like a sister. I love working with you and I think you're one of the most amazing detectives I've ever worked with, but if you keep this job, you're going to lose yourself and Sasha."

Aaron grabbed the almost-full bottle of beer from my hands. "As for that nutjob Evan, I suspect that envelope with Agent Fisher's handwriting may give you a lead."

I glared at the envelope. "I don't even want to open it. I'm afraid it's going to carry me further down the rabbit hole."

Aaron picked up the envelope and set it on my lap. "Read it. Finish the case and move on. Or move on and leave the case to the FBI. But do *something*, before you lose the girl you love and the girl I'm so jealous you get to see naked." Aaron winked at me as he flashed one of his cheeky grins. I laughed, punching him in the thigh.

We both paused at the sound of the front door opening. Aaron placed a hand on his gun. I winced when I reached for mine, only to find an empty hip.

"I grabbed some clothes, most of it dirty since I completely forgot about laundry day. Morgan wasn't home. I told her to call me and stop by here if it's okay with you." Sasha came around the corner, spotting Aaron and I frozen in ready poses. She and Aaron grinned at the same time.

"Hey you! I didn't know you were coming over!" She tossed her bag to the floor before grabbing him in a massive hug.

Aaron winked at me with arms around Sasha. "Our Lieutenant here asked me to come by and say hey." I rolled my eyes when he winked at me again before letting go of Sasha. "But I was just about to leave. I need to get back to the office and finish some paperwork." He turned to me. "I'll call you tomorrow. We can get coffee and maybe talk about your office changing hands."

I laughed. "A maybe on the office, yes on coffee."

Aaron gave me a thumbs up and gave Sasha a quick side hug before running out the front door.

Sasha sat on the couch, placing a hand on my thigh. I covered it hand with mine, lacing our fingers together. "How are you?"

Her hazel eyes were cloudy, but she managed a weak smile. "I'm tired and worried. Worried about you, us." She hung her head down. "I know it's stupid to worry about us, but everything is starting to digest and it's a bit overwhelming."

I pulled Sasha into my arms. "Well, I mean, you are involved with a woman who was forced into shooting a colleague who was working with her brother — and my foster brother serial killer — who's been chasing me all my life. And you almost died because of it, and I almost died twice. Yeah, I guess it's a lot to take in." I frowned. It was a lot to take in. It was a lot for me to take in and hide the utter terror I felt if I sat in silence for too long.

Sasha shook her head, my feeble attempt at humor falling flat. "What happens next, Emma?"

"What happens next? I don't know. I do know I won't go back to work for another week, leaving plenty of time to think about the future." I motioned to the envelope on my lap and explained what it was "This will be the deciding factor." I kissed her temple. "As for us, what happens next is we work through this. I love you and I want to keep fighting for you. The rest of it, I can take or leave."

Sasha half smiled. "What about Evan? He'll come back."

"He will. But I can't live in fear of him. I know he'll come back. I'm his number one focus in life. But if I live looking over my shoulder, always wondering what if, when and where, he wins."

Sasha wrapped her arms around me, nuzzling into my neck. "I'll keep you safe, Sasha. I promise."

She whispered softly, "I love you, Emma."

*　*　*

Sasha had left for work, leaving me to stare at the manila envelope that lay on the kitchen island. It'd been two days since we came home. We spent most of those days talking as much as possible. Talking was the only way for us to process in private with each other, on top of the individual therapy sessions the department forced upon us as standard operating procedure after an incident.

I ignored the file until Sasha left. I then clenched my hand around my coffee cup and engaged in a staring contest with an inanimate object. I had less than a week left of leave before I was back at the office and my growing stack of caseloads.

I let out a breath and set the cup down, pulled the envelope over and ripped it open. The files that slid out were blazoned with the FBI seal, with a small note clipped to the top.

Emma,

One way or another, the reason why you have these files in your possession is because you've discovered who I am. It was bound to happen. All secrets eventually come to light. In here are all the cases Evan has ever been involved with, his foster records, and my records. It may help you as the chase continues and give you an advantage over Evan.

I am sorry for everything,

Rachel.

I set the note down. I now knew for certain Rachel had always planned to end things her own way. Her guilt had consumed her, preventing her from killing her brother and driving her to attempt suicide by cop. Filling another cup of coffee, I sat down to read through the foster records.

Evan had been disruptive in all the foster homes he was placed in, but I was the only foster sibling he'd focused on. I was the one he became obsessed with. He bounced around from home to home. From a state mental institution to the streets at eighteen. His criminal record was extensive for the next three years, until he suddenly disappeared at the age of twenty-one. I pushed through the files Rachel had built on her brother, her hand-written notes in the margins. She had an idea Evan was randomly killing to satisfy whatever drove him, until he found me.

At the bottom of the stack was the case report on Rachel's wife. I quickly flipped through crime scene photographs. Her death was brutal and far too familiar. I swallowed hard as I read over the report.

Evan had kidnapped Rachel's wife from their home in Fairfax, Virginia and taken her well out into some farm fields in the southern half of the state. There he lured his sister. He'd handcuffed her to a chair and forced her to watch her wife die a slow and painful death. The couple was not found for hours. One of Rachel's coworkers had tried to call her and received no response, sending her office into a panic.

Rachel was in the hospital for a week, and had — remarkably — passed her psych exams. I set the report down. It wouldn't have been hard to manipulate the psychologists. A determined mind will overcome anything to continue on the path set by its owner. Never mind the fact Rachel was a brilliant manipulator.

I read the entire file, absorbing the type of person Evan had become. Very little had changed from the destructive child he had been. I had an advantage, now that I knew his background. I would be better prepared the next time I came to face him. I just had to worry about how to protect Sasha.

I looked out at the lake for answers.

I sighed. Why hadn't I killed him when I had the chance?

* * *

One week later, I walked into my office to find Aaron sitting in the chair in front of my desk. I smiled when he sat up, looking me over. "I see the head shrinker passed you with flying colors. Welcome back."

I set my bag down on the desk and sat down, noticing someone had altered my chair's settings. I shot Aaron a dirty look.

He grinned. "Sorry, I sat in it a couple times. It's a really nice chair."

I fiddled with the levers. "Yes, I've been cleared with green flags, green lights, and anything else you can compare to me having a clean bill of mental health." I stared at him for a moment, waiting for the question.

"Are you really ok, Emma?"

I chuckled at his predictability. "One day I'll answer that honestly, but today is not the day." I straightened the huge stack of files that still teetered on my desk. "What's new around here?"

Aaron pulled out his notebook. "We have a few open cases that should be tied up in a couple days after witness interviews. We caught a body last night. I was about to head out to the scene, but someone told me you were gracing us with your presence." He flipped a few pages. "Oh, and lastly, the media is *in love* with you right now."

I frowned, groaning.

Captain Jameson had briefed me an hour ago about protocols and professional behavior around the media. I was told to exercise extreme discretion when approached by reporters. Rachel's kidnapping from the hospital had been leaked, and I was headline news, until the next bigger, better story came around.

The lower-ranked news outlets picked up the story and were calling the department daily.

"Jameson just gave me the media protocol manual." I pulled it out of my bag and threw it across the desk at Aaron. "At least he made sure they went nowhere near my house or Sasha's apartment."

Aaron picked up the manual, weighing it. "She still good? I've talked to her on the street a couple times as our cases overlapped, but she's super tight-lipped." Aaron shook his head at the manual. "I don't blame her. If I was her, I'd ask for reassignment in the suburbs and hide."

"She's grown quiet over the last few days since we both chose to go back to work." I leaned back in the chair.

Aaron shrugged. "The FBI are still looking into Fisher's great escape from the hospital. Evan made it to the infamous Ten Most Wanted list.

Our end is all tied up and we were able to get a real identification on the body Evan used at the docks, closing that case." Aaron ran a hand over his hair. "I hate to say it, but it's a waiting game with that piece of shit. Hopefully he gets gangrene and dies."

I raised my eyebrows. "Gangrene?"

"I heard it's painful." Aaron dropped his feet from my desk. "Maybe you need to investigate that early retirement plan you've been prattling on about since you made Lieutenant. Snatch up your sexy detective in District Six and move as far away as you can." Aaron stood up and leaned over the desk, looking in my eyes. "Emma, it's time to make the most out of your life. Evan has presented you with the perfect excuse to say fuck it all, and *live*."

We stared at each other for a moment before he straightened up. "That's my advice. In the meantime, want to join me on this new case?"

I was absorbing Aaron's advice. He was right, I had to make the most out of my life. I pulled open the drawer and grabbed my gun, sliding it onto my waist. "You can drive." I followed Aaron out, and hoped getting back to work would clear my head, or at least push me to make a damn decision.

Chapter 22

Ramming my way past the uniformed officers who held back the reporter I'd just thrown garbage at, I yelled at Aaron that I was going back to the station. We had been in the middle of processing the scene of his new case when a reporter pushed past the scene tape. I was knee deep in a dumpster, looking for the victim's bloody clothes, when I was hit with a barrage of questions about my lesbian lover, the FBI agent I shot, and how it felt to be at the mercy of a serial killer.

I played nice and answered no comment, until he asked about Sasha and what happened in the warehouse. That's when I lost it, throwing handfuls of wet garbage at the reporter until uniformed officers restrained me and pulled the reporter away.

Slamming the car door so hard it rocked the car, I closed my eyes to calm down. I'd been seconds away from dropping the garbage and using my fists on the reporter instead. I leaned my head against the steering wheel, only looking up to see the reporter being dragged to the backseat of a cruiser.

Anger filled me again, and I started the car to drive back to the station. As soon as I was back behind my desk, I opened the bottom drawer and pulled out the early retirement paperwork. Setting it in front of me, I stared at it, before grabbing the phone to call Sasha.

"Emma? Are you okay? Aaron just messaged me about the reporter." She was outside, the sounds of Chicago traffic mixing with the wind. She was on scene, and my stomach knotted up with mild fear.

"I'm fine. Just irritated." I swung around in my chair to look out the window at the sailboats, my calming point. "Can you come to the house as soon as you can? I want to talk to you about a few things." My eyes roamed over the boats. The different colored sails were calming me down with every new pattern offered to me.

"Of course. I'm just finishing a few witness statements. I can be over in an hour, hour and a half at most."

"I'll see you then. Be careful, Sasha." I hung up and put my attention back to the paperwork in front of me. I then opened the middle drawer and pulled out my medical school acceptance package. It had been shoved in there to be forgotten.

I took a deep breath and called the number on the letterhead.

* * *

"Hey, sorry I'm late. My prime witness kept changing her statement." Sasha walked in and draped her jacket on the couch. She sighed and ran her hands through her hair, then produced a bag of Skittles, which she dropped on the counter next to my hand.

I held out a beer for her. "No worries." I ran a finger over the bag of candy, my heart swelling at the small gesture.

Sasha took a long drink. "So, what's up?"

Before I started the diatribe I'd been practicing, I pulled her in for a deep kiss. She melted on first contact with my lips. We'd not been intimate, aside from sleeping in the same bed and hugs. It'd been a while, too long, by the way she eagerly accepted the unexpected kiss.

When we parted, Sasha grinned. "Wow. That was quite the hello."

I bit my bottom lip as my hands moved to hers. "I have a couple things to ask you." I let go of one of her hands and picked up the resignation letter I'd been staring at while I waited for her. I slid the letter, along with a small stack of emails I'd printed out, across the kitchen island to rest against her beer.

Sasha glanced at it as I spoke.

"I had a heart-to-heart with Aaron this morning when I went in. He told me it was time to make the most of my life in the way I saw fit. I... finally made a decision in that regard."

I watched as she picked up my letter of resignation and read over it, her brow furrowing until she read the final paragraph. Her face softened. "Are you serious?"

I nodded. "Very much so. I picked it up on the way home. My retirement paperwork is sitting on Captain Jameson's desk for his final signature tomorrow." I squeezed Sasha's hands. "How do you feel about dating a first-year medical student?"

She grinned, slipping her arms around my waist. "As long as we get to have sexy, late night study sessions, I'm totally fine with dating a freshman." She paused, cocking her head. "Wait, does this mean we're officially girlfriends?"

I laughed. "Officially." I pressed a finger against her lips, halting the incoming kiss. "Which brings me to the second part." Taking a deep breath, I spoke. "I want you to move in with me. Cohabitate, for multiple reasons. I like having someone to come home to, even though I'm home before you get off work. But I want to keep you close. And lastly—" I pushed the emails closer to her "—where do you want to live?"

Sasha was confused. "What do you mean?"

I tapped the stack of emails. "After I hot garbaged the reporter, I spent the day contacting the medical schools I'd applied to a few years ago. I'm apparently still a desirable candidate, and being a small media star, answers came quickly. These are the ones who accepted me based on my academic records and original application: Northwestern Medical. California, New York, Seattle, D.C., Toronto. Boston, and even England. It helps to have amazing test scores on file."

Her hands moved from my waist to sift through the emails. "I know I'm repeating myself, but are you serious?"

"I could stay in Chicago, but I think it's time to make the most out of my life. Follow through on so many things I've wanted to do. I can't continue being a detective after everything. Evan was my breaking point. It's time for change." I leaned over, snaking an arm around Sasha's waist. "And I want you to come with me."

She bit her lip, looking through the emails from different schools, different cities. "I don't know what to say. I mean, I still love my job and the reporters are finally starting to back off." She gave me a small smile. "Can I have a day to think about it?"

"Of course. This is all short notice and a bit of a surprise for you. I mean we've only known each other for barely eight months." I looked out the window. It felt longer as fall continued to creep in. But it was only early spring when I was assigned a rookie.

Sasha laughed. "Eight months feels like eight years, but I know what you mean. I want to think about it. I have Morgan to keep in mind. She's like a sister to me and I just settled into being a detective here and..." She sighed. "But I can't imagine not being with you."

I nodded. "Think about it. I file in the morning either way. I can sit at home all day and collect dust." I softly kissed Sasha. "I hear Seattle is nice this time of year."

Sasha playfully slapped me and went on to talk about her latest case. I let her words wash over me, daydreaming of a day when homicide wasn't the topic of the day. Every day.

* * *

The next morning, I sat outside of Captain Jameson's office. He had called me in, first thing, and I knew it was because he walked into my retirement paperwork on his desk. I could hear Jameson talking to someone in his office. It was a female voice, but as hard as I strained to hear, I couldn't pick up on who it could be.

Fifteen minutes later, Jameson's door opened and a tall woman with auburn hair exited. She was beautiful, and carried the same elegance Rachel did, and wore the same standard issue black pantsuit of the FBI.

As Jameson issued his goodbyes to the woman, her dark brown eyes drifted over to land on mine. She smiled as she shook Jameson's hand. "Thank you, Captain, for your time. I'll be in touch." The woman threw me another glance as she passed.

Something about her made me very uneasy.

Jameson folded his arms, leaning against the doorway. "In the office now, Tiernan. We need to talk."

I stood, smoothing out my button-down before brushing past him to sit in front of his desk.

He sat, folding his hands over the paperwork I submitted yesterday. "You want to retire for real this time?"

"I do. That's why it's sitting on your desk." I met his eyes, then blurted out. "Why was that FBI agent here? Detective Liang told me we wrapped up the Latin murders on our end. The rest was handed over to the feds to deal with."

"Unfortunately, that is way above your pay grade and you're about to retire." Jameson sighed. "Are you sure you want to retire? You have maybe five years left until full benefits. You could be living happily at forty." Jameson fingered through the papers in front of him.

He was pulling rank on me, and it irritated me. "I know, but I don't really care about full benefits. I'll get at least twenty percent of what I'm supposed to. Bottom line is, I don't think I want to do this job anymore. After everything that has happened, it's changed how I feel about so much." I calmed down a bit. "Liam, I won't make it to forty."

"We need you, Emma. You're the best detective out there. I don't want to lose you. What if I promoted you to Lead Inspector? You keep your office, no more field work unless you want it. You just look over other detectives' work and you won't pull cases?" Jameson was negotiating. Becoming a Lieutenant Inspector would be a big bump in pay. And I would be a desk jockey.

"Tempting offer, but I want to completely change careers. Follow through on things I planned a long time ago."

Jameson gave me a hard glare. "Captain. I'll give you Captain. I have approval from the Superintendent to make you Captain. Any district you want. Shit, you can have my job, I'm close to retirement anyways."

I laughed. "You want me to forgo my retirement, so *you* can retire?"

He shrugged. "It was worth a shot." He leaned forward and grabbed a pen. "Give me at least two months to find your replacement."

"Fine, I'll even help you find my successor. But keep in mind I might be leaving the city as soon as I settle on which school I want to attend."

Jameson scribbled his signature on the dotted line. "Please tell me you're at least going into forensic medicine?"

I shook my head. "General surgery, with a minor focus in research medicine. I don't want to look at any more dead bodies. I'll leave that to Dr. Willows."

Jameson handed me the signed paperwork. "Good luck Emma, you will be missed. Both you and your reputation." I reached to take the sheet, but he held it firm. "I'll leave the door open for you. If you ever want to come back or change your mind, I'll find a place for you. I promise."

"Thank you, Liam." I shook his hand. "Thank you for everything. You took good care of me from the moment I walked in this station, in those awful brand-new creased blues."

Jameson grinned. "You were one of the best, kid."

I nodded once, suddenly feeling emotional. I held up the sheet as a final goodbye and walked out of his office.

I stared at the signature the entire elevator ride to my office. Aaron was in his usual spot with his feet on my desk, sifting through a case file. I walked past him, and set the sheet from Jameson into my bag.

"Is it true? You've flown the coop?"

"Quite the analogy, but yes. Captain Jameson just signed off on my request after offering me two huge promotions."

Aaron leaned an arm on the desk chair. "How big of a promotion?"

"First Inspector Lieutenant, then Captain of any district of my choosing." I looked around the office, trying to calculate how many boxes I'd need for my things.

"Whoa! You're telling me you could be Captain and you turned it down? That's like the cake of cake jobs in the department. You wear fancy dress whites, drink coffee and have discount lunches at the best restaurants in town. That, and it's one step closer to becoming Superintendent of the entire city." Aaron sighed. I knew he had bigger ambitions but was constantly passed up when promotions rolled around.

"You know how much I hate wearing the uniform, especially the white one. It has 'public complaint department' written all over it. I also hate, *hate* politics and that's all that job is. Complaints and politics." I sighed. "Yeah, I could be making six figures, but at the end of medical school, if I choose to, I can be making twice that and doing good in people's lives."

"You think you don't do good for people in this job?" Aaron raised his eyebrows.

"Aaron, I don't need you to negotiate with me as well. I've made up my mind. I want out." I let out a breath. "I've done good things here, yes, but Evan has tainted that. Sasha and I will carry scars, mentally and physically from him, for the rest of our lives. Never mind the families who suffered at his hand. I can't keep on working cases with that in the back of my mind."

Aaron had nothing to say, so he pushed the case file to me. "This is the witness statement from the murder the other night, the one where you threw garbage at that reporter." He leaned back as I read over the reports.

I saw him looking around the office. "Aaron, I'll make sure you get my office."

His face broke out in a wide grin. "Can I have your chair?"

I laughed. "Yes, my one at home is way better than this one."

Aaron threw up his hand in victory, and I smirked. I'd just made his day.

I watched him as he silently measured the walls, picturing where his silly *Die Hard* posters would fit. I shook my head and turned my focus to witness statements and evidence reports. I was still a detective, for now.

* * *

I left the office early, leaving Aaron to size up my office and begin to phase me out of the remaining cases we had. I also had an appointment to get my right hand checked. It was slowly healing, even after I'd pushed it once again during the incident with Rachel at the hotel room. Sitting on the hard wooden chair, waiting for my turn with the doctor, I sifted through emails on my phone.

A text from Sasha came in as I deleted some joke emails from Aaron.

- Emma, I'll be over later. But I thought about it, and yes to moving in with you. I've always wanted to live down south. -

I smiled at the text, genuinely surprised that Sasha would want to return to D.C., but Virginia was beautiful, and she had mentioned how much she liked it during the short time we were there.

Before I could text her back, I was called into the exam room. I prayed my hand would recover enough to hold a scalpel in a few months, and grinned at the idea of never having to worry about holding a gun and firearm qualifications.

Retirement was already looking good on me.

Chapter 23

I asked Sasha to meet me in the park instead of back at my place, giving me a chance to walk around the city. The evening was cool for late summer, and for the first time in a long time, I enjoyed it. I sat on a bench facing the lake, watching the water and listening to the sounds of people soaking up the last few days of summer.

Sasha sat next to me. "Hey you." She leaned over to kiss me on the cheek. "Sorry if I'm late. I caught another body over on the Southside. It looks like a drug deal turned murder." She looked tired and it echoed in her voice. "Did you get my message?"

I nodded. "I was at the doctor, getting a check-up on my arm."

Sasha lifted my arm, running her fingers over the thin pink scar. "And? Are you cleared for duty, and maybe extra side duties?" She smirked as I blushed. Sex was a bumbling feat for us as of late. We were both healing, and anytime we started, one of us flinched in pain.

"Physical therapy starts in a couple days. I should be back to normal in four to six months." I shrugged at Sasha as she frowned. I reached up and pushed some hair away from her face, grinning. "Good thing I'm ambidextrous." I ran a hand down her neck, running a thumb over her pulse, drawing a smile out of her. "Back to your message: Georgetown? Right?"

"If that works for you, but there's one thing. Morgan's my best friend. I can't leave her here and when I told her you and I were talking about moving, she said she'd follow." Sasha gave me a questioning look. "She's like my little sister. She won't be living with us, but is it okay if she follows us down there?"

It wasn't that strange of a request. In the small dealings I'd had with Sasha's best friend, I saw how important she was to Sasha. I also knew how important it was to have some sort of family where you had none before. "I think it would be a good idea. I'll be tied up in classes for most of the day and I'd feel better if you had someone you trusted around." I sighed. Evan was always in the back of my mind. Morgan was street smart and could be an extra set of eyes. I was also sure I could bribe her to watch Sasha while I was in late night lab sessions.

She squeezed my hand. "Thank you. I know it's weird, but she's part of my family." Her eyes grew wide. "What about your house?"

I smiled. The house meant a tremendous amount to me and there was no way in hell I'd ever get rid of it. "The house is mine. I own it and I'll never sell it. When I'm old and grey, I'll want to spend the last of my days in that chair." I drew Sasha closer. "I'm renting it to Aaron. He's taken over the guest bedroom over the years, and he's part of my family. He'll take care of it until I roll up with my walker and false teeth."

Sasha laughed, laying a warm hand on my thigh. "I started my transfer paperwork after I sent that message. Captain Jameson agreed to help me get a spot in the Metropolitan Detective Division in D.C. He told me it shouldn't be too hard, even with the little experience I have here."

"You don't have to do this, Sasha." Guilt washed over me. She was about to change her entire life for me. As if she hadn't already given up so much. She moved her hand to rest on my stomach, making the little butterflies in it flutter.

"I don't, but I want to." Sasha scooted up, her hand leaving my stomach and moving to my chin, tilting it up. "I want a life with you, not a police department or a city."

She closed the small gap between us and kissed me. The butterflies in my stomach started fluttering to the point they felt like they would push through my stomach and explode out, over the lake.

I loved this woman wholly and was ready to start a new life with her.

* * *

With my hands on my hips, I stared at the boxes scattered over the floor of my office, sweating more than I liked from filling box after box with my reference books. I was set to leave in two days. The house had been packed up with the stuff I wanted to take to D.C., and the rest I'd leave for Aaron. The window was his, no raffle needed. The rest of the unit didn't dare fight me when I handed it to Aaron. He'd saved my life and been a hero at the Corn Cob Towers. I sighed looking out the window; these were his sailboats now.

Staring at how much I still had left to pack, I debated just leaving it all there. I wiped my forehead, frowning at how sweaty I was. It was unusually warm for this time of year and the air conditioning in the station was struggling to keep up. Grumbling to myself, I reached for another handful of psychology manuals. As I dropped them into the box at my feet, I heard a light knock on the door.

I turned to it, and was met with the tall auburn-haired woman I'd seen leaving Captain Jameson's office the day I retired.

"Lieutenant Tiernan, may I have a word with you? My name is Dana Reagan. Well, my formal title is Special Agent Dana Reagan. I'm the Unit Chief of the Behavioral Science Unit based out of Washington D.C."

Running a hand through my hair, I shook my head. "I'm retired, Agent Reagan. Two days out from never having to be called Lieutenant again."

Agent Reagan's smile lit up her brown eyes. "Exactly why I'm here to have a few words with you."

I closed my eyes. "What is it now?" Why couldn't the FBI piss off and leave me alone?

The agent closed the door behind her and moved a box from the chair to sit down. Agent Reagan looked around as she spoke. "I understand your exasperation with the FBI, but I'm here because of your retirement."

I pushed the box I was filling with my foot — not quite a kick — and shot a look at the agent. "In two days, I'm leaving Chicago and leaving my police career with it." I looked at all I had left to do, then sighed and sat down in my chair. "But I get the feeling you're here to offer me some sort of a job."

"In a way, yes, but that's not exactly why I'm here. I'm here for the files Agent Rachel Fisher provided you. It appears she 'borrowed' them, and I need them back as we continue to look for her and her kidnapper."

"Of course." I reached into the bottom drawer, removing the envelope Rachel had left for me. I set it on the desk, glaring at Reagan. "How did you know that I was in possession of these case files and reports?"

Agent Reagan picked up the envelope, dropping it into her briefcase. "I have sources." The woman crossed her legs. "Now, for that job offer. I understand you're officially retired, and your classes start in a week." She paused. "The Georgetown medical program is quite impressive. I also know your mind is impressive and I'd like to throw out an offer to do consultation work. As Agent Fisher was initially sent in to meet with you for... but became distracted."

I stared at the woman as she continued. "You won't be required to pick up another badge and slide on a gun, but we desperately need your help in locating Evan Carpenter and Agent Fisher. I can pay you a consultation fee to help with tuition." She cocked an eyebrow, studying me.

"I have more than enough money to take care of my tuition." It came off harsh, but I was tired of everyone around me trying to keep me in a badge.

Agent Reagan raised her eyebrows and provided a smug smile. "Fair enough, but I know otherwise." Her words had an edge as she leaned forward. "What I'm asking is that you use the brilliant profiler's mind you possess to help the FBI. It can be on your own terms and own time. I, in turn, can offer you a steady paycheck and protection until Evan Carpenter is dealt with."

This elegant woman had a steely gaze far more intense than Rachel's ever had been. It seemed the FBI made immovable women when it came to interviews and interrogations. "I can also offer protection to your girlfriend. Because you and I both know she's equally a focused target of Mr. Carpenter."

I took a deep breath to hold back my rising anger. "I, again, appreciate your offer, Agent—"

Reagan cut me off. "Think about it before you say no." Reagan, the more I stared at her, was incredibly attractive but incredibly agitating to be around. She stood and grabbed her briefcase. "Enjoy your move to D.C. I'll be by to talk to you in a couple weeks." She reached into her jacket, pulled out a business card, and tossed it on my desk. "My direct number. If you come to a decision that will appease us both, call me. As for the files, only law enforcement personnel will be allowed to view them."

Agent Reagan issued a hasty goodbye and left my office. I was now sweating more from irritation than the broken air conditioning.

I sat and stewed for a while, wondering why I was the constant focus of a federal agency. This whole ordeal started out as a local case then spiraled out of control. I knew after the incident with Rachel I'd be on the FBI radar, but it should've dissipated as I was leaving Chicago and law enforcement. I was now just a future victim.

I sat, staring out the window, enjoying the sailboats for the last time, when Sasha walked in.

"You're going to miss that view more than anything else, aren't you?" She was smiling, holding an iced green tea. I smiled at the gesture. It was too hot for my usual.

I nodded. "More than Chicago deep dish and the Cubs." Sasha walked over to kiss me as she handed the drink to me. A bold move, since the entire division could see in my office, but I no longer cared.

She sat in the chair Agent Reagan had just vacated. "Almost done with the packing, Lieutenant?" She smirked as my formal title came out.

"Almost. Then I was interrupted by a visit from the FBI." I took a sip from the tea, the ice doing its job in cooling me down. Sasha seemed to tense up when I mentioned the FBI was in my office again.

"Oh, what did they want?"

"To pester me to become a consultant. An Agent Dana Reagan from the BSU. She wanted the files Rachel left for me back, then offered me a job I shouldn't say no to." I shook my head. "I just want to be a doctor. I want to hang up my gun and badge for a white lab coat and comfortable clogs."

Sasha giggled. "Hmmm. You in a white lab coat. I think I like that image." She sipped at her coffee as I blushed. "What kind of consultation work did she want you for?"

"Profiler. Profiling Evan completely, and then possibly other serial killers and criminals." I leaned forward on the desk, "She offered me quite a bit of money, and protection for the both of us until Evan is found."

Sasha began to fidget. "I hate when he comes up. It reminds me how safe we really aren't until he's caught." She met my eyes. "Maybe you should take the offer? Aside from the protection, the extra money would be an added bonus." Sasha latched onto the protection aspect, and I didn't blame her. Evan had proven to be a sneaky and formidable opponent.

"Emma, you're really good at what you do. You are one of the best detectives I've ever seen and you're incredible at profiling. Why not do it?" I felt as if Sasha was pushing me like Reagan had, and it made me swallow hard. But as I stared at her, at the hazel eyes I couldn't resist, I knew my ultimate goal was to keep her safe.

I held a handout to her, and when she took it, I smiled. "I'll think about it after we get settled in the new house."

She leaned over the desk to kiss me. "That's all I'm asking." She kissed me once more. "I'll be home late tonight. The boys at the 6th are taking me out for my last day on the job." She stood, smoothing out her shirt. "You're invited. Morgan would love to buy you a shot."

I smiled, shaking my head. "I'd rather leave quietly and leave the Ice Queen behind in this office." I sighed. "Which has way too much shit in it."

Sasha laughed. "You know the department has eased up on you since you were hurt. They truly respect and admire your steel balls. Maybe they'll buy you a drink?" She gave me a look that said, think about it. "And as for the shit in here, leave it. You already have ten tons of books in the moving truck. Maybe Aaron will get bored and start reading these instead of those silly graphic novels he has stashed in his desk."

I smirked at her. "I'm a maybe on joining you." I sighed, kicking the box at my feet for real this time. "You're right. The rest of this crap, Aaron can sort through. It's his office now."

Sasha chuckled, shaking her head. "I'll call you later." She turned to walk out of the office. "Oh, think about Agent Reagan's offer, please?" She left me there, with half-filled boxes and the heat. I sucked down the rest of my green tea and called Aaron to come help me carry them out.

Chapter 24

"Iceman, how am I supposed to help you when I can barely pronounce the words on these flashcards?" Morgan blinked and held up a card scrawled with salpingo-oophorectomy in my messy handwriting.

I sighed as I looked at it. We were sitting in the living room of the rental house Sasha, and I'd moved into. The furniture came with the house, making me miss my things in Chicago. What little crap we brought with us, was unpacked and shoved on shelves in the bedroom and spare bedroom. The house felt distant, cold, and like we weren't really living there. It felt strange, and I couldn't justify it outside of being homesick.

I was three months into my first year of medical school, and enjoying it, but wasn't used to this kind of overload. There was a basic anatomy exam in a few days, and I was cramming my brains out. I was the oldest kid in the class, and felt the need to try harder than the rest. Morgan had stepped up to be my study buddy.

Morgan had become a larger part of my life when she followed Sasha and me to Virginia. She had a habit of showing up at the house unannounced, and I grew to like her more and utilize her as a study partner when Sasha was working.

"Morgan, just read the definition on the back. I'll guess the word." I rubbed my eyes. I was tired. Morgan and I had been studying all day. "Let's take a break."

Morgan jumped up from her chair and ran to the kitchen. "You guys still have leftover pizza?" She buried her head in the fridge to dig for leftovers. I'd known football teams that ate less than this tiny woman. I mumbled about her eating me out of house and home as she found the leftovers.

Stretching out my arms, I laid back on the couch and checked my phone for messages from Sasha. She had transferred into the D.C. Metro police department and had been assigned to the narcotics division until a spot in homicide opened.

Sasha was excelling at the job. She had the street smarts, and knew how to talk to people. It also helped that she wasn't looking at dead bodies on a daily basis.

The house we had rented was smaller than my Chicago home, but worked for us. In Richmond, it allowed us to be close to the city but still live in the quiet suburbs. Life was beginning to feel perfect. Perfect and normal.

Everything felt super domestic, except when Morgan and Sasha disappeared every Sunday for hours at a time, claiming it as 'best friend time.' When I'd ask Sasha about it afterwards, she'd only say they went shopping, ate all day and hung out.

When I brought it up to Morgan, she told me it was tradition, and no boys or girls were allowed in the best friend club. I found it odd, but didn't want to upset Sasha. She was starting to relax and not be so jumpy every time the house creaked from the wind.

My mind drifted to Agent Reagan. She'd not been in contact with me since that last day in my office, but I often flinched when the doorbell rang. I expected to find the elegant, infuriating woman standing at my door, waiting for me to agree to her terms. Becoming her coveted consultant.

I let out a breath and watched Morgan walk back to the couch with a pile of cold pizza precariously stacked on a plate. "You want a slice, Ice?"

I shook my head. "But I'm glad you feel comfortable enough to call me strange nicknames."

Morgan flopped down and balanced the plate on her lap. "Feel free to return the favor, but you can thank Sasha for that particular nickname. She couldn't stop talking about how frigid you were that first day, but how hot you were. So hot, she wanted to melt the ice off your pants before she ripped them off with her teeth." Morgan winked. "You definitely caught her by surprise. She kind of broke her own rules when it came to you."

"What do you mean break her own rules?" I watched the small woman chew on her pizza like a starved cow.

"Never get involved with a..." She paused, catching herself. "Um, never get involved with a boss." She smiled, batting her eyes. "I want some ice cream. You want some? Before we hit the big nerd words?"

"No, I think I'm done for the night. I memorized all these terms the first day. I'm just being obsessive." My eyes followed Morgan as she jumped off the couch and went to pillage the freezer.

"Hey, what did you mean never get involved with? I know she wouldn't have said boss. I technically wasn't ever her boss, just her training officer." Morgan paused her rummaging, then straightened up, her eyes wide with panic, widening more as the front door opened.

"Look who's home! Sasha!"

I turned to see Sasha, still wearing her vest and police badge draped around her neck. She was dressed in loose-fitting jeans and a grey Metro PD t-shirt. "Hey, Morgan, Emma." She dropped her large duffle on the floor and headed towards us. "I just finished a raid on a drug house on the east side. We seized twenty kilos of cocaine and a ton of cash. It took forever to catalog the evidence and interview all the jackasses in the house." Sasha sat in my lap, wrapping her arms around my neck and kissing me. "How was your day, doctor?"

I grinned, kissing her back. "Classes went fine. We started work on a cadaver, and Morgan was helping me prep for tomorrow's test."

Before Sasha could say anything, Morgan rushed into the living room grabbing her jacket. "Yo! Sash, hate to say hi and bye, but I need to get some laundry done." She shrugged her jacket on. "Walk me out?" I watched the two silently communicate.

Sasha slid off my lap. "Sure thing." Morgan walked out the front door, and Sasha leaned down to whisper in my ear. "Give me a minute to send her off. After my shower we can play strip flashcards."

I couldn't contain my grin, and pulled her down for another kiss. "Hurry up."

Sasha walked out, closing the door behind her. I waited a second before walking to the front window and peering around the edge of the curtain to watch Sasha and Morgan talk. I couldn't hear what they were saying, but by their movements, it was something intense, something that had my gut poking at my brain to pay attention. I caught Morgan looking back at the house and Sasha moving her hands from her hips to a folded position across her chest.

After a few moments, they hugged, and Morgan scrambled into her tiny beat-up sedan. I quickly sat down on the couch as Sasha walked back into the house, smile once again on her face. She tugged off her vest, setting her gun on the side table. "I'm going to shower, then meet you in the bedroom?"

"Sounds like a plan. I'll grab the flashcards and be right up." Sasha blew me a kiss and ran upstairs.

Gathering the notes and my lab homework, I waited until I heard the shower turn on before acting. My gut was begging me to indulge its nosy desire. Sasha had been acting weird the last few days, her and Morgan. It could be the case she was working, or not. I never ignored my gut, and sighed at the guilt of thinking like a detective when it came to Sasha. I trusted her — it had to be the drug bust. Nothing more.

I dropped everything into my school bag and set it by the door. Looking down, I sighed. Sasha's vest and gear sat in a messy pile. I picked up her vest and hung it in the closet, then grabbed her duffle with one hand. It was heavier than I anticipated, and one end dropped, spilling some of her gear and files onto the floor.

I shook my head as I knelt, shoving her gear back in the duffle and reached for the files. Most were for cases she was working on in the narcotics unit. Drug dealer rap sheets, informant profiles, and requests for surveillance forms were all jammed together. I felt thankful I never had to look at this type of paperwork again, when my eyes fell on a familiar blue logo.

I paused, then pushed the other papers and file folders out of the way, my jaw clenching on its own accord when I uncovered the bright blue FBI logo. I quickly looked upstairs. The shower was still running, with Sasha — poorly singing — inside. I picked up the file with the FBI logo and scanned the cover. There was nothing preventing me from opening it.

Sasha had never mentioned that she was working with the FBI, or even the DEA. Every night she would tell me her latest case or sting operation, obviously excited to be back on the streets in any investigative capacity.

I sat back on my heels and opened the file. The curiosity was killing me.

The cover sheet was on Bureau letterhead, signed by my second favorite FBI agent, Agent Reagan. It was addressed to another agent, but the rest of the name was removed, blacked out with a marker like I'd seen in spy movies to protect the identity of the agent in question.

The cover sheet introduced the progress report on an undercover project that appeared to have been going on for the last year or so. I read it over, skimming past the basic federal cop lingo. Fifty-dollar words replaced the five-dollar ones I used in my own reports.

I turned the page and my phone blasted Aaron's ringtone at the same time. The page held my personnel information sheet from the Chicago PD. There was also the sheet Rachel created in the short time she interviewed me. My phone vibrated as it rang around the coffee table, and my heart raced. I'd call him back.

I frantically flipped through the file, but pages were clearly missing. They'd fallen out with the others when I'd dropped Sasha's duffle. Searching through the pile, I heard the shower turn off. I paused when Sasha called my name and then began to shove her files back in. I shoved the duffle into the closet, and ran to grab the phone before it went to voicemail. "Hang on, Aaron."

Sasha came downstairs wrapped in a towel. "If that's Aaron, tell him I said hi and that I miss him." She winked, mouthing for me to hurry up before turning and bouncing back upstairs.

My heart was racing, and it wasn't at the sight of Sasha, wet from her shower.

"Hey, Aaron, sorry about that."

"No worries, Lieutenant." Aaron had promised he would never stop calling me Lieutenant. It was his way of keeping me humble. "You alone?" The tone in his voice had me worried.

"Sasha is in our bedroom getting ready for bed." I kept my eyes on the closet. I wanted to dig into that duffle to find the missing pages. To know why my personnel file was in the hands of the FBI and my girlfriend.

"Ooh. Am I interrupting something?" Aaron was turning on the perve.

"Not yet, but if you don't hurry up, I'll hang up on you."

"Ok, ok. This really isn't a social call. I got word through the grapevine, and my contacts. Evan was spotted at the Kentucky-West Virginia border. A local sheriff spotted him as he tried to get gas at a truck stop. The sheriff went to pull the car over, a chase ensued, but Evan and his companion escaped."

"A companion?" Nausea struck me in a rush.

"They can't get a good enough ID from the truck stop's security cameras to determine if it's a male or female, let alone a face to run through the facial recognition programs." Aaron sighed hard and I heard the creak of my leather couch in the background.

"How do you know it's Evan?"

"The fucker made sure his face was seen on camera, multiple times. He still has a limp but appears to be back in action. I'm worried he's headed for you, and it pisses me off I can't do a damn thing. I called the metro chief and informed her what the deal was. She's promised to discreetly attach units to you and Sasha."

"That's not necessary. He'll slip past them even if they're sitting on my lap." I walked around the living room, to the desk pressed into one corner. Pulling open the drawer, I looked down at my gun. Loaded and ready, it had sat in the drawer since the moment the movers had placed the desk there.

"Don't tell Sasha about this." I lifted the gun with my right hand. It felt foreign, but I finally could grip it without too much pain. "Keep me updated if you hear anything more. But in a strange way, I want him to come for me, because this time I'll be ready."

"Jesus, Emma, you sound like John McLane."

I laughed. "You really love those movies, don't you? How many of your *Die Hard* posters are hanging in my office?"

"All four movies are gracing the walls of *my* office. I figured since I didn't get your Lieutenant spot, no one would yell at me for spicing up the walls." Aaron sighed. "I'd feel better if you'd let the locals watch you."

I shook my head. "I don't want more dead bodies because of me. He'll kill to get to me, and I'd rather leave him a clear path. As morbid as that sounds." I looked up when Sasha called me again. "Aaron, I have to go, but can you maybe do me a favor?"

"Anything for you."

"Can you send me Sasha's full police record? I want to try and pull some strings and get her out of narcotics. She always smells like weed when she comes home." My instincts were telling me something, and I needed to keep it quiet until I had hard proof.

"Ha! Sure thing. By the way, how are you two doing?"

"Living the domestic dream, a cop and a medical student. Kind of like the plot to that porno you have stashed in your bottom drawer." I smiled as Aaron choked on whatever it was he was drinking. "Goodbye, Aaron."

I hung up and set my cell phone down. Sliding my gun back into its holster, I dropped it in my school bag by the door. Then took it up to the bedroom where Sasha was waiting, wearing nothing but flashcards.

* * *

Two days later I sat alone in the library at school. I'd finished my afternoon class and was waiting for an evening study session with my lab partners in the cadaver lab. I sat down in a private booth in the library and pulled out what Aaron had sent me of Sasha's police record. I'd never got a chance to get back to her bag. She'd taken it to work with her the next morning, and left it there.

Sasha appeared a little different, almost wary, when she came home the next night, and when I asked her about it, she claimed she was tired from her shift. She then called Morgan and the two disappeared for drinks as I headed in for my evening class.

I loved Sasha with everything I had and was falling deeper in love with her as we lived together. I was showing signs of finally being happy. But there was something eating at my gut and I had to sort it out. I no longer had any contacts in the FBI aside from Agent Reagan, and the moment I called her she would pounce on me, shove her job offer in my face. The FBI started to leave a bitter taste in my mouth ever since I saw the files in Sasha's bag. It's like they were always a step behind me, hunting me like Evan.

I trusted Sasha, but there was something in that FBI file that begged me to look deeper. I wanted to ask Sasha straight up, but the cop in me wanted to gather a little more intel before I laid it all out. Strengthen the evidence before I made any accusation. Rule number five in my personal rulebook of detective work.

The police record stared at me until I picked up the front page and began reading. Sasha Garnier was a very straightforward police officer. She'd been hired two years after me and excelled at road patrol work. She received a commendation for saving a fellow officer after a gang shootout on the Southside.

The rest of her record was standard. She took the detective test and almost matched my score, but fell five points short. Sasha was well-liked by her supervisors and coworkers and had glowing reviews from supervisors.

I couldn't find anything suspicious in her record, which in itself was suspicious.

My police record was dotted with commendations and complaints — every cop had at least one or two citizen complaints. It was unusual if you retired without a single citizen complaint.

I read over her resume and the initial application Aaron had graciously included with my request.

Aaron had written a note on the application, explaining his findings.

I did some digging and it looks like Sasha applied to the FBI two years ago. She went through the full interview process and all that jazz but wasn't selected for further consideration. She took a four month leave of absence. Losing the FBI devastated her, and it looks like she wanted to take time to rethink her career in law enforcement.

Aaron had circled the date she moved to the homicide division. It was dated right after she returned from her leave of absence.

Blankly staring at the pages, I knew something was off. It made sense that Sasha had been shaken by being rejected, and had moved to the homicide division for a new lease on her career. She'd been tentative and new while I was her FTO, always making the usual fumbling rookie mistakes.

My brain was working in full blown detective mode, tearing things apart and reorganizing them into critical puzzle pieces. I scribbled some notes and texted Sasha that I wanted to talk to her after my study session. I would put the pressure on her in person. I hated doing it, but I had a growing feeling she was hiding something from me.

As I collected my things, stuffing them back into my bag, my fingers grazed the edge of my gun. I sighed. I'd been carrying it with me every day now that Aaron told me Evan was moving in on us.

Leaving the library, I moved down to the basement cadaver lab. As usual, I was the first one there. I looked at the clock. The rest of my lab group wouldn't arrive until at least eight-thirty.

Everyone in the group hated the evening study sessions, and most would show up with beer on their breath, agitated at me for being already set up and impatiently waiting for them. Dr. Ice Queen was about to make her appearance. I set my bag down and began to pull on my lab coat.

Crossing the room to our cadaver, I pulled the plastic sheet away, exposing the work we had done the day before in class. I sat on a rolling stool to review my notes, glancing up at the clock every few minutes. It was now a quarter to nine and the lab was silent, with just the rustle of my notes filling the room. I rolled over to my bag, and dug around for my cell phone, to message the rest of the group.

As my fingers wrapped around the phone, the entire lab went black.

My cell phone offered the only light in the incredibly dark and eerie room. I tried to dial, but the thick, ancient concrete walls of the basement prevented any signal from getting through.

An uneasy feeling flooded my veins and I reached back into the bag for the gun, then slipped it into the pocket of my lab coat. Standing up and using the cell phone as a light, I crept to the door, and flicked the light switch on and off. Nothing. The power was out.

I then reached for the doorknob, only to find it locked from the outside. Someone had locked me inside the room.

"Should I start calling you 'doctor' now, Emma? Or do you still respond to Lieutenant?"

My hand jammed into the pocket, fingers wrapping around the gun. "How do you always find me?" I spun in the dark, facing the direction of Evan's voice.

"Honestly? It's not that hard when you have a federal agent at your disposal. You see, my sister still has access to all the databases necessary to track someone. The FBI is slow to revoke privileges, but then again, I think they want her to access the databases. They have their own secrets to hide, but I'll get to that in a moment. Where was I? Ah, Rachel! When coerced, Rachel always gives me what I ask for."

Evan's voice was steadier than the last time I spoke to him. He had to be standing at the other end of the cadaver lab. His voice carried across the cold, concrete room.

His soft footsteps echoed as he moved closer. "If you're worried about my sister, don't be. She's still alive, but not for long. As soon as I finish with you, she's next. She's only alive to help me keep track of you." Evan paused. "I don't like talking in the dark. It reminds me of the days at St. Mary Francis when they would forget to pay the electric bill." I heard a hard click and the lights flickered back on.

It took a minute for my eyes to focus in the harsh fluorescent light. When they did, I looked straight at Evan, sitting on a stool, spinning around with a grin on his face.

"Ah, much better!" He stopped spinning, cocked his head and looked at me. "You look different, Emma. Healthy, and dare I say happy?" He smirked as he rolled the stool to a table, leaning on the edge to play with the plastic sheet that covered a cadaver. "I can't recall the last time I saw you happy. It does look good on you. I hate that I have to ruin it, though."

"I promised I'd kill you, and I will."

Evan laughed. "Promises, promises. And yet I'm the only one who ever follows through on promises." Evan sighed and stood, reaching behind his back to pull out a large knife. "Before we get started, I want to tell you a story." His evil grin took over. "I got a kick out of it when my dear, sweet sister told me. It was what actually fueled my inspiration to come and find you. I wanted to wait a little while longer. Maybe wait until you were closer to becoming a doctor. I had it all planned out! I'd wait until your graduation day and make it a night to remember." Evan shrugged. "Then Rachel spilled the beans on one very painful night for her." He looked me dead in the eyes. "How is your lovely little girlfriend, Sasha, by the way?"

I sucked in a calming breath, gripping the gun tighter, walking slowly as I moved towards Evan. "You leave her out of this. This is between you and me."

Evan took slow, jovial steps in my direction. "This is going to be fun! Do you even know who you sleep with at night? Do you really know her?" Evan was balancing the knife in his fingers. "By the look on your face, you don't."

"I know who my girlfriend is. You almost killed her, and now I'll make sure your death is far more painful than you could ever imagine," I hissed as I pulled out the gun and pointed it at his chest.

Evan frowned, pausing. "Not this again, Emma. I wish we could do this like gentlemen."

I aimed the gun at his head. "This ends now!"

Evan cackled. "Stealing my own catchphrases! You *are* adorable, my dear Emma. But you know better." Evan ducked quickly as I fired the first shot. The bullet pinged off the concrete walls, and the lights flickered out.

The shot ricocheting off the walls rang loudly in my ears. I didn't hear Evan move close to me until I was knocked to the ground. The gun was kicked out of my hand, making me groan as my still healing arm twinged with pain. I scrambled to get up, but a heavy boot kicked me in the back, dropping me to the ground before it pressed between my shoulders.

"When will you learn, Emma? I'll always be faster and smarter than you." The lights flickered back on and Evan stood over me. I groaned — someone had to be helping him. I tried to roll away and scream Rachel's name.

Before I could react, his hands shot down, jabbing two scalpels deep into my thighs, making me shriek in pain and lose feeling in my legs. Evan had sliced through nerves.

He laughed as he watched me try to pull the scalpels out like a broken crab. "You aren't the only one who's been studying medicine. It's fascinating how one small nick can keep a person down."

Evan yanked my arms behind my back as he dragged me to an empty table. I tried to fight him, but he pressed on my wrist and I was riddled with pain.

He handcuffed me before hauling me up onto the steel table. Careful to avoid my attempts to headbutt him, he laughed again. "Come on now, Emma, you need to learn better moves." He strapped me down and watched me writhe in anger.

"I'll fucking kill you!"

Evan smiled as he picked up my gun and set it on my stomach. "Feel free to. I'll leave this here as incentive. But in the meantime, I need to finish the story you so rudely interrupted. I *so* want to see your face when you find out you've been betrayed by the one you love."

"Sasha would not betray me. Stop trying to get in my head!" I kept wiggling, trying to slip my hands out of the handcuffs.

Evan grabbed a stool and pulled it over to the table, sitting down. "You trust far too easily, Emma. You trusted I wouldn't know you had a gun in your pocket. You trusted it would be too hard for me to find you. You trusted you'd be safe in the basement of an empty medical school, closed for the evening for cleaning." Evan grinned. "People will follow signs like ignorant little lemmings." He spun in a slow circle on the stool.

"And lastly, you trusted the woman you love to have no secrets at all. That her ineptitude as a police officer is just that, and not a cover up. A well-acted ruse."

"Shut up! All you know is lies." I winced in pain as the handcuffs bit deeper into my wrists. The adrenaline surged through my veins, keeping me conscious and fighting.

"Oh really! Well, I guess the file you found in sweet Sasha's bag from the FBI has nothing to do with you. Her strange leave of absence from the Chicago Police Department was just that. Her leaving because she was sad about being rejected. I bet you even believe her name is actually Sasha Garnier."

He raised his eyebrows at me as I swallowed hard, and he laughed with glee. "I can see it on your face, so I'll answer your question. How do I know these small things? Rachel. And I never stopped watching you. I just waited while I watched." Evan leaned closer to me, his breath curling around my ear. "Your dear, sweet, girlfriend is not who she appears to be."

I stared at Evan hard as I slid a handout of one handcuff, scraping large chunks of skin off, hissing the words out to cover the pain. "*I will kill you.*"

Evan stood up from his stool, rolling his eyes. "You repeat yourself and it's very annoying. I'm tired of this. You never want to listen when I want to tell you something important." He reached down to the slash in my thighs, twisting the scalpels, the renewed agony making me scream. "Such a shame. Now you will die knowing nothing." Evan shrugged. "I do hate cliffhangers."

He twisted the scalpels once more, then reached for his knife.

I couldn't breathe as I sobbed from the pain he was inflicting. "My final goodbye to you, Emma. I'll make sure Natasha knows how you died when I visit her next." I met his eyes, clueless to who he was talking about.

He saw the confusion in my eyes and grinned, bringing the knife to my throat. "Let's be quick about this, this time around, shall we?"

I flailed my arm up to grab his hand, blood covering my fingers, handcuffs swinging from my wrist. when I heard the lab door crash open. Evan looked up, giving me the chance to roll and punch him hard across the jaw, throwing him against the steel cadaver table across from us. I didn't waste time looking at what forced the door open, working on freeing my other hand and willing my legs to respond, when I heard Sasha's booming voice.

"You move, and I shoot! Drop the knife!"

Sasha was red faced, her gun aimed at Evan. The intensity in her eyes, directed at Evan, frightened me. She made no move to look my way, solely focused on the maniac next to me.

Evan smirked. "Ah! The good agent finally arrives to save the day!" Evan stood, rubbing at his jaw then turned to me. "Shall I make the introductions?" He nodded at Sasha. "Emma, may I present to you Special Agent Natasha Clarke. Federal Bureau of Investigation."

I looked between Evan and Sasha, watched her flinch, but she never broke her focus on Evan. "One last warning. Put the knife down." She growled the command out.

I couldn't pull my eyes from her as my stomach rolled. Things were coming together in my head, making my heart hurt.

Evan shook his head. "You agents and your warnings are so very annoying." Evan acted quickly, throwing the knife at Sasha just as she pulled the trigger.

A handful of shots rang out. I watched them hit Evan, all of them landing on their mark. Only one of them needed to be fatal.

Evan crumbled to the floor, lifeless.

The air thickened with the smell of blood and gunpowder. Sasha lowered her gun, looking at her stomach. Evan's knife had struck her abdomen on the right side. She pulled the blade out with a groan, quickly covering the wound with her hand, but blood seeped through her fingers.

Sasha stumbled over, set her gun down on the edge of the table and uncuffed the dangling handcuff, then reached for my bloody hand. I flinched away from her and yanked the scalpels out of my thighs with a scream, falling to my knees when I tried to stand. I winced, limping the two steps to Sasha, blood soaking through my jeans. Covering her wound with my hands, I swallowed and asked her, "Is he dead?" It felt like a ridiculous question, but nothing was ever certain when it came to Evan.

Sasha swallowed hard, nodding as she leaned against a table. "He should be. Nine shots to the chest and one to the head isn't survivable, unless you're Superman." She gripped the edge of the table, wincing.

I looked back at Evan and saw she was right. He had a neat bullet hole in the center of his forehead. His cool blue eyes were open and lifeless, staring at the ceiling.

Ripping off my lab coat, I balled it up to press against Sasha's stomach. "We have to get outside. There's no signal down here and I need to call you an ambulance."

Sasha nodded weakly. Morgan burst into the room with a gun in her hand and a gold badge flopping against her chest, shouting, "Jesus Christ, Sasha! I told you to wait for my signal!" She paused when she saw Evan's body on the floor, then looked back at Sasha and saw the blood on our hands. "Oh shit, oh shit, oh shit. Did he shoot you?"

Sasha shook her head, pale and woozy. Morgan wrapped an arm around Sasha as she pulled out a radio. "Yeah, we're all clear. We got one fatal, one agent injured, and we need a bus now. Send the guys in." She tossed the radio on the table, helping Sasha sit.

"Can you walk?" Morgan glanced at my bleeding legs.

"I think so." I wobbled, wincing at the immense amount of pain radiating from the slashes on my thighs where Evan had twisted the scalpels.

Morgan nodded. "I'm taking her out okay? There'll be a bunch of dudes in black tac gear swarming the room in about thirty seconds."

I tuned Morgan out, limping to stand over Evan. Staring at his lifeless body, I knelt down, fighting through the pain. I needed to know for sure. I pressed two fingers against his neck, checking for a pulse.

When I didn't find one, I took a breath and whispered. "It might have not been me, but promise fulfilled, you bastard." I stared at him a little longer, before Morgan grabbed my arm.

"Iceman, help me with Sasha. We need to get her to the ambulance."

I stood up, flinching and groaning, and eyed the gold badge around Morgan's neck. The letters FBI mocked me. When I met her eyes, she gave me a weak smile. "We have a lot to talk about, Emma. But first we have to make sure she survives this." I said nothing, but I helped Morgan roll Sasha towards the paramedics as they burst into the room.

They scooped her up, dropped her on a stretcher. She was pale and on the verge of passing out, but blinked as Morgan whispered something in her ear.

Our eyes met, and she tried to smile as hers welled up with tears. My view was cut off by a paramedic suddenly in my face. Asking if I was okay. When he finally moved, I was left alone in the room. The eerie silence mixed with the smell of cordite. And yet, it felt like the nightmare had started over.

I was placed on another stretcher, my thighs bandaged and an IV jammed into my arm. Looking past the paramedics that hovered over my legs, I watched as a crew of techs in their blue FBI jackets with big yellow letters on the backs placed Evan's body in a bag and hoisted it onto another stretcher. I continued to watch until the body was rolled out of the lab. My eyes caught Agent Reagan standing off to the side, talking to Morgan.

She saw me, excused herself from Morgan and came over to where I waited on my stretcher.

"Lieutenant Tiernan. Evan Carpenter is dead, for good this time."

I frowned as my former rank fell out of her mouth with ease. "Who is Sasha?"

Agent Reagan looked down at her folded arms. "There's a lot we have to discuss with you, but I will tell you this much. Sasha Garnier is actually Special Agent Natasha Clarke. She's part of an undercover unit attached to the BSU." She nodded towards Morgan, who was talking to other agents. "Morgan is also a Special Agent, and Sasha's partner for the last couple of years."

Tears streamed down my face. "Why?" My heart was breaking. The woman I was hopelessly in love with was not who I thought she was.

Agent Reagan sighed. "Like I said, we have a lot to talk about. After you get checked out at the hospital. Those thighs will need stitches." Reagan motioned to the paramedics to roll me away. I reached out, grabbing her arm.

"Is Sasha okay?"

"She's alive, and they have her stabilized. She saved your life, in more ways than one." Reagan motioned to the paramedics, and they rolled me away, shoving me into the back of an ambulance. My last sight was Evan's black-bagged body being rolled into a plain white coroner's van.

His reign of terror had finally ended, but I was now faced with so much more. More lies and deceit. I swallowed hard and let the tears fall, looking at hands stained with Sasha's blood.

Chapter 25

I sat on the edge of the bathtub in my rental house, and stared at the bandages in my hand, trying to remember what the nurses had said about how to wrap my thighs.

I'd spent a night in the hospital before I, once again, checked myself out. This time I did take the offered cane. The slashes in my legs made it difficult to properly bend and walk without looking like a broken robot. I had asked about Sasha once, while filling out the discharge papers. The nurse smiled, only telling me she was doing fine. I tried to go and see her, but when I stepped around the corner to her hospital room, I saw Agent Reagan standing next to her bed, obviously talking about what went down in the lab. Sasha's face was wracked with emotion, holding back tears. I stared at her for a moment, my heart tightening as I questioned who I was looking at. The tears slid down my face. I couldn't shake the feeling I'd been lied to, used, and left with a shattered heart. I'd turned away, limped to the lobby, and took a cab home.

I closed my eyes, holding back the tears. It had been a week since Evan had cornered and attacked me.

It had been a week since Evan was killed.

A week since I watched him die in front of my eyes.

A week since it was revealed the woman, I loved was not who I thought she was. I hadn't spoken to Sasha since we were carted off in different ambulances. I saw Morgan for a few minutes after my thighs were cleaned and stitched. She profusely apologized until she was pulled away by another agent. She apologized but never explained what the fuck was going on and why Sasha had been lying to me.

Aaron called, worried as ever. Two days later, he showed up at my doorstep with his bags and took over as the big brother he couldn't help but be. I tried to ask about Sasha, but he would only tell me she was fine and move onto different topics. He knew me better than I knew myself. Picking at an open wound wouldn't let it heal.

A shiver ran through my body, I'd just gotten out of the shower, had half-dressed myself, was still sitting on the edge of the bathtub wearing a blue button-down shirt. I paused halfway through the buttons as my mind drifted away, then looked back down at my legs. At the bandages with tiny dots of blood seeping through. A soft knock on the door dredged me from my spiraling thoughts.

"Emma? You okay?" Aaron was trying to give me privacy as he spoke through the door.

"I'm almost done in here." I stood up, and my legs buckled again. I frowned. I'd had to ask Aaron for help as my legs were still stiff and sore. It was embarrassing when I needed help — especially from Aaron — but he never said a word as he helped me to stand or helped pull on my sweatpants.

"If you need help, shout." Aaron's footsteps trotted away from the door.

I reached over, and grabbed the grey dress pants that sat on the edge of the sink. Aaron was driving me down to the FBI headquarters to meet with Agent Reagan for my final debriefing. Well, what I hoped to be my final debriefing. The FBI could kiss my ass. And kiss it hard.

I felt a small victory when I pulled my pants on and got ready by myself. Gathering damp hair back into a ponytail, I left the bathroom, using my cane like a frail old woman.

Aaron was waiting for me, grinning as I slowly descended the stairs, each one testing my pain tolerance and patience. "Looking good, Lieutenant."

I gave him a blank stare. I was so not in the mood for much lately, not his positive attitude, or just still living a home of lies. My days had fallen into an easy routine of crawling into bed where I would sleep for hours, then making my way to the couch. Where I would stare at the TV for hours with Aaron next to me. Rinse and repeat with no end in sight.

I had lost focus and the point. The school semester was lost. It was hard to miss days in medical school, even after the university offered to keep me on the roster until I healed. I was already six months ahead of the rest of the class, but I politely declined. I couldn't deal with the thought of going back to the cadaver lab after what had happened. It wasn't the fact Evan died in the room or that I had been beaten down once again. It was the sickening amount of betrayal that stained that room and my life.

I took Aaron's offered hand to help me down the rest of the stairs. He said nothing else until he handed me my grey suit jacket. "Ready?"

I nodded through a tight smile, fighting back tears.

"Emma?" Aaron looked sideways at me as he navigated traffic. He had yet to ask me if I was okay or needed to talk, which is why I appreciated him being around. He never picked or dug when I was hurt, sad or emotionally broken. He just sat and waited for me to break the silence.

My parents wanted to come down for a visit. Aaron ran interference, telling them he would take care of things. Honestly, I didn't want anyone to bother me, and Aaron was the only one I could tolerate at the moment.

I was looking out the window, staring at the hills and old houses of Richmond roll by. "You already know what I'm going to say."

"I know, but I have to ask." He paused, then blurted out, "She really loves you, Emma. Don't be an idiot."

"Save it." I shot him a dirty look.

"Emma, I'm serious. We talked a lot while you were in the hospital after the first attack. She never left your side. Sasha was always there, always asked about you even after she transferred out of our precinct. I can see it in her eyes. She truly loves you. Even if she was working undercover, her feelings for you are real."

"Or she's one of the best actors in the world. I really don't want to talk about this, Aaron." I hissed through clenched teeth.

Aaron nodded, biting the inside of his cheek. "For what it's worth, Emma, even a blind man could see she's in love with you."

"Shut up Aaron."

His jaw twitched. "Yes ma'am."

The rest of the ride was soaked in silence.

* * *

A gracious intern allowed Aaron to walk me to the door of Agent Reagan's office before he was ushered away to the lobby to wait. I was left with a faceless secretary who escorted me to a side conference room.

"Ms. Tiernan, please have a seat. They'll be with you in a minute."

I nodded, and eased myself into a seat in the large room. I spun it around, so I could take in the view from the large floor-to-ceiling windows, peering out onto the bustling streets below. My head hurt and felt painfully empty. I was drowning in so much emotion that my mind was blank. I felt nothing. I zoned out, watching the traffic patterns of cars and pedestrians merge and mingle.

Hearing the door whisper open, I swung around in the chair to see Agent Reagan walk in, closely followed by a young man who carried a stack of files.

"Good morning, Ms. Tiernan." Agent Reagan offered a warm smile as she sat across from me. The young man handed her the files and she flipped the top one open. "We'll get started in a few minutes when the others arrive." She glanced up. "Would you like anything? Water? Coffee? I can have Brian grab anything you need." Reagan's tone was softer than it ever had been with me. She appeared to be kind, or at least wanted to appear kind.

"Water would be fine."

Reagan motioned to her assistant, who hopped up and poured water in glasses. He set one in front of me with a soft smile. I went to open my mouth, to thank him, when the door opened again. Morgan walked in, wearing a black pantsuit with a red shirt underneath and her hair up, away from her face. I couldn't help but stare for a moment. I'd only ever seen the woman in ratty goth clothes, and here she was, sitting next to Reagan, looking like the professional she truly was.

Morgan smiled at me, throwing me one of her patented winks and mouthing a hello. I nodded at her, a small smile pulling at the corners of my mouth. I was mad at her, but more amazed that she was an undercover agent. My anger was muted. She'd hid things from me while becoming a close friend. Looking at her now, I saw she wasn't hiding anything from me other than she had a job to do, and I had been a part of that job. That, I could understand.

The door creaked open again and as I looked up, my heart dropped into my stomach. Hard.

Sasha slowly walked into the room, dressed in a dark grey pantsuit, her hair up in a similar fashion to Morgan's. When her eyes met mine, she paused. Morgan had to clear her throat and wave her to take a seat. Sasha broke the stare and sat in the chair, wincing as she leaned back.

Sasha and I had not spoken since we were in the cadaver lab, and I had no clue about her recovery, but as she moved gingerly in her seat, I knew her abdominal wound must still be painful.

Agent Reagan clasped her hands on top of the files. "Now that we're all here. Let's start the debriefing." She motioned to Brian, who set a small recorder in the middle of the table and hit the record button.

He leaned forward, speaking in an even tone. "This is the final debriefing for undercover Operation Eclipse. In attendance is Special

Agent in Charge Dana Reagan, Section Chief of the BSU. Special Agent Brian Athens, administrative assistant to Agent Reagan, Special Agent Morgan Adams, Special Agent Natasha Clarke, and lastly, retired Detective Lieutenant Emma Tiernan of the Chicago Police Department."

I looked at the swirls and knots in the large maple table in front of me. I'd stopped paying attention the moment I heard Sasha's real name and official title. Pain shot through my heart. It took me a minute to focus on what Reagan was saying, to realize that she was speaking right at me.

"Ms. Tiernan, I understand you may have some questions and concerns about what exactly this debriefing is all about."

"That's quite an understatement." I glared at the woman.

She just smiled, leaning back in the chair. "Operation Eclipse started about a year ago. We had leaks in the BSU unit that desperately needed plugging. We know now it was because of Agent Rachel Fisher, also known as Catherine Carpenter." Reagan picked up pages from the file. "She had been using federal resources to track down her brother after the horrific murder of her wife. She actually knew about you before Evan Carpenter did, and took it upon herself to track you down. Knowing you'd be the one thing Evan couldn't resist. You fell on our radar shortly after she first pulled your foster records eight months ago."

She set the pages aside. "We decided, during this time, to send in undercover agents to work with you and determine if you were also working with Rachel or Evan. Since your past with Evan was of a criminal nature, our profilers suggested you could've been brainwashed into being his pawn once again. Then it became a matter of keeping tabs on you as that theory was proven wrong, as his attention and violence towards you amplified. Then Rachel started to use you as bait, and I felt it was best to keep agents on you for protection."

Reagan looked at me. "You have to understand, the FBI has been hunting Evan Carpenter for almost a decade. We attributed almost thirty-five murders to him and we had no evidence to link him to it.

Until Agent Fisher found you. Agent Fisher understood the significance you held and became further obsessed in time with her need for morbid revenge." Reagan waved a hand at Sasha and Morgan. "Agent Adams and Agent Clarke were assigned to investigate you. Agent Clarke was a perfect fit since she'd already worked in the Chicago Police Department and was quite familiar with you. It made for an easy integration. Agent Adams was sent in as backup."

My eyes locked on Sasha's. She wouldn't hold my gaze for long without looking away, her tears begging to fall. My anger at being a number one suspect was incomparable to the anger of being lied to.

I kept my eyes on her as I spoke. "Why did you go through this much trouble? You could have easily come to me and asked for my help, like Agent Fisher did. I would've enthusiastically helped you, and it would've saved me a few new scars, let alone almost bleeding to death in a filthy parking garage. And maybe three people would still be alive." I returned my focus to Reagan. "This was all unnecessary. Two agents were almost killed. My trust and love have been compromised to a degree I may never get it back. You strung this operation out like a bad cop movie, leaving breadcrumbs for a killer to hunt me, trap me, and almost kill me a fourth time? All so you could lure him into your hands." I didn't care that I was in a room full of federal agents. I was done being professional. I was hurt, and throwing verbal jabs wherever I could.

I caught Morgan trying to calm Sasha down by squeezing her thigh. My words had landed exactly where I wanted them to, with venom.

Reagan pulled out another page. "We had no idea where Evan was at any given time. Agent Fisher was an incredible agent, which made it difficult for us to track her personal investigation of her brother. It was easier and proved to be beneficial to keep an undercover agent with you after we eliminated you as a threat, and Adams and Clarke are two of my best. The results show this was a successful operation. Evan is dead, and I've collected enough evidence to tie him to other murders."

"So, you used me."

"Not at all, Ms. Tiernan. We tried to bring you into the operation, but you were very resistant. Then *feelings* got in the way." Reagan shot Sasha a dirty look. "We had you under surveillance for months before Agent Fisher discovered you were in the foster system with Evan; unbeknownst to us, she found a connection we never thought of. I sent her in to pull you into the Bureau and hopefully end the operation with you in our employ and working together. Sadly, she did not do that, and it was Agent Fisher who delivered him right to you. We continued watching over you. But Evan moved faster than we expected, resulting in Agent Fisher's kidnapping and Agent Clarke's injuries. All unexpected occurrences."

I laughed, fighting down my rage. "Really? You do realize your agent brought this monster back into my life? I was living a very quiet life until then." I turned to Sasha. "And the feelings that got in the way? Was that all just bullshit too? Just a way to keep tabs on me? The bumbling rookie detective façade was obviously an act as well, wasn't it?"

"The feelings were true." Sasha's voice trembled, just above a whisper.

I laughed again. "The fuck they were." I turned back to Reagan. "You should be ashamed of yourself, whoring out an agent to get under my skin and into my bed, just so you could make the nab of the century with a serial killer and his insane sister." I pushed myself up from the chair, wincing as my legs wanted nothing to do with it. "Fuck you. I almost died chasing the bastard you brought into my life." I pointed at Sasha. "She almost died, twice, unless that was another orchestrated plan of yours."

Morgan stood up, yelling. "That was real, Iceman! Her feelings for you, all of it!"

Her unprofessional outburst made Reagan cringe. "Adams, sit down." Reagan glared at Morgan, who kept a hard stare on me even as she dropped back in her seat. Sasha remained quiet, her head down, as Reagan spoke. "Agent Adams and Agent Clarke saved your life and killed that man, Ms. Tiernan. If it hadn't been for them and their quick action, I fear I may be reviewing your own murder." Reagan had an edge to her tone that pushed me right over the edge into full blown rage.

"I'm done here. Fuck all of you!" I looked Sasha dead in the eye. "Especially you, *Natasha*." Every syllable of her name came out laced with poison. "You knew me, you knew my life, and you played my heart so I'd trust you. You played me until I thought my heart was whole again. You used the pain of losing Elle to gain advantage, for what? All for the stupid fucking Bureau to have an advantage in catching a serial killer? If you'd just asked, I would've caught him without leaving a trail of bodies behind us. You told me you'd fallen in love with me. That's all bullshit lies now, isn't it?"

I snatched my cane, dipping to grab my bag, and angrily limped past the four agents, now sitting in silence. I stopped behind Sasha.

She was trembling, her head tilted down, refusing to look up. Brushing her arm as I reached past her, I shut off the recorder before I spoke in a hard whisper. "I loved you, whoever you are. I loved you more than you could ever imagine." I took a breath, leaning closer. "Fuck you for lying to me and breaking my goddamned heart."

I hobbled out of the conference room as Morgan hopped up again, trying to defend her best friend. I walked away as she sputtered a handful of curse words at me.

Leaning against the wall by the elevator, I was on the verge of losing it in a tearful rage. I'd never been this angry, not even when I lost Elle. I'd been lied to, used, and worst of all I'd opened my heart to Sasha and she filled it with lies.

A soft click of heels on the tile floor was followed by Sasha's voice, shaking with choking tears. "Emma, please let me explain."

I closed my eyes, and put more weight on my cane. "Let me go, Agent Clarke."

"No. Not until you hear me out." She moved closer. I stepped closer to the wall, praying for the elevator to hurry up.

"I think I heard enough." I turned to glare at her. She looked exhausted and pale. "You really aren't an inept rookie detective, are you?" I flashed through memories of how Sasha stumbled through the basics like a green rookie, then turned around to surprise me with shining moments of the kind of impressive detective work that only came with training and experience. I frowned. She'd purposely pulled the wool over my eyes when I began to fall for her. I'd traded in my normal sensibility for the feeling of loving again.

Sasha shook her head. "I was recruited from the department after the gang shooting where I received a commendation. I was then pulled into the undercover unit by Agent Reagan, and assigned to you." She paused, cringing. "I didn't mean it like that."

The ding of the elevator broke the moment, and I was grateful for the escape. "You're quite the actor. Maybe you should leave police work and become an actress." I stepped into the elevator, and the doors started to shut.

Sasha quickly stood between them, holding them back with her body. She looked in my eyes, hers filled with so much sadness and regret.

"Emma, everything that happened between you and me was real. I fell in love with you. I fought it so hard because I knew it wasn't right to get so deeply involved with you." The doors pushed at her, begging to close, like I was silently begging them to push her out of the way and save me. "It wasn't a game for me. What I felt for you — and still feel for you — is real." She blinked back tears.

I sucked in a breath. "Can you move out of the way? I'd like to leave." I stared her down, watching as the tears fell. They ran down her cheeks as she stepped back, whispering, "I love you, Emma." The doors closed, cutting off my view of her.

I didn't stop as I passed Aaron in the lobby, only grumbling out, "We're leaving now." Aaron had to jog after me.

Silence filled the car for the second time that day.

The moment I was home, I stripped off my jacket and threw it on the floor in a crumpled ball. Aaron came around the corner with my bag. "Whoa, Emma. You good?"

I sucked in a shuddering breath and completely let go. I shook my head, finally let the sobs pour out of me as I leaned on the arm of the couch, gasping for air. Aaron was quick to embrace me, holding me tight. "Let it all out, Emma. You need to."

And I did. I let everything out in heaving sobs, crying until I couldn't breathe or feel anymore.

* * *

I woke the next morning on the couch, a blanket tucked up to my chin. I was still wearing the pants and button-down I'd worn to the debriefing, and as I stretched, I felt pain everywhere. It even hurt when I rubbed my face and looked at the coffee table. There was a bowl and a box of cereal with a note taped to it.

I'm at the gym, be back in an hour.
Eat something.

Aaron

The cereal box went untouched. I walked past the coffee table and slowly tackled the stairs to my bedroom. I sat on the edge of the bed and stripped off my pants, cringing when I saw my bandages needed changing. I pulled off my shirt, throwing it on the floor and leaned forward on my knees, holding my head. I felt like crying, but I'd cried myself empty the night before.

Scrubbing at my face, I glanced around the room. Sasha was everywhere. Her abandoned clothes sat in the closet, a picture of us from my last day as a Chicago detective sat on the dresser, and her perfume soaked the room. I stood and shuffled to the closet, dragged out one of her suitcases and started to throw her clothes into the bag. I picked up the picture of us where we were smiling and happy to be starting our new life, and turned it face down before placing it on top of random t-shirts, jeans and jackets. I was still frowning as I hobbled to the bathroom. I started the shower and abandoned the good memories, desperate to push through my anger. I was overwhelmed with too many emotions, I had no idea where to start. I hoped the hot water would beat some sense into my thoughts.

* * *

I was back to sitting on the edge of the bathtub, clumsily bandaging my thighs. I was exhausted, and steam radiated off my body from the boiling hot shower I'd just taken. Desperate to burn away the heavy feelings.

The front door opened, and I heard Aaron drop his keys on the table. I dried myself off, pulled on an old comfy t-shirt, and held onto the edge of the sink to drag myself to my feet.

Aaron's footsteps entered the bedroom, and I spoke before he could. "Before you ask, no, I didn't eat. I'll eat when I feel like it and no, I don't need help putting my pants on." As I stood, I twisted the wrong way, sending a jolt of pain through my legs. I lost my balance, scrambling to grab onto the sink before I fell flat on my face.

I didn't hit the floor as expected. Two very familiar strong arms caught me, and pulled me close. I gasped at the feeling, also feeling my stitches pull a little too hard.

"Emma, you should really learn to be more careful in bathrooms."

Sasha's voice was gentle but shaky as she held me, her heart pounding as hard as mine.

I grabbed the sink edge and pushed out of her arms. "How did you get in?" It was a stupid question. She used to live here, and I hadn't asked for the keys back.

Sasha stepped back as soon as she saw I was steady on my feet. Her eyes drifted up, saw I was still pantless before looking at the ceiling to protect my modesty as I sat down on the toilet to pull my sweatpants on.

"I still have keys, Emma."

Huffing, I struggled to get dressed and Sasha took a step out of instinct to help me, then caught the hard look in my eyes. She paused, clenching her hands together in tight, nervous fists. "I thought — I didn't think you'd be home. I came over to grab my things." She was stumbling over her words, then she closed her eyes. "Actually, I was hoping you'd still be here."

I snapped at her. "Where else would I be?" She flinched at the harsh tone.

"Back home in Chicago. Aaron told me you were talking about moving back."

"I'd appreciate it if you refrained from asking my friends about my intentions." I stood and hobbled out of the bathroom, careful to avoid touching Sasha in any way. I snatched my cane, poking at her suitcase as I walked past it. "I took care of the closet. I don't know what else is yours, but you can take care of what you have to. Aaron will be back in a few minutes, and he can take me anywhere but here." My words were edged and sharp. They cut deep, and when I turned to Sasha, her arms were folded tight against her chest. She was visibly biting the inside of her cheek to check her swirling anger.

She swallowed hard. "Emma, I need to tell you what I couldn't in that conference room."

"Are they the same things you couldn't tell me while we laid in bed together, professing our undying love for each other? Or while you gathered intel every moment of every day you were with me?"

"Emma, that's not fair."

I cut her off, yelling. "What's not fair is, you got to me! You're quite persuasive, I'll give you that. But you got to me, completely! Made me lose my sense of caution and I became ignorant to what my instincts wanted to dig deeper into. I'm a profiler. I see through the worst and best, and yet I couldn't see through your masks. I ignored the signs, because I fell in love with you. Hard and fast. I became weak and doe-eyed." I turned away from her to stare at the dresser. I was angry, and I had no reason to hold back.

"Even geniuses fall in love, Emma." Sasha mumbled the words out.

I hobbled to the edge of the bed, my back to her. "I was just a job, wasn't I? Everything was an act. The bumbling interviews, your sweet little childhood story. All of it was scripted, even down to knowing my favorite drink order. All fed to you by the FBI agents watching me." I turned to look at her over my shoulder. "What happened — *actually happened* — when we were interviewed separately after the warehouse, where you almost died?" My breath suddenly hitched. The memory was painful and now even more, knowing it might've been a set up.

Sasha's voice shook. "You were never a job, Emma. Everything I told you about me and my feelings for you, it's all real. The complete truth."

I cocked my eyebrow in disbelief. "Did they ask you to whore yourself out to me? Or was that an improvisation on your part? Knowing I'd most likely share more with you during pillow talk?"

I'd hit a nerve, and I watched Sasha turn a bright red color, then explode. "Fuck you, Emma! Use your brain to look at me and see I'm not lying when I say every moment we shared, that was me. Natasha. You got me, not the undercover agent. Me." She tapped an angry hand over her heart, fuming. "Agent Reagan was right when she said my feelings got in the way. I fell in love with you. Completely, unexpectedly, and with all of my being."

I snapped back. "No, fuck you Sasha — *Natasha*. You're avoiding the questions I'm asking! I don't think you'll ever answer them honestly. It doesn't matter anymore. The case is closed, over, and you're free now."

I stood up, stepping closer to her, our noses almost touching. "The only person in this whole fucked-up ordeal who ever told me the truth was Evan." Pausing, I watched Sasha fight rage and tears in her eyes.

"You're free to go, *Natasha*." I looked at the overstuffed suitcase to drive my point home, then wobbled out of the bedroom. I hit the stairs as I heard Sasha let out a choked sob.

I hobbled downstairs and across the foyer, bursting out the front door in desperate need of fresh air. I stood in the front yard, letting the hot sun beat down on me.

Aaron pulled into the driveway, and I rushed to his car. I had to go. Leaning out the window, his grin faded. I growled as I walked across the front bumper. "Aaron, get me out of here."

He glanced at his ratty gym clothes. "Can I change first? I had to sit on a towel on the ride home and I'm pretty sure I smell like shit."

I threw him a death glare and shouted. "Just drive the fucking car and get me the hell out of here."

"You miss your nap, Emma? You're a big crab ass."

I reached for the door handle while Aaron asked what was up my ass, then he paused. I looked up to see Sasha at the front door. Her face was streaked with tears and she clutched the suitcase with clenched fists. I heard Aaron mumble. "Oh fuck."

Sasha caught my eyes as I gripped the passenger door, my knuckles turning white. She cocked her head, silently asking something, anything from me.

I broke her stare, trying to get into the car without looking like a broken doll. "Aaron, now." I flopped onto the seat, cringing as I smacked my leg on the center console and bit back a scream.

He looked between Sasha and me, then back to Sasha. "Sorry, Emma. You can bitch me out later."

He slid out of the car and ran lightly over to her, and grabbed the suitcase out of her hands before walking her to her car, an arm around her shoulder. The two spoke while I watched through the rearview mirror. Sasha glanced back at the car, and wiped her face when Aaron gave her a hug then jogged back.

He started the engine, looking over. "Don't say it. I get you're pissed off beyond belief, and hurt too much to see what lies beneath. Doesn't mean I can't thank her for saving your miserable life, Emma." He backed the car out of the driveway. "I think you need a drink. The first round's on you."

I rolled my eyes and leaned back just enough to see the rear of Sasha's car drive out of view. My heart ached and for a split second I felt horrible for how I'd treated her. Then I remembered the sea of lies I was drowning in, and huffed.

"There's not enough alcohol in the world, Aaron."

Chapter 26

Two weeks later, I sat alone in the rental house. Aaron had gone back to Chicago. His vacation time had run out and Jameson needed him back immediately to cover new cases. He reluctantly left, asking at least two times for me to come back to Chicago with him. I had to shove him out of the door, and told him I'd call if I needed him. My legs had healed to the point that I could move on my own with ease, and I didn't need someone to put my pants on for me anymore.

My laptop sat open, notes and flash cards haphazardly strewn all over the coffee table. I was attempting to study, hoping it would fill my head with knowledge and not pain since I honestly had no clue where to go next in my life.

I didn't know how long I'd been blankly staring at the screen filled with lab notes. I sighed, rubbing my stomach, and headed to the kitchen. I missed Aaron's cooking and his mother's old Chinese recipes. I flicked a look at the empty takeout containers strewn all over the kitchen counter. Yeah, I missed him for sure.

I recanted this sentiment when I bumped into the massive piles of magazines he had collected and left on my desk. I lifted a stack with weird video game art on it, with nthe intent of tossing them into the recycling bin, and paused when I saw the lone silver key sitting atop of a picture of Sasha and me.

She had left it the day we fought and I kicked her out. I found it that night after Aaron brought my drunk ass home from the bar. I'd tried to throw it out, but was too drunk to remember where the garbage can was. It remained there, until it eventually became covered with video game and sports car magazines.

I stared at the picture, Sasha's handwriting scrawled across the bottom. Four words written in black ink. Four words that stung as I read them.

I love you, Emma.

I couldn't bring myself to touch the photograph. I covered it again with magazines and continued on to the kitchen.

The doorbell rang as I stared at the beer and ice cream Aaron left for me, trying to decide if I wanted to get drunk, or fat, or both. The doorbell rang again as I wobbled to it, picking up my gun on the way. I held a steady hand against the door as I looked through the peephole.

I sighed as I opened the door to reveal a smiling Morgan standing on the front porch. "Hey, Emma."

"Agent Adams." My voice carried an edge.

Morgan frowned. "Knock that shit off. I'm still Morgan, your favorite study buddy." She saw the gun in my hand, and pointed at it. "Maybe you want to let me inside and put that away?"

I leaned over, setting it on the side table. "What do you want?" I wasn't in the mood for visitors or conversation.

She brushed past me. "Why, thank you! I'd love to come in!" She flopped on the couch, kicked her feet up on the edge of the coffee table and eyeballed my messy attempts at studying. "Back on the doctor horse? Already missing those big nerd words?"

"Why are you here?" I kept an even tone. I wanted to be left alone but for some reason couldn't be mean to the woman.

She chuckled. "Nice to see the Ice Queen has returned." She toed the pile of notes next to her foot. "I came to have a bro to Ice Queen chat with you in regard to my best friend and FBI partner."

I said nothing, prompting Morgan to continue.

"I know you're real pissed off at her and the situation. You want nothing to do with her. That's fine, that's your jacked-up prerogative, but after a few days of pulling pieces together and drinking all my booze, Sasha told me things. The things she tried to tell you, but you didn't want to hear nor believe." Morgan pushed back into the couch. "You might want to sit down. This will take a minute."

"Morgan, there's nothing I want to hear."

She ignored me. "Sasha and I've been best friends and partners for about two years now. She saved me from the streets and took me under her wing. Then pulled a few strings and got me this sweet undercover job. I know what you're thinking. I don't look like federal material, but it helps when you speak fluent Russian and most of your family is connected to one Russian mafia or another."

She tapped her temple. "I'm also super smart, just never cared to apply myself." Morgan's ice-blue eyes turned serious. "Sasha is my sister. We know each other inside and out, up and down. My girl was so excited when she moved into the undercover unit after graduating from the FBI academy, but then they assigned her to Eclipse on day one. All because she knew of you and the department and was somewhat familiar with your past. She got nervous, real nervous. Ya see, my Sasha always had a thing for you. A crush, hero worship, whatever you want to call it, while she was working the road. Then to top it off, the suits deluged her with your background, your habits, patterns, everything but what your favorite color of underwear was. Mix that with your awesome ice box attitude in the first days she worked with you and it made for a fun time at home. Sasha would come home bitching and fuming about you and how big of a dick you were."

She smirked. "But every night, I saw there was more to it. She was falling for you, and it was *frustrating* when you threw ice cubes in her face."

I was overcome by the urge to sit down, as I absorbed what the fast-talking agent was spewing forth. My sore legs begged for me to sit and I fumbled into the chair across from the woman. "Morgan, this is all irrelevant. I was just a job."

Morgan chuckled. "Sometimes the smartest people are also the dumbest. Sasha broke protocol the day she kissed you outside that victim's house. Something she never did. Either in Chicago or the FBI. But when it came to you, the stunning Detective Lieutenant Emma Tiernan, she threw the whole damn rule book out the window faster than you could say Ice Queen. After your steamy awkward kiss in the street, she knew it."

Morgan glared at me. "She came home freaking out. She'd 'broken' her own rule of never getting too involved with victims, witnesses, etc. Let alone she just kind of cheated on her boyfriend."

My head shot up, eyes wide and dead on Morgan's.

She winked. "Yeah, Sasha was dating a dude, had been for quite some time. They'd met at a bar while we were celebrating becoming sweet ass agents. They became pretty serious for a while. He even confided in me that he was going to marry her. But after that kiss, shit fell apart in her world. She couldn't hide the love brewing for you and broke up with the poor sucker right after you left her on the curb."

Morgan paused for a moment to see if I was still listening. "Sasha started to lose the purpose of the operation. She was falling in love with you and struggled with the fact she was hiding things from you. It caused her to fuck up, and fuck up a lot. Her transfer out as your partner was her idea. She had to create distance and you really hurt her with the stupid shit you said. Then you and Evan tangled, and she forgot about keeping the distance. She never left your side while you were in the hospital. Then you told her you loved her, and it changed her completely — but then her focus became you and you alone, and she began fucking up more. That's how Evan nabbed her. We had intel come in that night the shitbag was in your neighborhood, but Sasha had turned her phone off. She always turned it off when she was with you. I can't vouch for you, just for her. But when it was you two, you got the real deal. The real Natasha and not the FBI agent. The girl whose eyes lit up like diamonds when she saw you or when she ranted about the little things you did and said." Morgan stopped for a moment, her cheeks pinked with anger.

I spoke before she could tear into me. "It doesn't matter. She stuck with it. The lies and the operation. She did her job."

Morgan hopped up from the couch, startling me. I watched as she walked into the kitchen, helping herself to the fridge. "That's where you're wrong. Not your fault, though. The FBI was adamant on keeping your ass in the dark." She came back to the couch with leftover Chinese. "Sasha tried to quit, bail on the entire operation. Those nutty-ass interviews Koo Koo Fisher did with you? Yes, Fisher was directed to separate you. One, so Sasha could be debriefed and updated on the sitch, and two, they were waiting for you to see through Fisher's bullshit and go rogue."

Morgan wiped her mouth with the back of her sleeve, speaking through a messy mouthful of noodles. "Sasha wanted to quit. I was in the room with her when she went apeshit on SAC Reagan. Asking to be removed from the operation. She couldn't keep lying to you and dragging you through the shit that was the Carpenters. I was shocked. She openly admitted to the suits in the room she'd fallen in love with their prime witness."

I sat silent, fixated on a point on the wall as Morgan continued.

"She had to play the game and the suits were rough on her. SACkface denied her requests, explaining we were at a critical point in the operation. Blah, blah, more bullshit. They scared Sasha into thinking if she pulled out of the operation, she'd lose you to Evan. Then the suits threatened to transfer her to the other side of the damn world if she didn't finish out the operation. They laid a thick mindfuck on her."

Morgan propped her feet up on the coffee table. "Sasha wanted to move down here so she could be closer to the FBI headquarters. The

Sundays we'd disappear, we were down at headquarters looking for loopholes to get her out of the operation without making things worse than they already were. You were getting suspicious, and it didn't help my big mouth almost blowing it during our study date. Sasha was happy down here — that was legit — and she'd found her out a few weeks before the lab shootout. An ancient loophole from the twenties that would allow her to pull out of the operation free and clear to pursue a future with you. She was a day away from setting it in motion when I got a weird voicemail telling me Evan had you cornered. Sasha left in the middle of a drug bust, ignoring my command to stand back until I had the boys in place."

Morgan grinned. "Yeah that. SACk-face put me in charge after Sasha went wonky." She set down the empty takeout container. "My girl kicked down that door for you. Killed Evan for you, but it totally sucks balls that Evan laid down Sasha's semi-secret like he did." Morgan met my eyes. "Sasha loved you, still loves you. She made stupid decisions because she was trapped. Trapped in wanting to keep you safe and loving you to the point she'd throw it all away... and tried to do just that."

I remained silent as Morgan finished her speech. She leaned over, slapping my back. "This is the honest to God truth, Ice. I've never seen her so far in love with someone."

I took a steady breath. "So many lies, Morgan. I was used."

The dark-haired woman stood, shrugging. "So was Sasha." She walked past me, squeezing my shoulder. "I have to jet. I meet my new partner in a few hours."

She noticed the look in my eyes. "Sasha left the UC unit a week ago. She's a desk jockey over in the intelligence division." Taking steps towards the front door, she spoke over her shoulder. "I hope one day, now that you know the truth and maybe when you're a fancy doctor, you can forgive her. You both love each other more than you want to admit, and before you tell me I'm full of it, it's written all over your face right now. You love her just as much as you hate her."

Morgan saluted me and left, the door clicking behind her, leaving me in the hard silence of an empty house. I was furious with myself. I hadn't let Sasha talk, and I'd let my unchecked anger consume me. I stood, walked to the pile of magazines, and pushed them off the picture lying at the bottom.

I slipped the silver key into my pocket, lifted the picture, and stared at it for a moment before I set it on my laptop to prevent my tears from smearing her words.

* * *

A month passed, and I fell into the same old habits I'd created when Elle died. I became closed off and distant, and eventually dropped out of the semester until the next year. I was too far behind, even for my own liking.

Making decisions in the silent house, I closed out the lease and called Aaron, telling him he would soon have his favorite landlord as a roommate. I then called Captain Jameson to set up a meeting for my possible return. Thankfully, his offer to ride a desk was still on the table. I was running out of money and applying for random jobs I thought might be interesting. Low paying, but interesting and free of dead bodies. But the job was the only thing I knew I could do on autopilot.

* * *

When I walked into the station three days later, it felt like I'd never left. There were some new faces, and some old ones who offered up a smile when they saw me, versus the Ice Queen stares I once received. I met with Captain Jameson and the Superintendent of the department, who were both eager for me to come out of retirement. We negotiated, and I settled on taking the captain position Jameson had offered me months ago. While I was gone, Jameson had taken my lead and filed his own retirement. I'd be taking his spot until a proper replacement was found, then I'd move to the training division and become the head of detective training.

I took the interim promotion for the pay bump and negotiated holding the Captain position for two years. By then I'd have saved up enough to be financially free from work and could focus solely on medical school. In truth, I had no stomach for going back to school right now. I just wanted to fly on autopilot until I worked through my tangled mind. Being a cop was a job I knew and still could do better than anything.

And there was an added bonus to returning to a full-time job in the department. They would pay for my therapy.

I walked out of Liam's office. The new Captain bars dug into my palm before I dropped them into my pocket. I was met with Aaron leaning across Jameson's secretary's desk, trying to pull a date out of thin air with Betty's younger replacement. It seems I'd started a retirement craze.

I walked up behind him. "Excuse me Detective Liang, but do you think this is proper office etiquette?"

Aaron froze and turned. "Holy shit, when did you get back?" He punched me in the shoulder, grinning like an idiot.

"A couple days ago. I've been staying with my parents. I had to make sure things were taken care of and it's been a while since I saw them."

"Your mom was getting close to busting in your rental door and laying down mom law on you." Aaron laughed. "But what are you doing here? In the station?"

Before I could answer, the Superintendent walked out of Jameson's office behind me, and shook my hand. "It's great to have you back, Captain Tiernan. I look forward to a long future of working with you." He briskly walked away as his assistant handed him a phone.

Aaron's mouth fell open in shock. "Shut. The. Shit. Up. *Captain* Tiernan? You didn't?"

I shrugged. "I had to. I needed a job. I can't afford school right now and I really don't want to work at Barnes and Noble, even though they called me for a second interview." I shoved my hand in my pocket, fingering the gold bars.

Aaron shook his head and motioned me to follow him. "My office." He turned, walking towards the elevator.

We said nothing until we made it to his office, my old office. I smiled when I saw the giant *Die Hard* posters hanging perfectly on the walls I'd once filled with books and diplomas. Aaron closed the door as I sat in his old spot. "Emma, are you kidding me? You're back?"

"I don't need a lecture, Aaron. I need a job. I'll be taking over for Jameson until they find a better replacement, and then I'll move to the training unit, teaching rookies. Which I think is the only thing I can handle until my head and heart..." I drifted off. "You can keep your office. I now have one with working air conditioning."

Aaron shook his head, ignoring my lame attempt at humor. "Have you talked to her?"

I shook my head as my stomach twisted. "No. Last I heard of her was when Morgan stopped by the house explaining the point behind Operation Eclipse and the fallout. All the things Sasha wanted to tell me, but instead I yelled at her and walked away." I fidgeted in the chair. "I can't expect you to understand what I'm feeling, but I haven't let go of the pain and the hurt. And before you tell me it's like when I lost Elle, it's not. It hurts more because of the lies, the betrayal. Everything is still very alive in my heart and I'm struggling with it along with my feelings for her."

"You still have feelings for her?" Aaron offered a hopeful look.

"I don't know if they're feelings of hate or love, Aaron. It just hurts, a lot. More importantly, my trust has been lost." I had to stop as tears blurred my vision.

"Well, Lieutenant, or should I say Captain Tiernan, welcome home." Aaron dug in his pocket and removed a key, sliding it across the table. "The moving van showed up this morning. All your stuff is inside. I've moved into the basement, since I practically lived down there anyways, in that glorious man cave."

I rolled my eyes. "Woman cave. I bought the TV to entertain guests during football season."

"Well, it's my room and 55" TV now." He squinted at me. "Is it against the rules if command and grunts live together?"

"If it is, I don't really care. Just as long as I still have my leather chair and my window." I stood. "What are they going to do? Fire me?"

The sound of Aaron laughing followed me as I left his office in search of mine.

Three months passed quickly. I'd begun to settle in as acting Captain, taking over for Jameson. The job was not as bad as I'd thought. I did have to deal with a bit of politics, but my reputation as a Lieutenant followed my promotion and many stepped lightly around me. Aaron would come into my office at least once a week to fill me in on what he was doing as I checked over case reports, complaints, and other mindless administrative paperwork.

He and I fell into an easy living arrangement. It was like living with my brother. I enjoyed it more than I wanted Aaron to know. His mere presence was healing.

The thing that irritated me the most was my uniform. Wearing the white shirt and gold accents again made me feel weird, especially when I was ogled by men and women alike. I'd been hit on in the coffee shop and a few times in the lobby as I checked on an incoming citizen complaint.

* * *

Even with the mindless piles of paperwork as a distraction, I thought about Sasha every day. Some days they were angry memories, others would give me glimpses of her in my arms in the first light of morning. I often found myself staring at the desk she'd once occupied as I sat in Aaron's office discussing lunch options.

I'd not heard anything from her since our fight at the rental house. Morgan called here and there, sent random emails and even called to congratulate me on moving up in the world, and to also remind me she still held rank over my gold bars. But in the times my office door was closed, or when I would sit and look out the front window at the lake, I would start to think about her and how much I missed her. The pain drifted away as days passed and I was left with a numb feeling. I couldn't place it, but there was something there and it wasn't always anger.

Today, I was lost in a particular memory — her sitting by my hospital bed — while analyzing the clues I'd missed about her being more than just a rookie. I was starting to realize that what Morgan told me was true and I'd been too emotional to see it.

My daze was broken by my secretary, who came into my office with a small package. "Captain, here are your travel arrangements and the updated conference itinerary."

"Come again?" I took it with a hesitant look.

The young woman smirked. "I figured things would get lost in transition. You're leaving in three days for the National Police Chiefs and Command Conference in Washington D.C. Captain Jameson was scheduled to attend this year as the Superintendent's representative for the department."

I blinked, still confused. "Excuse me?" Tearing open the package, the letter from the Superintendent and flyers for the conference scattered across my desk.

"It's an annual conference to improve upon policing across the nation. There are special guests, and seminars held by all the federal agencies. It's truly a cop convention." She smiled as she said it. "Apparently you're the jewel of the Superintendent's eye and he's selected you to be his ambassador."

I frowned. "Those were his exact words?"

The girl nodded. "Of course, but I took care of the arrangements. I've upgraded you to a suite at the hotel, and a car will pick you up. All your meals and expenses will be covered." She winked at me. "Those gold bars are good for something."

She left my office briskly as I stared at the flyers. Normally, I loved seminars and conferences when it came to psychology or new evidence collection techniques. I even once attended a conference on the human genome project in Iowa, but this conference sounded like a straight up dog-and-pony show. Groaning, I collected the flyers, plane tickets and hotel bookings and shoved them into my briefcase. I then looked at the calendar. It would be another three months until my replacement arrived, and I could fade into the training division, not running the homicide division. There was no way I could put this conference off.

I hit a button on the desk phone. "Aaron, my office now, and bring the good scotch you stashed behind Die Hard 2."

The last thing I wanted was to go back to Washington D.C.

The epicenter of lies.

Chapter 27

I felt uncomfortable in this sea of pompous, uniformed men and women. I'd just walked into the welcoming event for the conference, and I felt stiff in my dress uniform, a shining beacon of black, white and gold, and matching hat.

My discomfort amplified when I saw the ratio of men to women was sorely not in my favor. Squishing my dress hat under my arm, I navigated towards the open bar, where I received even more inappropriate looks. I stood out. It was rare to see a thirty-six-year-old woman wearing a tailored uniform, let alone one with gold bars on the collar.

A few times I was stopped by police chiefs and other high-ranking officers who knew who I was from the media coverage of Operation Eclipse and the downfall of Evan Carpenter. Many of them skirted around asking the questions I knew they wanted to ask. The ones about Evan and how I didn't know I was part of the FBI operation. Some of the details of Operation Eclipse had been made public through the FBI's media representatives to highlight to the public their federal agencies were still doing a good job keeping the world safe.

With a whiskey firmly in hand, I navigated back through the sea, making my way to the far side of the room where there were sign-up sheets for seminars and the other networking events. I scanned them over, only finding a few that interested me. One in particular caught my attention. 'The Psychological Effects of Serial Killers on Victims.'

I scribbled my name down, intrigued about how the information would be presented.

Scanning the other sheets, I heard a familiar laugh off to the left. I froze, pen in hand, until I heard it again. I grimaced and took a deep breath before turning in the direction it came from, but couldn't see anything over the crowd of people.

I was about to abandon the search and seek out another whiskey, when I heard it again. I swallowed and pushed through the crowd, my heart racing just as my eyes found the owner of the laugh, when a chief from some small town in the Midwest stopped me, excitedly introducing himself. Ambition shone in his eyes.

"Captain Emma Tiernan of the Chicago Police Department. I heard you were attending! I'd love to sit down and talk about your profiling and the work you've done through the years. I want to bring new training tools into my own detective unit."

I looked down at the smaller man. "I appreciate that, but I'm here to learn like you. I'm not sure I can provide you with..." I stopped when I glanced up and saw her.

Sasha stood in a circle of police chiefs and obvious federal agents with matching dark suits and government haircuts. She was laughing with the Boston police chief, her laugh echoing around me, drowning out the man standing in front of me. In her pale grey and blue pinstripe suit, she stood out in the bland crowd, a blue button-down hugging close to her curves.

I stared at her. It had been a long time since I'd seen her without tears in her eyes. Her smile was wide and bright, and the dimple I used to kiss while she slept was out in full effect.

Her long light brown hair was up, and I found my heart pounding uncontrollably. A wave of emotions was crashing over me. The chief in front of me had to half yell my name to pull my attention back to him.

Not only did it break my stare, it also caught Sasha's attention. Her smile faded for a second as the small man shouted my name and she turned. Our eyes locked.

It was as if someone hit the pause button on the whole room. Her smile faded, and sadness swept over her eyes. I couldn't look away from her, until the small man in front of me put a hand on my elbow, breaking my focus.

Frowning, I hissed. "To be honest, I'm only here for show. I don't give two shits about anything other than free food and drinks. If you want to know about my profiling techniques, read the article I published three years ago for the American Psychological Association. Please excuse me." I looked up to see Sasha moving through the uniforms and suits towards me. I panicked. I left behind the shocked, irritated little man and shoved through the crowd until I was out in the main lobby. I took a deep breath, trying to slow down my heart. I was shaking, clutching my dress hat harder against my side as I searched out the nearest elevator.

I found a large bank of elevators to the left, and rushed towards it, politely smiling at the endless number of uniforms walking past me. I hit the elevator button once, then twice, fifty times, hoping to speed up its arrival.

"Emma?"

Her voice made my heart skip.

"You might be in uniform, but I'd recognize you even if you were wearing a chicken suit." Her voice was soft, but tentative. I turned to see Sasha standing a few feet away. She smiled, but there was pain in her smile.

I swallowed hard. "This is pretty close to a chicken suit." I looked down at my uniform with its blazing gold accents. I whispered. "I didn't think you would be here, Natasha."

Hearing her full name from my lips, Sasha shifted from one foot to the other. "I'm part of the intelligence group leading the seminar on the legalities of wiretapping and inter-departmental intelligence gathering."

She chuckled. "Now I sound like a genius." I flinched at her words, and she caught it. "Sorry." Sasha cleared her throat. "So, a police Captain? What happened to medical school?"

Her words stung. "You know what happened." It came out harsher than I wanted.

I looked at the elevator doors, cursing their slow descent to my rescue. "Jameson retired, and I was offered to come back and become an instructor in the training unit. I'm acting Captain for my old district."

Sasha laughed, her temper flickering, turning her cheeks pink. "You, a teacher? Hmm."

"You, a mole? Hmm." I glared at her.

"Emma, I didn't find you to start a fight. I wanted to see you. It's been a long time." She was doing her best to rein in that infamous quick temper. She moved closer. "How are you?" I could tell she wanted to reach out and touch me, even if it was in the slightest way.

When I looked in her hazel eyes, I knew I wanted her to, as well, but the lingering anger held me back.

"Good, but I'd be better if this fucking elevator would hurry up." I sighed, turning to face Sasha. "I had a long flight and I'm tired." The elevator finally dinged its arrival, the doors whispering open. I smiled. "Maybe I'll see you at a seminar."

I stepped into the elevator, facing the back and trying to hold a pounding heart in my chest. I waited for the doors to close behind me, then let out a breath.

That was close.

"Morgan told me she came to the house." Sasha's voice startled me. I spun around and came face to face with the woman. "She told you everything, didn't she?" Her eyes were wide with hope.

My heart skipped as I stared at the woman I'd given it to, completely. "Cornering me isn't going to help, but yes. Morgan told me everything. How you fought to get out of the operation, to quit, everything."

Sasha nodded and shifted to the side of the elevator, leaving me more room to breathe.

"Everything she said was true. It was everything I wanted to tell you that day, but couldn't. You were so angry with me and it wasn't worth fighting. I let you win and gave you what you wanted."

Leaning my head back against the cool steel wall, I squeezed the dress hat in my hands. "Sasha, I don't think we need to do this." I closed my eyes. My hotel room was only two floors away. I could change my flight for the morning, save the city a few dollars and go home early.

The elevator came to my rescue once more when the doors opened, and I rushed out. "I'm sorry if I distracted you from your colleagues. Thank you for walking me to my room." I dug in a pocket for the room key.

I felt her hand on my arm, stopping me. "You do distract me Emma. Every damn day I wake up, I think about you. I can't stop thinking about you and what was between us. The things I left so painfully unsaid. Every day I wake up and regret not telling you to shut up like I'm about to now. Shut up and listen to me, Emma." Sasha gripped my arm. "Look at me, give me at least that. Look at me as I tell you there's not a minute that passes my heart does not ache for you. A minute does not pass where I don't wish I'd done things differently, pushed harder to leave the operation and just grab you and tell you everything after I almost lost you in the garage." I absorbed her words, staring at Sasha, speechless. Her eyes were brimming with tears.

"I meant it every time I told you I loved you, Emma, and I mean it now. I still love you, almost more than I can bear, as we stand here." She slowly let her hand fall from my arm. "The operation was nothing but lies. I was supposed to put on a show and play up bumbling skills to make you believe I was a stupid rookie. But I fell in love with you for real. That was real." She took a shuddering breath. "And as I stand here, looking at you in that uniform, you're still the most beautiful woman I've ever met."

Her words hit deep in my heart and my anger dissipated. And yet, I still didn't know what to think or feel. "You took my trust for granted." It slipped out in a rough whisper.

Sasha nodded as a tear escaped. "I know, and it's the one thing I regret the most. You lost your trust in me." She swiped the tear on her cheek with shaky fingers. "Maybe I should've died that day in the warehouse, then the lies would've ended that night."

It shattered my heart to hear her wish she'd died in the warehouse at Evan's hand.

I was holding back as much as I could but couldn't ignore how still very much in love I was with the woman standing in front of me, pouring out her soul.

She swallowed. "I made a promise to myself, the first night I sat with you in the hospital. I'd never let anyone hurt you again. That's why I killed him. But then I hurt you in the process, and it was better if I walked away that day in our house. I broke so many of my own promises." She paused, looking up and down the empty hallway, tears now streaming down her face unchecked. "I still fucking love you, Emma."

I squeezed my hat harder, and heard the plastic brim creak under the strain. This was everything I needed to hear but had prevented by pushing her out of my life as fast as I could. I looked at her teary hazel eyes as she waited for me to say something.

I didn't speak, moving to close the gap between us. Dropping the bent hat to the floor as my hands came up to Sasha's face, pulling her into a startling kiss. My hand fell to her waist, pressing into her with my hips. It took her a moment to respond, to give in. Her hand fell to my back, pulling me closer.

Our lips met in an angry, passionate way, taking and giving as much as they had in our first kiss against the squad car.

I broke the kiss, gasping for air. Sasha was breathless and flush. I looked in her eyes as I ran my fingers across her cheek. "You should've told me to shut up a long time ago." She closed her eyes as our foreheads met, swallowing hard.

I kissed the tip of her nose. "I can't keep hating you, Natasha, because I'm still very much in love with you."

I heard a noise off to our right and saw a random hotel guest stumbling down the hall had taken notice of us. They wore a hooded sweatshirt, the hood pulled deep over their face. I backed away from Sasha. "We have an audience. Let's go to my room. We need to talk."

Sasha glanced at the pervy guest and nodded, bending down to grab my hat. She held it out to me, mumbling. "You do look amazing in that uniform." I felt the blush creep up my face as I opened my room door and let her in first. I glanced one more time at the hooded stranger as they turned to walk back down the hall. I swore I could hear them humming Reunited, by Peaches and Herb.

* * *

"Wow, this room is three times the size of mine." Sasha was attempting to break the lingering tension between us. I tossed the hat onto the small couch in the room. "My secretary upgraded the room to a suite."

"You have a secretary now?" She chuckled. "Has Aaron tried to...?"

"He tried but I threatened to take my office back and put him in the cubicles if he couldn't control himself." I stripped off my jacket, laying it on the back of a chair. "Sasha, I...." She cut my words short.

"I know, the trust between us." She stood in the middle of the suite, looking as if, any minute, I'd ask her to leave. "I can't go back in time, Emma, and I can't change what happened. I can only change what will happen. There was a time when you completely trusted me, right?"

My hands fell to my hips. "I trusted someone."

Sasha moved closer. "That someone was me, is still me. Things won't be magically fixed in a matter of minutes or in one kiss. But, if I have to beg on hands and knees, Emma, I will. Give me a second chance. Maybe we can try to be friends again." She searched my eyes.

I took a slight breath. "You make me weak and fearful."

Sasha inched closer. "I make you human." The closer she got, the more nervous I felt.

I spoke softer. "You make me angry and nervous."

She chuckled. "Really? Because you make me strong and frustrated." She was now inches away from my face.

I swallowed hard. "I can't ever be friends with you, Sasha." My jaw twitched as I said it.

I watched her temper flare as she stepped back out of my space. "Why did I bother talking to you? Morgan told me the Ice Queen had returned. Looks like she was right." She turned towards the door. "I guess we are what we will be." Sasha nodded at whatever was settling in her mind. "I'll see you around this weekend, Captain Tiernan."

"I can't be friends with you Sasha, because I'd be jealous of anyone who had your full attention." My voice sounded shaky, frail, desperate in my ears. "Jealous of anyone who would touch you or steal your heart from me. I can't sit back and say yes to trying to be friends and not ignore how much I want to be with you. Regardless of the bullshit between us, I couldn't bear to see you with anyone else. I might or might not overcome the fear I have about us, our future. Who wants to think that far ahead? All I know is I won't be your friend, Sasha. I can't be your friend."

I pulled off the clip-on tie and threw it on the chair with my jacket. "That's the truth." I met Sasha's eyes as silence fell between us.

I held up a hand in defeat. "Maybe I'll sit in on one of your seminars. It was good to see you." I began to unbutton my dress shirt to release some of the heat I felt building up as a flash of anger overwhelmed me.

My hands shook. I kept my head down, hoping Sasha would make a silent exit and I wouldn't have to watch her leave.

Sasha's hands covered mine, stilling my fumbling fingers, her voice soft. "Let me." She brushed my hands away to take over the unbuttoning. "I can't be friends with you either, Emma. To see another woman stand where I stood, touch you like I did and want to every moment I look at you. To see anyone fight with you the way I do." She paused, licking her lips. "I miss the way you wanted me." Her hands finished unbuttoning my uniform shirt, pulling it open to reveal the plain white t-shirt underneath. She sighed as I shivered at the look in her eyes. "I don't ever want to imagine it, Emma."

Her hands tugged the edge of the t-shirt, pulling it free and tentatively slipping a hand underneath. Her fingers brushed against my bare stomach, sending more heat coursing through my body.

Slow, nervous fingertips grazed my scar. The new ones and old ones collided together as she connected them with her soft touch, making my breath hitch. I lifted a hand to push away the few messy strands of hair that fell across Sasha's face. "What if?"

Sasha smiled and shook her head, holding my hand as it rested against her cheek. We lingered for a moment, staring at each other. My hand moved further down to trace her lips with my thumb. Sasha closed her eyes at the touch, kissing my thumb and leaning in to brush her lips against mine, staying for a moment before pulling back.

"I should go." Her voice was a low rasp, the air filled with tension and nerves. It felt like this was both of our first times, the first time we fought the darkness to push towards the light. To give into our hearts, not our minds. I could see it reflected in Sasha's eyes, this was real. This was *our* first time.

I didn't speak. I just leaned in, closing the gap between us, bringing our lips together. I sucked gently on her lower lip and brushed my tongue against it. Sasha closed her eyes and drew me closer, slipping her hands around to my back. I couldn't hold back anymore. There was little room between us, but I lowered my hand to her neck and followed it with soft kisses to her collarbone then back up to the edge of her jawline.

Sasha moaned lightly, and our lips came together again. I meant for the kiss to be brief, but lost myself in the softness of her lips and her tongue against mine. Strong hands moved up into my hair, pulling me closer.

Before I knew it, she had pushed me backwards until I bumped into the edge of the massive bed, and fell back on it.

Sasha climbed on, straddling my waist as she pushed herself into me, her lips meeting mine in a deep, searching kiss. My hands went to her hips, squeezing hard as I pulled her closer, desperate to have all of her.

My head was swimming. We kissed for several moments until Sasha reached down to the edge of my shirt and slid her hands underneath. She caressed my stomach with her warm fingers. I moaned and arched into her hands. Just as Sasha's palms were at the swell of my breasts, I pushed her back to sit up. The taste of her lips made me ache to touch more of her, taste more of her, and I had to stop and gather myself. I didn't want to rush this moment like so many times before.

I reached up and shoved Sasha's blazer off her shoulders. She shook it off and watched; my once fumbling fingers were now steady and determined as they tugged at the buttons of her shirt. When her shirt was free, Sasha removed her bra and what I saw made me want to immerse myself in every inch of her.

I slowly reached my hand up, fingertips grazing the scar on her stomach. The sight of it sent a sharp pain through my body, I sucked in a shaky breath, pulling my hand away as the guilt crept in. Sasha took my hand, guiding it up to her breast, leading me to trace a finger across a hard nipple. She quietly moaned, squeezing my hips with her thighs.

I did it again, harder, and Sasha leaned into my touch. "Emma."

Before I could answer I felt her hands move from my waist, up and under my shirt. Rubbing the skin across my ribs and stopping at my bra. She bit at my neck, kissing lightly as her hands pushed my bra out of the way to tease my nipples. I whimpered as Sasha's hands covered my breasts, squeezing as her teeth gently raked across my neck.

God, I wanted her.

I took a moment to look at Sasha, her pulse racing in the veins of her neck. I couldn't hold back. As I bent to kiss her, I pressed my thigh up between her legs. She pushed down hard, moving back and forth as she moaned into my mouth. I didn't waste any more time. Her need was rising fast and hard, and I needed to touch her.

I reached down, unbuttoned her pants, and slipped my hand between the waistband of her dress pants and the thin cotton material that blocked me from where I wanted to be. I felt the heat radiating from her. I took my time drawing circles along the length of her, feeling Sasha squirm under my touch.

"Emma, please just touch me."

I smirked, pushing the fabric to the side, and, slipping a finger inside, took her breath away. I started slow. Taking my time, I increased the movement of my fingers until Sasha matched my rhythm. Within minutes, I felt her tighten around my fingers and she cried out in ecstasy. I covered her mouth with mine, biting her bottom lip.

Sasha didn't give herself a chance to recover. Her eyes were hazy, full of pent-up desire. In a second, she pulled me to my feet and stripped me of the simple white undershirt I wore, then tugged my pants off.

She pushed me back down onto the bed, climbing on top of me, stripping away the last fragments of clothing that stood in her way. She spared no time, working her way down my body, kissing my neck hard, biting at the tender skin around my nipples. My breath caught in my throat as I felt her tongue drag down from my navel to between my legs.

At the slow, purposeful touch of her tongue, my hips lifted off the bed and pushed into her. Her hands dug into my hips, pressing me back down as she slid two fingers in. I felt my heart stop. Gripping the sheets as my intense orgasm hit me, I couldn't control the moans Sasha wrenched out of me with every flick of her tongue. I collapsed back into the bed, breathless and exhausted.

Sasha's tiny tingling kisses traveled up my thighs, my stomach and finally my mouth. We kissed, the desire once rising between us. I slid my hand between our bodies as she laid on top of me. She gasped and broke away from the kiss when she felt my fingers dip inside her again.

I smirked. "You might miss that seminar."

* * *

My eyes fluttered open. The bright white bed sheets reflected the morning sun pouring into the room. I adjusted the pillow, propping myself to get a better look at Sasha, who was standing in front of the window, wrapped in a blanket.

"If you're cold, come back to bed." My voice was tired and raspy, and all for a good reason.

Sasha grinned, looking over her shoulder. "The sun was coming up and I wanted to watch it." She turned back to the window as the sun slowly rose, bringing morning with it. I crawled out of the bed, shivering as I walked over to her. I pushed her arms open, to stand with her inside the blanket. She scanned my naked body, her eyes pausing on my scars.

I held her closer, cutting off the view. "When do you have to leave?"

Sasha nuzzled against my neck. "In an hour. I have to meet the rest of the guys and get ready for the wiretapping seminar. I'm the lead speaker and can't skip it, as much as I'd like to." Her hands ran along my bare back, sending shivers through my body.

"I understand. I should probably show my face around the convention." I kissed the top of her head. "Apparently I'm the crown jewel of the department. That's how I got this suite."

Sasha laughed. "I should write the Superintendent a thank you letter. That bed is amazing."

We both looked at the bed. It looked like it had been in a war and it had, to a point. Sasha laid her head against my chest. "I should shower before I go back to my room and change." She looked up at me, with a small smile on her lips.

I kissed the corner of her dimple. "You don't even have to ask." I wound my hand in hers and led her to the bathroom, leaving the blanket in a pile on the floor.

Chapter 28

I stood in front of the bathroom mirror, adjusting my badge and name bar on a fresh white shirt as Sasha ran around behind me trying to collect her things. I clipped on my black tie and turned to her. "If I find any of yours, I'll bring it to you later. You're going to be late."

Sasha stood up from where she had been looking under the bed, and brushed her hair back. She smiled as she ran her eyes over my uniform. "You, in that uniform, are hard to resist."

"So were you in those patrol blues." Walking out of the bathroom, I picked up her jacket and held it out to her. "I'll meet you at the hotel bar in a few hours, and then dinner tonight?"

Sasha grinned. "I wouldn't miss it." She took the jacket and walked to the door. She paused before running back to surprise me with a kiss.

"I love you." She turned to run out the door.

I grinned. She was going to be extremely late to her seminar.

* * *

I suffered with a smile as I milled around the convention. Too many chiefs and federal agents droning on about their career achievements and boring the living hell out of me. I managed to sneak into a small group of female agents and chiefs who were fairly — relatively — interesting to talk to.

I missed most of Sasha's seminar, and only caught the end. It was fascinating to watch her. She was engaging and charismatic, and held everyone's attention. A far cry from the bumbling detective I'd met, it now made sense why the FBI had chosen her. She easily adapted to any situation.

At one point in her speech she made eye contact with me and couldn't hide the grin and slight blush creeping over her cheeks. I left the room before she spotted me again. I didn't want to distract her any more than I already had, but I couldn't wipe the stupid smile off my face.

As I walked through the hotel, trying to find a quieter bar to continue nursing my drink until dinner, I thought about last night. Sasha and I had reconnected, through and through. I still had doubts and lingering trust issues, but that was on me and me alone. I'd work through them. In time I'd forgive Sasha, if I hadn't already.

Glancing at the clock in the lobby, I saw it was almost time for me to meet her. We'd agreed to dinner and conversation to continue working on the rebuild of our relationship.

While I waited, I fidgeted with the small pamphlet given to me by an attractive CIA agent who'd been trying to recruit me in more ways than one. I laughed to myself as I read the paragraph that was obviously written by someone who had nothing to do with the CIA. The mission statement had me chuckling and wondering how it won anyone over, when my phone vibrated in my pocket.

I grinned when I saw it was a message from Sasha.

-Emma, meet me on the roof. The view is amazing, and I want to watch the sun set before dinner. Join me? I will be waiting at the west end. -

I shook my head. Sasha was more of a romantic than I thought.

I asked the concierge how to gain access to the roof. The young man gave me directions, not questioning anything. Who would, at a cop convention? He probably thought I was part of a SWAT team who wanted to spontaneously rappel down the side of the hotel. It appeared

I could go anywhere I wanted in the hotel as long as I was wearing a uniform.

Pushing open the roof access door, I squinted into the bright sun dipping lower into the horizon with every passing minute. I walked around HVAC units, shaking my head at the rooftop pool and patio a hundred yards away. This hotel had at least ten pools, so why not throw another one on the roof?

Gravel crunched under my polished boots when I saw Sasha sitting on a rooftop unit looking westward, her back to me.

"Hey, there's a perfectly good patio over there, with chairs and fancy drinks."

She didn't turn around as I moved closer.

"Did you lose your voice at the seminar?"

Sasha turned to me, and my heart sank. She had thick silver duct tape over her mouth with two sets of handcuffs around her wrists. Tears streamed down her face as she shook her head. Her eyes burned with fear, the setting sun catching the tears that flooded them. Sasha was petrified.

I reached for her. "What the hell happened?"

Sasha pushed me away. I frowned, reaching for the duct tape. "Sasha, stop. I have to get you out of these handcuffs."

"You should stop and step away from her, Emma." I looked up and saw the hallway gawker from the night before walking towards us, hood pulled over their face. The voice was female, raspy, unrecognizable.

"Step away from her," she continued. "I don't want either of you getting ideas. You are both very talented officers of the law." I focused on the familiar voice as I crept away from Sasha.

The gawker yanked the hood back. The woman tilted her face up to the setting sun. "It's nice to have us all together again. A bit like an awkward high school reunion." Rachel smiled as her blonde hair settled around her shoulders. She reached into her sweatshirt pocket, pulling out a gun. "Don't try anything, Emma. Not like you would anyways. You always seem to freeze under pressure."

"Rachel? What are you doing?" I stared at her in disbelief. Rachel was thinner and my eyes were drawn to an angry red scar across her face. And she was alive, not on the verge of death by my forced hand.

Rachel moved to sit next to Sasha. "I'm doing what has to be done." She nudged Sasha with her shoulder, smirking. "This lady is very sneaky. I had no idea she was the agent watching me until I dug it out of the database on my brother's request."

She reached up, idly tracing the scar on her face. "He had a way of getting me to do his bidding." She looked at me with the same blue eyes I had stared at far too many times, but this time she was dead behind them. Rachel had lost herself a long time ago.

"Oh! I have something for you. I'm not sure if you're the type who appreciates keepsakes, but here." She reached into her pocket again, tossing something on the ground near my feet.

Evan's knife skittered across the roof gravel. I swallowed the bile down, my breath coming in a shaky stutter. His knife had been a part of my life longer than my birth parents. It evoked the same sickening feeling I'd had the first time I saw it as a kid.

"You can have that, I have no need for it." Rachel wrapped an arm around Sasha, forcing her to whimper. "I should really thank you for killing my brother. In a way you saved my life. Evan had every intention of coming back and killing me after he finally killed you."

Rachel reached over and kissed Sasha on the side of the head. "But you, Sasha, are my hero! Emma's hero! You saved the day and put ten bullets in my dear brother!"

Rachel stood, the gun dangling at her side as she walked to lean against another HVAC unit. "I do have one question I was never able to ask you in our interviews, Emma." She rolled her head to look at me. "You've never killed anyone. Why is that?" She pointed at herself, then Sasha, with the gun. "My fellow agent here and I have both killed without hesitation, and yet you stared my brother down three times and couldn't pull the trigger. Why is that, Emma? Why were you so scared?" She gave me a hard stare. "Why *are* you so scared?"

I maintained eye contact as I laid my hands on my hips. My right hand touched the concealed holster specifically made for this dress uniform.

"Let Sasha go. Evan is dead and there's no reason for this, Rachel."

Rachel cackled. "Oh, there's plenty of reasons for this. I'm going to kill her, because she killed my brother. Well, that's the excuse I intend to use. Family revenge. But in reality, Sasha betrayed me. Much like she betrayed you."

Rachel pushed off the HVAC unit. "You see, after Evan kidnapped me from the hospital, after you failed *again* to kill me, he punished me as the details of Operation Eclipse leaked out. Severely. He wasn't happy I'd used you to bait him." Rachel reached up with her gun hand to rub at the side of her head. "I've lost my mind, plain and simple. The cracks appeared when I watched Annie die in that field, then they continued to widen as I spiraled deeper and deeper. I was so close, so close to killing him." Rachel shot the gun out, pointing it directly at Sasha. "Then she ruined it! He kidnapped her to get to you! And I was too busy covering your back as you tried to play the hero! You were supposed to kill me in that hotel, to set me free from him and everything in here."

She tapped her temple with the muzzle. Rachel had gone over the deep end, and seemed to think killing Sasha would make me understand her pain. "Because of her, he did this to me." She pointed at the scar on her face. "He did far worse things to me than he ever did to you, Emma." Rachel turned red with anger, her eyes welling up.

I spoke softly. "Rachel, I understand. I almost lost the woman I love by Evan's hands. You don't have to do this." I held out my other hand to try and calm her as the other inched further down on the concealed holster.

Rachel dropped the gun away from Sasha. "I brought you and Evan together at the lab. The anonymous voicemail to Agent Adams? It was me! All me! He made me drive him to the school. I begged him not to kill the sheriff who chased us. He didn't, but for that, I faced more punishment." She was all over the place.

Rachel paced, laughing maniacally. "God, it was so simple! You had the advantage, all you had to do was pull the trigger! You! It was supposed to be you who killed him! But you couldn't, you left it for your girlfriend to display her FBI heroics."

Rachel turned, suddenly rushing towards me as my thumb quietly flicked the latch on my holster, allowing free access to my gun.

"Emma, how is it you can dig deep into the mind of every evil person in the world without fear, but you cannot confront your own fears? Fear to love completely. Fear of taking control of the situation when you would rather be under someone's thumb?" Rachel paced back to Sasha, snatching her by the elbow.

Rachel screamed at me. "You failed me, Emma! You failed the one thing you had to do!" She pulled Sasha closer, pressing the gun against her temple. "This one has to die, and you need to watch her die, just like I watched Annie!"

I saw rampant fear run across Sasha's eyes and had to look away before my fear overwhelmed me. I glanced at Rachel's gun hand. Her finger was on the trigger, slowly pulling back. Sasha closed her eyes.

Rachel laughed, leaning into Sasha. "It'll make sense when it's done, so just sit and watch like only you know how to do, Emma." She laughed as the trigger inched back almost imperceptibly.

Two gunshots rang out.

Sasha flinched and kept her eyes shut until the sound of a body hitting gravel made her open them. I stood still, the gun in my hands still pointing where Rachel had stood, smoke snaking out of the barrel. Rachel was on the ground, coughing as blood blossomed across her chest from two dead center shots.

I lowered my gun and ran to Sasha, ripping off the tape before I used my extra handcuff key to release her.

As soon as her hands were free, she grabbed me in a crushing hug.

"Go get help." I whispered against her ear. Sasha nodded as she pulled back and ran to the roof access door.

I went to Rachel.

She coughed up a mouthful of blood, a wicked smile on her face. "Not so afraid anymore, are you?"

Bending down, I made no effort to slow her bleeding. "You didn't have to do this, Rachel. He would've never bothered you or me if you just left him alone. But you drew him out, you woke the evil." I could feel the latent fear I'd carried for years leaving my body. I was watching the last link to Evan die before my eyes, and it was oddly freeing. I felt light, like thirty-plus years of dread suddenly slipped away with her blood.

We were alone on the rooftop. I bent down closer to Rachel, and whispered to her. "I'll watch you die, just like I watched your brother."

Rachel met my eyes, laughing with difficulty. "I don't regret any of it."

She faded away, a twisted smile frozen on her face. I stood up and stepped over the knife Rachel had thrown at me. A handful of hotel security and local police burst through the roof access door and ran past me to Rachel's body. I kept walking, sliding my gun back in its holster. Never once looking back.

Sasha ran to me with another officer on her heels. "Emma?"

"It's finally over." The look in my eyes conveyed to her exactly what I meant.

Sasha swallowed hard as the officer held up his hand, stopping me.

"Ma'am, I think you need to come with me." He gave me an awkward look. I was a police Captain who was just involved with a rooftop shooting at a police convention. It wasn't surprising that he was confused about what to do.

I nodded, then looked back at Sasha and held my hand out to her. She took it and we both followed the officer as the scene behind us bustled with activity.

For the first time in my entire life, I truly felt free.

Chapter 29

I was interviewed in a side conference room, answering questions as I looked out the side windows, watching Rachel's body roll by before it was placed in a coroner's van. Sasha was once again separated from me while I spilled my guts to the locals and a sole FBI agent who had been first to make the rooftop scene.

My statement was taken, and I handed in my gun as evidence until everything was sorted out. When I was free to leave, I walked past another side room, where I caught a quick glimpse of Sasha through an open door, giving her statement to two other FBI agents and Agent Reagan. She looked in my direction and I paused. Sasha looked tired but relieved. It was over.

Agent Reagan closed the door on me, and cut off my view.

* * *

I waited twelve hours in my hotel room until the agent I'd dealt with came to my room and cleared me, returning my gun. When I asked about Sasha, he couldn't give me any details other than that Agent Clarke was still being debriefed and it was undetermined when she would be cleared. I rolled my eyes, making an offhand comment how federal agencies never made anything easy.

After he left, I finished packing my bags and pushed through the rest of the convention, ignoring the hard stares and proud grins, and hailed a cab. I had my secretary book a new flight back to Chicago to leave within the hour. I wanted to go home, more than anything now that it seemed the nightmare was over.

I left a message for Sasha. I didn't want to sit around or deal with Agent Reagan or any more FBI agents, knowing they'd keep Sasha from me as long as possible.

Walking into my house, I didn't respond to Aaron, who followed me up to my bedroom, asking a million questions. I began to pull off my uniform, stopping in the middle of unbuttoning my shirt to sit on my bed, after Aaron had pestered me to the brink of insanity.

"Tomorrow. Over eggs and pancakes I'll tell you everything. But right now, all I want to do is to crawl in my bed and have my first peaceful sleep in months." The look I gave him told Aaron everything without saying a damn word. Everything was too much right now. I was too tired, still in shock and waiting for the adrenaline to finally leave my body.

He nodded, sighing. "Sure thing, Emma." He smiled, turning to go back downstairs.

"Aaron, wait. If Sasha calls, wake me up."

Aaron paused. "*The* Sasha?"

"The one and only." I smirked.

He squinted. "Are you sure you don't want to tell me anything?"

I shook my head and continued removing my uniform. "Tomorrow. Everything."

As soon as Aaron left, I threw my pajamas on and collapsed into the bed, passing out in less than two breaths.

Three days passed, and I'd not heard anything from Sasha. I struggled, wondering if the FBI had imposed silence upon her once again while also dealing with what I'd done on the rooftop. For the first time in my life I'd killed someone, and it resonated within me. It wasn't a selfish, needless kill. I hated that I felt perfectly fine killing Rachel. I almost enjoyed watching the light fade out of her eyes, like with Evan.

Killing her was something I'd had to do and was justified in doing it. It didn't make the fact any easier to digest. It was also harder to digest without the woman I loved by my side. I needed to know she was okay, and I just needed her.

I missed Sasha on levels I'd never imagined. I wanted her to knock on my front door and hold me in her arms as I poured out my heart to her, the way I'd been craving since Agent Reagan closed the door between us in the hotel. I sent a few texts to her with no reply, and experienced a sinking feeling I couldn't fend off.

Morgan called a few days after that, only to tell me Sasha had gotten the messages I left for her, then told me to suck it up buttercup. I hung up, cursing the FBI.

I returned to work the next week. My replacement had been chosen and he would be taking over in a matter of days. I was eager to ditch the paperwork and fall into teaching new recruits until my contract ended.

By the end of that week, I cleared out the small number of items I'd brought into my temporary office as Aaron sat in a chair with his feet on my borrowed desk and watched me.

"It's so weird you haven't heard anything from her in weeks. You think this is another secret agent trick?"

I dropped files into a box, shaking my head. "No, not at all. What she said to me in the hotel room, and the pure fear I saw on her face, was honest and raw. I think the FBI likes to keep us separated." I laid my hands on my hips. "I honestly don't know, Aaron. All I know is I miss her. It could be because the media is all over my ass again and the FBI is keeping her from me to avoid unwanted exposure."

The media had picked up the story and was hounding me, asking for exclusive interviews and comments. I'd even received offers for television movies on that one network aimed at strong women viewers.

A light knock on my door distracted me. My secretary smiled as she poked her head in. "Captain, the Superintendent is here to see you." She looked down at Aaron, who immediately hopped up, grabbing his coffee and half-eaten bagel.

"I'll catch you later, ride home tonight?"

I sighed. "Sure. Meet you as soon as I'm done?"

Aaron winked at me. Ride home was our code word for afterwork drinks and hot dogs at the bar closest to the house. It'd become a habit since I moved home and it stuck. I was happy to have some sort of routine back in my life.

As soon as Aaron left, my secretary brought in the Superintendent, closely followed by my least favorite FBI agent, Agent Reagan. The Superintendent spoke first.

"Captain Tiernan! I'm glad I was able to catch you! I know you're enjoying your last few days in this office." He took a seat, motioning for Agent Reagan to do the same.

"Yes sir. I'm cleaning up the little bit of things I have around here. My replacement should be in by the end of the week." I sat down across from them, after moving the box to the floor. "I'm looking forward to moving into the training unit. It'll be a nice change of pace." I smiled tightly, baring my teeth at Agent Reagan.

The Superintendent nodded. "That's good to hear!" He nodded to the agent. "I've come here with Agent Reagan to discuss an offer with you." He reached into his briefcase and pulled out a small black folder accompanied by a small black box. He set the box on my desk. "First, this is a commendation for your actions down in D.C. You will be properly honored next month at our yearly ceremony, but I wanted to get this to you myself."

I looked at the commendation, signed by the Superintendent, Governor, and Mayor, and the medal. It was for bravery in the line of duty and saving the life of an officer. I smiled, and pushed them aside.

"Thank you, sir, but I was just doing my job."

The Superintendent grinned. "That's what they all say, but I'm very proud of you, Captain. Which brings me to my next order of business." He glanced at the FBI agent again. "As you know, Agent Reagan is the new head of the Behavioral Science Unit for the FBI. She and I had an interesting meeting this morning. We've been in contact since the shake out of Operation Eclipse and we've agreed that our two agencies working together is something we both want to pursue."

I felt my temper spike. "How do you mean, sir?"

"I'll let Agent Reagan take it from here."

Agent Reagan nodded. "Thank you. Emma, I'm going to present it to you as simply as I can. You are beneficial to the FBI. You have a profiling skill that has yet to be matched within our own agency, and as I told you that first time I met you, I'd return in time." She gave me a smug smirk. "The Superintendent has agreed to let me borrow you for an undetermined amount of time as I rework and reorganize the BSU unit. It's obvious we had some holes and leaks that need plugging. You're the perfect fit for the job. Before you say no, let me explain. You'll be working with new agents and training them as you would new detectives here, but you'd also be working on cold case files left abandoned by Agent Fisher."

Agent Reagan met my eyes. "You'll be assigned an experienced FBI agent as your partner and the two of you will work together as the BSU is reorganized." She smiled warmly as she finished.

I sat back in the chair. "Why on earth would I want to work for you? After everything your agency has put me through? The lies, the deception, the crazies who chased me and my loved ones?" I paused, staring at her. "Speaking of which, what has happened to Agent Clarke?" It was less of a question and more of a demand. I was done playing nice with Reagan.

Agent Reagan held her professional smile. "Agent Clarke has received a new assignment." She crossed her legs. "As for why would you want to work for me? Simple as this. If you give me two years — or the remaining time you negotiated with the Superintendent here — I will provide you with a full federal retirement. Your medical school will be paid for and as soon as you retire with us, you're free and clear. Never again will that uniform, or another badge see your closet. You will also have full access and privileges to FBI resources as any other agent would, but without the badge and title."

Agent Reagan took a breath. "We need you, Emma. You know what it's like to be chased by a madman and maintain your humanity when it's needed most. You look at cases with an analytical fine-tooth comb and never give up. I need that in the BSU."

I sighed. The offer she extended was too good to ignore. On top of that, if I had FBI access, I could be closer to Sasha. It would be worth playing the game, to keep her close. No matter where the FBI decided to send to keep her away from me.

The Superintendent looked at me with eyes full of political excitement, waiting for me to accept. He wanted to parade around the fact he was now working with a federal agency.

I took a deep breath. "Two years. No more."

The Superintendent couldn't hold back his smile.

Agent Reagan nodded with her own shitty grin. "Perfect, Emma. I will have everything set up for you. You'll be meeting your partner today or tomorrow, as soon as they arrive in the city. After that, you'll be moved to the Chicago office and work out of there until the internal investigation at the home office has finished." She stood and held out her hand. "I'm glad to have you with us. Regardless of our past meetings, I look forward to working with you."

I said nothing more as I shook her hand and the Superintendent's. They left me as quickly as they had come in, leaving me alone with my borrowed desk and my boxes.

After almost a half hour of staring at the desk, I called my secretary and told her I'd be leaving for the day and to tell Aaron to grab boxes before he left for the afternoon.

I stopped by the Superintendent's office on my way out of the station, to speak briefly to his assistant, then stepped out, squinting into the early afternoon sun, bright on my face. It was an abnormally warm day, and I found my dress jacket and uniform on the whole were far too much for the weather. I hailed a cab and rushed home, changing out of the dress uniform in favor of a pair of jeans and comfy, worn boots with one of Sasha's old white V-necks I'd kept from when we lived together.

I was determined to find her, and hoped my new partner wouldn't throw a wrench in the works. I was half tempted to request Morgan as my partner, or at least request her to work with me.

I walked out of the house and crossed the street, mesmerized by the clear blue water. I sucked in a large breath of lake air, letting the sun and water ease my decision to work with the FBI. I would be teaching, and the lure of cold cases was a little too much to ignore on top of having access to Sasha's location.

The lakefront was empty, only a handful of runners and people skipping work dotted the boardwalk. I walked to my favorite spot. It was on a small, isolated bend that gave me a perfect view of Navy Pier. I could look in any direction and see nothing but water. I sat on the edge of the concrete walls sunk deep into the lake, letting my legs swing over the water.

A kayaker paddled past, their movements rhythmic and hypnotizing. I heard footsteps behind me, but paid little attention, thinking it was a runner, pausing to enjoy the view for a moment. Then the footsteps stopped right behind my back, and a bag of Skittles landed next to my hand.

I hung my head down, staring at the water lapping at my feet.

"Where have you been?" I sounded irritated. I *was* irritated. It'd been two weeks since I'd heard anything from her, and I let my anxiety get the better of me.

I was also resisting the urge to grab her and never let go.

Sasha sat down next to me, our shoulders touching. "I've been trying to find my way to you." She looked at me and it was the first time I saw her smile since the morning in my hotel room. A genuine, happy smile because there was no lingering fear behind it. "You know this lakefront trail is eighteen and a half miles long?" She reached into her pocket, pulling out the wrinkled piece of paper where I'd written *meet me where the sun and water become one* and passed it to the Superintendent's assistant to pass onto Agent Reagan's after the meeting. I smirked. I owed them both a bottle of whiskey.

I smiled as she set the note on my leg.

"I had to ask Aaron what it meant. He told me this is where you sometimes sit and watch the sun set."

I looked out onto the lake. "When the sun sets into the lake, they both become one." I paused and looked at her. Sasha wore her hair up and was dressed in the usual black pantsuit. Even though she wore sunglasses, I felt her eyes bore into me.

"I thought you'd still be in D.C." My voice was softer as it resonated at how much I missed her over the last three days. My trust issues be damned, when I looked at her, all I wanted was her, close to me. I suddenly rethought my agreement with Agent Reagan.

"I've been reassigned. Aaron and Agent Reagan told me I'd find my new partner down here." Sasha's voice had a twinge of humor as she continued. "I'm hoping it's just one case and then I can go back to solo work."

"What?" I gave her a blank stare as my words from her first day as my partner were thrown back in my face.

Sasha held out her hand. "Hi, I'm Agent Natasha Clarke, Special Agent in Charge of the new BSU project here in Chicago. You must be Captain Emma Tiernan. It's lovely to meet you."

"Wait. I don't understand." I scrambled to my feet.

Sasha stood and stepped closer to me. "Agent Reagan gave me the same deal she gave you. Two years and we're both out of the FBI. We can spend our golden years of retirement together." She grabbed my hand. "Her words exactly. She let it be known that once upon a time she fell in love with her partner when she was a new agent and my story sparked the dead romantic in her. This was her idea to bring us together and keep us on. Win-win for her?"

I looked down at Sasha's hand in mine. "Why are we doing this? Continuing to work in the minds of monsters?"

"Because if we do, we may stop other Evans and Rachels. And because it's the only thing we know how to do, aside from love each other." She ran a hand down my face, cupping my jaw. "And the last because is, after two years, we can move to wherever you want to go to medical school and live without looking over our shoulders."

I sighed, rolling my eyes for effect. "You know I hate having partners." Sasha just nodded and kissed me, pulling me against her.

When she leaned back, she whispered. "I love you, partner. You won't be able to shake me loose as easily as you did my first week as a detective."

I sighed, pressing my forehead against hers. "I never really tried that hard." I closed my eyes as I felt her heartbeat mingle with mine. "Sasha, how do you feel about having a man as a roommate?"

She smiled, kissing the corner of my mouth. "Aaron already gave me a set of keys."

I wrapped her in my arms. "I love you, Natasha." She squeezed me harder as I whispered it in her ear.

Looking out over the lake, I watched the waves seem to echo the sense of serenity that washed over the both of us. They calmed, became motionless and seemed to still as we held each other.

I could feel my heart let go of the tension it had carried for far too long. I smiled into the setting sun, knowing it was because of the woman I held in my arms.

Whatever monsters waiting around the next corner for us would have one hell a fight ahead of them.

We both knew there would be more monsters.

Lightning Source UK Ltd.
Milton Keynes UK
UKHW021823241122
412725UK00012B/1290